DEMON CHASER

David Berardelli

DEMON CHASER

"Death is Hell, but the shoes are great!"

GRAVESTONE PRESS

PART I - "THE CHANT"

CHAPTER 1

Friday Night at the Dump

Todd Bochner eased his refurbished '67 Camaro convertible off the main road at the crest of the wooded hill and suddenly stopped.

In the twin headlight beams, a large, wavy pile of barbed wire and an old tricycle blocked their path. "I ain't goin' in there, man," he said, and crossed his arms over his skinny chest.

Beside him, Darcy McGill twisted in her seat. She suspected he'd do something stupid. But right now, she just wasn't in the mood. "Why not?"

"There's shit all over the place. Don't wanna get Cammie scratched and all messed up."

"It's *trash*," she said. "We're at the *dump*, remember? Go around it."

"It's barb wire."

"Same thing."

"Know what barb wire will do to paint and metal?"

She hated when guys whined. "I give up. What'll barbed wire do to paint and metal?"

"Scratch it up."

"Only if you get too close to it."

He shook his head. "Don't wanna go anywhere near it…"

Leon Bellson, his glossy eyes blinking from the grass he and Todd had just sucked up on their way over, poked his face between the front seats. "Heavy duty," he

5

whispered. "That trike looks like it'll scorch up some highway!" He giggled.

"Flick your dickhead button in the off position," Todd said, frowning. "And keep your zits off the upholstery. I just cleaned it."

Darcy cursed herself for asking them to bring her out here. When she first asked Todd during Study Hall, his face lit up like neon. She knew what that meant but decided not to give it another thought. If her Nissan hadn't been sitting in the shop all week, she wouldn't have even bothered. Todd was the only one available on such short notice on a Friday night. If he wanted to think something else would happen, let him. All guys were swimming around in testosterone—she couldn't help that.

She asked Leon to go along because she didn't want to be alone with Todd. Todd and Leon were tight, so Todd didn't mind so much. They were jerks, although Leon could actually manage an intelligent conversation at times. But right now Leon wasn't himself. The weed had kicked in. But at least he wasn't the perv Todd was. As they cruised out of town, she'd caught Todd drooling. Probably because the low cut of her tank top showed the mole over her small left breast. But that didn't bother her too much. Todd was a hopeless slobberer—he'd soak his chin if she was covered in burlap.

Right now, getting Todd to budge was the main issue. The City Dump sat a mile farther down. People brought out their trash at night and made a mess of the area. Some obviously didn't mind pulling off the shoulder and dumping right there at the entrance.

Todd's Camaro was his pride and joy—she should have known he'd be funny about taking it into the woods. But she had gotten him this far.

6

She opened her door.

"Goin' for a walk?" His eyes sparkled. "Want company?"

"I'm going to clear the way so I don't have to hear you whining about scratching up your lady." She stepped into the overgrown grass and, ignoring the tingles of the tall weeds brushing her bare arms, approached the tangled clump.

Todd gunned the Camaro, making it roar like an angry lion. He chuckled. "I could leave ya here, ya know."

She patted her pocket. "I could call my uncle, ya know."

His grin vanished.

Mentioning her uncle, Clancy Hawkins, Raven's finest deputy, had gotten her out of some tight spots. Not that she'd actually call Uncle Hawk unless it was an emergency. But it sure kept jerks like Todd in line.

Using the Camaro's headlights to scan the area, she found a foot-long section of rusty wire containing no barbs. She carefully wrapped her fingers around it, making sure no barbs were close enough to catch her jeans or tank top. Just as she started to pull, she heard footsteps behind her. Leon reached out to help.

"You're makin' me feel like a first-class jerk," Todd said sourly.

"Nothing about you is first-class," she said.

Leon giggled, and together they dragged the barbed wire clear of the path.

Leon rushed over to the tricycle and straddled it.

"Leon…" She couldn't understand how so little weed could affect him so much. Quiet and considerate one minute, he turned back into an idiot in the blinking of an eye.

After a couple of tumbles, he pushed the tricycle into the brush. "Growing up's a bitch," he said.

"Because you're too big to sit on a tricycle?" she asked.

He giggled. "I knew someone would understand."

They got back in the Camaro.

"You two finished playin' around out there?" Todd asked.

"Now it's safe to go down that hill," she said, pulling the door shut.

He groaned. "I see shit farther down. Wanna get back out and clear the path?"

She gazed into the headlight beams. "I don't see anything."

"You don't see that pile of crap down there?"

"*Weeds*, Todd. Those are *weeds*. No one mows out here."

Leon had stuck his head between the seats again. "Heavy-duty. Looks like a little Nativity scene."

"You're *so* totally a dorkster." Todd put it back in gear and eased down the slope.

"Where's this party again?" Leon asked.

"The abandoned mine," Todd said. "And you heard what I said about those zits."

Leon sat back and rubbed his cheeks. "Guess I should've popped 'em before you picked me up."

The mine had been the subject of folklore for years. A cave-in made the headline just before World War II. Casualties were minimal, but ghost and demon stories abounded anyway.

8

Darcy had grown up hearing all sorts of yarns. The theories outnumbered the tall tales. Evil had caused the collapse of the mine. Several of the religious miners painting crosses on the rock walls had angered Lucifer. The Dark Force retaliated by shaking the earth, making it crack, resulting in the cave-in.

Four years ago, when she started high school, she discovered black magic and read everything she could find about it. It quickly hooked her, and she got further into it than many of the other kids. She also read that it strongly influenced acid rock of the late sixties, creating its own culture. San Francisco boasted more devil worshipers than gays back then, with Anton LaVey starting up his own church. With the help of the Beatles, Aleister Crowley enjoyed a triumphant rebirth during this time. The greatest classic bands—the Stones, Megadeth, Black Sabbath, and others—all dealt with the Darkworld. Or so the rumors went.

During the last few years, the culture experienced a strange resurrection. What with Rap, Goth, Grunge, vampire flicks and demon shows, and the growing hatred in the world, Satan had slithered into the spotlight.

Local rumors also persisted of a secret society that supposedly met in the abandoned mine years ago to worship Satan. Darcy wasn't sure she believed it but grew curious last Saturday night, as she and her friend Sheila McKay came home after watching the Union Local High School football team practice. A quarter of a mile straight ahead, Mayor Holeridge's shiny Cadillac pulled off Raven Road West, without lights, onto the dirt path.

Surprised and curious, Darcy immediately engaged in a heated debate with Sheila.

Why would the Mayor drive down to the dump at night?

To drop off trash...

Trash? In a Cadillac?

To dump a body...

In the Mayor's personal ride?

To meet a girlfriend...

At the dump?

To take a leak...

At the dump?

There didn't seem to be *any* reason—other than the age-old legend of the secret society—to explain the strange occurrence.

"Guess I shoulda brought my player and some sounds," Leon said. "A party ain't a party without sounds."

"Don't need sounds," Todd said. "Our favorite cheerleader babe wants to conjure up a badass demon. He'll provide the sounds."

Darcy wanted to backhand Todd square in the face. Lucky for him he was driving. She abhorred violence, but Todd raked on her nerves.

"Really?" Leon asked. "A genuine demon?"

"Horns, pitchfork, and a long, pointed tail," Todd said, cackling loudly.

"You really think you can do it?" Leon seemed interested.

Darcy shrugged. Best keep this low-keyed. She didn't want to hear any more of Todd's tasteless jokes. "I keep hearing demons are out here. I wanna see if there's anything to it."

Todd shook his head." Man, just 'cause she looks like Buffy, she thinks she oughta—"

"*Please* stop that Buffy talk. I look *nothing* like her. She's blonde, for one thing—"

"Only one way to know for sure," Todd said, grinning devilishly.

"Todd Bochner, you can be really crude when you wanna be."

"Just 'cause demons might be out here don't mean you can conjure one up and take the sucker home," he said.

"Demons. Heavy-duty." No longer serious, Leon went right back to being silly. "Think they'd go for a buzz?"

"They're *spirits*." She pushed an impatient hand through her hair. "They don't *need* a buzz."

"Everyone could use a buzz once in a while…"

She turned around and gazed into Leon's glossy eyes. "If you could fly around, disappear, and make weird stuff happen, would *you* need a buzz?"

"Heavy-duty." Leon bounced on the seat. "I'd make mean old Mr. Amos Boswell Gordon pull down his pants and moon history class. Serve him right, giving me a frigging *C* on that last pop quiz!"

Darcy sat silently and tried ignoring them.

The city had sliced a wide path in the ground to accommodate Frank Miller's garbage trucks. A toxic dump spoiled the old farmland a mile or so down the path beyond the mine. This suited Darcy just fine. She didn't want to venture out too far. She had heard enough to know to avoid going near a place oozing noxious chemicals.

The path leveled off. Beyond the felled trees, a dome-shaped mound the size of one of those earth houses she

11

had seen on the Science Channel sat like a giant animal sleeping in the darkness.

Another roll of barbed wire lay half-hidden in the weeds. Broken bottles glittered like fireflies in the Camaro's headlights.

Todd stopped. "Here we go again."

"Does your steering wheel work?" Darcy asked curtly.

"You know it does."

"Then shut up and use it."

"Babes." Todd reluctantly did as she said.

When they could go no farther, Todd turned off the ignition but kept the lights on. The eerie glow flickered like critters running around in the bushes.

"Sure this is the spot?" Darcy asked.

"Fuckin' A."

Darcy shot him a glare. Todd could be so vulgar. No wondered he never got dates.

He found his flashlight and slammed the glove box shut. His knuckles brushed her left thigh.

She ignored the contact. "Where's the entrance?"

"Straight down the slope."

"I heard a secret club of rich guys comes out here." Leon giggled. "Maybe they left some neat stuff in there."

"Like what?" Todd asked.

"Money? Jewelry? Maybe a Snickers bar?"

Darcy sighed. Leon sure was outdoing his silliness tonight.

"You that wasted?" Todd asked.

"Just a little spacey. I've also got the munchies." Leon squinted. "Did you know you've got a long black hair sticking out of your nostril?"

"Which nostril?" Todd asked.

12

"The left one. Want me to pull it out?"

"Don't be such a total dorkster." Todd switched off the low beams. He grabbed his stash and a bottle of Wild Turkey from under the seat.

Darcy picked up her witchcraft book and the printout of the spell she had found online. Her pulse thumping, she followed Todd and Leon down the wild, uneven path.

CHAPTER 2

Helluva Way to Leave a Party

Tiffany LeBouf opened her eyes and found herself standing in the middle of a gray field.

She had not heard anyone say Johnny Rock's North Hollywood estate included any pastureland. But where else could she be? She couldn't even remember walking away from the pool.

Last thing she recalled was she had taken a drink from the bright-eyed, good-looking guy starring in that new reality show. He sure knew how to ramble on. All that stuff about the classic Porsche he had bought with money from his new contract had bored her half to death. She must have just zoned out, excused herself and went down the stone steps leading to the rear of the estate.

This pasture, beautiful and serene, certainly was strange. The colors were all wrong—the tall grass a light gray, the flowers a dull white, the plants a washed-out brown. At least it smelled pleasant. Mixed scents of mint and cinnamon filled the air.

Well, except for that dark backdrop close behind her. Its foulness revolted her. Smelled like a line of porta johns close by.

Porta johns? At a Hollywood party?

She couldn't imagine these Hollywood people going *near* a porta john, let alone *using* one. To hear them talk, you would think they didn't even bother with bodily functions like the rest of the population.

Even so, that didn't explain how she got here.

What did he put in that drink?

She didn't want to take it. Aside from not being much of a drinker, she didn't want to accept anything fixed without her watching. These shindigs often turned wild. People she didn't know usually came to them and many had reputations for being perverts. Tiffany showed up only because her agent suggested her presence could earn her a TV spot.

She made her grand appearance wearing her caramel two-piece by Chio with the maroon sarong wrap, and the gold laminated leather sandals by Ferre' with the four-inch heels.

Shoes were her thing. Her passion. She would rather buy shoes than anything. She didn't have much money, but her closet was crammed with the best shoes. The right look on a girl's feet turned her into a princess.

That was what Daddy always told her. And, judging by the stares from both men and women, she figured he was right.

The outfit had set her back four hundred bucks but really showed off her figure. Show them the product, her agent urged. Make those folks back in Peoria realize you're one high-class babe they should never have let slip through their fingers.

She wanted to tell him he didn't know what he was talking about. Her parading around like a hooker was anything *but* high-class.

But you didn't dare tell an agent what you really thought. You only did that if you were famous and could pick and choose who you wanted to represent you.

To be nice, she took the glass from the reality show hopeful and smiled politely. A promising young director wandered over not too long after. He'd been eyeing her legs so much that he nearly fell into the pool. Her open-toed sandals had obviously done their job. But the distraction made her forget herself. Before she knew it, she coaxed some of the cool, tangy liquid into her mouth.

Whatever it was, it sure worked fast. She had wandered into a strange field, her eyesight had gone all wrong, and her nose had picked up some really strange smells.

But she knew she couldn't just close her eyes and wish herself back at poolside.

She turned to go back. Her sandal twisted in the grass, turning her ankle, and forcing her foot down hard. A sharp pain scurried up her leg. She hopped backward, almost disappearing in the foul backdrop.

Before she could move away, something large and cold yanked her from the soft gray field, into the dark wall.

The ground instantly turned cold and wet. Tendrils of ice slapped her bare legs and stomach. Her skimpy two-piece was perfect for the pool party but totally inappropriate for jungle exploration.

She was dragged deeper into a darker section of woods. Maybe Johnny was taking her back—or the guy who had slipped her the drink. She tried resisting, but the viselike grip on her arm did not yield. She feared that if she didn't keep up the pace, she'd stumble and be pulled along anyway.

Should she struggle? What if this was one of those guys her agent had told her about? One of those well-connected producers she'd been seeking, perhaps? *Do whatever they say,* her agent had told her. *Show them what they're buying.*

It sure was dark, though. And muggy. Faint voices pierced the air as she passed. Maybe some of Johnny's friends were having their own party in the woods behind the estate.

The darkness gradually lifted.

Large claws tipped the hand gripping her arm. Fine rust-colored fur covered the arm that extended from a tall, lean, furred body. The creature's head resembled that of a wolf, although when it first turned in her direction, its face reminded her of an actor from days long past. Lee Van Cleef. That's who it looked like, anyway. But this creature couldn't be human.

She had entered a miserable, trembling forest. Crippled trees and broken limbs hunched around them. The warm air leaked heavily with sulfur. She covered her nose with her free hand and took short, quick breaths. Fumes from a distant fire burned her eyes.

A California brush fire? And she was being dragged right into it.

Terrific.

The furry wolf guy shoved her against an uprooted tree trunk. Sharp sticks jutting from its root base scraped her back.

The grip on her vanished.

Slobber soaked his hairy chin. Was this another promising young director?

A Hollywood director dressed in a wolf costume?

She knew they were weird, but this was way over the edge, even by their standards.

"Look what *I* found. Cool beans!" His eyes lowered, taking her in eagerly. The Lee-image appeared, but the glinting red eyes of the wolf remained. "Nifty outfit, babe. Plenty of smooth, pink flesh and other mouth-watering goodies, but you're dirty and smell kind of funky. Can't take you anywhere, can I?"

17

She massaged her stinging arm and tried focusing on the Lee-image, but the wolf kept coming back. What did those guys put in those drinks?

"What happened to the pool party?" she asked.

The red eyes blinked. "Pool party?"

Weird. Everyone knew about pool parties. "You know. Half-naked people standing around a pool, drinking, making out and pushing one another in."

"You mean like an orgy? With water pumped in?" He rubbed his furry palms together.

"Not exactly. I don't go to orgies."

"What else happens at these shindigs?" he asked eagerly.

"Everyone says they'll call and line you up for a job."

"Then what?"

"They never call or line you up for a job."

"You're not coming across as a happy camper, baby. Why were you there?"

"You have to do a lot of unpleasant things when you're struggling to be an actress."

"Is that what you were?"

Were? Whatever did he mean?

"I'd like to think I still am."

Ah. Cool. A babe with a sense of humor." He extended a hairy hand. "Pull that finger."

What a jerk. "No thank you."

"Heard that one before, eh?"

"A few times." Was he for real? "So where did everyone go?"

He shrugged. "No idea. Doesn't matter, though. Solitude turns me on. Especially with a female." He scratched the back of his head. "Then it's not solitude, is

18

it? Unless the female's not listening. But it's not her ears I'm interested in—if you catch my drift."

This was making less and less sense. "There were more than forty people at that party."

"Maybe they just faded quietly into the sunset with the passage of time." He giggled. "Sometimes I'm so full of myself. Anyway, what's wrong with a cozy evening for two?"

She had heard that one before as well. "Where *are* we?"

He waved an arm at the sick-looking woods behind him. "Welcome to my humble abode. As you can see, it needs a little, um, straightening up. The servants all seem to be on strike at the moment."

She couldn't tell if he was serious. With some men you never knew. "Who *are* you?"

"Your date for the evening—ain't it great?"

Figures. She sighed. "And I thought my day couldn't get worse."

He wrinkled his nose. "Not your type?"

She wanted to tell him that a furry Lee Van Cleef didn't do much for her. She just smiled politely. Producers and directors came in all shapes and sizes. He could be important, for all she knew.

"What don't you like? My abrupt manner? Take-charge attitude? Light-heartedness?"

"Your slobbering doesn't really do much for me."

"What's wrong with it? Not enough? Too much?"

"*Some* girls might like it, I guess…"

"I take it no one slobbers at your pool parties."

"Everyone's much too drunk to notice."

"So maybe if I don't slobber, you'll be warm for my form?"

"I'm not too warm about how you dragged me here. A girl doesn't like to be manhandled."

"How else could I get you to come with me?"

"You might have asked me."

He blinked. "You would have come, then?"

"No, but the gesture would have been nice…"

"You don't find me dashing? Debonair? Ruggedly handsome?"

"Hardly." He was no Cary Grant.

"How's this?" His image instantly changed to Cary dressed in a dark two-piece suit he wore in *Philadelphia Story*. "Dashing enough?"

"How did you *do* that?" She didn't remember Johnny saying anything about a magician showing up at the party.

"It's all done with mirrors."

The stumps and rotting deadfalls revealed nothing.

"I don't see any mirrors."

"They're invisible."

Terrific. Another guy who considered her gullible and stupid. She should be used to this. But that wasn't the main issue. "Where did the slobbering wolf guy go?"

Cary vanished. "Miss me?" The wolf guy returned, his grin just as bright as before.

Her heart sank. "No."

"How's this?" Humphrey Bogart appeared in his white dinner jacket from *Casablanca*. "Play it, Sam…"

"Stop doing that and just take me back. I'm getting depressed."

"Me? Take you back? Where? You're depressed?"

"You. Take me back to Johnny's. Yes, I'm depressed."

"Who's Johnny? Why are you depressed?"

20

"This place is really creeping me out. And it smells awfully—" The realization hit her hard. Her temples pounded. "You…don't know *Johnny*?"

"I'll bring air freshener next time. I keep forgetting, babes don't like things that smell bad, do they? Mint okay with you?"

She forced herself to stay calm. There had to be a logical explanation for all this. Losing her cool wouldn't help. "Johnny's the one giving the party."

His blank look caused an icy tingling to slide down her shoulders.

"Well?" she managed weakly.

"I'm thinking of a really dynamite answer."

She was in no mood for this. "Take me back. Right now."

"Have a peek at this first." Fred Astaire, in tails and top hat, held out his cane. He tried one of his old spins and nearly tripped on an exposed tree root.

She shook her head.

Another flash. Clark Gable, as Rhett Butler in *Gone With the Wind*, winked devilishly and tipped his hat. "Frankly, my dear—"

"I'm not having a good time, whoever you are." But she couldn't help wondering how he knew about her favorite stars.

"Tell you what. We can just mosey on over to that humongous deadfall and have our own little pool party. But we'll have to improvise. The closest body of water lies on the other side of those dead trees. It's not bad if you ignore the smell. Usually, the sludge doesn't make it this far south. Anyway, if you're still bummed out, later on I'll give you the bad news about where you are."

Tiffany had the sinking feeling she wasn't going back to Johnny's.

CHAPTER 3

A Summoning—sort of

Dead limbs forming skeletal fingers blocked part of the tunnel opening.

A fist of hanging moss punched Todd's forehead when he squeezed through. As he stepped over a jagged heap of rotting lumber, something poked him in the leg. He gasped, cursed, and pulled away. His unsteady flashlight beam splashed the uneven rock wall with a bright sheen of irritation.

Something flickered in his roving beam.

Darcy grabbed Todd's wrist, forcing him to keep the glow steadied on the shaft. "Look."

A pentagram sprayed in neon white covered the center of the rock floor. Half-melted candles were arranged there, too—black ones placed at each corner of the pentagram.

"There's even incense," she whispered.

Todd pulled away sharply.

"Someone must come out here. That's the Seal of Solomon." This was really strange. "Do you know what that means?"

Todd shrugged. "Some dude named Solomon who gets off on black candles and incense came in here?"

Darcy wondered if Todd was genuinely stupid or just trying to be funny. "It means the force is here, silly."

"What force?"

"The dark force. It's an aura. A strong, negative aura. That's what evil is. Some people say every bad deed conjures up a demon."

23

"The force be with you." His arms straight out in front, Leon shuffled around on stiff legs like a zombie. "Beam me up, Scotty!"

Todd lifted his bottle of Wild Turkey. He had a healthy swallow, then placed the bottle gently on the uneven rock floor at his feet. His loud belch vibrated through the shaft. "Two points," he said, snickering.

Ignoring him, Darcy squeezed out a book of matches from the back pocket of her jeans and lit the candles. The shaft brightened with an eerie glow. Tense shadows caused by the flickering flames slid erratically along the wall. She leaned an incense stick against the rock and lit it. A strong sandalwood odor rose.

"Who are we trying to bring up?" Leon sat cross-legged in the corner. He pulled in some fresh weed and let it back out in a loud, steady hiss.

Darcy sat in the center of the pentagram. The printout covered her left thigh. "I thought I'd start out small."

"You mean like one of those Munchkins in *Wizard of Oz*, only pissed off and slightly more radical?" Leon asked.

"No, silly. A subordinate."

"What's that?"

"They're not as powerful." She glanced at her witchcraft book. "Demons come in three categories. Superiors, subordinates, and inferiors."

Leon giggled. "Three categories. Plain, with nuts, or sugar-coated."

Todd shook his head. "Man, you're *such* a dorkster."

"I'm getting the munchies. Bring anything with ya, Todderino?"

"Just some warm Kielbasa and a pair of nuts."

Leon giggled.

Todd sniffed loudly, no doubt from the weed. He turned to Darcy. "Why waste your time on a radical midget?"

She couldn't believe him sometimes. Everyone knew what could happen if you summoned a superior spirit. But she didn't think he'd understand. They were both too messed-up to pay attention, anyway. She suspected the spell wouldn't work but knew better than say that. Todd would pitch a fit if he realized he had come out here for nothing. Better tell them something to ease their minds. "I don't want to be responsible for bringing up a full-blown superior, thank you very much."

Todd belched loudly again. "You've seen too damn many Buffy shows."

"Heavy-duty." Leon's eyes were glazed and out of focus. "Buffy and the pissed-off Munchkin demon dude."

Sighing, she picked up the paper. "We have to bow our heads."

Todd sniffed some more. "What *is* this? Church? I ain't bowin' my damn head."

"Just do it, all right?"

"Man oh man…"

"Let's do this right."

"I didn't come here to do that right. I came here for…for a good time."

Some guys were such dreamers. "Work with me here, okay?"

Todd and Leon bowed their heads.

She cleared her throat and consulted the spell. "We, proud followers of the Prince of the Seraphim, Lord of the upcoming Reclamation of Man, kneel humbly before you and respectfully plead that our benefactor, a subordinate

Prince of the Thrones of the Dark Angels, appear before us."

Silence.

"You're supposed to say 'Hail, Satan,'" she whispered.

"Hail, Satan dude!" Leon shouted.

Todd sighed. "Hail, whatever."

Darcy repeated her conjuration. "Say it again."

"Hail, Satan baby."

"Hail...man oh man..."

Darcy repeated it one last time.

"*Ahhhh...kuuu-cheeeellll*!" It came without warning, exploding from Todd's throat and thumping off the rock walls. Groaning, he wiped his nose and chin.

Darcy glared at him.

"Sorry. Incense sorta messed up my...ahhhh...*guuu-chilllll!*"

"Do you mind? We're in the middle of –"

"Kuuu-*chilllllllll!*"

"Todd Bochner, you're *such* a creep..."

"Wow!" Leon's glazed eyes sparkled in the candlelight. "That last load flew clean over her head and splashed the wall! Think you can do it again, chief?"

Todd wiped his nose with his shirt sleeve. "Man, that stuff does a serious job on the old sinuses!"

"Can't you take *anything* seriously?" She wanted him to disappear. It was such a shame that she probably couldn't find a chant to actually make that happen.

"Can't help it. That incense crap—"

Rumble...

"Heavy-duty!" Leon gaped at the shaft opening. "Sounds like somebody's going seriously nuclear out there."

26

Another rumble, this one louder.

"Sounds too heavy for a pissed-off, radical midget from Munchkin Land…"

A white flash flickered, lighting the entrance.

Todd sat bolt upright. "Oh, shit!"

"Now what?" Darcy asked.

"A storm's headed this way!"

"So?"

"My Camaro!" Grabbing the whiskey bottle, he scrambled to his feet. "If we don't get that top up quick, the seats'll be ruined!"

CHAPTER 4

Tiffany in the Valley of Decay
A Gathering of Demons

An explosion from above shook the clammy ground.
And another.

At the end of a third, a blinding flash forced Tiffany's
eyes shut. When she opened them, the wolf guy was gone.
A strange howling pierced the blackness above her,
trailing off into heavy silence.

Now who did he turn into? Claude Rains from *The
Invisible Man?*

She studied the terrain straight ahead. The broken
limbs and twigs covering the ground revealed nothing.
"Are you going to take me back or what?" she asked
nervously.

Silence.

"You're still here, right?" She checked behind her,
just to make sure. He had snuck up behind her once
before, hadn't he? "You're just playing another one of
your stupid games."

Still nothing.

She was in no mood for this. If he were going to
continue to play games, she would have to find her way
back to Johnny's estate all by herself. She would tell them
what she thought of their stupid pool parties, then find a
phone and call for a cab.

Rustling behind the trees ten or twenty yards to her
right made her jerk her head.

"Is that...you?"

More rustling. This time, it was coming from
somewhere else. On her left.

Fear gripped her, and she shivered. He wouldn't leave her here alone, would he? He was weird and silly, but he wouldn't leave her here by herself. Especially since he obviously wanted to party.

"Where...are you?" She glanced behind her. He wasn't there, either.

He had to be *some*where. He couldn't just disappear, could he?

Or *could* he?

He *had* turned into Cary Grant, hadn't he? And Bogie. And Fred Astaire. And Clark Gable. Anyone who could do neat stuff like that could certainly disappear.

He also seemed the type who liked having his ego stroked. Maybe if she appealed to his better nature, he'd stop this foolishness and reappear.

"Could you *please* do Cary Grant again? How about Cary in *Bringing Up Baby?* That was another of my favorites. He had these thick glasses, but he was still cute, in a nerdy sort of way. His name was David Huxley, and—"

Two huge dark shapes emerged from behind the trees. The harsh echoing sounds of breaking limbs and snapping twigs slammed through her.

Instinct told her to run. If she found her way back to the wall of darkness, she might be able to return to the gray pasture. Maybe they wouldn't follow her there.

Her soaked sandals were gone. She had also lost her sarong wrap—probably when the wolf guy dragged her through the trees. Darn. It took three months to save enough money to buy that outfit. She had only worn it one other time.

The crunching of dead leaves behind her made her flesh break out in knots.

The stench of rotting flesh reached out for her. Its rancidness made her gag. They were probably only yards away.

Mindful of her footing, she glanced behind her. Panic swept through her in a hot, violent wave.

There were more than two of them after her.

***

From the castle window, Balberith could see the slithering flames lighting up the darkness in the valley beyond the woods.

The Mortanites did their job well, rounding up wandering lawyers, paparazzi, and other dregs, tossing them in the pit and making sure the fire continued to sputter and sizzle.

Mortanites loved their work.

Pyromaniacs *should* know how to keep a fire going, shouldn't they?

"How did *that* abomination happen?" asked a throaty voice behind him.

Balberith turned. His four hooded companions huddled around the stone table in the center of the candlelit room. This was going to quickly turn into another session of name-calling and finger-pointing if they weren't careful. Demons could be so radical at times. "How should I know?" he said. "A mortal sneezed."

"And summoned a colossal idiot." Mastiphal, the dark figure on the far left, peeled a maggot from his snout and swallowed it whole. "Don't ancient spells matter anymore?"

"Gutrillus Canus should not have escaped." Braithwaite, the broad figure next to Mastiphal, straightened in his seat. His black eyes glowed like hot

30

embers. Froth bubbled between his cracked lips. "What's it matter how it happened?"

"Modern technology has seriously changed things up there," Balberith said.

"You *would* say that," Mastiphal replied. "You and Braithwaite were the two responsible for enabling mortals to develop computers in the first place."

"We didn't do it so those idiots could use it to make spells." Steam rose from the Braithwaite's hood. "We did it to hasten their demise."

"Doesn't matter. We all know how mortals destroy everything they touch. Every bit of technology being made up there now becomes a new toy."

"But it's working. They're using it to destroy one another, aren't they?"

"As well as creating spells…"

"We're getting off the main issue," Balberith said. "Gutrillus must be brought back quickly."

"Now *there's* a revelation," Braithwaite said sourly.

"Don't cop an attitude. I know that's your thing, but—"

"My *thing* is turning mortals into idiots." Braithwaite's broad, bull-like face scowled inside the hood. The large silver ring piercing his short, wide nose glinted in the candlelight.

"That isn't difficult," Mastiphal said. "Any inferior could manage it."

"That's right." Olivier, the vulture-faced figure on the right, nodded. "Most mortals are already borderline idiots."

"But I'm able to nudge them the rest of the way better than anyone," Braithwaite said.

31

"This isn't the time to show your horns." Mastiphal wiped drool from his snout with a hairy paw. "Balberith did an admirable job during his reign."

"You'll see a definite improvement once I'm up there," Braithwaite said.

Olivier mashed the large fly perched on the tip of his beaky nose. "Let's concentrate on what has to be done to bring Gutrillus back."

"An inferior must be sent." Situated between Braithwaite and Olivier, Asmodeus busily sharpened his three-inch nails with a large rusty file. "Gutrillus can sniff out any one of us a mile away."

"One inferior can't handle Gutrillus," Balberith said. "We'll need at least two."

"We can spare two. A trickster would suffice."

"What about the other?"

"A distraction will do. Gutrillus is a space cadet. Toss him a rat or a female and his brain turns to mush."

"I'll be leaving for Central Florida," Braithwaite said. "I vote on having this done quickly. I don't want that dunderhead making a shambles before I get up there. He's a horrible excuse for a demon. Everyone knows demons don't *improve* things for mortals."

"We don't even know where he went." Asmodeus shrugged.

"He surfaced in America." Mastiphal snatched the large black beetle descending his forehead, held it delicately between two sharp claws, and popped it into his mouth. "In southeastern Ohio."

"How do you know *that*?"

"One of my inferiors recognized the tunnel." Mastiphal's munching resonated loudly within the room.

32

"It's a coal mining shaft intermingling with a toxic landfill."

"Toxic dumps are everywhere up there."

Braithwaite wrinkled his nose. "Those damned things are making *this* place reek."

"There goes the neighborhood," Asmodeus said dryly.

Balberith joined his companions at the table. "I spent a few years in the Ohio Valley. Several of our associates live in Raven."

"Oh yes," Mastiphal said. "Those whiners who keep bugging us."

"They're frightened," Balberith said. "They miss me."

"Quick," Braithwaite said. "Someone find a violin, a box of chocolates and someone who gives a healthy damn."

"Save the sarcasm," Balberith snapped. "You're the one who keeps insisting on multiple ballots. Otherwise, this issue would've already been voted on."

"It isn't my fault we have so much trouble assembling. If the subs and supers weren't wandering around out there in the Valley, looking for fresh stuff—"

"Braithwaite needs to be up there *now*." Asmodeus pocketed his file. "Six mortal months have passed. Mortals can't be left unsupervised that long."

"Sonneillon is presently temporarily handling the middle section of the United States," Olivier said. "Maybe he could take some time off—"

"He's much too busy arranging tornadoes from his Omaha offices," Braithwaite said. "And obviously having lots of fun doing so."

"I envy him," Mastiphal said. "Tornadoes are fun to watch. Especially when you let them loose on trailer parks."

"Lots of trailer parks up there," Asmodeus said, chuckling.

"The mortal who sneezed might have been one of our associates," Balberith said. "They were probably trying to contact me and pulled up Gutrillus by mistake."

"Let them have him, then," Asmodeus said.

"They wouldn't tolerate Gutrillus," Balberith said. "He doesn't respond well to authority."

"How do we keep mortals from sneezing and summoning just anyone?" Asmodeus asked.

"Agaliarept could send over some planes from Egypt to wipe out another batch." Olivier studied his webbed hands.

"It would take too many planes," Braithwaite said.

"Is Gutrillus aware of our associates?" Olivier asked.

"Of course not," Balberith said. "Because of his classic blunders, Gutrillus can't even enter the Castle. He can do little harm in the Valley."

"By the way, where *is* everyone?" Asmodeus asked.

"In the Valley, hunting down that delicious blonde Gutrillus dragged in," Olivier said.

"Little harm, my huge, hairy ass," Braithwaite said irritably.

Asmodeus groaned. "I told you it was a mistake to let him wander. No wonder we can't get everyone together for a quorum. He'd do less damage if we kept him in one of the cellars, feeding the Malamores."

Olivier, short and blocky in his long robes, got up and waddled over to the archway.

"Where are you going?" Mastiphal asked.

"To my rock garden."

"Now is *not* the time for your infernal puttering," Braithwaite snapped.

"I don't intend to putter. I'm going to pick out a trickster."

CHAPTER 5

Back Among Mindless Mortals

Buck-naked, Gutril sat in the wet grass beneath a buckeye tree while the last of the black storm clouds slammed east.

Last he remembered, he was all set to sample that hot blonde wandering too close to the Meddaworld. A knockout, but a little ditzy, whining about some stupid pool party. Judging by her costume, it must have been a real sizzler.

That ear-splitting explosion moments ago turned everything into chaos.

Thunder from the storm?

Actually, it sounded more like a *sneeze*.

Because of it, he was back up here among the mortals. Cool beans. Not much entertainment down there in the Valley. But since they ordered him to stay there for the next two hundred years, he had no choice. Ever since his clever bit of tweaking at Belias' Watch Tower, no one wanted to be anywhere near him.

A shame he wasn't able to have his way with Blondie first. But she wouldn't be lonely in his absence. Alachua and Jouvart were close by, looking for fun and excitement. Plenty of choice stuff abounded down there— the place had been getting crowded lately—but everyone loved hitting the new kid on the block. Too bad she wouldn't stay fresh. That heat and humidity did a heavy number on silicone. Collagen bit the dust not long afterward, too.

He wasn't even supposed to be up here. After his screw-up in Chicago, they told him couldn't ever come up here again. He gave demons a bad name, they said. Did the same sort of stuff a goody-two-shoes angel would do.

Were they kidding?

They could be *such* dickheads.

They could all rot down there, dammit. He was up here again, and that was all he cared about.

Some idiot mortal with a brand-new spell must have called for him.

Looking around, he figured he had obviously come up through the crack in the ground a few feet to his left. The rich aroma leaking from it turned just as bitter as the River of Blood. A toxic dump, obviously. Toxic dumps weakened the soil.

Time was crucial. He had to act fast. They would surely send someone to take him back down very shortly.

No way would he go back. Nothing to do but wander around in the woods, finding ways to amuse himself.

First, he had to find out where he was.

He didn't want to bump into Astaroth or Baphomet. They both went nuclear when you ventured too close to their Asian or European turfs. Agaliarept had been managing inbred camel jockeys in Africa the last fifty years and turned super nasty when someone infringed on his territory.

South America was out of the question, as well. As overseer for the drug cartels, Leviathan turned intruders into sacks of cocaine lodged in the bellies of drug mules.

Australia was cool beans. That is, it would be if you kept clear of Saalah and his gang of Outback Badlanders. More rats there than anywhere else. Gutril considered the little critters cuddly and didn't know what the fuss was about. Rats were much cooler than mortals. They were

37

industrious, determined, interesting and especially succulent deep-fried.

Hopefully, this was Balberith's former stomping ground. Since the Legion had so much trouble getting everyone together to vote on a successor, the area been unsupervised for six mortal months. If he was lucky, he could hide or find a mortal host long before another super was sent up.

America was great fun. Hordes of shallow-minded idiots wandering around, their heads in a fog. Americans worshiped the young and the worthless, serial killers and athletes. Any inferior could control such gullible sheep. And there were seldom consequences to face. Their judicial system, fashioned ages ago by Balberith, kept the laws favoring the guilty.

Gutril remembered someone saying that a foul-smelling tunnel meant an abandoned mine. Since so many mortals had died from inhaling coal dust more than half a century ago, society had closed most of the mines. Now, due to modern technology, toxic dumps had taken their place.

Something tangy lay in the bushes.

Most of the skin and fur had been chewed away but Gutril could tell it was once a rabbit.

Maybe he could find a dog lying along the road, tenderizing. Or a raccoon. His mouth watered. Possums were okay if you caught them at the right time. He couldn't remember the last time he'd enjoyed fresh meat. Not much tender stuff in the Valley. Sibrius usually got first dibs and rarely shared. You just didn't want to antagonize a bad-tempered, salivating two-headed pit bull.

At least the rain had stopped. His soaked red pelt caused a shiver billowing down his limbs. He hated being wet—it made him smell funky. Mortals didn't care for funky, dead-rot, or morning dragon breath. They preferred perfumes, colognes, sweet-smelling soaps, and minty mouthwashes.

He shook himself off.

Clothes. He needed to appear appropriately dressed to blend in. Mortals couldn't cope with nudity in public. It played havoc with their brain cells.

He had no idea what the present fashions were. In those Third World countries, outerwear was simple—crap-wrap around the head, a burnoose covering the bod, and a pair of J. C. Water-walkers for the feet.

Not long ago an American rock star showed up down below in bell-bottoms, leather boots, flowered shirt, beads, and weird hair. But the athlete sent down more recently wore a baggy t-shirt, shorts pulled down to his knees, exposed checkered undershorts, tennis shoes, and tattoos covering his dark flesh—one of them on Mr. Happy that said *PEEKABOO* on good days, *POO* on bad ones.

Gutril wandered down the rain-slicked path.

Battered couches languished in the damp overgrown grass, giving off more sourness. TV sets with shattered screens lay in a muddled pile. Old tires, courtesy of Goodyear, no longer rolled. Beer bottles congregated among mashed Coors cans, some of them standing upright. Bullet holes riddled three cans.

Bullet holes and beer cans. That definitely meant America.

Far out. Casual wear.

Gutril preferred the hippie look; it reflected his independence. He also admired their lingo, which reflected his personality.

Besides, he didn't want to wear his pants so low that his crack showed. It just wasn't dignified—not even for a demon.

He closed his eyes. His lean figure immediately revealed a white tee shirt with the logo *KEDS ARE FOR KIDS* displayed prominently on his skinny chest, faded Levi's with frayed holes at the knees, and scuffed tennis shoes.

Half-hidden in the wet grass, a squirrel carcass blocked his path. *Cool beans*.

He bent and sniffed.

Bummer. Only an hour or two past how he liked it.

No problem. He'd find something shortly. This area looked promising for fresh smorgasbord.

CHAPTER 6

Tiffany Finds a Frisky Flower

A flower protruded from a swell of pine needles just a few feet away.

Irregular in shape, it stood about a foot high. Its petals were bright yellow and veined with purple, its leaves a lush green.

Tiffany scowled. Flowers? Out *here*? In the middle of a forest of dead trees, mud, and that really gross sulfur smell?

It was so colorful and pretty. Maybe she had gotten closer to that other place than she realized.

But the flowers in the meadow were drab and lackluster. This one actually *sparkled*…

The rustling in the bushes a few yards to her left wrenched her alert. She took off running.

The flower reappeared farther down, poking out behind a rotting deadfall.

Was it *also* following her?

Silly girl. Flowers couldn't do that. Maybe they grew wild out here. Otherwise, she was trapped in an insane dream—probably from that drink.

Of *course* it was that drink. What else could it be? It would explain that weird wolf guy who kept changing into her favorite movie stars and then disappearing. And those disgusting, smelly shapes chasing her.

And a flower that seemed to be *staring* at her…

That drink had certainly done wild, scary things to her head.

It was her fault for sipping it. Her fault for even going to that party in the first place. It *had* to turn out badly. She didn't know anyone, for one thing. And she'd accepted a drink, for another.

If only that director guy hadn't distracted her…

She had to get back to her place and clean up her act, maybe take more acting lessons. It would also help to find an agent who wouldn't toss her in with the wild crowd. The right agent might land her decent acting jobs. But it was almost impossible to find a good one when you weren't already famous…

Another pursuer—this one a giant bird—peeked at her from behind a tree. Two huge claws appeared, groping for her.

She backed up, spun around and—

Someone else

(a red blur)

grabbed her wrist.

A cold hand yanked her in the opposite direction, through the trees, and upward. Tiffany no longer felt the cold wetness numbing her feet.

She was actually *flying*!

But how could that be?

How could anyone *fly*?

But it was true. She was climbing higher and higher, into the growing blackness. The trees grew smaller beneath them, blurring into a dark mass of bad memory.

Darkness blanketed her again. The air turned rotten eggy. The blackness dimmed, revealing a jagged vertical shaft lined with cracks and crevices. Light gray gooey stuff clinging to its sides like bubbly snot trickled from its fractures.

Gross. This was even worse than the cold, clammy ground.

But it wasn't nearly as bad as dodging those scary creatures…

If only she hadn't lost her sandals.

They were her favorites. They cost her a bundle. She promised herself that when she got out of this mess, she would find the best sandals money could buy.

CHAPTER 7

The Party Animal

Todd finished the weed and sat back in his seat, waiting for his head to deflate back to its normal size.

The storm had passed, trickling down to a light drizzle gently tapping the windshield like a bunch of pygmies with tiny ice picks. Nasty one, too. Good thing they got the top up in time.

However, sitting here in the middle of the woods, coming down from a mellow, sure was weird. All those freaky sounds and shadows among the trees made his flesh crawl.

"Looks like a creature moving around in there," Darcy said softly, staring at the trees moving in the wind.

Leon giggled. "Bigfoot wants to take our favorite cheerleader babe into his cave to bear his children."

"Funny," she said flatly.

"What's wrong?" Todd asked. "Still pissed you couldn't conjure up your demon?"

"You ruined my spell," she snapped. "You and your sinuses from Hell."

Todd snickered. Her tattoo was doing a number on him. That long black hair wasn't hurting, neither. Or those tight jeans. "There are other things we can do, you know."

"Don't even think of it. I'm not in the mood. Just take me home."

Todd glanced at Leon's dark shape in the rearview. "How come chicks ain't in the mood when they're ticked off?"

Leon shrugged. "Ask her."

"How come you chicks ain't in the mood when you're ticked off?"

"If I have to tell you, you don't really need to know," she said.

Todd groaned. Chicks never made any sense—not even when they weren't getting wasted. He flicked on the ignition. No use staying here anymore.

"I hope you're taking me home now." She shot him a suspicious look.

"Nothing else to do, right?" He was tired of dealing with her shit. At least his buzz helped a little. Chicks were much easier to take when you were mellow.

"You're not even going to give me a hard time?" Damn if she didn't look worried.

"I thought you wanted to go home."

"Well, yeah…"

"*Now* what's wrong?"

"Nothing."

Todd couldn't believe how weird chicks were. They pitched a fit when they weren't in the mood, then weirded out when you didn't give a damn. Like his old man always said, you can't live with 'em, can't shoot 'em.

No wonder the old boy walked around mumbling all the time.

***

Halfway back to town, a long black shadow broke through the Camaro's headlight beams.

Todd's foot mashed the brake pedal to the floor.

Leon yelled, "Geronimo!" and ducked behind the seats.

Darcy twisted sideways and covered her face.

The Camaro fishtailed. Gritting his teeth, Todd clutched the wheel so tightly, his fingers went numb.

45

Squealing in protest, Cammie skidded past the center line. His mind switched off. He couldn't remember which way to turn. Everything in Driver's Ed Class had become a swelling emptiness heightened by the pot, the whiskey, the fear, and all the heavy Z's he'd grabbed in the class. Cammie slid off the road, thumping into the wet grass, then slammed against a bush, rocked unsteadily, and finally stopped.

He sat rigidly, the back of his neck damp. He wanted to wipe it dry but had to peel his clenched hands from the wheel first.

Moments later his heart slid back down where it belonged, and his breathing returned to normal.

"Wow!" Leon, grinning stupidly, propped his chin on the back of Todd's seat. "That was some rodeo, Chief!"

Darcy lowered her hands. "Did we…hit somebody?"

"How should *I* know?" He couldn't see any better than she could. But he was reasonably sure everything was okay. No thump, no harsh impact. Maybe just an animal scurrying across the road.

He opened the glove box, grabbed the flashlight, and tried not to drop it. His heart thrashing, he climbed out and pointed the beam as steady as his shaken nerves would allow.

Something moved on the other side of the road.

Todd fought down the urge to dive back into the Camaro.

The dark mass rose, taking on a human shape. At first he thought it was some sort of

(*wolf?*)

animal.

A lanky dude in a tee shirt, trousers and tennis shoes approached him. His shirt said, *KEDS ARE FOR KIDS* in black letters. Looked fairly new but had some mud splatters on it – probably from landing in the wet grass.

Lee Van Cleef. That's why Todd thought the figure was a wolf. The same kind of face, only longer and thinner. And with more hair.

"Yo! Dude!" Todd's throat, scraped raw, barely functioned. He wondered if it was the grass or the Wild Turkey. Probably both. "You hurt?"

"Naw, I'm okay." He wasn't freaked out or upset. A good sign.

"Did I hit ya?"

"Missed me by at least an inch. No prob."

"Man…why were ya so close to the road?"

"Can't get picked up if no one sees you."

"Hitching?"

"You're good. You a psychic?"

Cool dude, putting him on like that. At least he wasn't spazzed for nearly being run over. "The old man won't let me appear in public without adult supervision," Todd said, grinning.

"Where are you guys headed?"

"Back to town."

"Where's that?"

"Raven. Aren't from around here, are ya?"

"You *are* good. South, a little ways."

"Moundsville?"

"Farther south. Could you give me a ride?"

Dude's tennies were soaked. Todd was just gonna have to suck it up. He'd almost smeared this dude—why quibble about a little mud?

"Sure thing."

"Nice wheels." He nodded at the Camaro, grinning, showing all kinds of glistening teeth. "I'll bet she flies."

47

"Zero to sixty in just over six." Todd puffed up.

"Far out."

Todd liked him. Dudes appreciating a monster machine should stick together. "Climb in, man. Let's torch some highway!"

***

The passenger door clicked open.

The interior light oozed over the man's features. His piercing

(*red*?)

eyes

(silly, they're light brown)

focused on Darcy.

His jeans fit nice. A little dated, though. His shirt was from the late sixties or seventies. And the glint in his eyes made her self-conscious about her tank top.

"Let him in," Todd said from the driver's door. "He's comin' back with us." Todd hurried toward the back, the flashlight beam jumping like a crazed firefly.

"What's he doing now?"

The stranger said, "Checking for damages, I guess."

She pulled her seat forward. He squeezed in, his head bumping the convertible top. Leon moved over.

"What were you doing out there?" she asked.

"Hitching."

"Kind of dangerous, isn't it? This time of night?"

"All kinds of weirdoes out there. You guys having a party?" He spotted Todd's bottle.

"Righty-oh, Chief!" Leon handed it over.

Todd slid in behind the wheel and pulled the door shut.

"Everything okay?" she asked.

"A scratch from that damn bush. I'll know better tomorrow, when it's light. But at least we ain't stuck." He grinned at their new passenger. "You a party animal, man?"

"Right on all three counts." He hoisted the bottle.

CHAPTER 8

Rat Salad

Leon's folks owned a three-bedroom ranch house on Ohio Street, a mile south of East Main. The subdivision was the result of *Project Revamp Raven!* the City Council organized a few years ago. Farmland bordering the area was bought up and cleared, the old houses north of it torn down, bulldozed, and replaced with condos and affordable homes. Winslow Landscaping & Development headed the deal.

Leon's dad ran errands for Old Man Winslow, mostly in Pittsburgh, which was two hours away. Leon's mom usually went with him. She liked the stores there and never passed up the chance to stock up on new outfits. Todd considered Leon one lucky dude for having the place to himself so much. It was almost like having your own place at eighteen. And it gave Todd a place to crash whenever Todd's old man wanted to kick him around after coming home drunk.

Todd parked along the curb.

"I thought you were taking me home," Darcy said, glaring.

"I figured since we're all in a party mood, we'd get down with some sounds."

"But—"

"Sounds cool," the hitcher said.

Darcy shut her mouth.

Whoa. Todd couldn't believe it. Some guys definitely had the knack. Better ask this dude about that a little later. A guy could never learn enough about shutting up women.

50

They got out of the car. The hitcher approached the curb. "Got any dogs or cats?"

"We had a Golden Retriever," Leon said, "but she got old and the vet had to put her down. Like dogs?"

"*Love* 'em."

Leon's pensive expression wrinkled his forehead. Todd knew something was coming. Leon always turned deep about the dumbest shit whenever buzzed. "Know who you look like?" he asked the hitcher dude.

"No. Who do I look like?"

"Lee Van Cleef?" Todd suggested.

Leon shook his head. "Wile E. Coyote!"

The hitcher didn't reply. He just tiptoed down the walk, almost like a coyote, in fact—or a wolf. He stopped and stared at the woods behind the houses. His nose crinkled. "Any critters in there?"

"Whaddya mean?" Leon asked. "Snakes and stuff?"

"Raccoons? Possums? Maybe a squirrel or chipmunk?"

"I thought you liked dogs."

He grinned. "I'm what you'd call an animal lover, Chief."

***

Darcy popped her well-used Black Sabbath CD into Leon's player.

Todd sprawled out on the living room couch with his Wild Turkey. Leon relaxed in the La-Z-Boy, a few swallows left of the Bacardi bottle in his lap. The hitcher sat in an armchair, drinking vodka.

Darcy fixed a rum and coke, diluting it with ice. She rarely drank and hated the taste of whiskey. She couldn't understand why so many people liked it so much. It

51

baffled her, something tasting so awful making people do stupid, dangerous things.

But she needed to calm down since their close call on Raven Road West. She'd have to keep an eye on Todd to make sure he didn't overdo it. She didn't want him taking her home drunk. Right now he was watching the inch or so of whiskey floating at the bottom of the bottle as if waiting for it to do something interesting. Maybe he'd doze off and sober up. In the meantime, she wanted to relax and enjoy the loud, penetrating strains of *Paranoid*.

Leon's high-pitched, off-key voice cracked horribly while he sang, drowning out the Sabbath.

The hitcher grinned, nodding in time to the song.

His grin made her want to cover up. She had the strangest feeling about him. She saw darkness in his eyes. Darkness and coldness. And despite what Todd said, she didn't think he resembled that movie villain at all. But he did look sinister—no doubt because of those eyes.

"Cool lyrics," the hitcher said. "How old are these charts?"

"From the seventies," Darcy said. She got up and picked up the CD case from the table. As she checked the copyright date, she realized something wasn't quite right. This guy looked way over thirty. Wouldn't he be familiar with the Sabbath?

"Mind if I have a peek?"

She handed it to him and sat back down.

"What were you guys doing out there tonight?" he asked.

She hesitated. Talking about witchcraft and black magic scared some people. "Well, it's Friday night and we didn't have anything better to do, so we decided to drive around and—"

"Conjure up a demon!" Leon yelled, and went right back to the opening strains of *Evil Woman*.

Darcy wanted to sew Leon's lips together with baling twine. How could he even hear what they were talking about? His horrible caterwauling drowned out everything. Todd's fault, of course. When you hung out with a moron, it rubbed off.

"A demon, eh?"

Darcy got up again, this time to drop another splash of rum into her drink. Getting smashed right now seemed a sensible way of handling embarrassment. "Just something to do on a Friday night."

"Any luck?"

She poured more Coke into her glass, wrenched the Bacardi bottle away from Leon, dropped some into her drink and shoved the bottle roughly between his thighs. He gasped between "play your games" and "with me." She sank back in her chair. "Todd ruined everything when he interrupted my chant."

"What did he do?"

He obviously wanted to make fun of her. That's what guys did. Everything was okay with just the two of them, but whenever they grouped together they became jerks. Too much testosterone in the air upset their chemical balance.

"Why so interested?" she asked.

"Just curious. How long did you stick around after your chant?"

"Not long. It started to storm. We had to leave. Todd had the top down on the way over. We had to—"

"Crap. No whiskey!" Todd crawled over to the cabinet, opened the door, and stuck his head inside. "Not much in here. Your parents AA?"

Leon said, "My folks don't drink *that* much..."

"Dude, your daddy runs errands for Old Man Winslow!"

"So?"

"That old boy's a nasty old fart. How can anyone put up with his shit sober?"

Leon finished the rum and pressed his left eyeball against the bottle. He appeared to be studying a strange new world. "Where'd all my rum go? We need more."

"And people in Hell need ice water. We ain't old enough to buy whiskey, amigo. Why do you think I stole this Wild Turkey from Denner's Restaurant?"

"Because you don't know any better?" Darcy couldn't resist jumping in. "You don't respect other people's property? You don't care about anyone but yourself?"

"Naw, the bottle just sat there, and nobody seemed to notice it." He grinned. "One of the perks of being a stock boy."

"You call stealing a *perk*?"

"How about that?" He snorted. "Buffy wants to be a nun."

"You need help," she said. "Serious help."

"All I really need is more juice." He pushed a clump of dirty brown hair out of his eyes. "Can't have a party without it."

"Go get some," the hitcher said.

"You deaf, man? Ain't old enough. Neither's Leon. How about you?"

"What about me?"

"You're old enough."

"I don't know my way around. It would take too long."

"You can ride with me. I'll—"

"There's no time."

Todd opened his mouth, but nothing came out. Darcy wondered if the weed or the Wild Turkey had gummed up his thought processes. She nearly laughed. You couldn't gum up something that wasn't there in the first place.

"You might get lucky tonight," the hitcher said. "But hurry. They'll be closing soon."

Todd stared wide-eyed at the hitcher, still saying nothing. Leon stared off into space.

"You guys okay?" Darcy asked. "You both look…spazzed."

"Spazzed," Leon said in a whisper. "Don't you play games with me, you evil woman."

"Man, what a total dorkster." Todd, back to his obnoxious self, reached into his pocket for his keys. "C'mon. Let's get some booze."

***

"That was big-time strange." The girl gawked at the closing door. "They both know they can't buy liquor. Why would they—"

"Like I said, they might get lucky this time," Gutril said.

"How do you figure?"

"All they have to do is take it and run."

"You mean *steal* it? Right out of the *store*?"

"He stole the Wild Turkey, didn't he?"

"Todd's messed up. I must have gone seriously brain-dead to let him take me out to the mine in the first place."

"You never did say how he screwed up your conjuration."

"He sneezed."

55

It was a sneeze, after all. They could try and keep him down there for hundreds of years, but all it took to bring him back was a mortal's *sneeze*? *Far out.*

"You might have summoned a demon without knowing it."

"How could you summon a demon...without knowing it?"

"Stranger things have happened."

"Scary." She fidgeted in her chair.

Nice when they were nervous. When they were distracted, you could get in their heads easier.

"Which demon were you summoning?"

"I didn't know for sure."

"That's kind of stupid, not knowing who you're summoning." Bummer. She was just as clueless as her two idiot friends. But that made this even more hilarious. "What if you'd brought up one of the bad boys?"

"That's why I wanted to start out small."

She really *was* as dumb as a stick. "Girl, all demons are bad. And when they're here, their power grows."

"Why's that?"

"The open air releases their strength. They're no longer confined."

"You sound like you know...something about this," she said softly. Her face had paled; she rose from her chair and turned for the door.

He said, "Stop."

She froze.

"Now sit back down."

She did it without hesitation. Her dark-brown eyes stayed on him. Tattoos of barbed wire encircled her upper arms. The stud piercing her left nostril suggested that she liked pain—an added bonus.

He glanced at the plastic CD case in his hand.

A title jumped out at him.

Rat Salad.

His stomach rumbled. The woods out back.

He tossed the case on the couch. "Make yourself useful, all right? You can start by straightening up this place. It's a mess. I might be a little while."

***

The Camaro cruised down the deserted rain-slicked street.

"Man, you okay?" Todd asked. "Looks like you were in a fucking coma."

Leon rubbed his eyes. "Don't remember much. Just that we ran out of booze."

"You don't remember *Paranoid? Evil Woman?* You're too young for Old Timer's, amigo."

"Too young to buy booze, too."

"Man, I hear ya."

"You know Ol' Lady Snitzer will call the cops. We won't have Darcy to bail your ass out."

"Shit. Shoulda brought her with us."

"Wanna go back and pick her up?"

"Take too much time." The liquor store would be closed by the time they went back, picked her up and came back.

"How do you figure we'll do this?"

Todd realized the whole thing was hopeless but wanted to try anyway. Old Lady Snitzer took off her specs constantly and wiped them with her apron. She couldn't see without them. Catching her off-guard wouldn't be hard. She was old and didn't move very fast—they could be halfway back to Leon's before she even found the stupid buzzer. "We'll think of something."

57

"Something about that dude we picked up," Leon said.

"Man, he sure knew how to handle Darcy. When did you ever see somebody shut her up that easy?"

"Not in *my* lifetime."

His foot jerked down to the floor, forcing them both back in their seats.

"Whaddya doing *now*?" Leon asked uneasily.

"Something just pushed my foot—"

His foot mashed down harder. The needle jumped to sixty.

"Chief...this isn't fun anymore!" Leon braced his palms flat against the dash.

At seventy, the Camaro fishtailed on the glossy pavement, missing parked cars by inches.

"Todd, slow down! I'm gonna freak!"

"Wish I could!" His entire body shook. A heavy sheet of ice slid down his flesh. Some invisible power kept his foot flush to the floorboards. Cammie turned loose at the intersection. A fire hydrant slammed into their right side, forcing Todd's head against Leon's skull and making everything a hot, mushy shade of brown with bright stars twinkling right in the middle.

Metal screeching against concrete sounded like Cammie screaming. The car rose on two wheels and slid on its left side for nearly half a block. It finally toppled over and smashed into the stone wall of Crenshaw's Five'n Dime at the corner.

PART II - THE MISSION

CHAPTER 9

Tiffany's Epiphany

Tiffany didn't dare move away from the buckeye tree. Weeds, sticks, and dead limbs covered the ground around her. Snakes and other gross things were probably crawling about, too. Garbage bags and beer bottles littered the grassy slope behind her.

She and her companion had come up through the crack in the soil just a few feet from where she was standing. Grateful the sulfur reek was gone, she took in the fresh smell of pine from the woods.

A glittering light

(*sun?*)

spat chunks of brightness through the branches of the trees towering above her.

Only moments ago, her companion said he wanted to look around. He sniffed the ground, pulled out a clump of grass and sucked on the roots while walking away.

She'd been with weird guys before. She'd also been with guys too macho to ask for directions. She couldn't remember the number of times she'd ended up in the middle of nowhere, Mr. Macho running out of gas.

This guy was skinny and only an inch or so taller than she was. With his thatch of unruly red hair, he resembled Tex, the sheepdog her aunt once owned. He wore a short-sleeve tan shirt, jeans, and white sneakers. Funny. She didn't notice him wearing that outfit on their way up through the tunnel.

Her companion emerged from behind the trees, scratching his pointed chin as he drew nearer.

"Any idea where we are?" she asked.

"We're in the woods, buttercup."

"The name's Tiffany. Tiffany LeBouf." No need for pet names. They didn't even know one another. "And I can tell we're in the woods. Anyone could figure that out."

"How can you tell?"

"The trees, silly."

He nodded. "Good point—did you say LeBouf?"

"What of it?"

"Sure it ain't LeMuff?"

"It's Le*Bouf*."

"Literally translated, I'll bet it means Tiffany-in-the-Buff."

"Why do you have to be such a jerk?"

He giggled. "Sometimes I forget myself. You tend to do that when you keep moving along, singing a song, doo-dah, doo-dah…"

She sighed. Getting a straight answer was obviously going to be a chore. "Do you have any idea what happened? I mean, where were we?"

"Down below—where do you think?"

"Below?"

"The Dark Place. Hell. Didn't the sulfur stench, the heat, and those nasty-smelling uglies chasing you around give you some sort of a clue?"

She shivered. "You mean…I was…*dead*?"

"Deader than a doornail. Or coffin nail. Or mackerel. Guess what? You still are."

Dead. My God…

A sudden numbness enveloping her, she moved stiffly down the grassy slope. She no longer cared about her bare feet. She could think only of the emptiness, the waste. The shattered hopes and dreams. She had never thought much of death. She was *twenty-two years old*. Who thinks of death at *that* age?

She'd boarded the Greyhound bus for Hollywood less than five years ago. With money she had earned from working evenings and weekends at the Paramount Theater in downtown Peoria, she found a tiny efficiency. A few weeks later, after pounding the pavement, she landed her first job as a perfume tester. A month later, a cashier. Four months after that, a receptionist at a tire factory.

It took her six months to find her first agent. He negotiated an appearance in a detergent commercial, won her a spot in a shampoo commercial, and finally a good-paying gig advertising an underarm spray.

The jobs tapered off. Her agent told her she might want to have her breasts altered because the big boys liked bigger boobs. But she was proud of her looks and had no intention of changing anything. Impressed with her sincerity, he respected her wishes. He even found her another job a few days later, and she thought her luck had finally changed…

Until the party at Johnny Rock's.

The realization tore through her.

The drink. The strange meadow. The sulfur smell. The dead forest. The complete darkness. The feeling of eternal hopelessness.

Tiffany LeBouf, formerly Tiffany Sedarski, the only child of Ralph and Sandra Sedarski from Peoria, Illinois. The girl everyone thought was pretty but dumb. The kind men dreamed about…but never wanted to marry.

Dead at twenty-two.

Boy. And I thought that slobbering wolf guy was the worst part of my day.

"Hey, it happens," her companion said close behind her.

She avoided looking at him. He had become part of the nightmare. A figment of her imagination. That little voice you heard when you did something wrong.

"That doesn't make it any easier," she told the voice.

"Anybody ever tell you life is easy?"

She didn't need this. "I was only *twenty-two*!"

"How was it?"

He was *such* a jerk. If he hadn't gotten her away from those nasties, she would've already swatted him. "How was what?"

"Your life."

"Short!"

"Were you successful?"

She spun around. Her face burned, but there were no tears. They just wouldn't come. Maybe it had something to do with being dead. "I really didn't have much of a chance."

"Things could be worse."

"How could things get any worse than this?"

"You could still be down there…"

Despite the situation, her anger subsided. He had a point.

But something didn't make any sense. "I wasn't evil or nasty," she said. "Never hurt anyone, even. So why was I down there?"

"You were shanghaied."

"From where?"

"The Meddaworld."

62

"What's that?"

"There's a strip of darkness separating Limbo from Hades. It's an overlapping boundary. Not much overlap, though. Something should be done. Everyone gets antsy about who owns who and where the property line is. Folks with so much real estate can be snippy. Methinks you ventured too close to the line."

"I wish I'd known."

"You really need to watch where you're going, sweet cheeks."

"But you pulled me out of there. I'm back. Because of you."

"Save the adoration, accolades, and blubbering for later. I merely did what I was told."

"I don't care *why* you did it. Thanks for *doing* it!"

"*No problemo.* But like I said, watch where you're walking. Pretend you're a dairy farmer or something. You have to be careful. Otherwise, you'd still be there."

"You mean in Limbo?"

"I'm *so* glad you're paying attention."

"What *is* the Meddaworld? I heard voices."

"The duds live there."

"Who are they?"

"A low class of mortal. That's a contradictory of terms, if you think about it."

"Are they bad?"

"Not good, not bad. They're nothing, actually. Just went through life making babies and not doing too much else. Sponged off their government, which let them make more babies. Also, celebrities who did nothing more than get drunk and shoot up live there as well."

"And they're in the Meddaworld?"

"No one else wants them. They're considered subhuman."

"Sad. They have to spend eternity in total darkness."

"Hey, they're used to it."

"So that's all the Meddaworld is? Total darkness? And they can't leave?"

"You got it."

"But who pulled me out of Limbo?"

"It wasn't a dud, honey buns."

"A demon can enter the Meddaworld?"

"A demon can enter the Meddaworld, but not Limbo."

"So…if a demon hadn't pulled me into…the other place, I would've stayed in Limbo?"

"Pure genius."

"Is there any way I can go back?"

"Only a subordinate or super demon can enter the Meddaworld."

"What would happen if I tried?"

"You'd spend eternity with the duds."

"But…why did that wolf guy shanghai me?"

"Got a mirror handy? Look at yourself."

He *couldn't* be serious. "You mean…I've got to spend eternity in Hell because of a horny *jerk*?"

"Correctamundo."

She had never thought much of such a place. She heard about it as a youngster in Catechism Class but always thought they'd made it up to scare you into being good.

But it was obviously true. "What does everyone call you?"

"The name is Chip."

"I take it you're not a demon."

"How do you figure?"

"Your name. It's not scary. It's kind of cute, actually."

He chuckled. "You wouldn't be able to handle my real name."

"Try me."

"What language would you prefer?"

She sighed. "Since we're already speaking English, why don't we just keep it up?"

"The name, Sweet Cheeks, is Cypripedium Calceolus. Third Hierarchy, servant of Olivier, Prince of the Archangels, at your service." He bowed and farted. "Oops…sorry."

"No problem. I've been with guys before."

"You're cold, girl."

"Olivier…" Had she heard him correctly? "Not Lord Laurence Olivier?"

"He calls himself Prince, actually. Ollie to his friends—if he had any. Who are you talking about, pray tell?"

"One of the greatest actors who ever lived."

"Never heard of him."

"You're kidding."

"We don't get much television down there, sweet pea. No place to plug them in."

He had a point. "So your name is…Repeating Calculus?"

He groaned. "Cypripedium Calceolus. Don't make me hurt you, now. It's a very old name from ancient Greece. Downtown Athens, on Main Street and Olympus Avenue."

"What's it mean?"

65

"Literally translated, it means 'always a king, even in the presence of deity.'"

"It means all that?"

"Just having a bit of harmless fun in the morning sun." He tried a dance step and nearly tripped. "You happen to know what Tiffany means?"

"It's a company that makes pricey lamps. And a movie they made years ago with Audrey Hepburn."

"Who?"

"Never mind."

"Tiffany is from *tiffan*, which means luncheon." His eyes lowered. "So, in your case, my palatable smorgasbord, the name fits."

"Very funny. You haven't told me why we're here."

"We're here to pursue, find, and apprehend a fellow colleague."

"Who? And why?"

"The gentleman answers to the name Gutril. He's the stud muffin who yanked you out of Limbo."

"That creep." Her face grew warm. "How did he get up here?"

"A mortal summoned him."

"So *that* was what I heard. I thought it was someone sneezing."

"We've been hearing weird conjurations down there lately. The Arabs, no doubt."

"The wolf guy. His name is Gutril?"

"He's known as Gutrillus Canus, and he's one nasty dude."

"I figured that out right off. He was slobbering…"

"He's probably got acid reflux." He turned toward the grassy slope.

"Where are we going?"

66

"You wanna stay in this dump?"

"But I left my sandals down there…"

"And?"

"I don't like walking around in my bare feet," she said testily. "Especially with things lying in the grass. And I'm really upset about those sandals. They were expensive and I didn't even get to break them in."

"Wanna go back down and look for them?"

"No…"

"Then stop your whining."

"But they were stylish. And looked great on my feet. Especially when my toenails were painted a certain shade—"

"Jeez Louise…" His eyes crossed.

"You okay?"

His eyes uncrossed. "I'll be just fine when you stop the stupid girlie talk."

"How come men always get ugly when a girl talks about looking and feeling good?"

"It's a gene we have that makes us all want to have lobotomies when that subject comes up. But like I said, stop your whining. Visualize a pair of shoes, say abracadabra, and those delicious digits will be swaddled in the footwear of your dreams."

"That's all?"

"You're a spirit, right?"

"But my body—"

"An illusion, princess. Lots of super yummy, tasty stuff there, but merely an illusion."

She hugged herself. "I *feel* the same…"

"Part of the illusion."

"You mean there's nothing there? I mean inside? Like organs and bones and blood?"

67

"Oh my…"

"Please be serious."

"You want serious? All righty rooty." His smirk vanished. He looked just like one of those zombies in *Night of the Living Dead*. "How's this?"

"If that's the best you can do."

"That's all I got."

"Please go back to being silly."

His smirk came back. "Thanks, lamb chop. I feel *so* much better."

"What you said about substance…was it true?"

"While we're up here we've got substance. But as soon as we take ye olde downward plunge?" He shrugged. "Back to being a pretty picture again, but with feelings... Nothing more than feelings..."

"Why do we need substance here?"

"You realize what would happen if a mortal shook your hand and felt nothing? You were a mortal once. You know how easily they freak."

"You got *that* right."

"Up here we have powers we don't have down there. Why do you think everyone's fighting to come back up?"

"I don't know. Why is that? The power thing, I mean."

"It was supposed to be put it in the Bible in the Revelations section, but I guess someone snoozed. Hard to find motivated translators, obviously."

"What kind of powers do we have?"

"Make some shoes. Go on. Give her a shot. I guarantee they'll fit."

She stared at her feet. Was he kidding? Hard to tell. But at least he wore something, while she was practically nude. And it made her uncomfortable, being out here like this. She didn't want to step on anything sharp or gross if she had substance.

"Abra…ca…*dabra*?"

"*Shoes* might work better in your case."

She closed her eyes. *Shoes*…

She opened her eyes, looked down, and gasped.

Gucci white leather sandals. The pair with a metal buckle, a green-red web stripe on the front strap, leather soles, and four-inch heels. It was oh *so* much fancier than her Ferre's. "*Wowzer*! Shut *up*! Know how much *these* puppies go for?"

Steam puffed out of his small, pointed ears. "Epiphany –"

"Tiffany."

"Listen. You may be perfect for a stroke flick, but how long do you think you can get by with those snooty spikes out here?"

"But they're pretty. I've always wanted—"

"Change 'em. We don't have that much time. Get it?"

She got it, all right. But she had no intention of going back down. It was even better now. She looked and felt the same, but now she had *powers*. *Wowzer*!

She closed her eyes and thought of her sandals. When she opened them, there they were. She had them back. Everything was wonderful again.

"How's that?"

Chip shook his head. "Still too fancy. Besides, you lost them before, right?"

"So…what should I wear?"

"Jeez Louise." He covered his ears and spun around like a top. He eventually slowed to a stop and frowned. "Something sensible. Something that won't get us arrested. We're trying to blend in."

"This is new to me."

"I would've never guessed. Now get it together or I'll leave you here by yourself." He hurried away.

She closed her eyes. Abra... Oh, heck...tennis shoes. And jeans. And a nice, tight-fitting tee shirt.

She opened her eyes.

Avia Tuned Trainer sneakers—white with silver and thermal red stitching. A hundred bucks, but comfortable and not too fancy. The form-fitting designer jeans weren't anything special. Same with the tee shirt. If Mop Head didn't like it, she could change into an oversized sweatshirt and cutoffs or something else boring enough to pacify him.

No matter what he said, a girl wasn't comfortable blending in.

CHAPTER 10

Hawk

Deputy Clancy Hawkins carefully squeezed out of the cruiser.

Known as Hawk since childhood, he was often compared to—at least by the kids in Raven—Buford Pusser. Many said he even favored the actor who played in the original *Walking Tall* movie, only more massive and with a brush cut. His six-foot-three, two hundred and sixty pounds filled out his uniform like spandex stretched over a choice slab of beef.

Hawk graced Raven High's top defensive line twenty-five years earlier, pumping iron at an early age to get stronger. He continued the iron-pumping until just a few years ago, when the demands of his post finally took their toll. His solid thirty-six-inch waist softened, easing well past the forty-two-inch mark and smothering his belt buckle with a thick layer of flesh.

But things stayed fairly tight in spite of the added girth. Getting fat and sloppy was the kiss of death when you were frequently called on to secure belligerent drunks, confiscate illegal substances from the undershorts of strung-out teens, or battle an angry female without getting kneed, clawed, or bit.

Keeping alert was the only way to survive. Folks had been switching off their brains more frequently lately, doing things that staggered the imagination.

Like last night.

Hawk had been guilty of the stupids a few times in his earlier years. But what happened outside Crenshaw's defied description. Todd Bochner had never been the

71

brightest bulb in the box. It was no stretch to see him smeared all over the pavement. Shame he had taken Leon Bellson with him. Leon, an honor student, had already been accepted at Ohio U. on a partial scholarship. Why he chose Todd to hang around with would remain a mystery.

But Saturday somehow made things more tolerable. Chief Joe Flynn spent the weekends drinking beer and watching Extreme Fighting on his sixty-inch widescreen. Everyone at the Station enjoyed his absence. The pace did get a bit much sometimes with less manpower, but without Joe around to upset the works with his inflated ego, things stayed less stressful.

His polished black shoes tapping the pavement, Hawk climbed the familiar stone steps of the brick ranch house. This wasn't gonna be pleasant. But it had to be done.

The door opened.

Denise appeared in the doorway, sleep dimming her big blue eyes. Although past nine o'clock, she wore her heavy red housecoat and fuzzy yellow slippers. Her thick auburn hair was pulled back, tied, and held by a white plastic clip. Amazing how much she resembled Rainey— the same delicate face, the same swelled cheekbones. But Rainey would never answer the door in her housecoat.

"Figured we'd be seeing you this morning," she said, sounding tired. "Wasn't that horrible what happened?"

"Yep. Pretty bad. Chuck at work?"

"Half a day." She led him into the kitchen. The heavy fog of coffee and crispy bacon perked him right up even with the full stack of Rainey's tasty flapjacks and that three-egg cheese omelet filling his gut. Two plates sprinkled with bits of toast and bacon and smeared with egg yolk blots covered the red checkered tablecloth. A crossword puzzle book spread out with half the puzzle filled out in red ink sat beside a black mug of coffee marked with a large white "*D*."

"Coffee?"

"Thanks, I'll just chat with Darcy, then leave you be. I heard she was with Todd and Leon last night."

"Figured that's why you're here. They went somewhere in that fancy car of Todd's. Darcy's car's in the shop, and she—"

"She came home with them?"

"Actually, she came home just a couple hours ago. By herself."

Something wrong here. "She still here?"

Denise sighed. "I'll tell you something, Hawk. That girl hasn't been right since she walked through the door."

"Can't say I blame her. I take it she already heard about her friends."

"It's not that."

"What's up?"

"Best if I showed you." She swished down the carpeted hall and stopped in front of the door at the far end. "Darcy, your uncle's here."

Silence.

"Darcy?" Denise knocked on the door.

No reply.

Denise pounded.

The door eased open. Darcy appeared in a loose-fitting white tank top and baggy dark-blue shorts. Her hair hung free. Her cheeks were pale. She wore no shoes or slippers. That stupid smiling turtle on the inside of her ankle and the barbed wire tattoos on her upper arms made him grimace. He never could see the point of marking up

73

perfect pink flesh with pictures you wouldn't dare hang on your living room wall.

Darcy's changing attitude the last couple years frightened him. Hawk believed TV, fashion, rock music and the drugs were the cause. Kids grew up much too fast nowadays, getting pierced and branded like cattle. He couldn't blame Darcy. Everyone else did the same thing.

The changes—the inwardness, the aloofness, the anger— were painfully clear. She remained the same sweet girl he used to put on his knee such a short time ago, but something was definitely missing. He feared that short of a miracle, things might not ever be the same.

"Hi, Uncle Hawk."

"You okay?"

"I'm fine. Fine, fine, fine...."

Her sing-songy voice made him uneasy. "You sure?"

"Positive. What brings you here?"

"Came to talk at you for a little while."

"Is it about Todd and Leon?"

"Sure is. Where can we chat?"

She slipped past him into the living room and plopped down in an armchair, bringing her legs up and wrapping her arms around them. "Shoot."

Hawk took a place on the couch. Denise leaned against the archway, arms crossed.

He didn't like seeing so much of his niece's pink upper thighs. Something was definitely off. Later he'd ask Denise to see if she could find any drug paraphernalia in the girl's room. "Tell you what. Let me start this off by—
"

Her eyes glazed over. She sat up sharply and looked around the room.

"Darcy?"

She jumped up. "I need to be doing something." She moved quickly, fluffing pillows, straightening the doily on the arm of the couch near Hawk's forearm and smoothing out a tiny wrinkle on the green throw rug. She picked up something he couldn't even see and ran from the room.

Noises came from the kitchen. Water poured into the sink. Dishes and silverware clattered.

"What's she doing?" he asked, alarmed.

"Straightening up," Denise said flatly.

"How long has she been like this?"

"Since she got home."

"This ain't right. What were those kids doin' last night?"

"I haven't been able to find out."

"Coroner said Todd Bochner's blood contained nearly twice the legal limit when they brought them in. Leon's was elevated, but not nearly as high as Todd's. Is Darcy hung-over?"

"That girl doesn't even like to drink. You know that."

"I thought I did. But you know how kids are now."

"I know they're wild. I just don't think Darcy would change that drastically."

He decided not to debate the issue. "How'd she get home?"

"She said she walked back from Leon's."

"From Ohio Street? That's more than two miles. Kids don't walk nowadays. Not if they can help it."

Breathless, Darcy came back. "I did the breakfast dishes. Then I put the butter back in the fridge so it wouldn't get all icky. That all right?"

"Fine, dear. Just remember, you've got to get ready to go in to Crenshaw's this morning. Don't you start at eleven?"

"I have plenty of time. I can even vacuum my room before I leave."

Hawk had the feeling he'd slipped into someone else's house without even realizing it. "I guess the questions can wait for now—"

"Hey, Uncle Hawk," she said smiling. "Sorry about that."

"It's all right."

She returned to the armchair and sat, this time with her legs crossed. "Shoot."

He turned to Denise for reassurance but saw only fear in his sister-in-law's face.

He had no idea how to handle this. He surely didn't want to aggravate the situation. However, personal feelings had to be put aside. Whatever the circumstance, get the job done. If it's an arrest, do it quickly and efficiently. If it's a high-speed chase, force the perp off the road with the Precision Idiot Tap maneuver before he kills somebody. And if it's questioning, ask calmly and professionally.

He pulled out his notebook. "I'll make this real quick—"

"*Now* I know what's bothering me," she said, jumping up again. "The bathroom. Earlier I noticed this really gross water stain on the counter. Just be a sec!" She ran from the room.

He closed his notebook and got up. "I'll come back later."

Denise followed him to the front door. "By that time, she'll probably have the house re-painted. And if she ever finds out we need to have the insulation in the attic replaced…"

"I don't recall her *ever* bein' this way."

"When Chuck comes home, I hope he doesn't come in through the garage. He'll find his tools soaking in buckets of soapy dishwater. How in heaven's name am I supposed to explain *that* to him?"

CHAPTER 11

Tiffany and the Trickster Hitch a Ride

Beyond the clearing, a two-lane country road cut through at the bottom of the weed-choked hill. Chip waited just off the shoulder, his feet submerged in a puddle of water. His unruly hair flopped in the breeze.

Her new sneakers mashing wet grass, Tiffany proceeded cautiously down the steep grade.

He looked her up and down. "Nice ensemble. A bit flimsy with the whimsy, though."

"Whaddya mean?"

"The puppy noses want out."

She crossed her arms over her chest. She should have seen *that* one coming. "Tell me why we're going after the wolf guy. By the way, you're standing in water."

"Really?" He acted surprised. "You know, I wondered why my feet felt so cold. Thanks for clearing it up."

"You're welcome. And silly. Now tell me about the wolf guy."

"He's not supposed to be up here."

"Why not?"

"I'll tell you in good time, my naughty nymphet."

He was so infuriating. "Look, I'm not naughty and I'm not a nymphet. Most of all, I'm not yours. At least tell me why we were picked."

"My master saw you when Gutril brought you over. What can I say? He's been a dirty old man for five thousand years. He ain't gonna change anytime soon."

"That's it?"

"And also because you happen to possess certain qualities we might need for this little errand."

"Like what?"

"Those delicious-looking bazoombas."

"You can't possibly tell me I'm the only one down there with these."

"The only one available."

"Why were *you* picked?"

"I'm a dynamite trickster. Only a trickster can coax someone like Gutril back down."

"A...trickster?"

"The bestest you'll ever see."

"You sure are full of yourself."

"It's hard to be humble when you're the best...."

"I heard that in Hollywood all the time. What do tricksters do?"

"Tricks and illusions for all occasions. You see, I'm the bestest who can out-jest the jestest jesters in the West."

"It's really hard to take you seriously. About anything."

"That's because you obviously never met a real best-of-anything before. Not in Celluloid City, anyway."

Hard to believe a silly guy like him could excel at anything.

"Maybe if you gave me some sort of demonstration?"

"You like snakes?" He pointed to the ground between them.

"What?"

A huge black snake encircled her feet, its coils wrapped around her ankles, its head resting on the right toe of her Avia. Its tongue poked out, sniffing her. "Kill it! Kill it!"

79

"Look again, my frightened fraulein."

The snake was gone. A crooked tree branch lay half-covered in the wet grass in its place.

"H-How…did you—"

He picked up the branch and tossed it. "Like I said, my delicious, doubting Thomasina, I'm the best you'll ever see."

She waited for her heart—or whatever was there now—to settle down. It dawned on her that she might be able to do the same thing. She could visualize clothing, couldn't she? She closed her eyes. *Turtle*. She looked down. Nothing.

"Why can't *I* do that?"

"Haven't earned your horns."

"You mean because I'm new?"

"Methinks the bimbo's got it!"

Her face grew warm. "Bimbos are stupid, shallow women who use their bodies to get what they want. How come men aren't called bimbos when they use sex to get what *they* want?"

"Men never do that."

"How can you possibly say that?"

"Because, my delicious wafer, sex *is* what they want."

She hated when he was right. But she wasn't a bimbo. She was forced to use her resourcefulness from time to time, but sometimes a girl had to do unpleasant things to pay the bills. "You said you were up here before."

"More than a century ago the first time, then half a century ago."

"That's unbelievable."

"It feels like only a few weeks. Time races down there. It only drags up here."

"Why were you here?"

"Which time?"

"The first."

"No biggie just tricked some screwy Russian anarchist into pumping a couple of live ones into the President. Astaroth was running things up here then. He thought America needed livening up."

Tiffany scratched the back of her neck. Was he kidding again? She couldn't tell. "I didn't know John Wilkes Booth was Russian."

He frowned. "How can someone so luscious be so incredibly brain-dead?"

"Oh, stop."

About a half-mile to their left, an Interstate highway extended east to west. The two-lane turnoff ran south, veering off and disappearing behind the hill about a mile farther down. Straight ahead, the woods blocked their view.

Chip's nostrils flared. He was either sniffing the air or just listening.

"Which way?" she asked.

"Off-hand, I'd say we turn right and follow the road."

"There's more traffic the other way. We stand a better chance hitching a ride."

"I was told that your boyfriend headed for a town called Raven. And that sign says Raven, seven miles."

"He's not my boyfriend. And how do you know where he went?"

"Someone in Raven summoned him. He's probably already there." He stepped out of the puddle and started walking.

She caught up a few yards later. "Are you sure we'll be able to hitch a ride?"

"Positively, sweet cheeks. Especially with you trailing behind me with that shapely behind of yours trailing you."

The approaching roar of a pickup truck gave Tiffany hope. The big vehicle slowed before hurtling past, belching a knot of foulness from its oversized exhaust.

"Did you see that?" Chip stopped walking and stared after the truck.

"See what?"

"His tag said *MACHO1*."

"So?"

"Looks weird."

"It's personalized."

"Is that a *new* thingy?"

"They've been around ever since I can remember."

"Mortals are even dumber than *I* remember," he said flatly.

"What makes you say that?"

"Say you get plastered and run over some poor slob. Someone sees your tag. Instead of working up a large sweat trying to memorize a bunch of numbers, he sees Macho One. It's like saying Here I am! I'm the drunken doofus that ran over that guy!"

"I never thought of it like that, but I guess you're right."

"I *am* right." He resumed walking. "By the way, did you catch the state on that tag?"

"Looked like Ohio."

"You're not only deliciously delectable, you're also nimble and quick. Can you jump over a candlestick?"

"Good grief."

"What's wrong? You didn't bring along a candlestick?"

"What's in Ohio?"

"What's wrong with Ohio?"

"It's so…so *boring*."

"Cheer up. And stop being such a girl. You're acting all whiny and tragic again."

"Men. You're all alike."

"Really?" He crossed his eyes, wiggled his ears, stuck out his tongue, rolled it back into his mouth, and farted.

"Maybe not *all* of you."

A tan SUV zipped past.

Chip studied his thumb. "I haven't hitched a ride in fifty years. I guess I've lost my touch."

"Want some advice?"

"Got someone in mind who could give me some?"

"Me, you idiot."

"Turn me on to this mighty morsel of mental mirth."

"I think I know the problem."

"Please. Let these righteous ratifications rip."

"I could manage better if you weren't…well, if—"

"Go on…"

Oh, what the heck? Let him have it. He had no feelings. Even if he did, so what? He was much too full of himself to care.

"I think somebody would stop if they didn't see you."

"How cruel. How callous. How cold." He blinked. "Please explain this sudden outburst of blatant nastiness."

"For one thing, you're…messy-looking."

"How *dare* you…"

"And really weird."

"Ya think?" His eyes crossed.

The growing hum of an approaching vehicle shattered the silence.

A blue-and-white convertible Chevy Bel Air steadily approached. It was an older model, with fins and whitewall tires. A skinny man about twenty-five years old wearing a blue police uniform sat behind the wheel.

Tiffany reached up and pushed her flowing blond hair away from her face.

With the screaming of rubber, the classic car came to a smoldering halt.

***

Groggy from too much bar whiskey and not enough sleep, Deputy Ernie Travis turned off I-70 and headed south on Raven Road West.

Picking up a few extra bucks playing eight-ball at Frankie's Stick 'N Slick in Cambridge seemed a good idea at the time. But now he realized the error of his ways. Really stupid, actually—a full-time deputy trying to beat a full-time professional pool hustler at his own game.

Ernie had stumbled back to his one-bedroom Fredericksburg pad just before four. Just six hours ago. His last thoughts before falling asleep centered on the fifty bucks that Frankie "the Stick" had pocketed so eagerly before bidding him a good night and telling him to come back soon for another game.

You're such *an idiot!*

But at least Chief Joe wouldn't be at the Station, watching him stagger in with a head the size of a basketball.

Hawk was cool—he might sympathize and let him answer the phones. Covering a padded chair in a cool office all afternoon sounded great.

Ernie Lee, why do you have to be such a moron?

The sight straight ahead dissolved his thoughts like that last shot of Jack's the night before.

Two women in tee shirts and jeans, walking along the road.

Squeezing the last of the sleep out of his eyes, Travis squinted and took in the delicious sight. But it wasn't necessary. Taking in an eyeful like that jolted a man alert in a New York second.

It wasn't every day you found something this fine wandering around. They probably broke down on I-70 back a ways.

But he hadn't passed anything on his way in. It might have happened farther west—possibly out toward Cambridge. He wondered why they hadn't been picked up already. But it was still early—not much traffic.

Why weren't they toting bags? Or at least a purse?

Funny thing, though. At first he'd thought the redhead was a guy. But when the blonde reached up to push back her long curly tresses, he could tell both were female.

His hangover had no doubt affected his eyesight.

His size thirteen slammed down on the brake pedal. High-pitched squeals of protest issued from the pristine whitewalls he had bought only weeks ago.

"Where you ladies headed?"

The hot blonde looked even better close up. She said, "Actually—"

"Wherever you wanna take us, Officer," the redhead said, grinning. She was all right in a tomboyish way. But nowhere near as hot as her friend. "It'll be just perfectimundo."

"I'm going into town. Is that all right?"

"Righty-rooty."

85

"Get in back. We'll be there in a jiff."

"Okey-dokie." The redhead opened the door and let the blonde climb in first. "A jiff sounds just spiff—eh, Tiff?"

CHAPTER 12

The Mayor

Whistling, Mayor Phil Holeridge stepped out of the shower, grabbed a navy-blue bath towel monogrammed *PGH* in elegant gold letters and wrapped it around his broad waist. He then spent the next half-hour shaving and carefully arranging his hair transplants. Then he splashed his tingling cheeks with *Obsession for Men* and treated his impeccable hairdo with generous mists of Aramis Malt-Enriched Conditioning Hairspray.

Beneath the brilliant track lighting in his dressing room off the master suite, the racks of imported Armani and Baroni suits hanging neatly in transparent garment bags before him, he went through the arduous daily task of deciding what to wear.

Saturday meant an hour or two in the office. Casual would suffice and be quite appropriate for his one o'clock meeting at the Country Club. Hell, half of his comrades would be sweaty and disheveled from their usual shenanigans on the golf course. Best not appear overly dressed. He selected a single-breasted light-gray silk with a hand-woven sage green cotton tie and patent-leather tan Gucci slip-ons.

The slacks were a little snug. Had he put on weight?

Absolutely not. On the advice of Doc Woodward two months ago, he lowered his personal quota of six evening martinis down to a paltry three and immediately noticed a big difference. An error at the dry cleaner's, no doubt.

He would call Andre, his St. Clairsville tailor, for a discussion about possible alterations.

A clear, cloudless morning radiated a sea of blue beyond the dining room French doors. The grounds gleamed a rich green. However, signs of weed activity near the flower gardens and at the base of the stone fountains spoiled the masterpiece. Manny would tend to it, first thing. The estate must always look spectacular.

Holeridge helped himself to a cup of steaming chicory from the porcelain pot on the serving cart, then took his seat at the head of the big oval dining room table.

Philly sat on his left, Betsy on his right. Both were busy with their iPads.

Hattie, her customary smile brightening her round ebony cheeks, brought out a large plate of scrambled eggs and set it carefully in the center of the table. "Mornin', sir," she chimed in her gentle alto voice. "Miss Holeridge comin' down for breakfast?"

The antique walnut grandfather clock in the corner said 9:57. Irene usually slept in on the weekends and made her grand appearance around noon. Hattie was being polite again. "In a little while," he said.

Hattie nodded dutifully, then waddled back to the kitchen.

The kids hadn't acknowledged his presence. The crunching of cornflakes and the slurping of milk echoed in the room. They both ate using one hand. The other busily clicked and tapped their electronic toys.

Holeridge couldn't understand kids nowadays. In the old days you played baseball and football. You even got into fights and found out how tough you were. You learned the value of friendship, competition, and communication early on. Nowadays you went blind in front of a stupid computer and carried an iPad, cell phone, and laptop everywhere.

No wonder kids piled on weight and were incapable of carrying on an intelligent conversation.

"So next weekend we've got a birthday boy," he said, grinning.

Philly didn't even look up.

"You still haven't told me what you'd like."

Philly gulped down milk and continued pressing buttons.

"I could use a little help, you know." Holeridge wanted to yank the damned thing from his son's pudgy hand, mash it with his heel and toss it in the trash. "I can't be expected to know –"

"He wants an arcade, Daddy." Betsy looked up briefly.

She had to be joking. "An arcade? You don't mean—"

"Place with games and other neat stuff," Philly said, still focused on his game. "All the guys can go there after school."

"This is awfully short notice. Do you have any idea how much an arcade costs?"

Philly shrugged.

"Why would you even *want* one?" he asked, confused.

"He wants Tommy and Kirk and the older boys to like him." Betsy pulled back to avoid a kick under the table.

"Is this true?" Holeridge asked.

Philly said nothing.

"What would you do if you had one?"

"I'd hang out there after school and some of the guys could play for free so maybe they wouldn't pick on me and tell me I'm fat," he said in a rush, then went back to his iPad.

"They call him Philly Dog," Betsy said, avoiding another kick.

An *arcade*, of all things.

Holeridge had been given a twenty-six-inch bike for his twelfth birthday. A Schwinn, of course. With wheel guards, padded seat, and all sorts of gears. But that was in the eighties. A much different world back then.

Twelve years old and the boy wanted an arcade. What would he demand next year?

The Taj Mahal? The Space Needle?

Life thundered by so fast. Kids lost their innocence so quickly.

But it was unavoidable. You couldn't keep them under your wing forever.

At least he could give them what they wanted while they were small. Even though they wanted something ridiculous and would probably be bored with it in a few days.

He dished out a generous portion of scrambled egg and picked up a wedge of buttered rye toast from the stack.

An arcade. That meant buying a building. A deserted building, preferably on Main Street, where he could keep a watchful eye on things.

The time element presented a problem.

But that was not a concern when you had friends in high places.

CHAPTER 13

Two Classy Chicks in a Classic Car

The deputy watched them in the rearview. His small blinking chestnut eyes kept shifting to both her and Chip. The Bel Air nudged onto the shoulder.

"I don't understand something," Tiffany whispered close to Chip's ear.

The wind flapped his heavy mop. It looked like a big red bird trying to take off. "What seems to be confusing you, buttercup?"

She leaned closer. "Why did he call us *ladies*?"

"Guess."

"You don't mean—"

"I did happen to mention I'm a trickster, didn't I?"

"He actually thinks you're a—"

"I figured we'd have a better chance if we were both female. Especially since you said I'm so messy-looking."

"You were right." She couldn't believe it. "You *are* good."

"You ladies live around these parts?" the deputy asked.

"No," Tiffany said. "Actually—"

"Actually," Chip said, "we're from out of town."

"The truth is, I'm from Hollywood," Tiffany said.

"You don't say?"

"I used to be an actress."

"You mean you're not no more?"

"You catch on quick," Chip said.

"Oh, stop," she whispered. "You want him to drop us off out here?"

"What happened?" the deputy asked.

91

"Her career came to a screeching halt," Chip said.

She shot him a glare. "I'm exploring other avenues at the moment."

"Anything I mighta seen ya in?"

"I did a few commercials."

"I'll bet a gal like you had a *lotta* jobs."

"Not really."

"C'mon, now. Pretty thing like you?"

"Don't you think I'm pretty, too, Officer?" Chip fluttered his lashes.

"Well…yeah. Sure do, lady." The deputy fidgeted in his seat. "Sorry. I didn't mean nothin'—"

"The competition is fierce out there," Tiffany said quickly. Chip could be so tacky. If he kept this up, the deputy was bound to get suspicious. "Everyone's having cosmetic work done to make themselves more marketable."

"Those…ain't real?"

"Bought 'em at Boobs R Us," Chip said.

She wanted to strangle him.

"You ain't pullin' my chain, are ya?" the deputy asked.

"She had them enhanced," Chip said flippantly.

He had just entered enemy territory. "I most certainly *did not*."

"He doesn't know that," Chip whispered. "C'mon, cupcake. Live a little, so to speak. Loosen up."

"En-*hanced*?" the deputy asked.

"You know," Chip said. "Turned the puppies into monsters."

"So *that's* what ya had done, eh? Got two monsters in there?"

"Yes. Two monsters." Tiffany sighed.

The deputy chuckled. "How 'bout that?"

"Satisfied?" she asked Chip.

"For the moment." A silly grin covered his features. "You'll know when I get bored again."

"Whoa!" The deputy swerved off the shoulder again and fought to correct it.

"What's wrong?" Tiffany asked.

The deputy shook his head. "Didn't get much sleep last night." He pulled off his service cap, scratched the brown stubble covering the crown and snuck another peek in the rearview. "Eyes playing tricks, I reckon."

"Any idea what he's talking about?" she whispered to Chip.

"He probably just got a gander at my true self."

"I thought—"

"Lighten up. I'm only a trickster."

"But the way you were talking—"

"I've got issues, all right?"

Then she realized what he meant. "Your tricks don't last."

"That's why I came up here. To develop and grow. To mature."

"Is the wolf guy more powerful than you?"

"He's a *sub*, sweetness. He has special powers."

"Like what?"

"He shape-shifts, for one thing."

"What's that?"

"He's able to alter his form."

That explained the images of Cary Grant, Humphrey Bogart, and the others. "So *that's* what he was doing down there. How is that different from what you do?"

"When I appear as something else, it's just an illusion. Shape-shifters actually change their shape."

93

"The wolf guy's really good. What else can he do?"

"He can read minds and make you do silly stuff."

That explained how the wolf guy had picked out her favorite stars. "And *you've* been sent to take *him* back down?"

"Righty-rooty. Actually, both of us are up here to do that."

Tiffany had the uneasy feeling that Chip was no longer kidding. "And just how do we intend to do that?"

He shrugged loosely. "How should *I* know? I just got here myself."

CHAPTER 14

Finding a Mortal Host

Ten more minutes and Mirabelle could enjoy her well-deserved break. Just her hourly nicotine fix. No one cared. Not even Mr. Crenshaw.

Anyway, Earlene could handle things for fifteen minutes. Barely thirty, the tiny thing weighed no more than a hundred pounds, soaking-wet. She knew how to hurry things along when the situation called for it.

A strange morning, though. As soon as the McGill girl came in, she started straightening things up like a SWAT Commando. Hard to figure. McGill was more mature than others her age, but no neat freak. She always looked good—hair brushed, makeup light—although Mirabelle didn't care for the nose stud or the tattoos.

But something odd was going on. The girl grabbed the feather duster, attacked the jewelry case, and rushed on over to Swimwear—not even her department. She straightened out the Bargain Bin, then arranged the hanging stuff. Even wiped the aisle mirror with a corner of her apron.

The girl obviously wanted a promotion.

Mirabelle wanted to laugh. Mr. Crenshaw was okay to work for but was tight with a dollar. If McGill thought cleaning up the place would get her more money, she had another think coming.

Kids these days…when would they learn?

Life was short and unfair, and nearly all the time the most deserving didn't get their due.

Although sometimes they did.

That's what she thought earlier, on her way in. The mess outside nearly blocked the side entrance. Looked like someone had used one of those big Army helicopters to pick up an old car and drop it from a hundred feet up.

She recognized the car. It belonged to Todd Bochner. Turned out the idiot splattered himself and his friend into the side of the building.

Mirabelle was a God-fearing woman, but that no-account racing his loud machine up and down Chestnut Street at all hours proved more than even the best Christian could bear. Mirabelle always suspected the boy would meet his Maker that way. Or bump into that other guy, most likely…

A quick glance at the wall clock said break time. Mirabelle grabbed her Pall Malls from the cracked wooden shelf beneath the register. She fastened the yellow plastic chain across the aisle with the sign attached that said *CLOSED*. Straightening, she bumped into someone.

"Oops…sorry."

"No problem."

Long and lean, he had a pair of tiny light-brown eyes that made a gal a tad self-conscious. He knew it, too. His half-smile stayed on her.

Where'd he get that shirt? She hadn't seen the slogan *KEDS ARE FOR KIDS* in ages. Not since she was growing up in Bridgeport. He didn't get it here. And it looked new.

"I'm…taking my break now," she said uneasily.

"Far out," he said. "You do look a little tired."

Was he putting her on? That grin told her nothing.

"I only said that in case you wanted to check out in the next couple minutes. Earlene'll take care of you."

"I came in to talk to that girl." He pointed directly behind her.

She knew who he meant. *Go for it, cutie*, she wanted to say. *If that's what you want, that's what you'll get*. Mirabelle was too old for him anyway. She had varicose veins older than he was.

She smiled politely. Mr. Crenshaw stressed being courteous, and if she had learned anything in her years working here, it was that a simple smile and a polite thank you was all you needed to stay out of trouble.

She ducked through Electronics on her way out to the back. Just before she slipped through the stockroom doorway, she glanced behind her.

Cutie had reached the jewelry case. Her back to him, McGill eagerly buffed the glass.

Hopefully, Cutie went for neat freaks.

***

Darcy smiled at her reflection in the glass. Probably the first time those cabinets actually sparkled.

Now, if she could just keep her customers from getting their prints all over it…

She bent, sprayed the glass doors, and gave them a thorough swipe with her cloth. Perfect. She saw herself clearly. And someone behind her.

She spun around.

"Hi, there." His red-tinted light-brown eyes glistened. Something different about him this morning. Last night he resembled someone dark and scary. Now he looked more like one of those hippies from that Woodstock flick, only with shorter hair.

"Shame what happened to your friends."

Todd and Leon weren't exactly her friends, but they didn't deserve to die like that.

Last night was really strange. First, the fiasco at the mine. Then, nearly hitting this guy on their way back to town. Then the bit with Todd and Leon leaving the party to get more booze even though they both knew they were too young to buy it.

What topped it all off was this guy telling her that stuff about demons. It sounded like he actually *knew* about them.

She had sat on the couch after he left, wondering where he'd gone off to. Then, for some bizarre reason, she got up and cleaned up the living room. She slipped into the kitchen and cleaned that up as well. When she was finished, she went back to the living room, sat, and waited for someone to come back. When no one came back, she decided to walk home.

She wanted to stay a little longer but had a feeling Todd wasn't coming back soon. Anyway, she needed fresh air. The rum had disoriented her.

She reached Chestnut, saw the wreckage, and went totally numb. Fire trucks blocked the intersection. A deputy roped off Crenshaw's side lot and part of West Main.

She couldn't remember much after that. She had no idea how long she stood there. Or if she turned away when the bodies were placed on stretchers. Or making it back to her house. Or going into her bedroom and getting out of her clothes. She vaguely recalled Uncle Hawk's visit later that morning, but not much else.

"Good thing you didn't go with them," the hitcher said, jolting her.

"I...still don't know why they left," she said. "Todd thought too much of that Camaro to do anything really stupid. They sure were acting weird..."

"Weird how?"

"After you told them to get the booze, they both got quiet and acted really strange. Even stranger than usual."

"You don't think it was the booze?"

"No."

"How about the weed?"

"I'm not even sure about that."

"Maybe it had something to do with your conjuration."

Her fear came back. She stared at him, trying to read his thoughts. "How could that have anything to do with—"

"Miss?" A short, squat woman around fifty leaned against the counter. Her chubby hands rested flat on the shiny glass counter. "Would you mind? I'd like to see one of your watches."

Darcy snatched up her cleaning supplies and rushed over.

***

Gutril was getting nervous. He needed a mortal host. Since the girl had been instrumental in summoning him, she would logically be his first choice.

It had to be done quickly. The Legion had probably already sent someone to take him back down. Without the protection of a host, Gutril would be totally vulnerable.

As her customer walked away, the girl sprayed the glass and rubbed it vigorously with a rag. She brought over her cleaning supplies and set them on the counter. "What did you mean about my conjuration?" she asked.

"Maybe you actually did conjure up a demon."

"I don't know anything about that stuff. I just found some things online and a generic spell—"

"The spell itself doesn't matter. What matters is where you work it."

"Are you saying the mine does possess an evil force?"

He grinned. Sometimes she displayed actual brain activity. "Cool beans. You finally figured it out."

Her big dark-brown eyes stayed on him. She wanted to believe what he said but didn't want to believe she'd actually brought up a demon.

He was convinced she believed him.

"I don't believe you," she said, and began vigorously scrubbing the counter with her towel.

"Why not?"

"I can't bring up a demon. Nobody can."

"Where do you think *I* came from?"

She stopped scrubbing. "Are you trying to say *you're* the demon?"

"In the flesh," he said proudly.

She laughed.

"What's so funny?"

"You don't *look* like a demon. At least, not like what I've seen in those sites."

"Sites?"

"Websites."

"Web…sites?"

A frown. "Computers. Don't you know anything?"

"Computers?"

"Don't tell me you've never—"

"No computers where I come from."

"You're so weird."

"I'm supposed to be. I'm a demon."

"Demons are scary-looking."

"What do you mean?"

"They look like Al Pacino."

"Who?"

"You've never heard of Al Pacino?"

"Who's that?"

"He played the Devil in a movie."

"You think demons look like movie people?"

"Actually, they're ugly."

"Movie people?"

"Demons, silly. They breathe fire, smell bad, and slobber." She lowered her eyes. "And they don't dress like you at all."

"This is my street outfit."

"Demons aren't supposed to be funny, are they?"

He gritted his teeth. *Calm yourself. She won't want to be your host if you make her throw up all over her nice clean counter.* "Several comedians down there are demons."

"You mean like John Belushi?"

"Could be." *Who the hell is John Belushi?*

She gave the counter another swipe. Her thoughts rang loud and clear. *He's crazy. He doesn't look like a demon. He looks more like someone who got wasted at Woodstock. If he really is a demon, what's he doing in Crenshaw's?*

"I came to see you."

"*What*?" She nearly knocked over the Windex bottle.

"You wondered why I'm here."

"How did you possibly…how could you…*do* that?"

"Close your mouth," he said. "You're drooling."

She closed her mouth and swallowed. "If you're really…if you're from *there*…how did you get…*here*?"

"You summoned me."

101

"Todd sneezed. How could a sneeze bring up…one of *you* guys?"

"My name is Gutrillus Canus. Gutril, for short. The name might sound like a sneeze from a distance. Among idiots."

"Don't buy it." She shook her head, sprayed another part of the glass, and rubbed it. "It doesn't make sense. No one can conjure a demon—not by sneezing. Can you imagine how many people sneeze? There'd be demons all over the place."

He grinned. "What makes you think there aren't?"

She stopped working the cloth. "How about a demonstration?"

"Of what?"

"Your powers, silly. If you're a demon, you can do a lot of weird things, right?"

"I've already given you a dandy demonstration."

"When?"

"This cleaning obsession. Last night I told you to straighten up. You've been straightening up ever since."

She dropped the cloth on the counter, stepped back, and frowned at it. "This is all…because of *you*?"

He nodded.

"I cleaned up Leon's living room and kitchen. My parents' living room. Their kitchen. The bathroom. The garage. Dad's tools." She blinked. "Because of *you*?"

"Busy little bee, aren't you?"

"I also straightened out Swimwear and have been scrubbing this stupid glass like an idiot."

"Now you've got the clear picture. Sorry for the pun."

She groaned. "I knew something was wrong. I *hate* cleaning. Why did you do this?"

102

He shrugged. "You needed something to keep you busy while I went outside."

"That's another thing I don't understand. Where did you go, anyway?"

"The woods. I was hungry."

"Miss?" Standing in front of Swimwear, a broad-hipped middle-aged woman held up scraps of red material dangling from a plastic hanger. "Is this on special?"

"What *is* that?" he whispered.

"It's a thong." She shot him a glance. "You've never seen one of those before?"

"We don't need stuff like that down there."

"Miss? I'm in a hurry…"

Distractions, distractions. He considered giving the customer a sudden case of diarrhea. He decided against it. Best be subtle. At least, until you have your host.

Banana peel. Much more subtle…

The woman stumbled, frantically grabbing some hanging swimsuits, and pulling them with her as she fell. The Bargain Bin display sign dropped on her head. She sat on the tile floor.

The Darcy girl went to help.

"I've got a question," he said after her.

She turned.

"What's a Woodstock?"

The Darcy girl's jaw dropped. She backed up, slipped on some bikini scraps, and fell right on top of the customer.

Gutril sighed. Venting was seriously cool beans…

Back from her break, the Mirabelle woman watched the commotion as he passed. "What's happening over there?"

103

A heavy rupture of foul cigarette-tainted breath rubbed his face. "Some sort of freak accident."

"She's gonna *love* cleaning that up. By the way, what's up with her?"

"She'll be all right. I just helped her kick the habit."

"Really? How?"

"That's *your* job now."

Blinking, Mirabelle immediately grabbed a dust cloth and vigorously wiped down her counter.

CHAPTER 15

Not in Hell Anymore—or Are We?

The Bel Air pulled away from the corner.

Tiffany couldn't help feeling depressed. First, dying. Then, finding herself in Hell because of some horny jerk.

Now this.

Raven, Ohio. Looked like the sets Hollywood used when they made those cheap B-movies in the old days.

Beat-up pickups lined the streets. Rolls of fencing, bales of hay and sacks of livestock feed filled their beds. Potbellied men wearing baseball caps, stained white undershirts, overalls, and mud-caked work boots waddled down the street.

"What a tacky town."

"Don't have a tiff, Spiff," Chip said. "What did you expect?"

He was right. But she just couldn't help herself.

"Look at those vehicles. They're covered with primer and Bondo. And that Olds over there. It has *duct tape* keeping the taillight on."

"You don't want the poor schumck to lose his taillight, do you?"

"That's *not* what I meant."

He stared at her. "Doing a TV Special for Lifestyles of the Tastelessly Tacky? Or is this something from your dark past?"

"I feel like I've gone back in time. I wouldn't be surprised if Richard Carlson or Beverly Garland walked out of one of these stores."

"Richard Carlson?"

"An actor."

"Beverly Garland?"

"An actress."

"I'm *so* glad you've explained it so well."

"At least where I came from, we had a Walmart. I don't see one of those anywhere, do you?"

"Baby Cakes, I don't even know what a Walmart is."

"A big store that sells everything."

"Like that Five'n Dime across the street?"

Orange police tape sectioned off the area from the stone wall to the streetlamp at the curb. Glass and trash littered the ground. Across the street, city workers hunkering behind a white truck worked on a fire hydrant. Two skinny boys in their late teens approached them.

"Walmart is ten times bigger and carries everything," she told Chip. "Clothes. Movies. Groceries. Lawn equipment. Guns. Even tools."

"Tools?" Chip seemed surprised. "You know what tools are?"

"Not exactly, but they have them at Walmart."

No one she saw carried a handbag looking remotely stylish. And the stores and shops looked ancient.

"Are you sure this is the right century?" she asked. "The last time I saw a meat market was in an old Andy Hardy flick."

"Andy Hardy?"

"Never mind."

"Cool it, all right? Look what you're wearing. Didn't need a store for that, did you?"

Across the street, the two boys shouted at the city workmen. The workmen ignored them.

"What's that all about?" she asked.

Chip chuckled. "Those two are dead."

"The workmen?"

106

"The boys."

"Dead? Like us?"

"Not like us, Munchkin. They're still fresh."

"Fresh?"

"See how blurry and out of focus they get when the sun hits them?"

"Now that you've mentioned it…"

"Dead, all right."

"Is that why no one's talking to them?"

"Nobody but us can see them. They haven't left yet."

"Left?"

He sighed. "Is something wrong with your hearing? You sound like a parrot."

"Sorry."

"Want to know why they're hanging around?"

"Hang –" She caught herself. "What do you mean?"

"They don't know they're dead."

"Is that possible?"

"*You* didn't know until I told *you*."

"Why is that?"

"I do *tricks*, my titillating turtle dove. Describing the mysteries of the Universe is something slightly more complicated." He stepped down from the curb.

"Where are we going?"

"To give them the good news."

"Are you sure that's wise?"

"It's something they really need to know, Trinity."

"Tiffany."

"Whatever."

***

Todd was about to kick some serious ass. He needed to find out where the cops had taken Cammie, and these city jerks were being a royal pain.

He tried to ignore the mess across the street, where Cammie's parts lay. Mostly broken glass, but he also spotted jagged red chunks of the taillight covers he had bought for her last month.

The events last night turned cloudy whenever he tried remembering. It probably had something to do with cracking his head on Leon's skull. That's when the blackness had engulfed him.

The pain was awful. You expected serious pain when you slammed into a building. But it wasn't nearly as bad as he thought it would be. And just when he suspected it would get worse, everything turned dark and mellow.

Someone laid him on a stretcher. Someone else pushed the stretcher down the walk, then into the back of a van.

Explosions of more bright light blinded him. He tried to shield his eyes, but his arms had gone numb.

Where was Leon?

The sky turned clear; the sun already climbing high as he and Leon crossed the street.

Where had Leon come from? Where'd the stretcher go? The sheet? The van? Cammie?

You're just messed up. The weed, remember? The Wild Turkey. The bump on the head.

"How come these guys are ignoring us?" Leon asked, frowning at the city workers.

"They're assholes, man. My old man says the city hires assholes because they don't wanna waste their money on dudes who know what they're doin' or wanna get things done right."

"They're really busy. Fixing that hydrant thing looks complicated."

"They too busy to talk to two young voters?"

108

Leon scratched the back of his head. "We're too young to vote, Amigo."

"They don't know how old we are, man. They can stop for a second and tell us where the cops took Cammie."

"Maybe they don't know."

"Then they can take two seconds to say that."

"This sure is big-time weird." Leon shook his fingers in front of his face. He looked like he was trying to scare himself. "I thought they all snapped when I was pushing against the dash. But they don't even hurt."

"We lucked out, Chief. I don't hurt, neither."

"We should at least have some bruises…"

"Maybe we were thrown clear."

"Into what?"

"The grass?"

"Maybe we didn't get hurt because we were drunk."

"Ever watch that show about the world's stupidest police chases? When a drunk totals a car, he jumps right out and runs away."

"Neat." Leon wiggled the fingers of his other hand. "Wonder why."

"Hey!"

A skinny dude with wild red hair crossed the street. The best-looking babe Todd ever saw trailed behind him. Awesome. The same face and body as one of those Victoria's Secret babes.

"Hey yourself, man." Todd couldn't take his eyes off her.

The skinny dude glanced at the city workers. He motioned for Todd and Leon to follow them back to Crenshaw's.

"Where to?" Todd wasn't walking off with someone he didn't know. He would have if it had been just the babe. But Todd didn't like the looks of the skinny dude with her.

"We need to talk."

"Man, what's wrong with right here?"

"I don't want to strain my pipes yelling over those guys and their irritating equipment."

Todd looked at Leon, who just shrugged and followed them.

"What's this all about?" Todd wanted the babe to take over. All she had to do was say jump and Todd would have obliged. Hell, she made Darcy look like a drowned cat.

"I hate to break up this party," the skinny dude said, "but I have something disappointing, unpleasant, and somewhat tragic to tell you two."

"This…sounds bad," Leon said uneasily.

"You're quick," Skinny said, winking.

"What *is* this, man?" Todd asked.

"To put it delicately, you're both dead."

"What?" Leon nearly tripped on the curb.

"You some kinda wise guy, man?" Todd wanted to belt Skinny. Why would anyone say something like that?

"Take it to the bank. On second thought, I wouldn't. No one will pay much attention to you there, either."

"You sayin' we're dead?"

"Nothing wrong with *your* hearing, is there?"

"No way, man."

"Read the old lipperoos. You're *dead*."

"You mean dead?" Really and truly stone-cold?" Leon gulped audibly.

Skinny glanced at his hottie companion. "And they say the younger generation never listens." He turned back to them. "Yeah, sport. Dead. No longer among the living. Worm food. Don't go taking out any new life insurance policies."

Todd didn't believe this guy. He and Leon *couldn't* be dead. They were standing here, weren't they? "We ain't dead, man. We *can't* be!" His voice rose dramatically. "We're as alive as you two."

Skinny chuckled. The babe just sighed.

Leon trembled. "My folks. I've got to tell my folks—"

"They already know, sport."

"How the hell do you even know what you're talking about?" Todd asked.

"I've got what you might call some practical experience here," Skinny said.

"I don't even *know* you guys. Never saw you before. Why d'ya wanna—"

"I'm in a rare charitable mood. And believe me, where I come from, charity just doesn't cut it."

"But how can you say—"

"Go take a stroll out in the middle of the street. I guarantee you won't turn into roadkill."

"Man, you must think we're total dipshits." Todd tried to elbow Leon. His friend was obviously out of range. "Stupid, eh, Chief?" Todd forced out a laugh. "Go out there and stand in traffic. How stupid d'ya think we are?"

"Actually, that's a *different* matter."

"Listen, asshole…" Todd couldn't be sure, but that last thing sounded like some sort of snooty insult.

Skinny shrugged. "Take my word for it—you're both dead. And very shortly, neither of you will be standing here."

"Oh yeah? And just where will we be?"

"You're probably gonna find yourself in the Meddaworld." Skinny turned to Leon. "I'm not sure about you. You may not be as much of a dud as your friend."

"*Who's* a dud?" Todd hauled off and let one loose. No one called him a dud unless they were bigger and stronger. He didn't know how strong this jerk was. He sure was skinny, and barely came up to Todd's nose.

Swish!

Todd's fist sliced through Skinny's face. The force of the blow knocked Todd off-balance. He stumbled, rolling on the walk. But it didn't hurt. He didn't even feel the concrete slamming his butt and side.

"What the hell?"

Skinny and the gorgeous babe walked away.

"What happened?" Leon bent over him. "How did you miss that guy? What's this all about? We *can't* be dead. I have to put that scholarship form in the mail. And what about those X-rated DVD's I keep in a shoebox in the back of my closet, so my folks don't ever…"

Leon's voice trailed off. Todd wanted him to speak up. That always chafed his shorts about Leon. He mumbled when he was upset. Todd was in no mood to put up with mumbling.

Darkness came out of nowhere and enveloped him.

***

Tiffany couldn't shake the sadness enveloping her as she and Chip walked away.

112

She remembered standing near the buckeye tree, afraid to move. Not knowing where she was or where she had been.

But the horror for the boys had yet to happen. If Chip was right, they'd both soon be in that foul-smelling place.

"Did they have to know they were dead before they went down?"

"Like I said before, I wanted to give them a heads-up. I was being nice."

"Really?" She found that hard to swallow.

"A guy can't be a smartass *all* the time, you know."

"I didn't know you took time off from that."

"Hate to burst your bubble, but—" He went silent.

"What's wrong?"

Two well-dressed men chatting away on cell phones crossed the street.

"Are those...two-way radios?"

"Didn't you ever talk with anyone new down there once in a while?"

"Olivier kept me isolated. He didn't want anyone stealing me."

"Those are cell phones."

"Where's the cord?"

"No cords."

"Where's the power source?"

"Batteries."

"You're kidding. They actually *work*?"

"Most of the time."

"Not always?"

"Too many signals in the atmosphere cause interference. It also depends on which plan you've got with which company, where you are, and if you're outside. They don't work too well in stores or in elevators."

"Are they expensive?"

"Very."

"I see... They don't always work, but they're expensive." Chip scratched his head. "Sounds like the human race is seriously headed right down the crapper. Tell me. When did they come up with this brainstorm?"

"They had them when I was little. They were bigger back then, but they keep making them smaller and more compact."

"So eventually they'll be so small that you'll lose them?"

"People lose them now."

"Who could they possibly be talking to?" He was still watching the two men.

"I'm surprised they even have them in this tacky place."

"Sugar plum, save the cattiness for someone who actually cares."

Middle-aged females glared as they passed. Men stared wide-eyed and craned their heads.

"They're staring," she whispered.

"Ya think?"

"Is it...because of these?"

"You see anyone else toting around a pair as perky as those proud puppies?"

"What should I do?"

"Turn 'em into monsters. These locals will have a coronary."

"That's so *vulgar*..."

"Vulgar is my middle name."

"Your parents didn't have much imagination, did they?"

"You're a riot, Alice. Make them smaller, then."

"Shouldn't I wait till no one's watching?"

"We don't have that much time. Just do it."

"I guess I can re-lace my shoe...or turn toward a store to look in the window—"

"Jeez Louise... Make believe you're carrying around a pair of basketballs with slow leaks."

"Oh, all right. I hope you realize how ridiculous this makes me feel."

"And I hope you realize just how much I really don't care."

While she did it, she changed her footwear into a comfortable pair of Nina Elisha Indigo clogs by Clarks Orange.

"Like the shoes, too." Chip nodded his approval. "Now keep those puppies deflated. You don't want Gutril interested. We won't be able to take him back down if he knows who we are. The element of surprise is our only advantage."

"But he's seen me. Won't he remember?"

"He's probably having too much fun to notice you."

"You're doing wonders for my ego."

"Forget the ego, precious. You're dead—remember?"

"How will we know it's him?"

"You've seen him—I haven't. You'll probably recognize him if he's using his human form. If not, neither of us will know who he is."

"Not at all?"

"He could've been that fat, ugly woman with a goatee we just passed."

"That was a guy."

"Whatever."

"I know one thing."

"I wouldn't doubt it," he said.

She glared. He was such a jerk sometimes.

"Sorry. Proceed with your revelation."

"If I see any dead Hollywood actors walking around, it's really the wolf guy in disguise."

"Can't slip anything past you, can we?"

Mixed aromas of coffee, bacon, and potato pancakes drifted outside the open doorway of Jake's Coffeehouse.

"Want some coffee while we're in the neighborhood?" he asked. "Maybe a jelly doughnut? My treat."

"You have money?"

His laughter bounced off the concrete wall as he mounted the front step leading inside.

CHAPTER 16

One Slightly Demented Demon for Hire

Denner's Restaurant, the big two-story brick building two blocks east of Crenshaw's, displayed a *HELP WANTED* sign propped up in a window.

Gutril stopped walking.

Interesting. The Bochner kid mentioned working here and stealing that bottle of whiskey from this place. Since he was dead, they would need a replacement.

Far out. If he had a regular job, he could blend in better. And if he couldn't convince the Darcy girl to be his host, finding someone else wouldn't be difficult in a place like this.

A well-fed mortal always offered the least resistance.

The strong smell of roast beef filled the cool, dimly lit lobby. The clinking of glasses and silverware rang out from the main area.

A tall, dark-haired young woman in a business suit posed behind a podium in front of an archway. She wasn't bad if you liked business suits on women. Gutril preferred skirts, but so far, all he'd seen on females were jeans and slacks.

This modern century sure was weird.

"Smoking or non?" She produced a large menu covered with glossy color photos of food.

"Pardon?"

"Do you smoke?"

He grinned. "Only when I'm with a hot female."

She was not amused. *A jerk*, she was thinking. "Which section would you prefer to dine in?"

"Actually, I'm here for a job."

She yanked a small silver gismo from her jacket pocket, pressed it against her left ear, and whispered into it. Some sort of technological telephone thing, no doubt. This century was notorious for expensive, pocket-sized gadgets. "Go right on up," she said. "The stairs are over there." She pointed to a small alcove on her right.

The sign on the door at the top of the stairs said *Office*. His superior sense of smell caught a whiff of minty perfume trickling out into the hall.

He knocked.

A muffled female voice said, "Come in."

The large area was sparsely decorated. Stacked boxes covered the far wall. A small table and two metal chairs provided a cozy setting beneath the rectangular white glare of the window facing the street.

A slender woman in a long-sleeve white blouse sat behind a large desk stacked with paper, books, tablets, and menus. She gestured to the chair beside the desk. "Have a seat. I'm Kathryn."

"Hi." He admired her thick brown hair.

"Your name?"

"Gu…" He hadn't prepared for this. Couldn't tell her his *real* name, could he? She'd think he was weird.

"Did you say Goo?" She stared at him above her reading glasses. Her long-nailed fingers remained frozen above the keyboard.

"Gutier." He pronounced it GooSHAY. "Bill Gutier."

"Is that French?"

"Bill?"

"Gutier."

"Cajun."

"Really? In Ohio?"

"I travel a lot."

118

"You're not very dark."

"My mother was Swiss."

"You're…Cajun-Swiss?"

"My father always wanted to see the Alps. He met my mom on one of the slopes. It was love at first sight."

She smiled. "Very romantic."

He knew she'd like that. Females went all soft and gooey for romance.

She asked him to spell his name. Her nails clicked in a flurry on the keyboard. He assumed the square screen in front of her was one of those computer monitors he'd heard about. Apparently they stored more information than thousands of notebooks piled miles high.

He didn't see the logic for such silly inventions— especially when everything could be lost during an electrical storm.

"All right, Mr. Gutier. I guess you know we need stock help."

"I heard. Shame, wasn't it? The Todd guy dying and all?"

"Yes, it was a shock. Todd had personal problems." She pushed her reading glasses farther up her nose. "Now…what sort of work have you done in the past?"

His brief career at Belias' Watch Tower on the outskirts of Hades City wouldn't give her a true picture. The work, stupid and monotonous, was no challenge to his superior capabilities. Operating a winch? Raising blocks? Come on, now… It was no wonder he grew bored. To entertain himself, he caused so much turmoil that Belias banished him from the construction site.

Anyway, mortals didn't believe you when you told them what you did a hundred and fifty years earlier. They didn't think you could remember that far back.

119

"Construction work," he told her. "I was a personal assistant after that."

"What sort of personal assistant?"

"I worked for a druggist. Ran errands."

"Interesting." Her fingers clicked busily.

His role in helping the Chicago pharmacist select his victims was something else he knew he shouldn't talk about. Influencing a sociopathic druggist to murder a hundred and thirty people sounded impressive but wouldn't help land a job.

He did a quick probe, found some interesting data in the brunette's brain matter, and forced her to apply it to his employment form.

"Fine." She stared at the screen as though she'd just woken up. "Now I'll need your Social."

"My what?"

"Your Social Security number."

This was getting complicated.

He penetrated her head once again. A short list appeared. Each group contained nine digits. He gave her suitable data.

She typed it in and sat back. "We have a Social and an employment history. You really worked on three major gambling casinos in southern Mississippi?"

"Yes. Why?"

"I saw a special about that the other day on the History Channel."

"*There's* a coincidence."

"Really. Date of birth?"

He did one last probe, found something, and made her type it in.

"Wow. You have the same date of birth as my younger brother."

120

"What are the odds?"

"But you don't *look* thirty-four."

"Vitamins. A natural diet rich in protein. Exercise. Plenty of fresh air."

She remained staring at the screen.

"Problem?"

"You lived in Miami before coming to Ohio?"

"I guess you could say I was confused at the time."

"You're awfully pale."

"I never liked the beaches."

"Now *there's* a first."

"I prefer the nightlife."

"And you came *here*?"

"I just said I was confused."

She nodded. "Have you done much heavy lifting?"

The huge blocks at the Watch Tower weighed a ton apiece. She didn't need to know that when he grew bored, he tended to let go of the winch and watched the blocks drop onto passing servants.

"Is there much heavy lifting here?" he asked.

"The beer shipment comes in on Monday mornings, the wine and whiskey on Wednesdays, the food Mondays through Wednesdays. Some cases weigh fifty pounds, but there are dollies you can use."

"I can handle it."

"I'm sure you can. Go downstairs and work your way to the rear of the building, through the dining room. Niles will show you around."

"Niles?"

"He's about twenty-three. Tall and broad-shouldered."

He got up.

"Where on earth did you find that shirt?" she asked.

121

"Just something I slipped on."

She laughed. "I haven't seen that slogan since I was a little girl. Most people don't even know what Keds are."

"Oldies but goodies," he said, grinning. "Outa sight."

CHAPTER 17

Successful Scoundrels Lunching in Luxury

The Raven Country Club sat nestled in a grove of pine trees overlooking a sprawling golf course. Once prime farmland, the parcel consisted of five hundred choice acres situated three miles north of Raven. Five years earlier, Mayor Phil Holeridge purchased the section, along with a large tract bordering the west side of the road. Half of the latter tract was given to the city to expand the City Dump. The northern half was turned into a chemical site.

Passing through the double glass doors of the restaurant, Holeridge mumbled his usual greetings to the bright-eyed staff as he entered the bright, spacious dining room and approached the large circular table in front of the bay windows overlooking the golf course.

George Trent, General Manager of the First National Bank, already sat at the table. Trent wore a gold cotton shirt with French cuffs and black dress slacks. The cufflinks matched the large onyx ring on the fourth finger of his left hand. His brown hair, cut and styled to perfection, gleamed with mousse. A half-finished drink sat on the embroidered doily in front of him.

Holeridge ordered a Manhattan, then sat back and unbuttoned his jacket. A lanky young man with small blinking blue eyes instantly appeared.

"What's the special?" Holeridge asked.

"Ravioli cooked in our special Alfredo clam sauce, sir."

"Sounds good, but I prefer a dozen chilled oysters on the half shell."

"Right away, sir." He took off, running.

"How are things at the bank?" Holeridge asked Trent.

"Routine. Nasty accident last night."

"I talked with Hawkins briefly this morning. He said Bochner's Camaro was flying when it slammed into Crenshaw's."

"Kid was an idiot."

"Like father, like son."

"Too bad we can't castrate idiots at birth."

"We don't know they're idiots until they're older."

"Idiots breeding with idiots can only produce more idiots. How much damage to the store?"

"That building's been sitting there since the Second World War. Solid block foundation. It'll withstand an earthquake."

"Good thing. Otherwise, Ira will be moaning."

The cute brunette waitress brought the Manhattan on a small silver tray and placed it carefully in front of Holeridge. Holeridge drank some. "Excellent." He put down his glass. "The item we'll be discussing with the others," he said, lowering his voice. "I wanted to give you a heads-up first."

Trent leaned closer.

"Denner's Restaurant. We need it to sew up that block. It's a terrific anchor."

Trent frowned. "But the new owner's doing very well—even better than Bill Denner when he ran it for thirty years."

"Immaterial."

"Why not take over the mortgage and let the owner run it?"

"I don't want to handle it that way. I intend to offer the man double what he paid. I want the deal sewn up in three days. We'll discuss it in the Gold Room after lunch."

"Are you sure you want me to—"

"You're our spokesman, George." Holeridge hated being challenged. He knew this matter was bound to be tricky. But he had to tread lightly. Bankers were a strange breed. "You've been our spokesman since you joined the Society. And you've been doing well ever since. Don't let us down."

"I'll try not to. We need to stick together. Now more than ever. Since we struck out so badly last time at the mine—"

"There will be other opportunities." This wasn't exactly a good time to discuss their latest failure.

Miles Ladner, President of Raven's First Savings & Loan, came in with Ira Crenshaw. Both wore their sporting attire. They took seats on Holeridge's right.

Ira reached for the cashew bowl. "How're we doing today, gentlemen?"

"Never better," Holeridge said. "How 'bout you?"

Ira tossed half a dozen cashews into his mouth and did a remarkable job of not spitting any pieces out when he spoke. "I've been better days."

"We heard," Trent said.

Holeridge shook his head. "Just consider yourself lucky no one else was hurt."

"I'd better not be served."

"By who?"

"Bochner's dad—who else?"

"Bochner never cared about his kid."

"I don't trust him. He could be looking for a windfall."

125

"Don't worry," Holeridge said. "Bill Elliot's representing us. No one can touch you."

"Hope you're right," Ira said. "After last week…"

"We shouldn't discuss that right now," Miles whispered. "Too damned public."

Noel Thomas, owner of Thomas Hardware, the Raven Drugstore, Mike's Garage & BodyWorks, and the Raven Gun Shoppe, came in. His bald head gleamed from the sun shining through the big window. He pulled out a chair.

The brunette rushed over.

"What's your thirst-quencher, Noel?" Holeridge asked. "Your usual Guinness?"

"The extra Stout," Thomas said. "And hurry. This boy's parched."

Bill Elliot and his son Tom tossed martini orders over their shoulders. They took their seats between Thomas and Trent. They'd come directly from the golf course. Both looked morose.

"Bad game?" Miles finished his vodka rocks.

Bill sat back and sighed. "I'd welcome a bad game over this past week."

"Fill us in," Trent said.

Bill glanced at the couples filing in. He lowered his voice. "Not to be a doomsayer or anything, but in the last month our firm has lost three major accounts. That makes six for the year. Any idea how much money that translates into?"

Holeridge sucked down an oyster and blotted his mouth with his napkin. "You've lost accounts before. You'll survive."

"This looks worse and worse," Trent said dismally.

"C'mon, gentlemen." Holeridge picked up his drink. "We've been without our benefactor for six months. Are we gonna blame everything on his absence?"

"You have to admit things haven't been, well, rosy," Noel said.

Holeridge didn't want to voice his fears. These men were antsy enough. "Don't panic, now."

"What do you expect?" Ira asked. "They lose three big accounts and a teenage idiot nearly makes a shambles out of my store. Still think things aren't going south?"

"Quite the contrary," Holeridge said with a grin. "We need to stay strong. Panic's our enemy. This theory goes all the way back to Alexander the Great."

"Alexander the Great," countered Ira, "didn't have to worry about drunken teenage morons slamming a muscle car into one of his stores."

"What about that other matter?" Noel said edgily. "Jim Denner's daughter selling our restaurant to an outsider?"

Holeridge finished his drink and signaled for another. He told himself he needed to go easy on the booze. It might affect his judgment later on. Best stop after the next one. He had to stay in control. He also had to convince them to buy back that building. "Gentlemen, try the oysters. They're superb."

CHAPTER 18

Breakfast with Tiffany

"They're staring again," Tiffany whispered.

The eyes of every male customer in Jake's Coffeehouse had stayed on her since she and Chip took seats in the corner booth.

She knew she should be used to this. She had always been told she was beautiful, that she should be in movies. Wasn't that why she went to Hollywood? For the attention?

And, of course, to get far away from Peoria. And, of course, her new stepdad.

She picked up a menu and held it close. "I feel like some sort of oddity."

Chip grabbed his own menu. "Take a gander at thyself. The puppies are back and have taken over the pound."

Darn. There they were again—as perky as ever. "I thought I'd fixed that."

"Hey, it takes practice. It took me hundreds of years to get where I am now."

"Um, you're in a coffeehouse in Ohio."

"Cut the crap. You know what I mean."

She closed her eyes. *Slow leak. There.* She lowered the menu. Some guys continued to stare. Others scratched their buzz-cuts. After a while, no one cared. "What are we having?" she asked.

"Whatever you want. My treat."

He had to be kidding. "I've been with guys who pulled that one. They always stuck me with the check."

Chip brought his face closer. "Don't get bent out of shape, cupcake. The check doesn't mean squat to us now— get it?"

"Sure means a lot in *this* place." The tall, matronly woman stood over them like a vulture sizing up its next meal. "You two got money?"

"What's with the attitude?" Chip asked.

"I heard what you just said."

"Oh, that…" Tiffany waved it aside. "I like giving him a rough time."

"All I cares about is the tab. Got money? Let's have your order. If not, there's the door."

"We feel so *welcome* here," Chip said amiably. "Right, love blossom?"

"I'm not your love blossom," Tiffany said flatly.

"What's your order?" the woman asked.

"I'll have a big pitcher of water," he said, grinning. "Also, a small glass of freshly-squeezed orange juice. And a hard-boiled egg. Make that two hard-boiled eggs. And make sure you leave the shells on."

The woman's broad forehead filled up with wavy cracks. "You want the eggs *and* the shells?"

"Correctamundo."

"Is that a yes?"

"Righty-rooty."

She waited to see if he was putting her on. When he didn't say anything else, she scratched out his order. "Is that it?"

"I smell coffee."

"You want coffee with your water *and* orange juice? Or instead of?"

"Just bring the grounds."

"You want an order of *coffee grounds*?"

"Abso-damn-lutely."

She sighed tiredly. "You want it right from the pot? Or from the pile soaking in the trash?"

"From the pot, please. I like my coffee grounds fresh."

She stroked her chins, then turned to Tiffany. "And you, missy?"

"A jelly doughnut, please."

"That's more like it. Coffee?"

"A small glass of diet coke. Have to watch my figure."

"You're watchin' your figure, but you wanna jelly doughnut?"

"I probably won't eat *all* of it…"

"Two funny bunnies at the same table. My lucky day." She finished scribbling, then shuffled off, shaking her head.

Tiffany gawked at Chip. "Coffee grounds?"

He shrugged. "I've got issues."

"I'll say."

"Don't throw stones, honey buns. Anyone who still wants to watch her figure when she's colder than a mackerel has one or two serious concerns of her own."

"Just because I'm…that way…doesn't mean I intend to let myself go."

He chuckled. "You're gonna be the talk of the town when we go back down."

"Tell me about the wolf guy." She didn't want to talk about going back to that horrible place.

"You already know about him. Didn't you two have a thing going down there?"

She wanted to reach across the table and see how much hair she could pull out. "We didn't have a thing going. He's a pig."

"Actually, he's a wolf."

"Whatever he is, he's not nice. But tell me what I need to know. You want me to help, don't you?"

"You've got a point, Tyranny."

"Tiffany."

"He's an airhead. He gets distracted. That can help us. But it'll still be tricky. His powers are pretty frightening."

"I've seen some of them."

"You saw what he can do when he wants to be cute. You haven't seen him pissed."

"Why doesn't anyone want him up here? He's a demon. He does bad things."

"Undris controlled the Midwestern section of this country nearly a hundred and fifty years ago. A psycho pharmacist living in a castle in Chicago wanted to summon a demon. Since Gutril excels at manipulation, Undris picked him to come up. Gutril started out doing his job just fine.

"The pharmacist eventually did in more than a hundred and thirty folks without getting caught. Then Gutril got a whiff of rats in the castle and went looking for them. Without Gutril's protection, the pharmacist was caught by the cops."

"Who's running things over here?"

"Balberith, but his time ran out. He did some nifty bad things, too. A few years ago, he got together with Agaliarept—the bad boy controlling Africa—and sent some inbred camel jockeys over here crashing into buildings in hijacked planes."

"Good grief. That was because of…Gallery Arp?"

"Agaliarept. And Balberith."

"You guys really *are* nasty, aren't you?"

"Lucifer and the G-man have this big-time rivalry. That's why mortals were invented. They've been using mortals to play their war games ever since."

"Is Lucifer down there? I mean…do you know him?"

"Socially?" Chip laughed. "You must be joking. He'd been down there, doing weird things in the basement for a long time. He doesn't see anyone where he is."

"How does he get things done?"

"By having the bad boys convince everyone the G-man ain't so cool."

"I don't get it."

"You've heard the phrase, in his own image?"

"Of course."

"When a demon causes a mortal to do something stupid or nasty, it's a spit in the eye – if you know what I mean."

"Why doesn't one of the super demons come up for the wolf guy?"

"Gutril's sniffer is top-rate. If he suspects a super is up here, he'll go into hiding. For this job they needed two little guys like us so Gutril won't suspect anything."

"Tell me something."

"That's why I'm here, my luscious wafer bar."

"How come you know all these names but can't get mine right?"

"I've been down there hundreds of years. How long have I known you?"

"Three or four hours?"

"Good math. Now. You were saying, Epiphany?"

"Tiffany. Tell me, if the wolf guy does some really bad stuff up here, won't they leave him alone?"

"The supers like to think they're running things. They don't appreciate it when someone they're trying to punish is brought up without their permission."

"I think I get it. I just don't understand how we're going to get him to go back down."

The sour-faced woman shuffled over with their orders. "Two hard-boiled eggs with shells. One order of coffee grounds. One glass of orange juice." She put the plates down. "And one jelly for missy here. I'll be right back with your pitcher of ice water and your diet Coke."

Chip sniffed the coffee grounds.

"Problem?" the woman asked.

"It smells funky."

The woman scowled. "They're *coffee grounds*. What did you expect?"

"What kind of coffee is it?"

"Decaf."

Chip handed her the plate. "I prefer regular."

The woman took it and groaned. "Be right back with your order of *regular* coffee grounds."

***

Ernie Travis parked the cruiser in front of Jake's.

Just enough time for a quick coffee to go before heading over to Raven High. Hawk wanted him prowling the parking lot to make sure nothing funny was going on. The jocks had football practice, which usually meant shenanigans. Maybe even a little pot-smoking.

After some aspirin and a cup of that battery acid Nancy Cunningham fixed at the Station, Ernie felt a little better. But Lois Becker made the best coffee in town. He

133

wanted some quality stuff and maybe a cream-filled doughnut before heading off for playground duty.

Lois hunched over the stove, flipping eggs.

Ernie leaned against the counter. The usual crowd. Everyone busily chowed down their roast beef sandwiches, some having a late breakfast. "How goes it, Lo?"

"Same old, same old. Need some java?"

"Just dump some in a cup. Got to head on over to the high school, see who's actin' stupid."

"Be easier seein' who ain't." Lois scooped up two eggs and slid them onto a plate. She nodded at Sylvia to take care of Travis.

The two sitting in the corner window booth made him stiffen.

No way. Couldn't be.

But the long, curly blond hair sure did look like—

"Somethin' wrong, Ern?" Sylvia capped off his steaming cup and slid it over. "Looks like you just seen a ghost."

"Somethin' ain't right."

Sylvia rang him up. He gave her change, then slowly approached the booth.

Sure does look like the same chicks.

*But some*thin's different.

He remembered his little brain fart from before, on the way into town. How the morning sun hit the redhead at a weird angle and made her look like a guy.

This *was* a guy.

What in holy hell is goin' on?

"Hi," the blonde said, nibbling delicately on a jelly doughnut.

"How goes it?" her companion said, munching noisily on something.

Something else odd here. The tiny hairs on the back of his neck straightened.

Where'd Blondie's monsters go?

"You're pale," the redhead said. "Getting enough Vitamin C?"

Screwy. Red's a guy, then a chick, then a guy again. Now Blondie's flat-chested.

"Maybe you're working too hard," Red said.

"I...think I might be." A solid mass of dizziness hit him. Damn. He needed to stay away from that cheap bar whiskey.

"I hope you feel better soon," the blonde said.

"I'll bet you're not getting enough Vitamin C." Red reached up and pushed her hair away from her cheek.

Her?

Working too hard. Yep, that was it.

"Their orange juice is terrificoso," Red said. "Vitamin C's the key. Your chemistry works better when you've got enough Vitamin C. Right, Spiff?"

"Tiffany," the blonde said sourly.

"Whatever."

Gotta get outa here...

In a daze, Travis found his way back to the counter.

"Sure everything's okay, Ern?" Sylvia's heavily-made-up face scrunched up with worry lines.

"Tell me something, Syl. Table I was just at? Who's sittin' there?"

"Some girl and a guy. Why?"

"Ya sure?"

"Course I'm sure. What's wrong? You okay?"

He rushed outside, nearly tripping on the concrete stoop.

CHAPTER 19

Taking Back a Restaurant

The Gold Room glimmered brightly from the afternoon sun penetrating its large bay window.

First Edition books, sculptures of Roman figures, and expensive European bric-a-brac filled the bookshelves lining two of the room's four walls. An elegant pool table occupied one corner, a round casino-type card table opposite it.

Beneath the ornate crystal chandelier, a large mahogany table stood over an imported wine-red Turkish rug. A bottle of Napoleon brandy and several snifters sat on a gleaming silver tray. Beside the bottle, hand-rolled King of Denmark cigars, priced at a hundred and fifty dollars per, lay in neat rows in a polished wooden box.

Coming straight from his St. Clairsville branch offices, Leonard Winslow joined the group. For the last ten years, Winslow Landscaping & Excavation had cornered the market in condominium and strip mall development in Belmont County.

Augustus Phelps, CEO and founder of Tri-State Building & Development, hustled in behind Leonard. His group of developers remained constantly busy, buying up Ohio Valley property. For a man pushing seventy, and forty pounds overweight, Augustus showed no sign of slowing down.

Alan Crenshaw came in a few minutes later. Alan's activities consisted primarily of maintaining his father Ira's apartment complexes and collecting rents from more than two hundred Raven tenants.

Holeridge dismissed the waiter, then closed and locked the door. Bill Elliot, Alan Crenshaw, and Augustus Phelps sipped brandy. Miles Ladner and Ira Crenshaw puffed on cigars.

Holeridge selected a cigar and lit it with his gold monogrammed lighter. He lowered his large butt into his chair. "Any concerns before we start?"

George Trent said, "I only care about what happened at the mine last Saturday."

"You mean what didn't happen," Noel Thomas said.

"That was the second time our conjuration went unanswered." Ira Crenshaw coaxed a lopsided smoke ring out of his mouth. It floated lazily a few feet and broke into light-gray strands.

"It's been a horrible year," Miles Ladner said. "The Savings & Loan has lost several major accounts. And look what's happened with Bill's law firm and that near-calamity last night at Ira's store."

"Gentlemen, please..." Holeridge hadn't expected things to escalate so soon. "Let's keep calm."

"What I'd like to know is why we're suddenly unable to be heard," Augustus said. "What could possibly be going on down there? Why aren't they listening?"

"They're listening," Holeridge said.

"Then why isn't anyone coming up?" Alan Crenshaw usually voiced his opinion only when asked. "I thought we were on good terms with them."

"Mr. Balbor was sent back," Augustus said. "It all boils down to that."

"We all know how they operate," Holeridge said. "We'll have a successor. He could be on his way up as we speak."

"You mean here?" Miles asked. "In Raven?"

138

"He'll be sent where he's needed most," Bill Elliot said. "That's how it was with Balbor."

"Balbor came here first," Augustus said.

"We requested his presence," Holeridge said.

"That's not the point," Bill Elliot said. "Except for a few minor annoyances, we have an excellent record."

"Won't do us much good." Miles tapped the glass ashtray with his cigar.

"Exactly," Noel said. "But how long will these annoyances remain minor without intervention? If they think someone needs help more than Raven—"

"We're toast." Ira stubbed out his cigar.

"I wouldn't rule out anything," Holeridge said. "We stand as good a chance as any to get the successor first."

"I'd bet on Miami," Miles said sourly. "All those damned Hispanics. And they breed like rabbits."

"What's that have to do with anything?" Augustus said.

"Hispanics don't need supervision," Alan said. "They just take over."

"Don't forget, our benefactors prefer being close to the Society," Holeridge said. "There aren't that many of us in this part of the country. Or in Miami."

"Hispanics don't believe in the Devil," Bill Elliot said.

"Of course they do," Noel said. "They're Catholics."

"Catholics believe in the Devil," George Trent said. "They just don't worship him."

"None of this would have happened," Ira said, "if Balbor hadn't been called back down."

"It was only a matter of time," Holeridge said. "Now we've got to deal with it."

"How?" Bill said. "It's out of our control now."

"We have to look at this logically," Miles said. "Without backing, we're sitting ducks."

"How do you figure?" Holeridge couldn't believe how easily these men were shaken. "We own eighty percent of all business enterprises in Belmont County and nearly fifty percent of all farmland for two hundred square miles."

"That doesn't mean we're not sitting ducks," Miles said. "Look what happened with the Denner deal."

"I'm glad you brought that up," Holeridge said. The meeting had finally moved in the right direction. "That's what I wanted to discuss."

"You want to discuss how we were swindled out of inheriting our own restaurant?" Leonard asked.

"I want to discuss buying the property from the new owner."

"You can't be serious," Noel said. "Denner's is doing better than ever. The new owner's bright, knows what he's doing. He'd be a fool to sell."

"He might consider for enough money."

"Why bother?" Augustus said. "The man's pulling in entirely too much business."

"I'm sure he's got his price. Everyone does."

"What'll we do when we get it?" Ira asked.

"Keep it running," Holeridge said. No need to let them know why he wanted the building. He'd tell them after the papers were signed. They wouldn't mind; they all loved making more money. Arcades made money.

"Why not assume the mortgage and have the present owner run it?" Leonard asked. "He's showing definite signs of successful bankability."

"We hand-pick our help," Holeridge said. "Look how efficiently this place is running. Every employee was personally selected, screened, and interviewed."

"You've made your point," Ira said. "So all we need now is to vote on it."

"That's right," Holeridge said. "Everyone agreeing please raise his hand."

Everyone but George Trent agreed.

"George?"

Trent studied his brandy. A painful expression had taken over his fine features. "I'm...not comfortable with this."

"Why not?"

"I don't want to ask a man to sell off his dream."

"What if he doesn't want to sell?" Ira asked.

"We're facing one of two options," Holeridge replied. "The first is to offer him enough money. If he doesn't agree, offer him fifty percent more."

"And then?"

"If he doesn't agree to the second offer, our next step is to locate and deal with his beneficiary."

CHAPTER 20

A Nifty Way to Make Money

Tiffany pushed away her plate.

Eating just wasn't fun anymore. You were dead, so why bother? It was probably just another way of blending in. Besides, watching Chip munching on eggshells, swallowing coffee grounds, and chugging a pitcher of water proved too much. More than enough on her mind, anyway.

She would probably feel better when she found a way of staying here.

At the counter, a well-dressed guy around forty with a buzz cut and a neatly trimmed black beard pushed small forkfuls of sliced roast beef into his mouth while talking on his cell.

"Who can he be talking to?" Chip asked.

"His wife. Girlfriend. Boss. What's wrong with that?"

"Is it necessary to chat with someone when you're sucking up food?"

Chip sure was weird. How could anyone not understand cell phones? Everyone knew you couldn't get by without them nowadays.

"Last time I was up here, everyone was freaked about the Bomb and the end of civilization. People ran around like scared rabbits because there weren't any underground shelters, and no one actually wanted to take the time to build one. Now, everyone's gone nuts about these funny little phones."

"There was a *bomb*?"

"That's right, you weren't born yet."

142

"My *parents* weren't even born yet—there was a *bomb*?"

"A big scare. This country thought Russia was going to blow everyone up."

That didn't make sense. "Russia?"

"Things were different back then, muffin."

"How had everything changed so much?"

"Mortals are crazy."

"You can say that again."

"Mortals are crazy."

"I asked for that, didn't I?"

"But they can't be crazy on their own. They need constant help."

"You mean...that Wheelbarrow guy?"

"Balberith?"

"Was he the one behind that bomb scare?"

"His gig, all right. Who do you think ordered Kennedy being shot?"

"Ted Kennedy was *shot*?" She didn't remember hearing anything about that.

He sighed. "Girl, you must have sucked down a batch of heavy Z's in History class."

"Oh. Now I remember. You're talking about his older brother. What was his name? Bobbie?"

"Let's talk about something else, like paying for the tab."

"We're not going to get in trouble, are we?"

"You've got new powers. You can already make your ta-ta's disappear, so at least you're getting the knack."

"Give me a hint. I'm new at this."

"Visualize a twenty and give it to Miss Sparkles."

"I can actually *do* that?"

143

"Just make sure she dumps the cash in the register before we leave."

"What cash?"

"The money you give her."

"The imaginary money?"

Chip's eyes twinkled. "Pure genius."

The big woman waddled over, scratching something onto her pad. "Everything all right?"

"Super," Chip said. "Great food, service with a smile. We're pleased as punch. Tell the management to give you a raise."

"Here." Tiffany handed her an imaginary twenty. "And thank you."

The woman studied the bill.

"Something wrong?"

"Thought I saw something weird. This real?"

Chip winked. "Printed it off just for you."

She shook her head. "Gettin' old, I guess. Be back with your change."

"Keep it."

"Thanks." The beginnings of a smile loosened her glower. She stopped halfway to the register and studied her empty palm. "Didn't you just give me—"

"You dropped it," Tiffany said quickly. "It's…under your shoe."

"Didn't even feel it slide out." With a cracking of joints, she bent and grunted back into an upright position. Then opened the register, shoved the bill inside, pulled out change and dropped it in her apron pocket. "C'mon back, now." She slammed the drawer shut.

"What did she see on your bill?" he asked her outside.

"Burt Lancaster."

144

"What's *that*?"

"A favorite actor. A big, muscular guy with lots of teeth and curly blond hair."

"Why him?"

"For a second I forgot which President was on a twenty."

"This Burt guy…he looks like a President?"

"No…"

Tendrils of steam trickled out of his ears. "You're killing me, you know."

"I got Burt confused with Charlton Heston."

"Who?"

"Another favorite actor."

Chip pushed both hands through his red mop. "Please explain this sudden plunge into hopelessly idiotic incoherency."

"Heston played President Jackson in *The President's Lady*."

"Huh?"

"A movie."

"So?"

"Andrew Jackson. The President on a twenty."

Chip rubbed his face. "I think I need a tad more explanation—"

"Oh, shut up and go see the movie."

"If I know you, it's probably sappy and sudsy at the same time."

"It's a wonderful love story."

"Damn. I left my spare box of Kleenex back at the rock garden behind the Castle."

"Well, how'd I do? I mean really?"

"A smidge more study and you'll be as good as me. On second thought, nobody's that good. But you'll be good enough."

They started up the walk.

"Where are we headed?"

"Hunting for the wolf guy, lamb chop."

"How will we know where to look?"

"Got to sniff out clues."

"That'll be tough in a tacky place like this."

He punched her playfully on the shoulder. "Ya know, Litany—"

"Tiffany."

"Whatever. You just might turn out all right."

"You're serious, aren't you?"

"Can't be the jostling jester of jocularity *all* the time."

"Why not?"

"I'd laugh myself silly."

"I should've seen that one coming. And thank you for the compliment."

"No big shakes, Miss Flake. And speaking of shakes… The puppies have wandered out of their kennel again."

"Oh, crap." This was getting old.

CHAPTER 21

Mysterious Phone Call from a Banker

Antoine's high-pitched shouting burst through the kitchen.

Gripping a long glistening knife, the enraged Frenchman followed stock boy Niles Cameron to the back doors like a hungry cat stalking a fieldmouse. Niles was younger, nearly a foot taller, and in much better shape, but Antoine was clearly the aggressor. Niles quickly escaped through the exit. Antoine shouted at the closing door, then returned to his butcher block and mercilessly chopped up an onion.

Hearing the commotion, Louis Gates slipped through the swinging doors separating the dining room from the kitchen. He ignored Antoine on his way to the stockroom. He avoided the surly Frenchman whenever he could.

Louis never regretted his decision to buy Denner's Restaurant six months ago. Finding a man with Antoine's cooking expertise had taken two months but hiring him presented a number of complications. Antoine was moody and cantankerous, with a violent temper. The only way to deal with him was to listen to his barrage of rapid-fire French, nod politely, and quietly walk away.

But everyone loved the man's cooking. With the food top-rate, overlooking outbursts and tantrums seemed an acceptable option.

Louis rushed into the stockroom. At least Niles wasn't bleeding or dying. "What's the problem? I heard him shouting all the way from Main Street."

Niles lugged a fifty-pound sack of potatoes over to the fresh produce area in the corner. "He's having a bird about the potatoes."

"What's wrong with them?"

Niles set it on a pallet in front of two unopened sacks. "This batch insults his creativity."

"What else did he say?"

"Everything else was in French."

"Terrific. The people in this town barely speak English."

"That new guy just started a couple hours ago."

"Kathryn told me. What about him?"

"His name sounds French." Niles shrugged. "Maybe he can understand Antoine."

"I'm part Italian, but that doesn't mean I can understand it."

"It's worth a try. Want me to get him?"

"Guess it won't hurt. But do it fast. That crazy Frenchman's liable to start tossing knives again. I just saw what he's doing to a helpless onion."

Niles left the room.

Louis needed a cigarette. He'd left the pack upstairs.

Trying to quit, remember?

Niles came back. A tall, lean guy with rust-colored hair, high cheekbones, and light-brown eyes followed him. Niles said, "Bill Gutier, this is our boss."

Louis nodded. "You speak French?"

Gutier shrugged. "Doesn't everyone?"

"In France, maybe. This is Ohio. How about doing us a favor?"

"Does it involve speaking French?"

"You sure are a quick study. Go ask Antoine who pissed in his Cheerios."

148

"Who's Antoine?"

"You can't miss him. The short, potbellied bald guy with the waxed mustache waving a meat cleaver and shouting in French."

Gutier nodded. "And what are Cheerios?"

"Ah. Stock help with finesse and wit. I like that." Louis nodded. "Good to have you aboard."

Gutier headed for the kitchen doorway.

Louis visualized trying to explain human blood spatter to the Raven cops. "On second thought, you don't really have to go in there."

"You just asked me to—"

"When Antoine's upset, he's liable to fillet anyone getting too close."

Gutier pushed open the swinging door and disappeared.

"Brave stock help?" Louis said. "That's a first."

"He's new," Niles said. "He hasn't met Antoine yet."

The shouting stopped.

"I don't know if silence is a good thing now," Louis said.

"You don't think Antoine would…?"

"I wouldn't put anything past him."

"It's hard to find a good chef—even if he *is* a fruitcake."

Gutier, still in one piece, emerged from the kitchen.

"What happened in there?" Louis asked.

"He said he couldn't use the potatoes. Didn't like the way they looked."

"What else?"

"He thinks it's really nifty that I speak French."

"That's nice."

"Far out for me, too," Gutier said wryly. "He told me about his mother, and some woman in Wheeling driving him crazy. He has a younger brother—"

"Sorry about that."

"Is that all you want?"

"Yeah. And thanks."

Louis peered into the kitchen. Antoine remained at the butcher block, chopping and dicing more onions—this time more humanely.

His cigarette craving stronger than ever, Louis hurried down the hall. These days he was down to ten a day, failing by five. He made a mental note to keep the pack with him.

He'd been living upstairs since he bought the place. The office and supply area took up half the second floor, but there was more than enough space in his bedroom to accommodate his modest wardrobe and his jazz collection. Jazz had been his passion since he was a boy. He had entered Duquesne University eighteen years ago on a partial music scholarship, but after visiting many of the jazz clubs in the area, he decided music proved too iffy a profession. Computer technology dominated the trend at that time. He switched his major halfway into his sophomore year and became a programmer five years later.

Ten years in that field left him with ulcers, a nicotine dependency, a drinking problem, and an intense hatred for modern technology. The hours were long, the money very good. After ten years of wise investments and a decent retirement portfolio, he left programming forever.

Kathryn replaced the phone when he came in.

"That was George Trent. Shame you weren't here ten seconds ago."

"My timing's always been good. Who's George Trent?"

"Manager of the First National Bank."

"A bank manager calling on a Saturday?"

"He didn't say what he wanted."

"Didn't he give you some idea?"

"He called and asked for you. Said it was personal. I didn't want to ask any questions and embarrass him."

"That never stopped you with me or any of the staff."

"We're like family. It's fun to embarrass family members."

"I *knew* there was something about you I admired."

"I thought it was my legs."

"I also find it impressive that you can sit there all day and handle just about anything."

"Nothing has actually taxed me yet. By the way, do you intend to return his call?"

"I don't like personal calls from men."

"He's a banker, silly. I don't think he'd call unless it involved some sort of business thing."

"That *was* silly of me. Is he going to call back?"

"He left his number." She handed him a scrap of paper. "He'd like to hear from you at your earliest convenience."

He took the paper and dropped it on the desk. "Maybe he wants to know what the buffet is this afternoon."

"He could've asked me."

"Maybe he wanted to hear it from the man in charge."

"It sounded important."

He opened a drawer and took out a crumpled pack of Winston.

Kathryn stared in her quiet, unsettling way. "What makes me think you're not going to return the call?"

"Because I probably won't."

"Why not?"

He lit a cigarette and pocketed the pack and the lighter. "First National isn't carrying the note to this place."

"So?"

"And I don't like bankers."

"Some of them are actually nice and don't beat their wives."

"I'm not concerned about that."

"What are you concerned about?"

"They mess up your checking account and charge you a fortune for returned checks. Then they smile and tell you to have a nice day. That's what cops do when they give you a ticket. Believe me, it's irritating."

"You've had *such* a rough life."

"I'm a walking study of injustice and social intolerance." He sat, propped up his feet and blew the smoke at the ceiling fan. Smoke bothered Kathryn. "By the way, that new guy we hired actually coaxed Antoine into not killing anyone today."

"How'd he do that?"

"Spoke to him in French."

"That's all?"

"Funny, ain't it?"

Kathryn shook her head. "And here I was thinking Antoine suffered anger management issues."

"What would make you think that?"

"Last week he threw a steak knife at you and called you a dirty name."

"He said he wasn't aiming at me."

"What about the dirty name?"

"He doesn't remember."

"I'm glad you cleared that up."

"It pays to be understanding. But I'm happy we hired Gutier. Now we have a translator."

"Should I adjust his salary?"

"Let's see how he handles the stock. Then we can decide on his new title and perks."

"Good decision."

"That's why I'm the boss."

"Really? I thought it was because you bought the place."

"That, too."

CHAPTER 22

Tiffany's Bathroom Escape Attempt

A bulky old man slouched on a padded stool behind the storefront window that said *Corner Newsstand*. His shock of curly white hair covered his scalp like a frosted Brillo pad. Thick-rimmed black bifocals balanced on the tip of his bulbous red nose. The Raven *Gazette* was spread out on the chipped wooden counter. He squinted while reading the funnies.

Chip stepped behind a paperback rack inside the door. He appeared to be scanning the books, but Tiffany could tell he was studying the people at the magazine racks.

Looking for the wolf guy.

Not sensing his slobbering presence in the room, Tiffany focused on more important issues.

A lime-green curtain stretched across an archway at the other end of the room.

A back door, maybe?

She stepped up to the counter. "Hello," she whispered.

The old man looked up from his paper. His veiny gray eyes narrowed above the bifocals, taking her in and immediately lowering.

Boys will be boys, she thought, even though this "boy" was probably well over seventy. "Is there a bathroom I could use?"

"Mosey on down to the other end, little lady. Through the doorway."

"Thank you."

"Where to, Travesty?" Chip asked behind her.

154

"I have to use the little girl's room."

"You're kidding."

"No. I'm not."

"Listen, buttercup—"

"Will you *please* give me a little privacy?"

Heads turned in their direction. The old man watched them over his paper. With a sigh, Chip returned to the paperback racks.

The small, tiled foyer led to the room marked *Office*. It was locked. The only other door said *Bathroom*.

The small room smelled strongly of Lemon Pledge. A naked bulb fixed to the faded plaster ceiling provided light. She crossed the scuffed linoleum, slipped inside the stall, then closed and latched the door.

A swiveling handle in the oblong window above the tank opened the smudged pane. It was already cracked a couple of inches.

She stepped up on the commode lid. If she climbed onto the tank and opened the window just enough to slip through…

The bathroom door squealed open. She scrunched down and froze.

"Baby cakes?"

She sighed. "Yes?"

"What are you doing in there?"

"What are *you* doing in here?"

"Looking for you."

"Are you a homely stick-girl again?"

"I prefer the term, lithe and coltish. But don't change the subject. Why are you here?"

"I already told you."

"You're up to something."

"What could I be up to in a bathroom?"

"You tell me. By the way, where are your feet?"

"They're attached to my ankles. Why?"

"I don't see them under the door."

He could be so aggravating… "I brace them against it so no one will break in."

"You're still worried about stuff like that?"

"Some things a girl never gets over."

"Listen…I don't think you can do that anymore."

"Do *what* anymore?"

"You've got substance. You just don't have *substance*."

"I just had a diet Coke."

She heard him sigh. "I just had a pitcher of water and a glass of orange juice. If *I* don't need to make wee-wee, why should *you*?"

Her plan shot, she climbed down. He was such a jerk.

She flushed. Just for spite. Then unlocked the door and pulled it open.

"What did you just flush?"

She glared at him on her way to the filmy mirror. "Memories."

"You can be really tragic at times. Learn that from those acting classes?"

She arranged her hair better. She didn't like him very much right now. "Maybe I'm not ready to, you know, give it all up."

He forced a hand through his thick red mop. "Let's can this stupid bathroom nostalgia and make tracks."

"Where?"

"Where else? Find the wolf guy. He's definitely not here. But there are forty other shops in this town. And no more of this crap—if you'll excuse the pun. We don't have the time."

CHAPTER 23

Feeding the Hungry

Her honey-blond curls mashed beneath her hairnet, Rae Larson dropped an extra piece of buttered toast onto the small plate and handed it to the skinny middle-aged man. He smiled through his scraggly black beard, picked up his tray and left a rough waft of stale cigarette smoke in his wake.

"*Pot Luck 4 One and All*," sponsored three times weekly by the First Presbyterian Church of Raven, boasted an impressive turnout. It was intended for the needy and the homeless, but a surprising number of people on fixed incomes weren't too proud to attend.

Reverend Edwin Spencer, nearly a head taller than everyone else and ganglier than ever in his charcoal-gray shirt and black slacks, edged through the crowd, offering a warm handshake and spiritual words of wisdom to those who had fallen onto rough times.

Rae had known Reverend Ed since she'd attended grade school twenty years earlier. When he stood behind his podium, lecturing in his commanding voice, the huge silver cross hanging high from the rafters made him appear larger than life.

The passage of years had softened the authority in his voice, but in her eyes he remained the same sweet man who gave his time to everyone.

Reverend Ed's caring and undying passion meant much to her, especially during the last few months. His kindness had aided her immensely in her recovery when Alan walked out of their five-year marriage two weeks before last Christmas.

Rae blamed herself for the divorce. Alan wanted to move to Columbus, but she had no intention of uprooting herself. Her unwillingness to compromise to help him proved a key issue. Alan's career in software consultation required a major metropolitan base to ensure financial success. But in spite of her love for her husband, Rae loved Raven even more. She'd grown up here; her friends and relatives lived here. Despite the pressure Alan placed on her, she couldn't possibly move away.

Reverend Ed snuck over to where she stood behind the steaming buckets of soup. "If you keep handing out extra portions, we'll run out," he whispered.

Unruffled, she carefully ladled chicken noodle soup to a short, slender man with yellow teeth and a smattering of curly gray hair poking out of his stained red ski cap like a shock of steel wool. The reek of whiskey emanated strongly from him.

"He needed the extra calories," she told Reverend Ed.

"They all do." He gently tapped her shoulder. "And don't worry, I was teasing."

"I knew that."

"Even though I had on my grim expression?"

"You wouldn't deny the needy an extra crust of bread, would you?"

"I guess *some*one's paying attention to my sermons."

"A couple of us are."

"*Touché*. Will you have time to talk later?"

"Anything wrong?"

"Not at all. It's been a while since we've chatted."

"I'll see if I can work you into my schedule."

"Wonderful." He hurried off to the kitchen to check on his wife Pat.

***

Dressed in a white tank top covered with blue sequins, maroon Capri's, and open-toed sandals, Sheila McKay slipped through the glass door of Crenshaw's Five'n Dime. While Darcy tended to her last customer, Sheila checked out the ear stud display. Her long platinum hair swished across the glass. Darcy knew Sheila wouldn't buy anything. She didn't have room for another stud—each ear held at least twelve. Sheila loved flash, sprinkling her hair with glitter, and gluing tiny stars to her cheekbones. She carried around tattoos and piercings in a dozen places. She also wore bracelets, rings, and necklaces.

Darcy rang up the purchase, bagged it and handed it over. The big woman nodded her thanks and lumbered away.

"Figured you might, like, wanna do something tonight," Sheila said. "I'm bummed out from hearing about Todd and Leon all day."

"What…did you hear?" Darcy asked uneasily.

Sheila pushed her hair away from her face. Her long acrylic nails were painted black. Tiny silver stars highlighted each glossy center. One of the perks of working in a nail place; you could do anything with them. "Just about everyone said something about it. You were with them last night, weren't you?"

Darcy didn't want to go there, but she had to tell her something. "We had…kind of a party."

Sheila frowned. "You didn't even *like* Todd. I know he's dead and all, but he sure was big-time lame."

Darcy thought about the hitcher. She couldn't even remember his name. But he sure acted nuts.

And he read my mind…

159

That frightened her. He had come into the store just hours ago, said some weird stuff and then did some really scary things to her mind. First, that cleaning thing. Then Woodstock. *My God*. How could he have done that?

But he had. He had somehow slithered right in there and—

"You okay? You're doing a major zombie weird-out."

"I just need some fresh air. I've been here since before lunch."

"You haven't eaten?"

Darcy shrugged.

"Sure you're okay?"

"Let's just leave." She locked up the cabinets and took the keys down the hall to the manager's office. She wanted to tell Sheila what happened but was afraid to. She really should confide in someone…

When she came back out, Sheila was checking out the thong bikinis. "Weird."

"What's weird?"

"When we go back to school Monday, they won't be there." Sheila put the hanger back on the rack. "Leon was cool when he was solo. How could anyone hang around Todd Bochner? Like, minus zero on a good day. He had a serious ride, but he only used it to get laid."

The urge to explain herself rocked through her. "Listen, my car's been in the shop all week."

"What does that have to do with—"

"I…wanted to go out to the mine."

"You mean…you actually went *out* there?"

Darcy hated herself for saying anything. Now she had to tell Sheila the unpleasant details. "We went out there right before the storm."

160

"What happened?"

"Let's go." Darcy led the way.

Mirabelle, the older lady who ran the front register, frantically scrubbed down her counter.

"What's *her* story?" Sheila whispered. "She was doing that when I came in."

Darcy bit her lower lip and said nothing.

The strong aroma of coffee, melted cheese, and garlic drifted down the street. Scattered crowds flocked in front of the Presbyterian Church one block north.

Sheila took some fresh air. "Ever eaten there?"

"No, but I hear they serve good food."

"Let's go chow down."

"But—"

"What's the prob? They don't turn anyone away."

"It's for the needy."

"Girl, that place is always packed. You know they're not all needy. Anyway, if you feel guilty, cough up a donation."

As she walked with Sheila, Darcy forced herself to ignore the broken glass of Todd's Camaro winking at her in the streetlamp haze.

***

Gutril relaxed on a green bench on East Main, thinking about his workday and trying not to work himself up into a frenzy again.

Working at Denner's was just as ridiculous as hoisting rocks at Belias' Watch Tower. Both involved taking stupid orders to accomplish a silly menial task.

But at least there was no need for winches in the New Millennium. Everything was technical and much easier. Denner's had a little white vehicle on wheels called a

161

forklift that hoisted palettes piled high with food and cases of beverages.

Dropping a palette on Niles from the forklift would be tricky. Niles would have to be wandering around aimlessly—which wouldn't happen because he always seemed to know what was going on.

But something had to be done.

Turning invisible—at least for now—proved the ideal remedy. Gutril performed his stupid task and then vanished. When it was safe to go back, he reappeared in the stockroom. But Niles quickly found him and barked out yet another ridiculous order.

Gutril hated taking orders. It made him lose perspective, forget who he was. When he lost perspective, he did nasty things.

But he had to be careful. He couldn't draw attention to himself until he found a mortal host.

Speaking of hosts…

Across the street, Darcy and a skinny female with long platinum blond hair left the Five'n Dime, heading north. Bummer. He hadn't planned on her being with someone.

Hard to convince a female to accept you as her personal demon with another female hanging around.

What would the logical remedy be in this situation? Make the skinny blonde evaporate?

No. Too many questions.

Push her out into the street to be run over?

No. The Darcy girl was already bummed out about her two dead friends.

Gutril got up. Where there was a will…

"Hi, there."

The girls spun around.

"Where did *you* come from?" Her dark-brown eyes swelled in their sockets.

"Who's this?" Wavy lines marked the blonde's forehead. "Friend of yours?"

"No." Darcy's eyes spat flame. "Are you *following* me?"

"I just happened to be in the neighborhood…"

"Go away."

"Listen, I thought we might have a nice little chat—"

"C'mon, She."

Arm in arm, they pulled away and filed into the church cellar.

Bummer. She was no doubt embarrassed.

Inside, knots of sloppy, foul-smelling mortals blocked the counter. The room was thick with a strange mix of chicken, garlic, B.O., whiskey, and tobacco smoke.

Mortals sure were disgusting.

The girls picked up trays and silverware. When she saw him again, she lowered her voice. His excellent hearing enabled him to hear her over the clattering of dishes, the clinking of silverware and the discordant barking of the crowd. "I hate being followed!"

They shoved their trays down the aluminum track, snatching up bowls and plates of steaming food.

Young females were difficult to deal with. Fiercely shallow, competitive, and obsessed with fashion and appearance, they behaved an "accepted" way for their peers. Their "code" nearly mirrored the Code of Demons. No wonder so many of them fitted in so well down below.

Gutril squeezed through the crowd and found an empty place facing the girls.

163

Darcy shot him another quick glare and whispered something to her friend. Both looked down at their food and simultaneously scooped up chicken soup.

This called for drastic measures.

"What we were discussing earlier in the store? I guess I need to be clearer."

She didn't look up from her bowl. "I don't even remember any of that. I don't like being followed..."

"That big boy sitting over there." He pointed to his left. Two tables down, an obese mortal with a shaved head shoveled food into his mouth. "Cue-ball head? His wardrobe right out of Hicks R Us?"

"I wish you'd just leave me alone."

"Watch and see the cool shit he does." Gutril quickly focused on the boy's large skull. "I think you'll be—"

The tangy aroma drifted in from outside, overpowering the stagnant odors inside the big room.

Fresh meat. The unmistakable fragrance made his mouth water.

"Gotta go!" Gutril jumped up and scurried down the aisle, bumping into mortals on his way out.

***

In the rear of the crowded cellar, Chip chose a small table near the hall entrance. This was as good a place as any to watch the festivities. He and Sweet Cheeks would have a good seat.

"How's this for a panoramic view, angel cake?"

No reply.

He spun around. Epiphany was nowhere to be seen.

Jeez Louise. Here we go again...

He squeezed through the collection of bodies. Outside, her golden curls fluttered in the night breeze, twinkling in the reflection of the streetlight. She'd reached the end of the block and was about to cross the street.

He ran down the walk. Just as she stepped down from the curb, he yelled, "Want to let me in on your latest adventure, problem child?"

She jerked sharply at the sound of his voice and turned. "You scared me..."

He stopped about ten feet away. "You didn't exactly do my ticker any good, either. That is, if I still had one. Where do you think you're going?"

"I thought I just spotted the wolf guy."

Vagrants crowded the walk near the church, smoking, coughing, and hawking into the street. "And you decided to chase him all by yourself?"

"I didn't want to...you know, lose sight of him."

"Well, where *is* he?"

"I...lost sight of him."

Chip groaned. Litany was great to look at—even smelled fantastic for a dead chick...but she sure was trouble. "Do me a large favor. Put a lid on the vanishing acts. If I don't know better, I'd swear you were up to something."

"Don't be silly."

"Me? Silly?" His hair stood up on end. His fart erupted like a firecracker.

"Was that the eggshells? Or the coffee grounds?"

"I think it's this foul Ohio air. Let's go back inside."

They slipped through the milling crowds and found a table next to the bulletin board wall.

Chip scanned the crowd. Since he had never seen Gutril, he had no idea what he was looking for. All he knew was what Olivier had told him. The wolf demon was long and lean, with sharp features and small red eyes.

The minister was long and lean, but Chip didn't think Gutril would assume the form. Ministers exuded an amiable, open manner. They talked to everyone. They were honest and sincere.

Demons just weren't very good with honesty and sincerity.

"My smeller's not sniffing him out," he told Litany.

She sighed. "Would a demon even set foot in a church?"

"He has to blend in. What better place to hide?" It was a pain, breaking in a newcomer. But he wanted to give her the benefit of the doubt. He felt sorry for her being pulled out of Limbo. She needed a break.

"If he can change his shape, I don't know how we'll spot him," she said.

"He can't stay altered very long. Shape-shifting takes concentration. Gutril gets distracted too easily. We'll just stick around and see what happens."

"What if nothing does?"

"Then we'll have to find a motel room for the night."

She went silent.

"What's the problem?"

Her lips pushed out. She looked like a little girl who had just been sent to her room. "Can...I trust you?"

"C'mon, Tuscany..." Why did females think that every living thing with a male member wanted to jump them? "You really don't think that's going to pop up—so to speak?"

"What is? And it's Tiffany."

"Whatever. The issue."

She squirmed in her seat. "You are a *guy*...I guess..."

"Guess something else. For one thing, I ain't interested. For another, this is a business trip."

166

"You wouldn't lie to me, would you?"

"Baby Cakes…" He moved closer. "We're both dead, remember?"

"The wolf guy's dead…"

"The wolf guy's a dog."

"Wolf."

"Same thing."

"No it's not." She shrugged. "I love dogs."

"Dog, wolf – what's it matter? I ain't the wolf guy."

She blinked. "You don't think I'm attractive?"

"Jeez Louise…" He definitely should speak with the Management when they went back down.

***

The man who had been given the extra toast by Rae Larson pushed his tray onto the towering heap. He winked at her while jamming a crumpled cigarette between his cracked lips. "'Night, little lady. Thanks again."

"Good night."

He hobbled toward the door, lighting his cigarette. A serpentine plume of gray smoke followed him outside.

"Got some time?" Reverend Ed pulled a Styrofoam cup from the stack on the table.

She tugged off her cap, fluffed her hair and unfastened her apron, then joined him at a small table near the side door. A sheet of cool night breeze swept in, refreshing her. Reverend Ed sugared his coffee. "So how have you been getting along? I occasionally stop in at the drugstore, but you're always too busy filling out prescriptions to chat."

"Much better, thanks to you."

"Don't give me too much credit. You've managed a few things on your own."

She smiled. Reverend Ed being his old humble self. "You helped me over a horrible rough spot."

His lean features fell into a frown. "I still don't understand how Alan could let someone like you walk out of his life."

"He outgrew me. People outgrow one another all the time. It's sad. I think I outgrew him as well."

"Well, you weren't the reason for the divorce. Remember that."

"Alan's career meant everything to him."

"You're a warm, caring person," he said. "Alan was the selfish one."

"Sometimes I have doubts about that."

"Why?"

"I have doubts about everything."

"You're helping people. You've been doing this since we started the program. That should be testament— in my mind, anyway."

"I just don't think I'm so wonderful. I could be doing this to escape the boredom of going home to an empty house."

"But you're not, are you?"

Two elderly ladies sat at the next table, chattering away. Just watching them made her feel better.

"It's a way of giving something back," she said. "No one's life is perfect. But each one of us has something we can be thankful for."

"I wish more people felt that way."

"We wouldn't need soup kitchens. Everyone would be taking care of each other."

"In a perfect world." He stared at his coffee cup.

"I didn't say something wrong, did I?"

"Of course not." He sighed.

"Please tell me what's bothering you."

He shrugged. "I feel like I'm losing my touch. I can't understand people as well as I should."

"But who does?"

"I'm a minister. It's my job to understand."

"What makes you think you don't?"

"Take the other day, for example. I was in the bank when someone tapped me on the shoulder. It was Lillian Tawber, but I didn't know it at the time. She had to tell me who she was."

"I haven't seen Lillian in quite a while."

"She used to show up every Sunday for Services. Now I don't see her at all."

"You forgot about her. I do that, too. If I don't see someone for a while, it's almost like my brain erases them from my memory."

"Lillian had a facelift. She also had collagen injections, a tummy tuck, breast implants, and electrolysis."

"Lillian and Fred split up a couple of years ago. Momma said Lillian was dating someone working at the St. Clairsville 7-Eleven. A much younger man. Maybe she wanted to look younger for him."

"The woman's changed. I don't mean just on the outside. I felt as if I was talking to a stranger."

"But what makes you think this reflects on you?"

"I preach the word of God each week, but it doesn't seem to matter anymore. Attendance is good, but people are different. Cold. In a hurry. I see blank, passing glances almost constantly. I can't help wondering why they even show up."

"I think this new information age is changing people. The whole world has opened up to them in their own homes."

"My point entirely," he said. "Computers should be bringing people together. We communicate with others all around the world. Shouldn't we be coming together as one?"

"In theory."

"Yes, unfortunately. And another thing—"

Something warm and gooey splashed Rae's right cheek.

A piece of toast whizzed past like a Frisbee.

CHAPTER 24

Food Fight
A Quick Snack at the Local Dumpster

Hawk trudged wearily down the stone steps of the Police Station.

It was nice, escaping the stuffy office and getting out into the clear, cool night. A few stars winked like the sequins on one of Rainey's fancy hats. Moon even looked like it was having itself a nice, cozy little nap.

Rough day for a Saturday. The Bochner-Bellson business was more trouble than it should have been, Leon's hysterical parents trying to be helpful but getting in the way. Good thing Todd's daddy was home, no doubt sleeping one off.

Best get home and relax.

Rainey might have her special beef stew ready. If not, he'd have to settle for leftover rice and beans. Didn't matter. Rainey could make doggy doodles on stale bread just as tasty as one of those fancy meals Denner's served.

His radio squawked to life, dang it, when he pulled onto Church Street.

"Hawk?" It was Nancy Cunningham.

"On my way home, Nance."

"Something just came in. Sounds *way* off-the-wall."

"What's goin' on?"

"You're not gonna believe this."

"Just tell it up front."

"Pat Spencer called, said a food fight's going on in the church cellar."

A food fight? On Pot Luck Night? Didn't sound right.

171

Nance had a playful side but was usually all business about the job.

"You gotta be kiddin' me."

"Wish I was. I'm sending Ernie over to help out. This might turn ugly."

"Nance, I never handled a food fight before. But going by what I've seen in those Three Stooges movies, it usually starts out ugly and goes south from there."

***

You could find all sorts of tasty goodies in a dumpster.

Gutril never understood why mortals always tossed the good stuff and kept the trash.

A skinny, middle-aged female wearing a stained white apron blocked the rear doorway of the church. She gripped a broom in both hands.

"What's up?" he asked.

"Over there." She gestured. "A *rat* under that dumpster!"

Cool beans. He was about to partake in a light snack before bedtime.

"What's the broom for?"

"Gotta kill it! Can't have *rats* comin' in!"

"Haven't you ever heard of a church mouse, lady?"

"*What*?"

"Just a little humor to lighten the moment."

The woman stared at him. Gutril never understood why mortals didn't appreciate humor when they were upset.

"What's a rat doin' there? Exterminator comes in once a week, we still got rats…"

"Rats have to eat, too."

The woman scowled. "You some kind of nut?"

"That's presently under investigation. But listen…you don't need a broom to kill a rat."

"I had a gun, he'd be dead. Thing's a monster!"

Gutril's mouth watered. "Tell you what. Take your broom inside. Give me a minute. I'll take care of this."

"You know how to get rid of rats?"

He grinned. "I have my own special technique."

She disappeared inside and slammed the door.

Gutril got down on both knees and peered underneath the dumpster. An almost inaudible *squeak*! issued from the darkness. His excellent night vision caught movement. Monster, my ass. With some mortals, anything larger than a bedbug freaked them out. The rat nibbled eagerly on a potato

skin. Gutril reached underneath and snatched it.

It was soft and warm, struggling beneath his long, slender fingers. Its heart raced. It looked up at him with its tiny blinking black eyes. Its whiskers twitched.

"How can anyone be afraid of a furry little guy like you?" Gutril popped it in his mouth. The hot blast of pungent tenderness exploded down his throat.

***

The church cellar looked like a bomb had gone off.

Tables lay on their sides. Overturned chairs cluttered the center of the room. Soup, rice, and mashed toast coated the floor. Noodles and sauce soaked the walls.

Several ladies from the kitchen and half a dozen helpful diners pushed mops, trying to clean up. Reverend Ed and his wife tended to an elderly woman bleeding from a cut on her left cheek. Nearly a dozen older folks huddled together in a group.

Reverend Ed had definitely seen better days. Blotches of food stained his shirt. His saturated trousers shined in

173

the overheard lighting. Part of his scalp showing through his thinning black hair had caught splashes of sauce.

The paramedics filed in.

Hawk stepped aside for them, then caught Reverend Ed by the elbow. "Rev, what in tarnation *happened* here?"

He shook his head. "I was sitting over there, having coffee with Rae Larson. One moment it was quiet. Then the place exploded. Everyone began shouting, tossing food, wrestling with one another, and shoving tables around."

"Many hurt?"

"Someone hit Mabel with a tossed fork. But everyone seems to be all right. Just shaken up, mostly."

"Miss Larson okay?"

"I managed to hustle her out in time."

"Any idea who started it?"

"Apparently Elroy Purdy instigated it."

Hawk stared at Reverend Ed to make sure he heard him right.

This didn't make a lick of sense. Elroy was a brick or two shy of a load, but never hurt anyone. He had straightened out considerably since he'd come home from Ohio's Early Release Program. Doing some time for the botched robbery of a local liquor store had taught him the error of his ways.

"I thought Elroy learned his lesson."

"I thought so too," the Rev said. "I tried talking to him, but he didn't seem to acknowledge my presence. Something's definitely wrong. If you don't mind, I need to help Pat and the others clean up."

Elroy slouched on a bench in a corner. He seemed to be gazing at a noodle lying on the wet linoleum. Ernie Travis stood over him, watching him closely.

174

"Find out anything?" Hawk asked.

"Kid ain't talkin'," Travis said. "Heard he grabbed a little guy sittin' next to him, asked for the salt. Elroy tried yankin' the man's arm clean out of the socket."

"Don't sound like the boy wants to stay out of the slammer."

"Sounds like he wants back in."

"Why?"

Travis shrugged. "Daddy workin' him too hard on the farm?"

That made even less sense. "Figure the County'll take it easy on him?"

Travis pushed his service cap up an inch. "Maybe you can get him talkin'."

Hawk dragged over a metal folding chair. He sat ass backwards and rested his huge forearms on the curved back. "What happened, son?"

Elroy kept staring at the floor. "Dunno, Sharf."

"You been doin' real good. Not one slip-up in six months. Your daddy tells me you're doin' fine work on the farm. What the heck made you do this?"

Elroy's eyes seemed to glaze over. "One minute I'm sittin' there, eatin' and havin' a good time. Then something happens."

"I'm listenin'."

Some people passed. Elroy went silent and lowered his head.

Hawk tapped the boy's beefy shoulder. "Let's talk somewhere else."

***

Elroy squeezed his massive frame into the passenger seat beside Hawk.

Just up the street, the paramedics slid a gurney into the rear of the ambulance. The curly white hair and bandaged face told Hawk it was Mabel Kirby.

"Go 'head," Hawk said softly.

"Dunno where to start."

The boy obviously didn't understand the situation. Maybe some brain cells had gone bad. Could be from the coke he'd done years back.

"Start where you think it's important," Hawk said.

"Fella next to me I ain't never seen before. Little guy, smelled kinda bad. Cigarettes, sweat and whiskey."

"What's he doin'?"

"Starin'. Last time somebody did that, I'm in the prison chow hall, everybody laughin', sayin' ugly stuff. Things like hick, redneck, hillbilly—all kinds of meanness."

"You're out now. What's it matter what cons think?"

"I know, but for a second it was like I'm back in. Can't explain it."

"Go on."

"Anyway, I tell myself I'm out and I ain't never goin' back in. Then the little guy next to me says somethin' and I go nuts."

"You go nuts when he asks you to pass the salt?"

Elroy cringed, making the car rock. "Coulda swore he said somethin' else."

"Like what?"

"Thought he said hillbillies like me shouldn't try to get laid in stir just 'cause we can't find ladies on the outside."

"Now why would he say somethin' like that?"

"I dunno. But Sharf, I *swear* he said that."

Hawk couldn't smell booze, but that didn't mean anything. Folks shooting up these days, you checked out their eyes for the glaze, quick movements, and body language. Elroy's eyes weren't glazed, and he moved just as slow as always.

"You straight, Elroy?"

"Yes sir."

"Don't let me find out you been boozin' or snortin' again—"

"No way I wanna go back to that awful place. Mean boys there, cut out your eyeballs while they're smilin' atcha. Ain't even had beer since I been out. Pop'll tell ya."

Elroy was telling the truth, but Hawk had to go through the proper channels. "I've got to take you in, have the doc look you over."

"Okay with me."

"But I need ya to be straight. You're lyin', I can't help you. You're on the level, I'm all you'll need. One last time. You sure about all this?"

"Positive, Sharf. Somethin's wrong with my head, I wanna know. Ain't natural, you think folks are turnin' ugly when all they're doin' is askin' for the salt."

CHAPTER 25

A Demon in my Bedroom

Darcy lay in bed, staring at the reflection of the streetlamp beam on her bedroom ceiling.

Each time she started drifting off, bright flashes slapped her wide awake.

A food fight in a church cellar. How seriously bizarre...

She couldn't stop thinking about the weird guy with the red eyes. He had said the strangest things at Leon's. Then at Crenshaw's. Then, to make the situation *totally* creepy, in the church cellar just a few seconds before it all happened.

Good grief. *Was* he a demon?

If so, what could she do about it?

Tell Uncle Hawk?

Was it even possible to arrest a demon? They weren't exactly regular people, were they? They were spirits. They *looked* like people—well, sort of. But they probably didn't have anything going on inside.

But *some*thing had to be done—there was no doubt about that. If he could make that food fight happen, what else could he do?

She still couldn't believe how quickly everything went bad. The whole thing was right out of one of those ancient slapstick comedies.

Good thing Sheila's Accord was parked down the street. By the time they scrambled outside, the cops and medical units had shown up. They couldn't let Uncle Hawk see them; he'd have even more questions she couldn't answer.

"Was that something from *Animal House* or what?" Sheila's arm shook finding her keys. It took her forever to get the right one in the ignition.

"You've got soup in your hair and on your shirt," Darcy said absently. She watched Uncle Hawk squeezing through the crowd gathered outside the church cellar entrance.

"Shit. It took, like, forever to get those sequins perfect before I zapped everything with hairspray." She turned on the interior light to check herself out, glanced at Darcy, then flicked it off. "You're wearing noodles."

Darcy carefully touched the top of her head. A sprinkling of cold noodles settled there and on her shoulder like a weird epaulette. She lowered the window and tossed out whatever she could find.

"I know you couldn't talk before," Sheila said on the way home, "but since we're solo now, I guess it's safe. Like, who *is* that weird dude?"

Darcy didn't want to believe he was a demon. If she told Sheila, it would be all over town in a couple of hours. "Some guy I met last night."

"At Leon's?"

"We picked him up earlier."

Sheila pulled up the drive and parked behind Dad's white Dodge 2500 pickup. "How come the truck isn't in the garage? Your dad always parks inside."

"There are buckets and things spread out on the garage floor."

"How come?"

"How should *I* know?" She forced the anger away.

"What's the story about that dude? He says, 'watch what he does,' and then Junior Samples jumps up and goes apeshit. You must know *some*thing about all that."

"I wish I did."

Now, as she watched the beam of light that split her ceiling in two, Darcy realized she had no idea what was going on.

Maybe you did conjure up a demon...

No. No way.

I came to see you....

What's a Woodstock?

No. He *hadn't* read her mind. It was a fluke, a coincidence. No one could read minds. It just wasn't possible. It just didn't make—

A sharp tap at her bedroom window jolted her upright.

A shadow moving around outside made the streetlight beam flicker.

She grabbed her robe and, shrugging into it, cautiously approached the window. The penetrating red eyes on the other side of the glass grew vivid.

How would he know where I live?

A finger of ice tickled the back of her neck.

Good thing the window was opened only a couple of inches. The lock Dad screwed in just above the frame kept it from opening farther. It made her feel safer. She wouldn't have to worry about him forcing his way in. If he caused a fuss, she could yell.

Dad was a very light sleeper. And he had a gun.

She warily brought her face closer to the windowsill. "What do you want?" she whispered.

"We need to talk."

"Go away…" Her heart pounded.

"Why are you giving me a rough time?" he asked. "I thought—"

"I don't *care* what you thought. Go away. I don't like being followed!"

She stiffened. Was that a noise out in the hall?

She tiptoed over to the door and pressed her ear gently against its cool surface. The humming of the refrigerator down the hall. Nothing else.

She turned around and nearly bumped into him.

Gasping, she jerked back, instinctively grabbing the chenille lapels of her robe.

He stood in the center of her bedroom, grinning, showing *way* too many teeth.

"What are you doing…how did you…get out of—"

"So this is your room, eh? Cool beans." He studied the dark, poster-covered walls. Images of the Sabbath, Megadeth, Jimi Hendrix, Guns & Roses, Santana, KISS, and other favorites bonded together in the semi-dark. How could he see anything with just the streetlight shining in? "Neat outfits. That KISS demon dude looks like Balberith on a bad day. Nice tongue—for a mortal." He opened his mouth and let his tongue slide down well past his chin. Then he sucked it back into his mouth and grinned.

Her pulse thumping, she gaped at the window. Still only an inch or two shy of being closed. How could he possibly have gotten in?

He wandered over to her CD tower. "I slipped in through the crack."

He had read her mind again. She shivered at the thought. But his window trick scared her much worse.

"You can't…do that. No one can do that."

He picked up a CD, sniffed it, wrinkled his nose, and put it back. "Demons can do all sorts of neat stuff."

181

She wanted to scream, to yell, to do whatever it took to get him back outside.

Think rationally. Force yourself. If you believe any of this, things will only get worse.

She had read tons of stuff about demons and what they did centuries ago— bewitching people, making them crazy…

But none of that made sense. People were much more superstitious and less educated back then. They didn't have TV or the Net. Despite her suspicions and those stories about the mine, demons couldn't possibly be walking around.

"I don't believe you're a demon," she said.

"You told me that before," he said. "In the store. And what happened? I made the fat lady undo all your hard work in Swimwear."

"That…was an accident."

"How do you explain what happened at the church?"

She shrugged. "Some dweeb went bonkers. It happens all the time. Some people just go nutso for no reason."

"What about your cleaning obsession?"

"Sometimes I do weird things. I have urges. I'm a teenage girl. Something about our hormones being out of whack."

"What about your friends killing themselves last night?"

No. He didn't cause that. No way. If he did…

"Todd was drunk. So was Leon. Todd liked getting drunk. He also liked getting high. You can't take credit for that."

He watched her tightening the sash around her waist. She hoped she had won the argument. She figured she had

182

because he wasn't saying anything. Maybe he would leave.

"How'd I get in here, then?"

Time to come up with something clever. Some dynamite bit of logic to make him leave in humiliation... But her mind turned just as blank as it did whenever she took a test in Mr. Moody's algebra class.

"Well?"

"I just don't think you slipped through that crack. You're too big."

A rap on her bedroom door.

Darcy froze.

Her father's voice. "Darce? You okay?"

"I'm...fine, Dad..."

"I hear voices."

She covered her mouth with one hand. If there was ever the time to come up with something brilliant, it was now.

But her mind remained empty.

"Darce?"

The guy behind her whispered, "Tell him you're okay."

She kept her hand over her mouth. "I'm...okay..."

"What was that?" Dad asked.

"Lower your hand," the guy whispered.

She did as he said. "I said, I'm okay."

"Can I come in?"

She gritted her teeth, closed her eyes, and held her breath. *Hold on. These last few seconds of your life are precious. Savor them.*

"Tell him to come in," her visitor whispered.

She spun around. "Are you out of your—"

"Darcy?"

183

This could prove what he wanted her to believe. But it would also prove that he really did cause Todd and Leon's death. And the church riot.

But did she really want Dad in here? What would it accomplish? It wouldn't be good. No matter how she looked at it, it just wouldn't be satisfying. Not with Dad and a guy who thought he was a demon. Especially when Dad caught this guy in his daughter 's room late at night.

A voice behind her, sounding remarkably like her own, said, "Come in, Dad."

The door opened.

Darcy held her breath and waited for the end.

The hall light spilled on the bulky figure, casting a gleaming oval window on Dad's bald head. His hairy gut covered the elastic band of his light-blue pajama bottoms. His squinty gray eyes puffed with sleep. "Why aren't you in bed?"

"I…I got up when I heard your voice."

"I heard you talking."

"I had the TV on a little while ago."

"Guess I must've been dreamin'. Go back to bed, baby." He yawned and pulled the door shut.

She didn't move until she heard his bedroom door close. Then she spun around. "He didn't…*see* you…"

"He would've ruined our cozy little pajama party."

"But how…why didn't he—"

"He needs a treadmill, you know."

She ignored that. "How come he didn't see—"

"When will you start believing me?"

"And my voice… How…did you *do* that?"

"He drinks beer, doesn't he?"

"What?"

"Your dad drinks beer."

184

"What's *that* have to do with anything?"

"His gut. It's not very attractive. I'll bet he'd look hilarious in one of those thongy things you sell at the store."

"Listen—"

"He'd better be careful. He might have a heart attack—"

This was ridiculous. "Forget my dad, okay?"

"You're cold, girl." He grinned. "I like that."

"Everyone knows demons don't exist."

She had no idea why she even said that. She'd believed in demons…and angels…and Heaven and Hell…since grade school. The 9/11 tragedy convinced her more than anything else that evil existed. But even in her fascination with black magic and witchcraft, she didn't want to accept the fact that a demon could leave Hell and roam the earth.

"Demons *are* roaming the earth," he said. "I'm living proof."

He'd done it again. "H-How do you *do* that?"

"Do what?"

"How do you know…what I'm thinking?"

"It's a hobby." He belched softly. "Sorry. I had a light snack a little while ago."

"Why did you come here?"

"I'm offering you the chance of a lifetime. The opportunity to have your own personal demon."

"Why would I even want that?"

"I can get you things. Make people do stuff for you. Cause all sorts of funzies to happen. Spice up your life, so to speak."

"Is this like a genie thing?"

He groaned. "Genies give you three wishes. Then they squeeze back into their bottles and snooze for a thousand years."

"How many wishes would I have?"

"No limit."

"What's the catch?"

"There *is* no catch."

"I don't believe you."

"There you go again. What's wrong now?"

"Demons are bad. Dishonest. Why should I believe a word you say?"

"As your demon, I can stay here."

"Why would you want to?"

"If you saw what it's like down there, you wouldn't ask."

"What's it like down there?"

"Hot. Muggy. Smelly. Crowded. All sorts of disgusting things lying around." He frowned. "You know, if someone doesn't straighten up that place soon, I'm gonna demand urban renewal step in—"

"In other words, if you do everything I say, you can stay here."

"You got it."

"And there's no catch?"

"Just one. I can stay with you only as long as you want me."

"Then what?"

"Then I'll leave."

"How come I still don't believe you?"

"Because you're young. Inexperienced. Immature. Naïve. You don't know much important stuff yet."

A rap at the door made her jump.

"Darcy?"

186

"Yes?"

It was Dad again. "Turn off the boob tube, Darce."

"Doing it right now…"

"'Night."

"Good night, Dad."

Her visitor stood over her desk, looking at her schoolwork. This made her feel violated, and she glared.

"Sorry." He straightened. "Don't want you to feel violated."

My God. How can you deal with someone who can read your mind?

"Just tell me to get out of there," he said, shrugging.

That definitely sounded like a plan. But would it work? Or was he just putting her on again?

"Get out and stay out. And get out of my room."

"No problem. Just tell me you'll think about it."

She stared at her bedroom door. Was Dad still out in the hall?

She found herself wishing she was little all over again. Whenever she had bad dreams, Dad came right in and held her until she grew drowsy. Then he covered her and checked under her bed and in her closet. When he was finished, he kissed her forehead and told her to go to sleep. And as long as he was around, no one would bother her or hurt her.

Now she was almost eighteen—nearly a full-grown woman. A demon had entered her bedroom, wanting to be with her forever.

The idea freaked her out. She couldn't possibly live a normal life with a demon hanging around. How would she explain him? How could she do anything, knowing he was always there, watching her? She couldn't even go out on a date…or go to the bathroom without—

She turned around. "Listen. I just can't—"
He had disappeared.

CHAPTER 26

Mr. & Mrs. Heller Retire for the Night

Beneath the cracked neon sign that said *RAVEN MOT L*, the L-shaped yellow block building formed a cul-de-sac one block south of East Main on Henderson Street.

Tiffany and Chip went down the walk leading to the building. Chip hadn't said anything since they'd left the chaos of the church cellar. He wasn't his usual talkative self, which worried her. Chip wasn't exactly the strong, silent type.

"Something's wrong, isn't it?" she asked.

"I just don't think these local yokels would cook up something like that food fight."

"You saw them. Most were homeless and probably drunk. Drunks are capable of anything."

"You sound like you actually know what you're talking about, sweet cakes."

"My stepfather's a drunk." The anger came back. She pushed it away. *Such things don't matter very much when you're dead.*

"I sure hope a drunk didn't start that."

"Why not?"

"I'm hoping that was Gutril's finest hour."

"Gutril?"

"The wolf guy. Tall and lean? Red eyes? Slobbers?"

He was so aggravating. "I meant, why Gutril?"

"It would mean he hasn't found a host yet."

"A host?"

"You're doing it again, angel cakes."

"Doing what?"

"The parrot thingy."

189

"Oops. Sorry."

"If he finds a mortal, he's untouchable."

"You mean we won't be able to take him back?"

"If a demon finds a mortal to bond with, he can stay here forever. Or until his mortal dies."

"Then what happens to us?"

"We go back down and hope Olivier's having a good hair day. But that's unlikely. It's hard having good hair with bugs and other nasty things crawling around under your hood. We'll probably kiss our butts good-bye for the next thousand years."

She kept herself from dwelling on that. "What are the chances the wolf guy has found a host?"

"If he found one, he has to do what the mortal wants."

"You mean a mortal actually has power over a demon?"

"Don't be silly. If the demon wants to stay here, he'll have to do some serious ass-kissing. In this case, the mortal will think he's in control. That'll work, as long as the mortal's looking."

"Then he might've done that thing at the church when his host wasn't looking."

"Unlikely. If he wants to stay here, he'll have to keep close to his host. For a while, anyway. He knows the Legion will send someone up, so he'll want to keep a low profile."

"Then you think he caused all that by himself?"

"A mortal smart enough to have his own demon wouldn't cause a food fight. Mortals want things. And position. And power. And wealth. A food fight? That would mean Gutril picked a host just as silly as he is. Like I said, unlikely."

"Then we might still have time?" she asked hopefully.

"We need to wait for morning. We'll be able to track him down better in the daylight."

"Don't wolves like the night better?"

"Mortals are more active during the day."

"But if you're right, he'll sniff us out."

"That, my pet, is a definite possibility."

A tired-looking clerk smiled weakly behind the chipped counter. Tall and thin, he wore a red bow tie and a plaid vest over his wrinkled white shirt. He perked up when Tiffany smiled at him. "Evening, folks." He straightened and adjusted his glasses.

Chip picked up a pen and signed the book.

The clerk pulled it over. "Mr. Heller." He blinked at Tiffany. "And you're *Missus* Heller?"

"Yes," she said flatly.

The clerk logged on to his computer. "Any preferences?"

"We'd like a bed," Chip said.

"They all have beds."

"This modern age really wipes me out." Chip shook his head. "Conveniences everywhere. Cell phones. Beds in every room. I'm amazed and bewildered."

"You're not serious," she said.

"Don't I look amazed and bewildered?"

"I thought that was gas from those eggshells and coffee grounds you ate."

The clerk typed busily. He pulled a bill from the printer beneath the console and snatched a key from the pegboard on the wall behind him. "Any luggage?"

Chip held up an imaginary suitcase.

191

The clerk scratched the back of his neck. "I...don't remember you bringing that in..."

"You might have been slightly distracted." Chip winked devilishly and jabbed a thumb at Tiffany.

The clerk reddened. He handed over the key.

***

The small room smelled of mint air freshener. Faded green curtains hung in front of the picture window. A small brown-and-red plaid couch sat in front of it. A dresser, TV, and writing desk lined the wall facing the double bed.

"Where are you going to sleep?" Tiffany asked.

"Need you ask?" Chip grinned at the bed.

She sighed. "A true gentleman always offers the lady the bed."

He looked around. "Lamb chop, just where do you intend to dig up a true gentleman?"

"I guess I was hoping..."

"I'm a *demon*, princess. Demons don't do good manners very well."

"I just thought you'd be nice and at least offer..."

"Nice? Me? You can be really cold, buttercup."

"I didn't mean for it to come out that way..."

"Got you going, didn't I?" He wiggled his ears.

"Can't you *ever* be serious?"

"Like I said, I have issues."

"I honestly hope you can get some of them resolved. I never know when you're putting me on."

"Hey, it beats watching TV. And speaking of TV..." He picked up the remote. "Is this a newfangled turn-on do-hickey for that?"

"Yes."

"No more channel flicking? Adjusting the rabbit ears? Climbing up to the roof to fix the antenna?"

She blinked. "What…are rabbit ears?"

"Children should be seen and not heard." He turned on the set. His eyes grew. "Why so many channels?"

"It's Cable."

"What's *that*?"

"Signals come from satellites now. Cable companies pull them out of the air and charge us for them."

"They steal signals out of the air and charge for something that used to be free?"

"TV used to be *free*?" Her mother never told her that.

"Ah. Yet even more evidence of Society's swan dive down the tubes. Forgive the pun." He flicked the button. "When I was here last, there were five channels. Six, if you wanted to watch that educational network that instantly cured insomnia."

Extreme Fighting blasted onto the screen.

"Cool! Malamores!"

"What?"

"The supers bet on them in the Castle of Demons. Olivier nearly lost me to Asmodeus when he almost bet on the wrong guy."

"Extreme fighters are down there?"

"In Hades City they're called Malamores. They're kept in damp little cells until they're called out to fight. The winners are tossed an extra slab of raw meat or a hooker the supers don't want any more. Gang members are also Malamores."

"Gang members aren't demons? They sure are nasty enough."

"The supers don't trust them." He flicked another channel. "Are gang members on TV, too?"

"They usually become rappers."

"Wrappers?"

"You've never heard of rappers?"

"Yepperino. Condoms. Or paper used to wrap gum or candy cars."

"Drop the w. Rappers stand on stage in messy clothes and rap."

"And they make money?"

"They're filthy rich."

"People pay *money* to watch a bunch of idiots chattering away on stage when anyone can do the same thing in the privacy of their own home?"

"You've got to hear them to appreciate what they do."

"You like them?"

"No, but a lot of people go crazy over them."

He flicked a channel. "What's a...reality show?"

"Programs with ordinary people stuck together in a group and stranded on an island."

"What happens?"

"They try and survive."

"Anyone die or get eaten?"

"Of course not."

He wrinkled his nose. "I thought TV was supposed to be entertaining."

"Some people think it is. You really haven't seen any rappers down there?"

"Describe them."

"They're young, black, dress sloppily, and talk rough."

"I thought those were athletes."

"These guys have funny-sounding names."

"Like Darius and Tyrone and Shaleem and Abdul?"

194

"No, more like NastyC and SweatBoy and I.B. Smooth."

"Ah. Then their names are the only difference?"

She thought for a moment. "Athletes are taller."

Chip switched to the Adult Channel. The screen showed two naked women and a naked man lying in bed. "Terrificoso." He sat on the edge of the mattress and grinned.

Tiffany couldn't believe him sometimes. "Don't tell me you're going to *watch* that..."

"Did you ever make one of these?"

"Of course not. What would make you think I would?"

"You *were* sent to Hell, cupcake..."

"I wasn't supposed to be there. Did you forget already?"

"Issues, remember? Short-term memory's one of 'em."

He flicked off the set.

"So where do I sleep?" she asked.

"In the bed—where else?"

"Really? Truly?"

"Watch the drool, now. The couch looks more appetizing anyway."

***

Later, as she lay on the hard, musty-smelling mattress, staring into the darkness, Tiffany thought about another possible escape. She might have succeeded at the church if she hadn't had so much trouble getting through the crowd blocking the side door.

But she hadn't lied to Chip. She was certain she saw the wolf guy rushing outside just seconds before, heading north. Not wanting to get too close, she turned south. For

195

one thing, she didn't want to risk the chance of his recognizing her. If he did, it would end their mission. If she could get away from Chip, she could hide until she had a more detailed escape plan worked out. But since he tracked her down, she had to bide her time again.

This new idea seemed simple. Just slip quietly out of the bed. Chip hadn't moved in the last twenty minutes; he might already be asleep. And if she had learned anything from those few years living in Hollywood, she knew how to silently sneak out of a man's bedroom.

"Chip?" she whispered.

Silence.

Her heart pounded. *Great. He's asleep. But make sure first.* "Awake?"

"I kinda think so."

Darn. He didn't even sound drowsy.

"Is that all you wanted to know, lamb chop?"

Since he was up, maybe she could find out a few things. "I have a question."

"I was afraid of that."

"Say we find the wolf guy."

"We find the wolf guy."

"Oh, stop."

"Let loose with your brief inquiry. I've got better things to do."

"Like what?"

"Like lying here, worrying about my issues. Let loose with the litany, Whitney."

"Tiffany. What happens when we find him?"

"Find who?"

"The wolf guy—who else?"

"I've already told you. We find a way to take him back down."

196

"Then what?"

"That's it."

"I stay in the Darkworld?"

"Unless they say otherwise."

"What are the chances that they'll let me back into Limbo?"

"How does one in a billion sound?"

"Lousy."

"That's why it's called Hell, muffin cake."

Darn. She was afraid of that. If only she could—

The flash of inspiration forced her bolt upright.

If a demon finds a mortal to bond with, he can stay here forever.

Wowzer! She just figured out what had to be done.

PART III - THE SEARCH CONTINUES

CHAPTER 27

Reverend Edwin Spencer

His tan sweatshirt damp beneath his dark-blue blazer, Reverend Edwin Spencer forced his exhausted frame up the stone church steps.

Due to noticeable physical changes taking place recently, he accepted the need to work some additional activity into his lifestyle. His rising blood pressure and growing fatigue gripped him more frequently. The blood pressure issue wasn't a big concern, but the fatigue factor bothered him. He would not tolerate weakness during a sermon or when preparing for Services.

On the advice of Rae Larson a few months ago, he began every morning with a fast walk down Chestnut. He turned right on West Main, covered the next full block, and made another right on South Broadway before returning to the church. Although not quite a mile, the trip never failed to stimulate his appetite and awaken his senses. It also contributed to an explosion of fresh energy. And the dreaded fatigue paid him shorter and less frequent visits.

The brisk morning walks also cleansed his spirit and cleared his mind for the challenges of a new day. And it didn't hurt for his parishioners to see him in action each morning. Several had taken up exercise as a result and attributed this new activity with eliminating negative emotions.

This morning taxed him more than usual. He hadn't slept much, crediting his restlessness as the reason for this lack of endurance and determination.

He spent most of the night thinking about the explosion of violence in the church cellar. He never saw the Purdy family in church but knew they were hard-working farmers who kept to themselves and never caused trouble. Despite previous run-ins with the law, Elroy wasn't what you could call bad. Just a weak-willed unfortunate who ran with the pack without considering the consequences.

Spencer entered the cool, dark nave. Light from the early morning sun shining through the stained glass of the Sanctuary sent hazy beams of colored light dancing on the pews. How packed would the big room be in two hours? Had news of the brawl reached the town?

Nowadays he couldn't be certain of anything. As he told Rae, he feared he was losing his grasp on human nature, on society, and on life itself.

But was it any wonder?

People didn't seem to care about anything anymore. Instead of talking out your differences, senseless violence had become the solution. Home invasions, road rage, carjackings and other irrational bloodshed were living proof of evil thriving in the New Millennium.

Everyone was more concerned about looking younger than worshiping God or helping his fellow man. The latest craze involved cosmetic surgery, body art, and six-pack abs. Plucking out thy left eye paled in comparison to facelifts, tummy tucks, nose jobs, dental cosmetics, breast enlargement, liposuction, and hair restoration. Young girls barely in their teens were having their breasts enlarged and their noses and chins altered.

But as people grew more apart, sex grew more rampant. Grade schoolers participated in sex parties. Live sex shows could be viewed in every city. Teen prostitution had reached epic proportions.

Mirroring society, TV clearly demonstrated a deep moral decline. Every conceivable form of neurosis, obsession, and repugnance could now be seen on major networks. Programs featuring dysfunctional people from all walks of life dominated Prime Time.

Spencer found his wife in the kitchen annex, removing the muffins from the oven. The warm room radiated with the sweetness of cinnamon and vanilla-flavored coffee.

Despite his initial depression, he found himself smiling. Pat exuded a special glow that had not dimmed in their years together. At forty-one, Pat was twenty years younger than Spencer. And even though many of the parishioners had voiced their chagrin at this age difference, the Spencer's had been incredibly happy the last twenty years.

"Did the walk help?" she asked.

"A little. I'm just tired. Didn't get much sleep last night."

"I was there too, remember?"

"Only too well. I was the one picking noodles out of your hair for twenty minutes."

Pat found plates from the cabinet. "That was a turn-on for me. How many women can say their men will do that for them?"

"I also got a kick out of watching croutons drop to the floor when you undressed."

"And they say romance dies after the first year of marriage. It could have been worse, you know."

200

Sometimes her sense of humor astonished him. "How can you say that? I found someone's tennis shoe floating in one of the soup bins. And I nearly broke my neck when I stepped on a plug of chewing tobacco and slid merrily across the room."

"Now *there's* a visual..."

"I'm serious, Pat."

She poured coffee. "At least we weren't hurt."

"You're right. It could have been worse."

"Aside from noodles and soup in my hair, I'm just fine."

"I was hit in the head with garlic toast, a spoon, and someone's shoe."

"If you weren't so tall, they would've missed you entirely."

"At least I was hit where it couldn't hurt me," he said jokingly even though he didn't feel jovial.

"That was strange, though..."

"Strange isn't the word I have in mind."

She brought over two cups. "What's on your mind?"

"Canceling Pot Luck."

"Why?" She pulled out a chair and sat. "People come from all over just to share a meal with us. And you know many wouldn't get to eat otherwise."

"I don't want to go through another night like that."

"What makes you think that'll happen again? It was probably just an isolated event."

"How can you be so sure?"

She shrugged. "It's the first time we've ever had trouble. Who knows what was going through Elroy's mind?"

"What about all those other gents who decided to make a tense situation worse by tossing food, chairs, silverware—"

"There are idiots everywhere. You know that. Opportunists automatically jump right in. They're sheep. They're always looking for an excuse to have fun."

"*Fun*? Is *that* what that was?"

"Idiots find great pleasure in the misfortunes of others. They blame their mothers for everything because they're too stupid to realize they're sick."

"I don't want them using my church to exercise their perversions."

"What about the good people who were there last night, having fun socializing with us? You're not gonna make *them* suffer for the actions of a few morons, are you?"

"Do you know what Rae and I were talking about just before that happened? We were talking about me. I just don't think I'm making much of a difference anymore."

"What would make you think that?"

"People have been changing so drastically lately."

"People haven't changed. The times have, but the same nice people we've known in this town all these years are good, honest, hard-working folks."

"I've been sensing something foul in the air." He could think of no other way to describe it. "Something that wasn't there very long ago."

"It's not another sewer leak, is it?"

Her question made him realize once again how frequently he was unable to get his point across. "Do I sound crazy?"

Pat opened a steaming muffin and smeared it with apple butter. "You're worried. You're actually expecting bad things to crop up."

"Well, I can't help being suspicious about that offer the Mayor threw at me a few weeks ago."

"I don't see the big deal. The church needs renovation."

"Pat, they want to change the cellar."

"I thought they wanted to remodel it."

"There's no place for Pot Luck in their plans."

"But the cellar's huge…"

"It won't be when they're finished."

"Why would they want to get rid of Pot Luck?"

"That's what's puzzling me."

"Well, you shouldn't have to worry at all if you cancel it."

He suddenly felt guilty. She considered him foolish for ending a program so many people loved. She was right. He was being foolish. And it wouldn't be fair.

"I'll keep it open. For a while, anyway."

She patted his wrist. "You won't be sorry."

CHAPTER 28

Chatting with Kathryn

Bars of late morning sun burning through the window blinds coaxed Louis Gates out of bed.

He had heard something a short while ago. Probably Kathryn or one of the waitresses quietly looking for something in the office down the hall. Amazing that the quieter you tried to be, the louder you were.

Sunday meant brunch at eleven. It also meant getting things done without Antoine, who refused to work Sundays.

No problem. Antoine usually left enough prepared food to handle a two-hour buffet and dinner. Morey, the weekend cook, had more than enough to work with.

After a shower Louis shaved, dressed in a dark-blue polo shirt, Levi's, and athletic shoes, and went down the hall.

Kathryn sat in her usual place behind the big desk. Her hair was pulled back, tied, and fastened with a green ribbon. A yellow pencil pierced the works. Kathryn always came in early, even on Sunday. He figured her as either obsessively conscientious or just bored at home.

"You're early," he said, heading for the coffeepot.

"And a cheerful and bubbly good morning to you too, Mr. Boss Man," she said in her customary dry wit.

"Refill?"

"If you'd be so kind."

He filled her cup, tended to his own, and replaced the pot. "Anything happening?"

"You've already had a phone call. Mr. Trent again."

"On a Sunday morning? Doesn't anyone go to church anymore?"

She blinked. "You want me to comment on that?"

"Are you referring to the fact that I no longer gratify the House of God with my presence?"

"That did cross my mind."

"And why, pray tell, are *you* here rather than spending your morning sitting on a hard wooden pew in a crowded Sanctuary?"

"I find this chair more comfortable."

"Is that the only reason?"

"I also enjoy the frantic expression on your face as you fumble around, looking for your cigarettes."

"I knew there was a legitimate reason for your madness. What could George Trent want so early on a Sunday morning?"

"He didn't say."

"Hmmm. A mystery."

"Did you return his call yesterday?"

"I don't remember."

"Then you deserve to not know what he wants."

He drank some coffee. The nicotine craving grew. It always did after the first jolt of caffeine. "I buy a restaurant and just six months later I'm getting mysterious weekend calls from a bank manager."

"And one of your most loyal customers. I've been told by various sources that he comes here every day for lunch."

"I wonder why."

"It's either for the food or the dancing girls."

"I've never seen Wendy or the others serving anything but food and drinks. What else did Trent say?"

"He'll call back in an hour."

"Lucky me."

Kathryn scribbled something in her ledger. "You're a popular man. I'm honored to be associated with you."

"I didn't realize you were an associate. I've always considered you the hired help."

Kathryn pushed out her lower lip. "Such a low blow. And here I was thinking we had such a terrific working relationship."

"You're right. You're much more than just regular help."

"Much better. Anyway, I prefer associate. It impresses my friends."

"Those middle-aged women with sex problems you know from the hair salon? The ones who come here for the Saturday seafood lunch buffet?"

"If I tell Sylvia you referred to her as middle-aged, she'll come after you with her walker."

"The woman's pushing seventy. How many people a hundred and thirty-six do you see running around? She's lucky I don't refer to her as elderly."

"By the way, Niles wants to talk to you. Something about the new guy."

"What's up?"

"He sounded anxious and upset."

"The new guy?"

"Niles."

"Niles is always anxious and upset."

"I've noticed. Why is that?"

"It's probably a hormone thing. Testosterone can be hard to deal with at times."

"You can say that again."

"I'd rather just smile politely and look macho."

"You do both so well. Were you that way at his age?"

206

"I believe I was slightly more sophisticated. Musicians must maintain their dignity, you know. Their audience demands it."

"And everyone knows how sophisticated and dignified young musicians are."

"Actually, it's taken me years to reach this level of style and finesse."

Kathryn drank a little coffee—possibly to avoid a snappy retort. "Anyway, Niles sounded more anxious and upset than normal. Maybe it's something other than his hormones."

"Lovely."

"Ah, the perks of owning your own place."

"The popularity factor gives me a constant adrenaline rush."

Kathryn pulled off her reading glasses. "Tell me something."

"What's that?"

"Why are you up so early? You're never up before ten on a Sunday. What happened?"

"The morning sun and the chirping of the birds nudged me awake."

"Sure it wasn't when I dropped your stapler on my foot?"

"I thought you came in to do the books. I didn't realize you were into pain and humiliation. Don't you have a husband for that?"

"You can be *so* funny. At times."

"It's a God-given gift."

"Sure it's from above?"

"Reasonably. What were you doing with my stapler?"

"I already told you. Dropping it on my foot."

CHAPTER 29

Spencer and "The Committee"

Tires crunched gravel as the church parking lot emptied.

Standing in front of the big open doors, glints of afternoon sun touching his robes, Spencer shook the hands of Mayor Phil Holeridge and Augustus Phelps and reminded himself to remain cordial. But despite the healthy turnout and the fact that many of his parishioners had praised his sermon on their way out, he found his bright mood waning in the presence of these men.

Spencer had little tolerance for the "Committee," as they called themselves. They were a small group of extremely fortunate individuals, yet Spencer seldom saw many of them during Services. And whenever he tried asking them to donate their time to church activities, they invariably begged off, blaming business pressures and prior engagements.

"Good, sound sermon, Reverend," the Mayor said pleasantly.

"Eloquently delivered, as usual." Augustus nodded his approval. "But you look tired."

Spencer smiled weakly. He had hoped his morning walk and Pat's delicious breakfast would return the color to his cheeks. The stress had obviously been too much. "What happened at Pot Luck upset all of us."

"We heard," Mayor Holeridge said grimly. "I've always feared something like that would happen."

Spencer didn't appreciate the Mayor's tone. "How so?"

"When you invite the destitute into your home—"

"It's the destitute who need our help," Spencer said defensively.

"Of course," the Mayor said. "However, that sort of behavior is totally unacceptable."

"To say the least," agreed Augustus. "The majority obviously appreciates your work."

"Which is why we're so eager to help," the Mayor said. "Have you given any further thought to our offer?"

Spencer had thought about little else during the past few days, but not in the way these men would have liked. Instead of voicing his views, he chose to select his next words carefully. It had been his diligent practice to avoid upsetting anyone after Services. If it meant coloring the truth a little, then so be it. "I'm sorry, gentlemen. I just don't know what to say."

The Mayor removed a pair of Polaroid shades from the breast pocket of his silk jacket and slipped them on. "A simple yes would suffice," he said. "As you well know, the Committee can be extremely generous."

Spencer did not trust the Committee. These men nearly always lost sight of the general good. The renovation on the west end of Church Street—which until just a few years ago boasted the oldest houses in Raven— ruined the look of that section of town. History could no longer withstand the current trend of mass renovation. Though most of its tenants had lived there more than thirty years, the houses were all torn down and replaced with condominiums and townhouses.

Augustus said, "The church is old, Reverend."

"I'm aware of that. I just don't know if I want to see such a huge project interrupting our schedules."

"The renovation won't compromise your activities," the Mayor said. "Winslow Construction and Landscaping can have the foundation revamped in just a few weeks."

"You've mentioned that your main concern is the cafeteria."

"The cellar is old and severely neglected. Major plumbing issues must be addressed. Those pipes haven't been maintained in years. The walls have shifted. The integrity of the building—"

"What about Pot Luck Night?"

Augustus said, "Surely you can postpone that...for a few weeks." The man's utterance of the word *that* sounded like a cough.

A gnarl of disgust scratched its way down Spencer's throat. "Pot Luck," he said with some difficulty, "feeds a great many homeless in Belmont County. For some, it's the only nourishment they can look forward to."

"Surely you can set them up somewhere else temporarily."

"For instance?"

"The Lutheran Church." The Mayor made the solution sound simple. "Their banquet hall would suffice. However, we will need to revamp that building as well. It suffers almost as many structural defects as this church."

"All older buildings have problems," Spencer said. "I just don't understand why the town elders are so interested in such an enormous project."

"It's a matter of progress. Everyone will benefit."

"It sounds like you're trying to phase out the cellar entirely."

"On the contrary. As we have said, a portion of the new area can easily be set aside for other activities."

"I've reviewed the plans that were sent to me. The allocated section of the new addition allows for approximately two hundred square feet of open floor space. That will be the only portion we'll be able to use for future cafeteria events."

Neither man responded.

Spencer bristled at their silence. It convinced him that they were not at all interested in helping the poor.

The disgust once again settled in his throat. It should not be necessary to convince anyone that a church could not be bought and sold as easily as the rest of the town.

"It's been a long morning, gentlemen," he said. "I hope you'll forgive me…"

The coolness and peacefulness of the Sanctuary welcomed him back.

CHAPTER 30

In Search of the Vanishing Stock Boy

Niles acted as if a hornet was loose in his undershorts.

As soon as Louis entered the stockroom, Niles jabbed an index finger at the loading dock area and led the way through the long plastic strips separating the two big rooms.

"Tell me this isn't a ploy just to get me alone," Louis said, following. "I really prefer the female gender."

Niles' tense scowl did not soften. Louis figured this must be serious. "It's about that new guy." Niles stopped near a palette stacked with crates of canned food.

"Gutier?"

"That's him."

"What about him?"

"He obviously doesn't like to work."

"What makes you say that?"

"I sorta got that impression when he began disappearing."

"There aren't many places to hide around here."

"Maybe not, but he's obviously found them all."

"What else has he been doing that isn't in his work description?"

"He screws around a lot."

"Describe a lot."

"All the time."

"Now describe screws around."

"I'll tell him what to do and what to bring in. Then I'll leave, come back in fifteen minutes, and he's gone."

"Did he do any work?"

212

Niles shrugged. "That's the weird thing about it. The work's all done."

"In fifteen minutes?"

"I'll give him what takes me half an hour to forty-five minutes to finish. He gets it done quicker than quick, then wanders off."

"How does he get it done if he doesn't like to work?"

"Beats me. I wish I could get my work done without actually being there to do it."

"Then what's the problem?"

"Boss, there's no way one man can get that much work done that fast."

"Is it done properly?"

"Hell, no…"

Louis waited for more of an explanation. When Niles didn't provide any, Louis said, "Now would be a really nifty time to tell me what you just meant."

"I'll ask him to bring in ten sacks and stack them neatly on a palette. They'll be stacked, but it looks like they were tossed."

"Twenty-pound sacks? Tossed? From here? That's more than fifty feet. The Incredible Hulk couldn't manage that."

"That's what I'm thinking."

"Gutier can't weigh much more than one-forty or so."

"That's also what I'm thinking."

"Where's he right now?"

"You tell me."

***

The dining room hummed with the hungry church crowd.

The bar wasn't open. Due to state law, Louis couldn't serve liquor on Sundays until one in the afternoon.

No sign of Gutier out here, either.

Louis didn't think Gutier would be out mingling with the customers. If he insisted on spending his time avoiding Niles, fraternizing out in the dining room among the waitresses, hostesses and busboys would not be the world's best hiding place.

A clean-cut, well-dressed man around forty sat alone at a table in the bar. The opened jacket of his blue silk suit revealed a red-and-gold checked cotton tie. A cup of coffee sat on a saucer in front of him.

"Lou Gates?" The man stood.

"Guilty."

"George Trent."

"Ah. The man making all those pesky phone calls."

They shook hands. Suddenly uneasy, Louis made the handshake brief.

Trent invited Louis to sit. "You're a hard man to nail down."

"When you've got a business to run—"

"Businessmen usually answer their phones."

"Even when they're not in their office?"

"There's a new invention." Trent's smile relaxed. "It's called the cell phone. You carry it around in your pocket. It rings, you take it out and *presto*! Someone's talking to you. They've been making them for some time, now."

"Never liked them," he said, ignoring Trent's sarcasm.

"The wave of the future."

"I don't think they'll last."

"You can't be serious."

"So many idiots driving around, jabbering away. If you knew how many times I've almost been killed because of some asshole on a cell phone, you wouldn't have asked. The highway people need to do a study. Then they'll outlaw them and I'll personally commemorate the occasion with the help of booze and a gaggle of strippers brought in."

"You hate them that much?"

"It goes back to when I was a programmer and was on call twenty-four, seven. Anyway, now I have a manager."

"She can't talk to me about this."

"I'm here, so talk."

Trent had some coffee. He put down the cup and stared at it for a few seconds. "It's simple. I'd like to buy your restaurant."

The uneasiness returned. "Sorry. This place isn't for sale."

"Just like that?"

"I've never been the long-winded type. People don't listen anyway."

"You've already decided to turn me down? Without hearing me out?"

"I like this place. As you can see, I'm doing pretty well. I'm told you even come here."

"I love the food, the service, and the atmosphere."

"But you want to buy me out. That's clear as mud."

Trent reached into his jacket pocket, pulled out a white envelope and slid it across the table. "The people I'm working with have authorized me to offer you double the amount you paid."

"Double?"

Trent nodded.

"Fair return on a six-month investment."

215

"You'll probably never make such a large profit so quickly."

"You're probably right."

Trent sat back. "What do you say?"

Louis pulled a cigarette from his shirt pocket. He'd smoked two in the last hour. That translated into a pack and a half in one day. He put it back.

Double the amount. No one could quibble about that. But why was it so important for Trent and his cronies to buy the place?

"I don't know…"

Trent scowled. "No one can pass up such a deal. No one in his right mind, that is."

"Who told you I'm in my right mind?"

"Why won't you consider this?"

"You're too eager."

"The people I'm representing don't care about price."

"Who are you representing?"

"I'm not at liberty to say."

"Now *that* makes me feel cuddly and warm inside."

"It's a generous deal. So generous, in fact, that most people would jump at the chance."

"You run First National, right?"

"I'm also connected with a select group of businessmen interested in acquiring property in the Ohio Valley."

Louis didn't know if the word *representing* raised the flag or the word *connected*. Either way, he didn't like where this was going. "Now why would a select group of businessmen be interested in buying my restaurant?"

"My associates specialize in obtaining businesses all over the country. They've instructed me to give you whatever your price happens to be."

216

Associates. Another word Louis didn't like.

"Blank check, eh?"

"Basically."

"And they won't settle for a simple no?"

"They prefer the negotiations to be kept open."

"Sure you're not a lawyer?"

"I'm a banker."

"You sound like a lawyer."

"You don't sound like a businessman, Lou."

"Actually, I'm a musician."

"I thought you were a programmer."

"I started out as a musician."

"Then why are you running this restaurant?"

"I'm trying to be a businessman, but you and your associates won't let me."

Trent finished his coffee and stood. "Will you at least look at this offer?"

Louis stuffed the envelope in his pants pocket. He didn't want to insult the man by leaving it on the table. "Sure."

"That's all we ask." Trent held out his hand. "Here's hoping we can come to a mutual agreement."

Louis made their second handshake just as brief. "One can always hope."

CHAPTER 31

A Takeout Order of Mexican for Lunch

The poodle growled softly behind the chain-link fence.

Despite his growing hunger, Gutril wasn't wild about poodles. The lanolin taste in their coats stayed in his mouth. To get rid of it, he had to eat something else right after. Rabbit pellets, or raw chicken gizzard. Might as well suck on a bar of soap.

Down the street, a Chihuahua yapped agitatedly in its front yard.

Cool beans. Lean and gamy, Chihuahuas tended to be spicy if you found them at the right age.

The little dog jumped at the fence. Snarling, it lashed out with its forepaws. Its rat tail quivered nervously.

Gutril licked his lips. About time he had something substantial. The two rats he sucked down since the Darcy girl summoned him had been his only decent nourishment. He thought it ironic that you could work in a restaurant and starve half to death. The only red meat Denner's served was swimming in chemicals. It made him doubly hungry for fresh.

How did mortals exist nowadays?

Didn't they care what they dumped in their stomachs?

No one visible from the house. Lunch should be a walk in the park.

He reached over the chain-link and grabbed the tiny critter by the scruff of the neck. Snout wrinkled, teeth bared, it snapped at him.

"Kinda scrawny, but you'll definitely hit the spot."

About a hundred feet farther down the walk, tall grass, trees, and overgrown bushes took over the vacant lot. He could enjoy his lunch undisturbed.

"Hey! Where the hell ya think you're takin' that dog?"

A bearded guy around thirty thumped down the porch steps of the house behind him. Big-boned and bare-chested, his hairy pot bulging over his jeans, he gripped a can of Bush beer in his right hand. In his left, he held a half-eaten bologna sandwich which, judging by the smell, was loaded with chemicals.

Beer and chemicals. No wonder mortals seldom showed brain activity.

"What's the beef—so to speak?" Gutril strolled back to the fence. The dog had already begun dozing peacefully in the crook of his arm.

"That's my dog."

Images of a woman named Margaret—huge tits, large ass, and a loud, screechy voice—blipped in the guy's head.

Gutril gave him a quick once-over. "You don't *seem* the Chihuahua type. You're more studly. Let me guess. Pit bull, maybe? Rottweiler? A Chihuahua's too scrawny. A girlie girl's dog. Not enough meat to satisfy a *manly* man—right?"

The guy puffed up. His thoughts immediately shifted to the set of weights stacked in a corner of the garage behind the treadmill Margaret used once and quickly discarded. "You're right. Mutt belongs to my girl."

Gutril winked. "I know a manly man when I see him." He turned to leave.

Mr. Macho snapped out of it. "But you *can't* just run off with—"

219

"You *like* this overgrown washrag?"

Mr. Macho glanced to his right, then his left. "*Hate* the damn thing. Always yapping when you're trying to sleep, watch football—"

"Then why the attitude?"

He shrugged a beefy shoulder. "You *can't* just take someone's *dog*—"

Gutril shrugged loosely. "It wandered outside the fence."

"How'd it get out?"

Gutril pointed. "That big hole over there."

Mr. Macho stared dumbly. Then his eyes grew. "How'd *that* get there?"

"You'd better fix it. You never know what's liable to squeeze through."

Gutril left him staring at the imaginary hole in the fence. After lunch he'd make an appearance at Denner's. He didn't want the Niles jerk having a bird looking for him again. Besides, Gutril was having fun. Disappearing and moving things in ways Niles couldn't understand was much more fun than dropping boulders on passing servants.

After playing hide'n seek with Niles for a little while, he'd visit the Darcy girl and find out if she'd reconsidered his offer.

He needed a host *fast*.

CHAPTER 32

George Trent's Story

Like a man approaching the electric chair, George Trent took his seat in front of the bay window in the Gold Room.

Depressed over his meeting with Lou Gates, he would have loved it if someone had suggested moving this gathering to another time. But these men wanted to hear news— especially bad news—quickly.

They were Trent's comrades. His true friends. Because of their help and influence, he'd been running the First National the last fourteen years. Before that, he was a lowly teller. His bank account and prospects were abysmal in those days. He lived in a one-bedroom apartment, drove a ten-year-old Honda, and brought egg salad sandwiches to work for lunch each day. His suits were off the rack, his shoes bargain basement. Women were impossible to snare when you had nothing but high ideals and unfulfilled dreams to your credit.

But Trent's life changed the night he bumped into Phil Holeridge in the Moonlite Lounge in St. Clairsville. In those days, Trent went there nightly to relieve the stress of long hours standing behind his cage, handling everyone else's money.

Spotting him almost immediately, Holeridge brought his drink over and squirmed onto the stool beside him. After casual pleasantries, Holeridge lowered his voice and said, "Like your job?"

Trent considered the question strange. Best choose each word wisely. Holeridge, possibly the most important man in Raven, knew Trent's boss, Bank President Leonard Stokely. "I like banking," he said.

"What about your job?"

"It's…not challenging enough."

"You prefer challenges?"

"Love them."

Holeridge watched him closely as he raised his glass to his lips. Trent had the strange feeling he was being evaluated. "How would you like to manage that bank?" Holeridge asked.

"Who would I have to kill?" Trent joked.

"Any objections to joining a private club?" Holeridge asked solemnly.

"What *kind* of club?"

"A very select businessman's association. A gathering of investors, if you will."

Trent had never heard of such an organization. He went to the Country Club once a month for their excellent buffets but knew a few of its regulars only because they kept such large holdings in the bank. As a member of the banking arena, he occasionally caught snippets of conversation from the big boys who went there but was never able to hear enough to understand what was going on. Not wanting to be caught eavesdropping, he always kept a low profile.

"What's it called?" he asked Holeridge.

"No one is permitted to know unless he's chosen as a member."

Trent visualized a group of old farts running half-naked down motel corridors, squirting seltzer at the motel staff. "Oh. A *secret* club," he said, forcing himself to appear serious.

"If you're chosen, the sky's the limit. You want to manage that bank? You'll be the manager in no time at all."

"Mr. Lanier might object."

Holeridge winked devilishly. "I'm sure Sammy might just want to consider an offer."

Trent knew all about Holeridge's clout. The man hadn't lost a mayoral election in three terms and stood an excellent chance to win the next one. But the matter of banking hierarchy posed a problem. In the great scheme of things, a teller just didn't cross the line. "This sounds too easy."

"If you're accepted, you'll be required to handle certain financial matters for us."

"Do I have to sign anything?"

Holeridge's broad cheeks swelled. "We don't need your *signature*, George."

"What *do* you need?"

"Only your soul…"

Trent hadn't believed in organized religion for years. He considered the situation laughable. "You certainly don't want much."

He met Holeridge the following Friday night after hours in the abandoned parking lot behind the bank. As soon as he slid into the passenger's seat of the Mayor's Cadillac, someone sitting in the darkness of the back seat placed a soft black mask over his eyes.

The big car immediately pulled out.

Fifteen minutes later, he was escorted, still blindfolded, through wild brush. The mask was then removed. Eight hooded, black-robed figures surrounded him in what appeared to be a foul-smelling mine shaft. The strong smell of burning incense filled the area.

Flickering candles cast undulating shadows on the rock walls. No one said a word. Trent was no longer thinking of seltzer or motel corridors.

Silently the men approached him. They stripped him of his clothing and forced him to kneel in front of a pentagram formed of lit black candles. Standing over him, Holeridge told him to repeat the "Pledge of the Thrones," absolving Trent of all former good thoughts and deeds, and allocating his soul, from that day forward, to the Black Prince.

Within one year, Bank Manager George Trent owned a luxurious eight-room penthouse apartment in one of Ira Crenshaw's high-rises. Trent also acquired a new Jaguar and Corvette, jewelry, stocks, bonds, and a hundred-thousand-dollar wardrobe.

In the years since his initiation into the secret society known privately as the Diocese, a tiny subchapter of the Legion of Demons, he had seen these men in action. Seldom did anyone stand in their way. When some problem did occur, the situation quickly resolved itself.

He was certain this issue with Lou Gates would prove no different.

Holeridge sat at the other end of the big oval table and lit a cigar. The Mayor's eyes stayed on him as the flame grew. Trent could tell the man was eager to hear about their proposal. They all were.

"Talk to us," Holeridge urged.

Trent cleared his throat. His pulse raced. He took a giant breath. "Gentlemen, our offer was…turned down."

Silence.

Miles Ladner shoved cigar smoke in Trent's direction. Ira Crenshaw sat back and glowered. Everyone else remained silent.

"You're saying the new owner won't accept this deal?" Holeridge asked softly.

Trent shrugged. "He doesn't want to sell."

Ira shook his head. "That offer's more than twice what the place is worth. What's his problem? Don't tell me he wants *more*…"

"I don't know *what* he wants."

Holeridge blew on the hot ash of his cigar. "Didn't he say what he wants?"

"He seemed more interested in why we're so eager to buy."

"This is insane." Leonard Winslow put down his half-empty snifter. "Whatever happened to good old-fashioned capitalistic greed? The last two generations have made fools of us in this area. Kids just out of high school, earning thirty K a year without degrees, certificates, or a working brain cell. The average college grad hitting the workplace nowadays starts out at fifty and reaches a hundred in two years. In high school I worked my butt off for a buck an hour and was damned happy to get it."

"That's right," Augustus Phelps said. "My grandkids aren't even in high school. They have High Density TV's, computers, and sound systems in their bedrooms. We're talking ten grand, easy, in equipment. Care to hear what their sucker of a granddad shelled out in Christmas gifts last year?"

"Not necessary." Holeridge didn't want to tell the men about his spoiled children. Or what his son wanted for his twelfth birthday.

"This new owner," Leonard said. "What's his name?"

"Gates," Trent said. "Lou Gates."

"That's right. Gates." Holeridge stroked his chin. "I never thought of it before. I wonder if he's related to—"

"I don't think so," Trent said.

"You're sure?"

"It's a fairly common name."

"If he *is* in that family," Miles said, "he would've taken our offer."

"How do you figure?" Noel asked.

"He'd certainly have a talent for making a fortune."

"I don't think that gene is inherited," Holeridge said.

"He might have picked up something from the dark side of the family. Maybe a mentally-deficient uncle or grandparent."

"He'd *have* to be mental to pass up more than a million," Holeridge said.

"How old is he?" Leonard asked.

"Around thirty-five." Trent poured more brandy. "What's his age got to do with this?"

"Generation X happens to be the target group for sociopathic tendencies, self-absorption, delusions of grandeur, and unadulterated greed," Leonard replied. "I've always called it Generation Extra Pampered, for obvious reasons."

"What's his problem?" Holeridge asked. "Wouldn't he like to be rich? A million bucks is a nice chunk of change."

"I honestly don't know," Trent said. Gates' aversion to cell phones had raised red flags but there was no need to mention it. It would sound petty. But it did say something about the man's peculiarity. Also, Gates obviously didn't like shaking hands. "There's something about him I can't put my finger on."

"Talk to him again," Holeridge said. "Find out what he wants."

"We need that place," Noel said. "When Denner died, we were supposed to get it."

"Denner 's oldest daughter sold it in spite of what her father wanted," Augustus said bitterly.

"You were handling that." Ira shot a glare at Bill Elliot. "Wasn't there anything you could have done?"

Elliot shook his head. "Sally Denner-Johnson is a self-centered, cold-hearted, obstinate—"

"Typical Generation X," Leonard muttered.

Elliot ignored the interruption. "She was having marital problems with her third husband. She sold to Gates and ran off with the money before I even heard about it."

Holeridge stubbed out his cigar. "We bought and paid for that place in more ways than one."

Leonard said, "Well, that's not how it ended up, is it?"

"Now I hear we're having problems with our Presbyterian minister," Miles said.

Holeridge shrugged. "Spencer is old-fashioned. He'll come along to our way of thinking."

"A lot of trouble," Ira said, "just to get that damned Pot Luck program axed."

"The church does need a facelift badly," Augustus said. "If you saw that cellar—"

"It won't take long," Holeridge said. "We'll rid the town of those worthless vagrants."

Ira grimaced. "They gorge themselves at the church, then sack out behind my store. I can't remember how many times my employees were forced to clean up the area. If you knew what those bums did back there…"

227

"I can imagine." Holeridge was getting stirred up again. "It makes the whole town look bad. And what about that incident last night with the Purdy boy?"

"Spencer's going to need a special insurance policy if he wants to keep taking in bums."

Holeridge poured more brandy into his snifter and glanced at George Trent. "Talk to Gates again. Do whatever it takes to get that property back."

CHAPTER 33

Bad Vibes

After Wendy brought up a tray of food and went back downstairs, Kathryn got up from the desk and followed Louis over to the table beneath the front window of his apartment. "What's for lunch?"

After searching the restaurant for Gutier and dealing with George Trent, Louis was famished. He raised a silver metal lid. Tongues of steam billowed out. "Fried drumsticks." He picked up another lid. "And green bean casserole."

Kathryn sat facing him. "Did Antoine or Morey make the casserole?"

"Antoine made it yesterday morning. But it always tastes better the second day."

Kathryn used tongs to pick up a drumstick and dropped it on her plate.

"Take two," he said. "They're small."

"Maybe later." With the ladle she scooped up half a cup of steaming casserole and smeared her dish with it.

Her diet nonsense again. Stick-thin and still watched everything she put in her mouth.

"If you're not careful," he said, "that waist's gonna balloon out to twenty inches."

"I'll probably skip dinner this evening if I'm too full."

"What was I thinking?"

Kathryn had some iced tea. "Tell me about our new hire."

"I need to talk to him."

"Doesn't that require you to find him first?"

229

"Sounds reasonable. I think I'll try it."

"What will you tell him?"

"I don't know. I'm new at this restaurateur crap."

"Really?"

"Maybe I'll mature over the years."

"That raises an interesting question."

"Shoot."

"Are you going to sell this place? And how much time will I have to find another job?"

He finished his first drumstick and dropped the bone onto his plate. "This can be answered in two parts. Part one? When hell freezes over. Part two? As much time as you need. Or you can just stick around until you get tired of the place. Or me."

"Decisions, decisions." She nibbled on her drumstick. "Why don't you want to sell? Wasn't the offer good enough?"

"It would give me more than enough money to pay off all my bills, buy a Harley and put down a hefty down payment on a condo in Rio de Janeiro."

"I didn't know you rode Harleys."

"I don't. But if I ever decide to withdraw from society and pull an Easy Rider, I can afford one."

"What would you do in Rio?"

"Same as all the other rich American men. Walk along the beach, toss money at the bikinis and develop skin cancer."

"Sounds lovely. And you're turning him down because…?"

"Bad vibes."

Kathryn had more tea. "I don't understand."

"When I have bad vibes about someone, there's usually a legitimate reason."

"Like the way you feel about Antoine?"

"Antoine's a crazy, psychotic Frenchman. I just stay away from him."

She put down her glass. "He can cook up a storm, so we'd better keep him."

"We'd be stupid not to."

"What about Mr. Trent?"

"Can he cook up a storm?"

"Be serious, now…"

"I thought I was."

She nodded. "I keep forgetting how well you hide your emotions."

"Thank you."

"I didn't realize that was a compliment."

"Men consider that a valuable and useful talent."

"Yes. I forgot. My husband does that too, but not as well as you do."

"Something about him doesn't feel right."

"My husband?"

"Trent. I've never met your husband."

"You'd like him."

"Trent?"

"My husband."

"Just so he doesn't act like Trent."

"I wouldn't know. But Arthur doesn't act like a banker. He can be silly at times."

"Good. I wouldn't trust you if you'd fallen for the banker type."

"Ah. Clear as a bell."

"This goes back to my childhood."

"Where's Doctor Phil when you need him?"

231

"I had this relative who liked hurting me when I was little. He was sort of an uncle. I've always been suspicious of people who remind me of him."

"George Trent reminds you of this man?"

"In some ways."

"Tell me about this uncle."

"He wasn't actually my uncle."

"Why'd you call him that?"

"He was married to my aunt."

"Doesn't that…make him your uncle?"

"He's dead."

"Doesn't that make him your dead uncle?"

"I never considered him my uncle when he was alive. Why should I change my opinion of him when he's dead?"

"Okay." Kathryn pulled another miniscule shred of meat from her drumstick.

"He was a fat, arrogant loud-mouth. When I was growing up, he and Aunt Maudie came to our place and stayed for days and days. Why is it that your least favorite relatives always stay the longest?"

"That's one of those Murphy's Law things. But please get back to this issue with your uncle."

"He liked picking me up and putting me on his knee."

"How old were you?"

"Four or five."

"If you'd been fifteen, I'd worry."

"I had strange feelings when I was on his knee. It's hard to put into words. I don't know if his touch or his smell messed me up. It scared me and made me uneasy. Things turned dark. When I saw him again years later, everything came back."

"He didn't put you on his knee then, did he?"

"No."

"You said he hurt you."

"He took my arm, twisted it behind my back and pushed it up between my shoulder blades. He also enjoyed twisting my thumbs in unnatural positions."

"Why?"

"He liked it when I cried."

"Why didn't you fight him? Or at least ask him not to do that?"

"I was told to respect my elders."

She nodded. "A fine philosophy for a child to live by."

Louis sighed. "He died around the time I graduated from college."

"You sound disappointed."

"I promised myself that when I grew up, I'd break his arm the next time I saw him."

"Then it was good that he died."

"For him it was."

"You obviously hated him because he manhandled you."

"I hated him because he was evil and manhandled me."

"You think he was evil?"

"He never had any financial worries and always lucked into things. That made me suspicious. He bragged about some club he belonged to in Pittsburgh. But whenever anyone asked about it, he changed the subject. I figured he made it up, but when Trent told me about his associates, it took me back."

"What religion was he?"

"Trent?"

"Your aunt's husband."

233

"Why?"

"This evil dynamic intrigues me. He wasn't a churchgoer, was he?"

"He claimed to be a Christian Scientist but never went to church."

"*You* never go to church..."

"I used to."

"Then why consider that awful man evil just because—"

"I never get scared or uneasy when I'm by myself."

Kathryn sipped her tea and watched the activity at the 7-Eleven across the street.

"Haven't you ever had uneasy feelings about someone?" he asked.

She put down her glass. "I had some when I applied for this job."

"Really?"

"I thought you were very good-looking."

"Thank you."

"Very bright."

"*Such* a flatterer."

"A fine figure of a man."

"I'm getting excited."

"But strange."

"My bubble just burst."

"You asked."

"Me? Strange?"

"How would you describe someone who turns down a terrific offer because he doesn't like the man handling the deal?"

"Shrewd? Cautious? A snappy dresser? A big hit with the ladies?"

"You can't stay serious very long, can you?"

"Not too long. I have to live with myself, you know..."

Kathryn shrugged. "I just don't know what any of this has to do with George Trent's offer."

"I had dark, uneasy feelings in the bar when I met him."

"Could this be because he runs a bank, and you dislike bankers?"

"He's also got a greasy handshake."

"Maybe it was mousse."

"I don't care if it was antelope. I won't do business with a man I don't like or trust."

"That associate thing. It could be legitimate, you know."

"Maybe."

"But you don't think so."

"Not really."

"Why not?"

"Anyone who wants to pay too much for something without trying to get it for a lower price has to have something up his sleeve."

CHAPTER 34

Darcy Goes to Town

Dressed in a red tank top and frayed jeans, Darcy lay on her bed while *Evil Ways* churned steadily from her CD player.

She spent the night huddled beneath the sheets, cringing at the slightest noise. Every couple of hours she got up, checked the window, and peered outside.

Her own personal demon...

What had she been thinking last Friday night? What made her go out there in the first place?

Her imagination had been her downfall. She grew up reading the works of Poe, Lovecraft, Bierce, and Blackwood. Films like *Frankenstein*, *Nosferatu* and *The Wolf Man* gave her bad dreams but also made life much more exciting. Make-believe was always much more exhilarating than reality.

That is, until just last year, when she actually saw evil faces in archive photos of the smoking Twin Towers. People said the images were merely illusions—computer-altered graphics fashioned to resemble demonic faces emerging from the smoke. But Darcy wasn't convinced, and suspected they were the faces of actual demons. And that they did indeed exist.

Had she conjured up something in the mineshaft?

Impossible. He was just some weirdo Todd picked up and brought into town. He could do a few strange tricks, but that didn't make him a demon.

Demons couldn't just *leave* whenever they wanted, could they? Couldn't come up from Hell when someone *sneezed*...

She knew all about mental cases. The only sensible way of dealing with them was to ignore them. They would eventually take the hint and go away.

Friday night was really weird. Wasn't it only natural that she would have crazy dreams about it? She felt so guilty about Todd and Leon dying. They would still be alive if she hadn't asked them to take her out there. Her guilt had obviously conjured up this imaginary guy.

Seemed reasonable, didn't it?

But Sheila had also seen him. And Mirabelle at the store.

Her cell buzzed. It was Sheila. "Hey."

"What's up?"

"Not working today?"

"I'm off."

"Wanna hang in town?"

That sounded better than hanging around here. "C'mon over and pick me up."

***

Tiffany opened her eyes and stiffened at the sight of the unfamiliar room.

A motel room. It came back in trickles at first, then a heavy wave. The church. The food fight. A tacky little Ohio town called Raven, with beat-up pickup trucks, men who chewed tobacco and wore bib overalls, and a slobbering wolf guy she and Chip had to send back to—

The empty couch grinned at her.

She sat bolt upright. Where was he? The bathroom?

Silly. What would Chip be doing in a bathroom?

But his absence immediately triggered something that had been weighing heavily in her mind.

A mortal to bond with.

237

If Chip wasn't around, it wouldn't be difficult to sneak out and hide until the coast was clear, then grab someone decent to bond with. That wouldn't be a problem, either. Once she made the puppies bigger, she could have her pick of any male in town.

Chip could no longer touch her. She could stay up here and do whatever she wanted. She had powers and wouldn't have to worry about going back to that foul-smelling place ever again.

She jumped out of the bed and closed her eyes. Something casual and inconspicuous. And the puppies needed to be small for now. Otherwise, it would be just as it was in Jake's Coffeehouse.

When she opened her eyes, she was wearing a short-sleeved black tee shirt, tan Capri's, and a pair of Kitten Heels by Donald J. Pliner Viola. The puppies were barely noticeable. Satisfied, she went over to the door and cracked it open. And groaned.

Chip, dressed as he was the day before, stood in a puddle of water. Ten feet from him, a mildew-stained fountain leaked at its base, forming the pool. He bent and yanked out a plug of grass.

Her heart sinking, she stepped outside and let the puppies fill out to their normal size. No sense looking inconspicuous now.

"How was the bed?" he asked, munching.

"Hard. How can you eat that stuff?"

"Minerals, baby. Did you say hard?"

"And lumpy. You're standing in water again."

"Really?"

"Why do you do that?"

238

"Cools the feet. You ought to try it. You'll have to take off those fancy tootsie holders first. They're cool, though."

"Thanks. Maybe I'll try the water thing later."

"Did you say lumpy?"

"Very. And hard."

"I should've let you have the couch."

"How was it?"

"Lumpy. And hard."

She should be used to this by now. "We're not making much sense, are we?"

He swallowed the dirt, tossed the grass, and started up the walk. "Sounds like one of those meaningless conversations mortal men have when they can't find anything else to do."

"Such as?" she asked, catching up.

"When males have nothing bright or important to say—which happens all the time—they indulge in idiot talk."

"*Idiot* talk?"

"Guys stand around, belching and farting. One of them bends over to pick something up. His friend says, "Wow, Bruce, looks like you're getting a little thin on top." Bruce says, "So?" The first guy says, "Just making an observation." Bruce replies, "You know what *I* just observed? You really *are* an asshole." Then they laugh and crack open another beer."

"A shame women don't do that."

Chip laughed. "What do you think would happen if a group of females were congregated together and one of them started on another's flaws?"

"A catfight?"

239

"With blood, torn clothing, and medical units involved."

"Good thing women are more sophisticated."

"Too bad they don't know how to belch and fart in front of one another."

Main Street hummed with traffic. Clots of casually dressed folks left Jake's Coffeehouse and filed into the stores lining the block.

"What's the plan?" she asked at the corner.

"Keep your eyes open."

"I have to. I can't see very well when they're closed."

He sighed tiredly. "Save the jokes, okay? Just tell me if you see anything suspicious."

"With my eyes closed?"

He stopped walking and stared at her. "*Must* you be a problem?"

"I don't want you to get bored."

"You're *such* a girl…"

***

Sheila parked in front of Thomas Hardware on East Main.

Across the street, Mirabelle Polsky gave the glass behind Crenshaw's storefront window a thorough workout with the Windex. The surface glistened like polished gems in the sunlight.

"That lady's big-time weird," Sheila said, getting out.

Darcy said nothing.

One block up, a couple of neat-looking antique clocks embellished the storefront display of Neely's Novelties. One of them displayed a hefty price tag stuck to its face.

Sheila joined her in the shade of the green store awning. "Two hundred bucks? What else does it do besides tell ya the time? Find you a software zillionaire?"

"For that price, it should," Darcy said.

"You can afford it," a voice behind them said.

They spun around.

He stood there grinning, those scary reddish-brown eyes boring into her.

"Here we go again," Sheila said flatly. "Why didn't you tell me you two were gonna hook up?" She glared at Darcy. "I could've stayed home and had much more fun shaving my legs."

"Why are you following me?" Darcy demanded. The heat climbing up her back made her unsteady. If she told Uncle Hawk about this—

"I wouldn't if I were you," he said.

She swallowed. "Wouldn't what?"

"Tell your uncle. He wouldn't know what to do. He's still too busy trying to figure out what happened with Big Bad Elroy last night."

"What's this all about?" Sheila edged closer to Darcy. "What's he talking about? How'd he…come up with *that*?"

"He seems to think he's a mind-reader."

Sheila shrugged. "Sounds to me like he's pretty good at it."

"Don't let him fool you." She had to stop this right now. "He's…into body language."

"Why don't we go somewhere and talk?" he said. "We didn't have much time in your bedroom last night. Your annoying father kept interrupting our party."

"Darce?" Sheila gawked at her. "What's he talking about now?"

"Now he's reading his own mind." No way would she let this jerk ruin her reputation by—

"Is your reputation that important to you?"

He did it again.

Stay cool. Keep your head.

"I don't know—or care—what foolish notions you've—"

"Foolish? When I left your room last night—"

"Darce?"

"Tell your friend what's going on." His grin made her tremble. "She wants to know. Look at her— she's all bummed out and nervous."

"You idiot." Fire singed Darcy's cheeks. This was much worse than what happened in her bedroom last night. If any of their classmates strolled by, she would be ruined. "Don't you realize what you're doing?" She tried keeping her voice down. "I *live* here! My *friends* live here!"

"You have *friends*?"

"Of *course* I have friends!"

"Wow. Cool beans."

"Darce? This is, like, big-time weird. What's goin' down?"

"It's simple." His gaze shifted to Sheila. The grin had vanished. "I'm—"

Darcy closed her eyes, gritted her teeth, and held her breath.

"Gutier! What the hell are you doin' here? You're supposed to be back at the loading dock!"

Darcy's eyes shot open. A guy she had seen working at Denner's jogged toward them, dodging traffic.

***

242

Half a block west, two young women and a tall, slender man argued beneath a green canopy in front of a novelty shop. A smirk covered the man's lean face.

Tiffany froze. Those eyes…

In the sun, they glinted a reddish-brown. And that smirk…

The foul-smelling woods flickered in her mind.

The brunette's voice grew louder as they approached. "I *live* here. All my *friends* live here."

"You have *friends*?" The slender man's smirk remained.

That voice. It was definitely

("Look what I found")

something she would never forget.

"Lamb Chop?" Chip whispered. "Problemo?"

She shook her head, then fell back into step with Chip.

Another guy dodged the traffic and joined the arguing trio. After the two men had a brief argument, they left the girls and crossed the street, heading for Denner 's Restaurant.

Behind Tiffany, the brunette said in a soft, dreamy voice, "What kind of demon works at a *restaurant*?"

Tiffany turned. The brunette's lips weren't moving.

"You sure nothing's going on?" Chip asked. "Your deer-in-the-headlights look seems to be switched on full."

The young girls watched the two men. The skinny blonde said, "What's wrong with that guy, Darce? And what was all that crap about being in your bedroom?"

The brunette ran both hands briskly through her long black hair. "He was…just trying to cause trouble."

"C'mon, now…you can tell me…"

The brunette's lips stopped moving again. "Sure. It would save me the bother of telling the whole school…"

"How about it?" the blonde coaxed.

"My reputation's ruined. I won't be able to show my face in this town."

"Some heavy shit's going down, isn't it?" the blonde asked.

"No…" The brunette turned away.

"Then why're you so bummed out?"

"That guy's weird, okay?"

"You picked him up the other night, didn't you? You told me yourself."

"How am I going to live this down?" The brunette was thinking furiously again. "He says he's a demon, but he's just some jerk working at Denner's. Now Sheila knows about it."

"I promise I won't tell anyone," the blonde said.

Tiffany nearly stumbled on the curb as the realization roared through her. *My powers. I might be able to help her. The wolf guy did something to her. I just can't let him get away with it.*

She stared at the blonde and thought: *I have no idea what just happened here.* Then to the brunette: *no need to worry, Darce, you're safe.*

Tiffany stepped down from the curb.

"You gonna tell me what *that* was all about?" Chip said.

"The wolf guy," she said over the passing traffic. "He was the one arguing with those girls."

"How sure are you?"

"Don't you think I'd remember the pig that pulled me out of Limbo and stuck me in Hell?"

***

244

Darcy cursed herself for leaving her bedroom.

Couldn't leave well enough alone, could she? She was bored and had to come into town. Now she was paying for it, big-time. Her reputation was going down in flames and that weirdo had found her again.

Now she was hearing strange voices.

A good day's work for a Sunday afternoon.

"Are you gonna tell me what that was all about?" Sheila asked. She seemed totally confused.

Darcy wanted to close her eyes and touch down back in her room. Suddenly the prospect of listening to Santana sounded terrific. If only she could manage that. If she could, she wouldn't dare answer the phone this time.

"What was *what* all about?"

Sheila shrugged. "That clock. You know you can't afford it. You make what? Like, ten bucks an hour at Old Man Crenshaw's? How's that doofus know how much you can afford?"

Something about the clock.

They were talking about the clock before all that happened. Now all Sheila wanted to know was—

No need to worry, Darce, you're safe.

The blond lady she had just seen crossing the street.

That strange voice in her head.

"Is *that* what we were talking about?" Darcy asked innocently.

Sheila flipped a long strand of glittered platinum hair over her right shoulder. "You zonin' out on me?"

"Not really. I—"

"That weirdo—the one with the funny red eyes. He works at Denner's?"

"I guess…"

"Then why was he here, puttin' the move on us?"

Across the street, the blond lady and the skinny redhead disappeared into the restaurant.

That voice in my head. Was it the blond lady?

Nothing else made sense.

She rescued me.

But how?

And, more importantly, why?

Darcy's temples throbbed. "She...how much money are you carrying?"

"Hell, I dunno..." Sheila clicked open her tan leather purse and pulled out a slim wad of fives and tens, a Lotto ticket and some wrinkled coupons from Arby's. "Forty, forty-five bucks. Why?"

"How about Denner's for a late lunch?"

"Denner's? Ya sure?

"Why not? Going by how he's dressed, that guy probably works in the kitchen. We won't see him at all."

Sheila shrugged. "Kinda pricey. But what the hey, it's only money, right?"

CHAPTER 35

Denner's Diners Destroyed by a Disgruntled Demon

His vision a misty red, Gutril fought down the urge to turn the irritating stock boy into a fresh cow patty as he followed him across the street.

Doing something like that right now wouldn't be such a cool move. Mortals were stupid, dense, and blind. They didn't notice what was going on right in front of their faces most of the time. But even the world's stupidest mortal would pick up on someone suddenly turning into cow shit. Questions would be asked. The cops would be called in.

"You're in trouble, Gutier," the stock boy said.

"What's the beef?"

"You're not taking the job seriously."

He had to be joking. "You lift boxes, crates and sacks. You move them from one room to another. It's not exactly brain surgery."

"It's a *job*," Niles snapped. "I've caught you screwing off a dozen times in just two days."

"I'm new to the area. Give a guy a break."

"I gave you a shitload of breaks yesterday."

How did mortals endure this nonsense?

No wonder they were neurotic, angry, messed up, and got drunk all the time.

Two vehicles down, a guy in an expensive suit slid out of a shiny black sports car. The image of a gun lying in the console filled the mortal's thoughts as he shut the door. Then he turned and headed for Denner's.

Cool beans.

Gutril injected

(protect yourself)

into the man's head.

The man suddenly stopped, turned around, went back to his car, opened the driver's door, and reached inside.

Gutril grinned as he followed the stock boy down the alley leading to the restaurant's rear entrance.

A little added entertainment was exactly what this boring job needed.

***

"How old are you?" The barman's thick black brows twitched over his crinkly gray eyes.

Chip winked. "Just a few years older than the carbuncle on my—"

"In *years*, Mr. Funnybone."

"I was a mere twenty-seven when I found myself buried up to my neck in the rock garden behind the castle walls. But that's been a while ago…"

The barman turned to Tiffany. "How about you?"

He's looking at my face…

Tiffany realized she had just messed up again. There was only one reason why a man stared directly at a woman's face. She had adjusted the puppies to make them smaller when she and Chip came inside. Bad move. Men didn't like a flat chest on a woman.

Time to fix things. She bent over, apparently to adjust something on her Kitten Heels, thought, *melons*, and slowly straightened. "Twenty-two."

The barman nearly dropped the glass he was polishing.

"Something wrong?"

The barman's eyes bulged. He cleared his throat. "Uh, no…nothin's wrong."

"You gonna serve us? Or just stand there, staring at my chest?"

He reddened. "Sure. Yeah. Uh-huh. What's your, uh, pleasure?"

"A big glass of ice water for me," Chip said.

"No chaser?"

"Chaser?"

"Mixer."

"Righterino. Orange juice. Freshly squeezed. No pits."

The barman groaned.

"I'd like a strawberry daiquiri," Tiffany said.

The barman hustled away.

She rested her elbow on the padded counter and used her palm to cover her left cheek. "I *hate* being that way."

"What way?"

"Mean. Nasty. And top-heavy."

"But you're good at it."

"So now I've got to keep them big."

"Why?"

"Won't he get suspicious if I make them smaller?"

"Sweet cakes, how many mortals actually pay attention to anything?"

"Men pay attention to a girl's breasts."

The barman brought over their drinks, then scurried away.

Chip sucked down half the pitcher of water, belched, then sipped orange juice from the tiny glass.

"Tell me something," Tiffany said. "Can you hear voices?"

"Those mortals pigging out in the dining room. They're almost as loud as the supers at the banquet table

249

when the hookers are brought in for their acrobatic exercises."

"I mean thoughts."

"Mortal thoughts? Or is this something about my sanity?"

"The mortal thing. I'm pretty sure about your, uh, sanity."

"I'm unable to develop certain powers. Tricks are about it for me."

Once again she tried to imagine what he had done to be stuck in someone's rock garden in Hell. "You never told me what you did in the mortal world."

"One day, maybe. When this job's finished."

She suddenly remembered the brunette's thoughts.

What kind of demon works at a restaurant?

She wanted to bring it up but thought it might offend Chip, so she decided to drop it—at least for now. "I wonder where the wolf guy went," she said, looking around.

Chip had more water. "That other guy was dressed in work clothes."

"A stock boy, maybe?"

"Gutril doing *stock work*?" Chip chuckled. "Some visual..."

"Maybe he's trying to blend in."

A skinny male around twenty-five with a shaved head and a pronounced Adam's apple grinned at her from across the bar.

She recognized the signs. "Uh-oh."

"I see him. Stupid-looking dork with a cue-ball head?"

"What do I do?"

250

"You might not have to do anything unless he actually comes over and tries hitting on – oh, crap."

He came right over, carrying his beer.

"Now what should I do?"

"Show him that humongous wart on your nose. Bad breath will also work wonders."

He slid onto the stool next to her. A heavy mix of Aqua Velva, stale cigarette breath, and B. O. brushed her face.

"Hey, baby, I been watchin' you –"

"You're drooling."

"Can't help it. You're a hottie. I mean *smokin'*…"

She hated that kind of talk. Hearing it constantly in Hollywood had ruined it for her. "I'm not your type."

"Lemme buy you a drink. Ya might change your mind."

She closed her eyes. *No teeth*. Then she smiled.

He swallowed loudly, his Adam's apple quivering.

"Uh…thought you were somebody else…" He nearly fell off the stool in his rush to get away.

"That was easy," she said.

Chip frowned. "I liked my humongous wart idea."

"Maybe next time."

***

Tall, slender, and smartly dressed in her tan suit, the hostess smiled at them behind her podium.

Darcy tried peering into the bar. Two large, well-dressed men engaged in a heated discussion blocked the entrance. *Darn. If they would just move away from the doorway or go inside, maybe I can sneak a peek and—*

"Darce?"

"Uh-huh?"

"Non, right?"

"Huh?"

"Non? As in, like, non-smoking?"

"You know I don't smoke."

Her eyes darting from table to table, she followed Sheila and the hostess down the tile-covered hall, into the warm, candlelit dining room. Big band music swept softly from its many speakers. Really old stuff, but relaxing. Rich aromas of baked seafood, fried onions, and charbroiled beef filled her nostrils. Darcy realized only then that she hadn't eaten since breakfast.

No sign of the blond lady. Several blond women sat at tables but were all much older. None looked half as terrific as the lady she'd seen outside Neely's.

The hostess led them to a small table behind a thick stucco pillar. She handed them menus, then whisked away.

"You okay?" Sheila asked.

"Why?"

"You're acting like Richard Kimble."

"Who?"

"The Fugitive."

"What does he have to do with me?"

"Don't tell me you're looking for that guy…"

"He weirds me out. Makes me want to take a shower."

"Hey, we both saw him head over here. Like you said, I don't think we'll see him out here at all."

"I totally hope you're right."

***

Morey had no trouble keeping up with the hungry crowd.

He had been a short-order cook for thirteen years and boasted that he could handle a dozen orders of eggs,

252

bacon, sausage, and hash browns in less than five minutes.

Louis thought it too bad that Morey and Antoine couldn't get along. In Antoine's view, Morey could do nothing more complicated than heat up canned food for rowdy truckers. In Morey's view, Antoine would be much happier sitting in a padded cell, poking out the eyes of people in magazines.

Luckily the two rarely encountered one another.

"Everything going all right?" Louis, looking worried, edged carefully through the kitchen chaos. All around him, waitresses snatched up orders while busboys lugged baskets filled with dirty dishes.

"Just dandy." Morey tended to a double order of *sautéed* shrimp and scallops. He slid the plate over to Wendy, who placed it on a tray. "I can do this in my sleep."

"Just don't try and prove it," Louis said. "Customers tend to get nauseous when they notice hair or drool on their plates."

Someone tapped Louis on the shoulder. It was Niles.

"What's up?"

"I've got Gutier at the loading dock."

"What's he doing?"

"I told him you wanted to talk to him."

"Where'd you find him?"

"Across the street, hitting on two high school chicks."

"How was he doing?"

"I got there just in time."

"You should be ashamed of yourself."

"You serious, Boss?"

"Don't I look serious?"

Niles shrugged. "I can never tell."

"Good. I'll keep up my mysterious persona."

"Your what?"

Louis followed Niles through the huge doorway.

The big room was stacked with palettes and crates. But there was no sign of Gutier.

Niles ran over to the forklift, peering behind it. "Dammit. He was just here!"

Louis sighed. "I guess I'm going to have to give that guy his walking papers."

"You'll have to find him, first—"

Gunshots roared from the dining room.

***

Overturned tables and chairs littered the big dining room. Dishes, glasses, and silverware covered the tile. Food sat in scattered heaps.

Screaming and yelling, customers tripped over chairs, tables, and one another to escape. A waitress crawled underneath a table while a busboy scrambled beneath a window booth.

His back to Louis, a tall, well-dressed man stood stiffly in the center of the commotion. The gun in his hand pointed at a tangle of limbs writhing on the floor.

Louis's thoughts slammed into overload.

Got to grab that damned gun...

The gunman was more than twenty feet away—how could anyone cover that much distance before another shot was fired?

Wait until he runs out of bullets.

That wouldn't work. More people might be shot and possibly killed.

The gunman took aim again. Another shot reverberated. The room shook. More screaming customers forced themselves through the doorway.

254

Louis's gut tightened. His pulse racing, he grabbed a tablecloth from the floor. Moving quietly and careful not to slip on tossed food, he veered left, until he was directly behind the shooter. His head had grown hot. His hands shook. He barely felt the floor beneath his feet.

He moved closer. The tablecloth weighed a ton. An illusion.

Your brain's running on pure adrenaline. Focus on bringing him down.

His arms trembling, the tablecloth gripped tightly in his white-knuckled fists, Louis lunged at the man.

***

After the bar cleared, Chip strolled over to the archway.

Tiffany stayed right where she was. She hated guns and wanted to leave. She knew she couldn't be hurt, but the memories from her past were still very painful. Her father was a hunter and was killed when she was five. Another hunter mistook Daddy for a deer despite his orange jacket, plaid shirt, and hat.

Watching the commotion, Chip munched on an eggshell he'd grabbed from a bowl of raw eggs on the counter. He motioned to her.

Reluctantly she tiptoed over.

The dining room looked like one of those disaster flicks Hollywood made from time to time. Everything had become total chaos. People were crawling around and fighting with one another to escape.

"That wuss isn't your basic killer," Chip said. "Look at the suit."

The well-dressed man standing in the middle of the room, holding a small handgun, made her think of Barclay Dunstan. "He reminds me of a guy I knew in high school back in Peoria. He wore white socks and studied all the time, even took notes."

"You always had an eye for high class, huh, baby cakes?"

"I didn't *date* him or anything..."

"Look at him. A real geek. All dressed up just so he can indulge in a little target practice after his meal."

They both saw the wolf guy and the stock boy come back to this place. Chip might actually be right. Tiffany strongly suspected Gutril had caused this. If so, a lot of innocent people were going to be hurt.

Then it hit her. Her growing powers.

I can fix this. I might even be able to do it without Chip suspecting.

She closed her eyes. *My aim is off.*

Two more shots exploded in the next room.

She opened her eyes. A dark-haired guy had entered the picture. His face was really nice to look at. Fairly tall and broad-shouldered, he picked up a red-and-white checkered tablecloth and held it in front of him.

The gun went off again.

The dark-haired guy tackled the shooter.

***

Once Louis had tossed the tablecloth over the shooter's head, panic set in. His knees quickly turning to mush, he collapsed, bringing the shooter down with him. The two men went to the floor together in one lumpy, red-checkered mass.

He lay on top of the other man, listening to his own heart fighting to thrash its way out of his chest. He played football briefly in high school and learned how to tackle an opponent. You grabbed him from behind, pinning his arms and using your own weight to bring him to the ground.

This was a much different situation. His fear had made him collapse, bringing down his opponent as he went down. A nice stroke of luck, considering an armed man lay pinned beneath him, unable to shoot anyone else.

Louis kept his weight firmly on the restless mass beneath the tablecloth. Terrified that the slightest shifting on his part would enable the shooter to regain control of the gun, Louis didn't budge.

Except for the customers scrambling through the doorway, the lack of gunfire sounded just as pleasing to the ears as the big band music drifting sporadically from the speaker system.

If only Niles, Morey, or some brave-minded diner will come over here to help me—

The gun. He suddenly realized he didn't know where it was.

Pulse racing, Louis groped frantically at the shapeless form beneath him, searching for an arm, a hand, an elbow, trying to distinguish hard metal among the warm, taut flesh.

The shape squirmed, moving in the opposite direction.

Still no gun.

Only one way to find it.

Gritting his teeth, Louis straightened, grabbed the tablecloth, and yanked it away.

George Trent lay struggling beneath him.

"What the hell?"

Trent twisted around beneath Louis's weight. Louis lost his balance and fell, landing on his side. He forced himself back up.

Trent's eyes looked glazed, unfocused. Both arms had already come up. The snub-nosed weapon was gripped in his hands.

His blood ice-cold, Louis numbly stared at the huge black hole at the end of the barrel.

***

Click.

Louis felt as if he had just been doused with a bucket of ice water. He could feel the hair on the back of his neck moving around like nervous ants. His mouth had gone numb; his throat had dried up.

Trent gawked at his weapon, then at Louis. The gun came up again. The trigger squeezed.

Another *click*...

Fighting nausea, Louis grabbed an extended wrist and pushed it down. He mashed his elbow into Trent's side. The gun clattered onto the tile. Louis grabbed the man's arm and twisted, forcing Trent down. Trent pulled free; his left elbow came up, catching Louis on the forehead. Louis's vision turned double. A jolt of sharp pain sliced through him. He struggled to stay in control. Hopefully, someone carrying around one of those damned cell phones would think to switch it on and bring the cops—

Someone tapped him on the shoulder. He flinched and spun around.

A huge, broad-shouldered police uniform towered over him, the name *Hawkins* printed neatly on the plastic nametag over the man's left breast pocket.

"About time you showed," Louis said, his voice weak.

"Got here quick as we could."

Light waves of dizziness wafted through him. God, he needed a cigarette. And a drink.

Two more cops appeared, their handcuffs clinking. One cop mashed a khaki-covered knee into the back of George Trent's neck while the other cuffed him.

The dizziness returned.

The room began spinning.

***

Tiffany loved happy endings.

Too bad Hollywood was so obsessed with sex and violence. That was probably why she never landed any of the better parts. They could tell her heart wasn't in it. She wanted them to make the kind of love stories they did years ago, with Clark Gable and Humphrey Bogart and Cary Grant. She would have sparkled in those kinds of flicks.

If only she had been given the chance…

If only someone had sensed her screen presence, her talent…

If only she had been able to begin her career without having to resort to those stupid pool parties…

She had run out of time.

But at least now she had powers and knew how to use them.

She would use them only for good. She had been pulled into Hell, but that wasn't her fault. She was good and intended to stay that way. She had already helped that young girl out in the street and had just helped that cute dark-haired guy. Chip didn't have to know. She was going to do what she was meant to do. She was going to keep helping people and eventually find a mortal host so she could stay here forever.

Anyway, it felt good. Everyone was out of danger, the gunman apprehended, the cute dark-haired guy the hero.

259

The same guy who had just fainted the moment he started walking away.

***

Chip cracked another egg, dumped the gooey stuff into the bowl, and popped the jagged white shell into his mouth. Behind them, the barman picked up barstools and slid them under the counter. A waitress knelt on the carpet, using a towel to coax broken glass into a dustpan.

Tiffany could tell Chip was trying to put things together.

"You didn't have anything to do with that, did you?" Chip said, swallowing noisily.

"Me?" Tiffany asked innocently.

"You're the only *you* I seem to be talking to at the moment."

"What could *I* have done?"

"His gun jammed."

She shrugged. "Guns jam all the time, don't they? Why would I do that…even if I could?"

In the dining room, the cops handcuffed the shooter and pulled him to his feet.

"Maybe he just ran out of bullets," she said.

"That's possible. In the excitement he mighta forgotten how many times he pulled the trigger. But it makes me really suspicious. Now I'm almost certain Gutril caused this."

Relief surged through her. "So…what do we do?"

"Got any ideas?"

Escape. The dreamy black-haired guy. Finding a mortal.

The plan had materialized almost without her realizing it.

"Why don't we split up?" she suggested.

260

"Whaddya mean?"

"I go somewhere, you go somewhere else."

"At the same time?

"That's usually how splitting up works."

"Please explain this sudden outburst of unexpected reasoning."

"We both suspect the wolf guy did this. We also know he works here. I might be able to find out what happened easier by myself. I might even be able to find him easier by myself."

"What's with all this by-yourself stuff?"

"It's just that, well, you don't make a very good first impression…"

"So?"

"When you ask questions, people cooperate more if you're nice."

"I'm a *demon*. We don't—"

"I got it, believe me."

"And they say blondes aren't capable of hauling around a brain cell."

She ignored that. "Nice happens to be right up my alley."

"I'm painfully aware of that, sweet cakes."

"You actually agree?"

"It's the only disgusting thing about you."

She should have seen *that* one coming…

"One thing I can't figure about all this," Chip said. "Why the gunplay?"

"That's something else we have to find out, I guess."

"So then, what am I doing while you're being disgustingly nice to these local yokels?"

"You could visit the Police Station, find the man who shot up this place and ask him why he did it."

261

"Without being nice?"

"I don't think they care about being nice in a police station."

"I'll be in my natural element, then. But what'll you do if you find him? Nothing stupid, I hope."

"I'll find out what I can and wait for you to come back."

"You know something, muffin? You're not as stupid as you look."

"You're full of compliments today. Are you sure that's *you* in there?"

"Loading up on Vitamin C and calcium does wonders for my charisma."

"Your what?"

"Heads up, folks." A short, potbellied man in a police uniform cleared a path for two paramedics. "Police business."

Tiffany stuck her head out in the hall. "Officer?"

He stopped cold. His eyes lowered. "Yeah, baby?"

"I was just wondering how the other man's doing. Wavy black hair? He's wearing black form-fitting slacks."

His eyes stayed focused on the twins. Tiffany could tell he wasn't paying attention to the sound of her voice.

"He took the gun away from the shooter."

It snapped him out of it. "Gates. Owns this place. He's upstairs. Shaken up a little."

Someone called for the cop, whose name was Joe. He saluted Tiffany and then waddled down the hall behind the gurney.

"I'll be back when I find out something," Chip said.

"I hope I find out something, too," she said.

Escape was now only a flight of stairs away.

CHAPTER 36

Tiffany Meets the Sexy Restaurant Guy

Slouched in an armchair, Gates looked all done in, Hawk thought. His ripped shirt collar showed a small cut across his collarbone. Food stains smeared his shirt and slacks. His eyes weren't focused.

Not exactly his day.

The razor-thin brunette coming from down the hall carried a cold compress. Gates took it and dropped it on the arm of the chair. He got up and moved almost like a drunken man on his way over to the desk. Then he picked up a pack of cigarettes and dropped three on the table. He stuck one between his lips and tried his best to get the lighter working. He had a helluva time doing it, his nerves shot and all.

"Any idea what got into George Trent?" Hawk figured this might be as good a time as any to find out what happened. It might even get Gates back to thinking rationally.

Gates sank back into his chair and put the compress over his forehead. "What makes you think I know what's going on?"

"Just an educated guess."

"Use your education to guess something else. I'm still trying to figure out why a banker brought a gun into my restaurant."

"When you handle money, it's smart to have one handy."

Gates dropped the compress. "He wasn't handling *money*. He was eating my food."

"Trent's always been solid and level-headed."

"I only saw him once before," Gates said.

"Where?"

"Downstairs."

"Talk to him?"

"For a few minutes."

"About what?"

"He wants to buy my restaurant."

Hawk scratched his chin. *Trent? Buying a restaurant?* "He say why?"

"He said he represents a group of investors who want it."

Now it was clearer. The old boys at it again, buying up whatever they could, then not knowing what to do once they got it. "The town elders."

"I don't care what they call themselves. I told him I didn't want to sell."

"How'd he take it?"

"He didn't."

"Those men don't like to be turned down."

"So then, he figures that if he comes back and shoots up the place, I might change my mind?"

"Don't sound quite right, does it?"

"That theory does have a glitch or two, doesn't it?"

"I've known Trent a long time. He's honest, respectful—"

"And likes to go ballistic every once in a while."

The brunette watched him closely. Hawk didn't think it was a romance thing; she just looked worried.

"We're not sure what happened," Hawk said.

"I don't think Trent did, either."

"What makes you say that?"

"His eyes were glazed over."

That didn't make sense, neither. "You mean he mighta been drunk? Spaced out, maybe?"

"He didn't seem to recognize me when I pulled the tablecloth away."

"You sure he was lookin' at you?"

"I took the gun from him, remember? We were nose to nose. I could smell the cordite coming out of that gun barrel."

Hawk couldn't get much of a grip on this one. A respected banker comes here for dinner, then shoots up the place. His eyes are glazed. Doesn't even recognize the man he'd talked to recently about a major business transaction. "This just isn't makin' sense."

"Do you realize what I'm facing? Lawsuits. Medical bills. Wrongful death. If I'm lucky, everyone who was shot or injured will wait for me to sell so they can –"

"Trent didn't actually shoot anyone."

"What about the tables, chairs, dishes, silverware, and glasses tripping people and knocking them flat on their asses?"

"Paramedics saw cuts, maybe some bruises. Nothin' serious."

Gates stared at his cigarette. "I heard at least five shots. The place was packed. Seems I've been doing a bang-up business, excuse the pun. Is Trent a lousy shot?"

"I saw him at the firing range. He could qualify as a sharpshooter."

"Well, I sure am glad he ran out of bullets…"

"Two rounds were found in the mag."

"The gun jammed, then."

Both Travis and Joe Flynn had examined the gun. Neither saw any reason for it to jam. But Lou Gates didn't need to deflect any more curve balls right now. He had more than enough on his plate. "Possibly."

"What kind of gun was it?"

"Didn't you see it?"

Gates sighed. "I caught a really nifty look at the barrel. You know, that big gaping hole where the bullets come out? I didn't think to check out the make and model."

"It's a Beretta compact. A Cheetah three-eighty. Mag holds seven, one up the pipe."

A knock at the door.

"Want me to get that?" asked the brunette.

Gates heaved out of his chair. "Seems I need the exercise."

A pretty young thing with thick blond hair and a nice figure appeared in the hall. She had on a black tee shirt, a pair of those fancy jeans ladies wear to show off their calves, and pricey-looking heels. "Mr. Gates?" she said in a soft voice.

"Can I help you?"

"I was wondering…if this isn't a good time—"

"Were you downstairs during the shooting?"

"That's why I came to see you."

"You really need to get with your attorney –"

She blinked. "My *attorney*?"

"Do you intend to press charges? Sue the restaurant?"

"You risked your life down there. I just wanted to thank you personally."

"*Thank* me?" Gates took a step back.

"That was really brave. You could've been killed."

Gates straightened, adding an inch or two to his height. "It was nothing."

Hawk held back a grin.

"It was, to *me*…"

"C'mon in," Gates said.

***

His smile warmed her immediately.

A tiny crescent-shaped dimple marked each cheek. His long-lashed dark-brown eyes settled on her.

He wasn't alone in the room. The big, broad-shouldered deputy who arrested the gunman blocked the front window. A delicate-looking woman about forty with thick brown hair sat in a chair beside a large wooden desk.

The deputy checked his watch. Trying not to stare, no doubt—unlike that Joe guy she had just talked to. The brunette watched her, too.

Darn. Lost your concentration again... I should have made the twins smaller.

"Have a seat," Mr. Gates said.

She lowered herself into an armchair.

"What's your name?"

"Tiffany." Should she tell them her real name? Or the one she changed it to in Hollywood?

"Just Tiffany?"

"Sedarski." Strange. She hadn't used that name in years. For some reason, it didn't make her feel self-conscious right now.

"I better head on back down, finish doin' my job," the deputy said. "Sure you don't need to get yourself checked out?" he asked Mr. Gates.

"I'm fine. It'll be a different story when the lawsuits start pouring in. Then I'll need a shrink and a case full of pharmaceuticals."

"Like I said, no one got shot or hurt bad. Don't make a lick of sense—not with that room bein' so crowded. The

267

sighting on Trent's gun mighta been a hair off, for all we know."

Tiffany tried hard not to smile.

"You might wanna get in touch with your insurance carrier, though," the deputy said. "Give 'em a heads-up." He tipped his hat and let himself out.

"You don't have to stay, Kathryn," Mr. Gates told the lady.

"Will you be all right?"

"Eventually. We'll have to close for a while."

"How do you want to handle the employees?"

"Everyone can use a vacation for a few days. I know I can."

"That sounds good. It'll give us time to find a cleaning service and someone to repair the tile and replace the chandeliers and everything else Mr. Trent shot up."

"You need a vacation too, Kathryn. Take a week off."

"Who'll make all these calls while I'm gone?"

"What calls?"

"A cleaning service. The tile and chandelier people. The insurance adjusters."

"You're hired."

"I already work here."

"Even better. Come in bright and early tomorrow morning."

"You don't want me working half-days until we reopen?"

"If you don't come in when you're supposed to, I'll have a talk with my manager and get him to—"

"Your manager's a woman."

"Get her, then, to dock your pay."

She frowned. "She'll *never* agree to that."

268

"That's right. She's cold and hard, isn't she?"

"I honestly don't know how you put up with her."

As soon as they were alone, Mr. Gates opened a cabinet door behind the desk, removed a pint bottle of Jack Daniel's and brought it over. "Want one?"

"Please."

He left the room and came right back with two glasses.

He poured and handed her a glass. "Now, Ms. Tiffany Sedarski, tell me a story."

"A...story?"

He sat in the brunette's chair and sipped the whiskey. "Tell me why you're really here." His eyes stayed on her.

Suddenly nervous, she drank some of the strong drink to give her courage.

This obviously wouldn't be as easy as she thought.

But she was mature, resourceful. She'd been this way since she was eight years old, when her new stepfather bullied his way into her life.

You've been on your own since before you turned sixteen. You did well, too—even without a formal education. You made it across the country and survived four years in Hollywood without becoming a hooker or porn star. You supported yourself honestly and without regret. If you hadn't trusted the wrong people, who knows where you'd be?

They killed her, but she had found her way back. If she kept her head and thought this through, she might even be able to stay here.

No, this wouldn't be easy. But the most worthwhile things never were.

"I was attacked...in your bar," she said softly, her pulse hastening.

CHAPTER 37

Chip Chats with the Local Chaps

The recently renovated three-story block building marked *Raven Police Department* sat proudly behind its trimmed bushes. The modern windows shimmered in the sun. The brightly painted gold block walls gleamed. The new shingled roof sparkled.

Half a dozen police cruisers filled most of the spaces out front. The vacant stall, painted *MAYOR OF RAVEN* in white block letters, sat just a few feet from the front steps of the building. Next to it, spaces for the Mayor's secretary and several city employees provided eight more.

Despite Chip's initial misgivings, Litany's suggestion made sense. They could cover more ground this way. However, what happened at Denner's still puzzled him. He didn't believe her when she told him she hadn't interfered with the shooting. She avoided his eyes, which made him suspicious. She definitely had a problem lying. Which wasn't surprising. The babe just wasn't demon material.

No problem. He could fix that if he had enough time.

He decided to give her some slack. Gutril had dealt her a bad hand down in the Valley.

Chip had a soft spot for women—no doubt because they loved flowers.

Inside the building, uniformed officers and men in suits wandered up and down the aisles. Two females sat at desks, handling calls. A wide aisle behind the reception area led to glass cubicles. Men in plain clothes slouched in front of portable TV sets displaying gray screens and tiny white lettering.

A busty redhead in a sleeveless white blouse chatted away on her phone. Bracelets, rings, several tattoos, and gold necklaces decorated her flesh. She put down the phone and asked what he wanted.

"That dude they just brought in. The one who turned the restaurant into a garbage dump."

"Yes?"

"I need to talk to him."

She stared at his clothes. "You from the *Gazette*? I don't remember seein' ya before."

She actually thinks I'm a reporter? That's even more insulting than Epiphany telling me I'm messy looking.

Everyone knew reporters were genuine dorks.

This called for a little trickery. But first, some distraction...

He tilted his head. "Do you know you only have one eyebrow?"

"Oh, *cripe*..." She yanked open a drawer. A pocket mirror magically appeared in her hand. She stiffened at her reflection. "So-called *buds* of mine." She opened another drawer and unclasped a large brown handbag. "Won't even let ya know when somethin's wrong..."

"Some people," he said.

She was too busy fumbling with her makeup kit to reply.

Now that she was preoccupied, a quick wardrobe change was in order...

A lawyer, maybe? They were slightly higher up the food chain. Lawyers were dorks, too. But they got things done without too much fuss and didn't upset as many people. He probably couldn't get to see the shooter otherwise.

Since the other two females were busy typing or talking on the phone, Chip covered himself in a tan suit and slipped quietly down the aisle.

A tangle of male humanity blocked the hall.

"Help ya?" asked a pencil-thin guy in baggy slacks. The knot of his striped tie was pulled down, exposing a large Adam's apple.

"The man just brought in. I'd like to see him."

"And who might you be?"

"I'm a lawyer from Columbus." Columbus, as he remembered, sat in the center of Ohio. It was huge and crowded. Probably boasted a bumper crop of lawyers. "I was just notified that—"

"Lawyer?"

Three simultaneous frowns. Everyone knew about lawyers.

"What firm?"

Time for a little fun. This batch looked like they could use some entertainment.

"Feeny, Feeny, Feeny and Fromm."

"And you're from Columbus?"

"Yeppers." He was surprised they remembered.

"You got here fast."

Chip shrugged. "Traffic was light."

A tall, sloppy-dressed guy with thinning black hair stepped into the picture. "Who notified you? And would ya mind showing us some ID?"

Chip pulled an imaginary billfold from his imaginary jacket pocket. He flipped it open. The first guy grabbed his wrist. Chip thought up something impressive and pocketed the billfold when the man released him.

"Who are ya? Feeny? Or Fromm?"

"I'm Fred Feeny. Frank's my father, who founded the firm. Frank and Ernest Fromm were forced to do some fancy finagling when they were figuring out how to finance the firm. Frank and Ernest are from downtown Frankfurt. I'm Phil's younger brother. Foley's the oldest but didn't want to have anything to do with law. Foley fixes fine furniture for his favorite friends."

A short silence. They looked confused and uncomfortable.

The tall, sloppy-dressed guy stared at Chip. "Your firm's in Columbus?"

"Yepperino."

"And you came from there to get here?"

"Actually, I came from Finley."

More bewildered looks.

"What's there?"

"My sisters Francine, Frieda, Fiona and Frederica live there. Figure I'd spend some time fraternizing with them. Family, you know? Family folks tend to fully frazzle a fella. Is there any way for me to talk to the suspect? I'm kinda rushed, fellas."

A flurry of puzzled looks. Chip knew he should act more dignified, even for a lawyer. But he just couldn't help himself.

"Better call Joe. He doesn't like it when –"

"Isn't that him outside?" Chip pointed to the glass doors.

"Joe? Outside?"

Chip winked. "As opposed to Joe inside."

More befuddled looks.

Chip figured the Joe dude was the guy at Denner's who couldn't pull his eyes from Trinity's perky puppies.

"Large square head? Low simian brow? Stupid-looking? With a huge butt?"

One of the men said, "Thought I just saw him in his office."

"I just saw somebody out front."

"He didn't say anything about leavin' yet."

"Wouldn't put it past him. He doesn't even wanna be here today."

"I'll go see if that's him…"

CHAPTER 38

Darcy's Rules

The wooden bench on East Main afforded Darcy a terrific view of the restaurant entrance.

Fifty feet away, paramedics escorted several customers outside and helped them into two of the three medical units waiting at the curb. Four other paramedics carried two elderly women on stretchers and slid them carefully into the back of the third unit.

Darcy's nerves still tingled. It was almost like being trapped in a *Die Hard* movie with people screaming and trampling one another while someone shot at everyone in sight.

Just like the food fight in the church cellar—

Oh my God. If that demon guy caused the food fight, did he also cause this?

And if he really is *a demon, who was the blond lady? Is she also a demon?*

No way. She has to be some sort of angel—or maybe a benevolent spirit. Only an angel would have helped Darcy outside Neely's.

But she hadn't come outside. Darcy had been sitting here for nearly twenty minutes now and hadn't seen any sign of her. But just a few minutes ago, her redheaded companion came out and disappeared around the corner.

If the blond lady was hurt, she would already have been brought out.

But that made no sense. If she was an angel, she *couldn't* be hurt.

So why hadn't she come out?

275

"This town's totally freaking me out, big-time." Her arms crossed in front of her, Sheila paced just a few feet from Darcy's bench. "Food fights. Shootings. It's like we're trapped inside a bad video game!"

Darcy said nothing. She was still watching for the blond lady.

"You're doing a number on me, too," Sheila said.

"How?"

"Like, we're in the restaurant, and suddenly some dude in a suit goes all schizoid with a fucking gun. Now here you are, mellow and serene."

"I beat you out here, didn't I?"

"Only because I had to climb over two blue-hairs fighting to get their walkers untangled."

"Then what's the problem?"

"You don't look like you're coming out of your skin. You look like—shit, you look like you always do."

"We got out in time," Darcy said. "That's the important thing."

Sheila sighed. "Wanna split before a bomb goes off or something? My ride's right across the street."

"I think I'll stay here a while longer."

"I just don't get you sometimes. We almost—"

"Hi, there." He appeared behind Sheila, his crinkly eyes sparkling in the sun.

Sheila spun around. "You again?" She gawked at Darcy. "Darce? How'd he...I didn't even hear someone..." She backed up toward the curb. Heedless of the passing traffic, she dashed across the street.

"When are you going to totally stop *doing* that?" Darcy wanted to scratch his eyes out.

"The popping-up thing?"

"Yes, dammit..."

"Whenever you tell me to."

"Stop doing it. It's annoying."

"No problem."

"And no more magic tricks."

"Magic tricks?"

"Disappearing. Making weird stuff happen. Mimicking my voice. Hurting people. It's so *freaky*..."

"I take it you saw what just happened," he said, grinning.

"I was *in* there!" It came back in a rush. His smugness and that stupid grin made her skin stand out in red blotches. "I could've been *killed*. My *friend* could've been killed. Why'd you *do* that?"

"I always get a little perturbed when someone interrupts my shtick."

Unbelievable. "You mean you did that because of what happened in front of Neely's?"

"We were having such a nice little talk—"

"You're an idiot."

He flinched. "But...it's what I do..."

His reaction betrayed him, told her he was sensitive. Weird. Demons were sensitive? Awesome. This suggested that she just might have the advantage. If he wanted to be her demon, she should be able to keep him in check while she thought up a scheme to get rid of him.

"You really want to stay here?" she asked.

"That would be *so* far out..."

"Then you have to do what I say. Isn't that what you told me in my bedroom?"

"I don't remember."

"Otherwise, you'll have to find someone else or go back where you came from."

His eyes grew. "Does this mean you want me?"

277

"Only if you agree to my conditions."

"Cool beans."

"Then you'll do everything I say?"

"Just lay it all out, baby."

"No more sneaking into my bedroom?"

"Check."

"Popping up when I'm with my friends?"

"Roger Wilco."

"Terrific. You can start by giving me back my space."

"Your space?"

"I like my privacy. Get lost for a little while. I'll call you when I need you."

"But what'll I do while—"

"Whatever you want."

"Far out." That creepy grin again.

"As long as you don't hurt anyone or cause people to do anything stupid."

"But—"

"Get to know the town. Make some friends."

"Make...*friends*?"

"Friends. Chums. Pals."

"We don't do *pals* down there..."

"You're up here, now, so you have to behave. I'll let you know when I need you."

"How?"

"I'll call your name. Three times, right?"

"Right."

Off to her right, one of the paramedics leaned against the first medical unit, talking on a cell phone. When she turned back to where the demon guy was standing, he was gone.

That was easy.

Or was it?

"You'd *better* not pull that invisible stuff again…"

His form reappeared in front of the Savings & Loan half a block down. He smiled sheepishly. "Can't blame a guy for trying."

She glared.

Head down, he limped away.

Her father's white Dodge Ram pulled up to the curb. "You okay?" Dad looked frightened. "I just heard. Some psycho—"

"I'm fine, Dad."

He sat back in his seat, pulled off his smudged red baseball cap and rubbed his scalp. "Just got back from Wheeling. Your mom told me what she heard." He stuck the cap back on. "Said you were in town. You weren't close, were you?"

"Sheila and I were window-shopping." Sometimes it was best to lie. Dad didn't need more stress right now.

"Climb in," he said. "Let's get you home."

She snuck a quick glance at the restaurant. Still no sign of the blond lady. "I thought I'd just hang around here and—"

"C'mon. Your mother 's holdin' supper."

CHAPTER 39

The Hero Cop of Belmont County

His feet propped up, Joe Flynn finished his second glass of Wild Turkey and hoped he could get the hell out of here before too long.

Damn that George Trent!

Joe hated being hauled in on a Sunday. Weekends were strictly for kicking back and watching sports on the flat screen. And, of course, soaking up the suds at Vinnie's Tavern every Friday and Saturday night.

And when you were known as the "hero cop of Belmont County," you did as you damned well pleased.

Joe's claim to fame took place outside Vinnie's five years back. Joe was shacked up with two local chicks, Hildy and Tildy, at the Shamrock Motel behind Vinnie's, on Belmont County Road. As usual, he'd brought along the old '79 Ford pickup for the occasion. It was important, keeping a low profile. He also wore his civvies—at least for the first five minutes.

Later, an elderly guest spotted six people standing around the open trunk of a TransAm, sharing a joint. The police were called, the DEA in Columbus notified.

Joe, in his slacks and shirt, was ready for a second trip to the ice machine when his cell went off. It took only seconds to reach the crime area. Since his handcuffs and plastic zip-ties were being used on Hildy and Tildy for entertainment purposes, he was unable to properly restrain any of the suspects. However, he always carried his gun, and it didn't take much time to get it. He was able to hold the suspects at bay until the DEA and the local cops arrived. Since everyone was stoned, no one resisted. More

280

than half a million dollars' worth of cocaine sat in plastic bags in the trunk of the TransAm.

Joe instantly became the local celebrity. The networks and news stations in the tri-state area covered his life story and career highlights. His high school wrestling pics were printed on the front page of the Raven *Gazette*.

The *Gazette* also included a photo of Joe standing over a huge bull elk one of his buddies had shot on a recent hunting expedition. Joe posed with his trusty Winchester 30-30, his Coors baseball cap dangling from an antler. The caption read, "*Joe Bags a Big One!*" No one seemed to care that Flynn wasn't the one who had actually "bagged" the thousand-pound animal. The only thing that mattered was the cocaine taken out of circulation.

In gratitude for his "performance in the face of adversity and great personal danger," Joe landed the position of chief law enforcement officer.

Not bad for a good ol' boy from Moundsville who had barely graduated from high school by the skin of his teeth.

Slouched a little more than usual, Hawk came in.

"Drink?" Joe knew Hawk wouldn't want one but figured he should at least offer.

"No, thanks." Hawk remained standing. He never sat unless invited.

Joe pulled a small cigar from his shirt pocket. "Damn busy weekend. Kids messin' up Main Street. Ol' Elroy tearin' up a church cellar. Now we got George Trent, our number one banker buddy, shootin' up our best restaurant." He lit the cigar. "Make sense to you?"

Hawk cracked open a window. Cigar smoke really bugged him, poor schnook. "None at all."

"Trent ain't talkin', by the way."

"He's probably waitin' for his attorney to show. What did he have to drink?"

"Barman said one Scotch rocks, double shot."

"Drugs, maybe?"

"Trent? C'mon…"

"Gates said Trent looked spacey."

"Gates?"

"Restaurant owner. Took the gun from Trent."

"Gates mighta been a little shaken at the time. You tend to be when you're starin' down the wrong end of a gun barrel."

"Gates was makin' sense while I was there…"

"Don't matter. Trent's strictly booze. Anyway, once Bill Elliot has a chat with him and the county shrink's brought in, Trent's their problem."

"What about Gates?"

"What about him?"

"He's gonna have problems."

Joe pushed some smoke toward the ceiling. "We all got problems."

"He can't get his place cleaned up, he has to sell. Some jerk buys it, can't make a go of it, and sells to a developer. Things go south from there."

"Won't happen. Mayor wants the place."

"Gates told me about Trent's proposal. What's goin' on?"

"How the hell should *I* know? The Mayor wants somethin'? He gets it. This oughta be a great time to pick it up."

A knock at the door. Ernie Travis stuck his head through the opening. "You in here, Chief?"

Joe sighed. "I'll letcha guess."

"Everyone says you're outside."

Sometimes Travis worried him.

"Pay attention, now. This is me, okay? I'm right here. I can't be outside if I'm here, right? Now…what's up?"

"Couple *Gazette* reporters say there's a lawyer here from Columbus."

"Trent's supposed to be talking to Bill Elliot – no one else."

"He said he wanted to talk to George."

"Don't sound right."

Travis scratched the back of his head.

"Somethin' else?"

"I dunno…"

"Spill it."

"It's about Nance."

"What's wrong with Nance?"

"She's walkin' around with one regular eyebrow and the other one lookin' like a squished caterpillar, and she's actin' really whacked out. I'm wonderin', maybe I oughta say somethin'…"

"You wanna live?"

"Well, yeah…"

"Then keep your big mouth shut. You know how females are." Joe stubbed out his stogy and got up. "Let's check out this lawyer fella."

CHAPTER 40

A Dissatisfied Customer

Louis was proud of his restaurant. He had had good luck building a great customer base and choosing loyal employees. Except for Antoine, everyone got along. Sal, the barman, wasn't the type to let anything weird or unpleasant go on in his room. Sal came from Bridgeport. He had worked as a longshoreman for a few years, boxed a little in the Navy and had been tending bar the last twenty years. If someone wasn't behaving himself, Louis was certain the troublemaker would be tossed out onto the street.

But as Louis stared at the beautiful young woman in the chair facing him, he could tell something had happened to put the worry in those big blue eyes.

"Someone actually *attacked* you?" he asked.

Tiffany Sedarski fidgeted. "Yes," she said softly.

"Didn't the barman see any of this going in?"

"He might have been busy at the time. My table…it was off to the side, behind the main doorway. It was kinda dark over there–"

"This guy who attacked you. Ex-husband? Boyfriend?"

"Just some guy who approached me just before the shooting."

She was obviously having trouble talking about this. She glanced at the door—definite proof that she was frightened. Either that or she was a damned good actress. And with those looks, she really ought to be. She looked every bit as good as one of those babes peddling perfume on TV. Or that drop-dead blonde he remembered last year doing that underarm spray commercial.

Why didn't she tell Hawkins about this?

Maybe she figured the owner of the place would do something about it. Maybe she wanted to tell Sal but in the heat of the fireworks, forgot all about it. Sal might have told her to come up and tell Louis her story.

Sounded reasonable. Louis really should be the one taking care of this. He was the boss, wasn't he? Like it or not, being the boss came with a few unpleasant responsibilities.

Couldn't have some asshole accosting his customers, could he?

At least this girl was honest enough to tell him about this in person. Someone else might have decided to let their attorney handle matters.

This made him appreciate her even more. "Is he a local?"

"I just got in town this morning."

"Where'd you come from?"

She hesitated. "California."

"You're a long way from home."

"You have no idea," she said softly.

"Tell me more about him."

"He saw me sitting alone and joined me without even asking. I tried being nice, even excused myself, but I just couldn't shake him. I guess the shooting turned out to be good for me. He just disappeared."

"I'm glad it was good for *some*one." Louis had another slug of Jack's.

"I'm so sorry…I didn't mean—"

"I know what you meant. What does he look like?"

"He's tall and thin. And he's got a bad temper."

"Whaddya mean?"

"When I got up to leave, he grabbed me and pushed me back down."

"He…grabbed you?"

She twisted in her seat and hiked up her shirt.

Over her lower ribs, a discolored imprint the size of a fist marked her smooth, pink flesh.

CHAPTER 41

Fred Feeny Flees the Fuzz

The small room marked *Interview* blazed with light from the overhead fluorescents.

The shooter hunched over the table. He didn't look anything like a shooter.

"*You're* our man of the hour?" Chip closed the door behind him.

No response.

"If you aren't, you picked a lousy place for a nap."

A mumble.

"I'll bet you'd rather be anywhere else right now."

"Yeah," came the muffled reply.

"Care to tell me what happened?"

He raised his head and squinted. "I was expecting Bill Elliot."

Who's Bill Elliot?

"He…couldn't come right now."

"Who are you?"

"I'm Fred Feeny. Call me Fred. Or call me Feeny. Hell, call me anything but late for dinner."

He blinked. "You're a *lawyer*?"

"If I'm not, I spend entirely too much time in courtrooms. And way too much money on fancy clothes."

"What kind of lawyer are you?"

"The kind who doesn't take life too seriously. If you knew me, you'd understand why."

"Fred Feeny?"

"Good memory."

"Never heard of you."

"I'm from out of town."

"I don't understand."

"Not local. I'm visiting. Taking advantage of the local color."

"Bill Elliot's the only one who should be talking to me. I'm his client. I don't even know you."

"But I've heard of *you*. You're the guy who shot up the town's favorite restaurant."

He sat back and groaned.

"Now that we've got the formalities out of the way, let's get down to business," Chip said. "Tell me what happened."

He rubbed his eyes. "I don't know what happened. And I'm only supposed to be talking to Bill Elliot."

"You just went into the restaurant and started shooting?"

"It…didn't happen like that. I intend to tell Bill all that when he gets here."

"Where'd you get the gun?"

"I brought it in."

"Interesting."

"But I don't know *why*..."

"Whose gun was it?"

"Mine."

"What were you doing with it?"

"I have it for protection. Carjackings—that sort of thing."

"Car…*jackings*?" *What was this?*

"Where have *you* been?" The shooter looked confused.

"Uh, out of the country, representing Arabs with mental issues and really bad hygiene. Enlighten me."

The shooter shrugged. "Someone robs you while you're sitting in your car. Don't tell me you've never heard of that."

"Isn't that called, um, robbery?"

"A robbery is when someone takes your money, watch, or jewelry. A carjacking is when the jerk points a gun in your face, tells you to get out of your car and drives off with it."

"Kind of risky…"

"For who?"

"The guy stealing the car."

"It's not exactly a picnic in the park for the owner. It's declined slightly, but it still happens. I don't want it happening to me. That Vette cost me a fortune."

Chip was amazed. In fifty years, they had forgotten all about the Bomb. Now their attention centered on cell phones, paying for things that used to be free, and making off with one another's cars…

"You keep your gun in your car?"

"Always."

"Why take it in the restaurant?"

"Haven't you been listening? I already said—"

"You just wanted to feel safe."

"That's about it."

"Then why did you take it out and start shooting?"

"Three guys at the next table were talking about someone. That's when my head sort of went fuzzy. They didn't know me—why would they be talking about me?"

"That's when you started shooting?"

"It was…a total blank. Now, if you'll excuse me, I intend to rest until Bill comes in and asks me what he needs to know." The shooter lowered his head and buried his face in his forearms.

Footsteps in the hall.

The door swung open.

***

With Hawk close behind, Joe Flynn pushed open the door.

No one there but Trent slumped head-down at the table. A wooden chair sat just a few feet from the door.

Joe rubbed his brush cut. Something odd here. "Who brought this in?"

"Wasn't here before?" Hawk asked.

"These rooms all have three chairs. One for the suspect, two for the interviewers."

"Coupla rooms have four."

"Even so, the fourth should be in the corner. Looks like somebody dragged it over. Why would someone do that with two at the table?"

"Last visitor we had was—"

"Me," Joe said. "With Travis outside."

Trent raised his head and blinked. "Where's the other guy?"

"What other guy?"

"He was skinny, with wild red hair. Feeny, his name was. Dressed in a tan suit. Said he was an attorney. He asked me all sorts of questions. Then you guys showed up."

"No one came out."

"He was here a second ago…"

"Where'd he go?"

"No idea."

Joe was getting perturbed by all this weird nonsense. Food fights in the church. A shoot-em-up in Denner's. Now a lawyer from Columbus hears about this, gets here damn quick, cons his way in, and asks Trent questions

Bill Elliot should be asking. And no one knows where the hell he is. "He just disappeared?" he asked.

"Like I said, I don't know. He asked his questions and when we were finished, I put my head down. Then you two came in."

"Hawk, go check around."

Hawk left the room.

Joe lowered his butt into the chair. It creaked loudly—even felt rubbery and bowing beneath his weight. He straightened. What the hell? Sucker was about to collapse. He pushed it behind the door. The wood felt soft and clammy. Had a weird smell, too. Somebody probably left it out in the rain. He'd have Maintenance stick it in the trash.

Joe pulled out another chair and sat carefully, facing Trent. "Anything comin' atcha ya couldn't remember before?"

"Like I told that Feeny guy, I don't know anything. I'm really tired. Any way I can get some sleep?"

"It would help if ya told us somethin'." Joe lowered his voice. "Mayor's gonna hound my ass to death about this."

Trent rubbed his eyes vigorously and yawned.

Hawk came back in.

"Find anyone?" Joe asked.

"Not a thing." Hawk looked around. "What did you do with that chair?"

"Pushed it over there." Joe pointed to the empty area behind Hawk.

Gone. The short reddish hairs on the back of Joe's neck bristled.

"What'd it do?" Hawk asked. "Walk out?"

Joe jumped up. "You ain't playin' games, are ya?"

291

"Joe," Hawk said, "when I left this room, there were four chairs. Now there are three. *I* see three. How many do *you* see?"

Suddenly nauseous, Joe sat back down. Drinking too much Wild Turkey, obviously. Or smoking too many of those damn Italian cigars.

He had a feeling he ought to stop doing *some*thing for a while.

CHAPTER 42

Tiffany Works Her Magic

"That jerk did *that* to you?" Mr. Gates's beautiful dark-brown eyes had grown as he stared at Tiffany's flesh.

Tiffany covered her imaginary bruise with her imaginary tee shirt. She hated lying but knew it was necessary. She wanted him to feel sorry for her and tell her she could stay here, where she'd be safe. Later she would tell him the real story. Maybe he would believe her and feel sorry for what the wolf guy had done. She would just have to be convincing enough where—

Her powers. They had just slipped her mind. She just used them to create an imaginary bruise. She had also used them to save this man's life. For some reason, she hadn't thought about using them for her ultimate plan.

You didn't have to be convincing when you had powers.

"He didn't tell you his name?" he asked.

"No."

"He didn't say anything about himself? Where he lives?"

"I didn't like him, so I didn't say much. If you don't encourage conversation, a guy will usually take the hint. But not him."

"But you obviously did something to make him—"

Please let me stay here with you...

He stopped talking. His eyes stayed on her. They had gone blank. He seemed almost hypnotized.

She hoped she hadn't done anything stupid. Or that she had hurt him in any way. That was the problem when you had new powers. You didn't know exactly how much to use.

"You're staring," she said softly. *Please. Show me you're all right. I have to know if I gave you a concussion or did something to your memory.* "Do you feel okay?"

"Sorry." He blinked. "I'm fine."

She sighed in relief. "You looked…funny."

"I just can't believe anybody could be violent with someone like you."

Her face grew warm.

He finished his drink. "I…didn't mean anything by that—"

"It's all right. That was very nice…" She couldn't remember the last time a man said something like that. The fake compliments she heard when she was alive had made her distrustful. When you put up barriers, they kept out everyone.

"Hawkins needs to know about this." He got up. "Or would you like me to take you to the Police Station so you can swear out a complaint?"

"That's really not necessary."

"He *hurt* you. We *can't* let him get away with this."

"Can we do it tomorrow? I think I'll feel better after some rest."

***

Louis massaged his temples.

The increasing dizziness had turned everything into a soft shade of gray. He should have gone in for a checkup after all.

No. This was something else. Something other than cracking his head on Trent's elbow. Or staring down a gun barrel.

The only thing he could focus on was the gorgeous young woman sitting just a couple of feet away, watching him.

This had nothing to do with what happened downstairs. He felt sorry for her. And a hot surge of anger for the idiot that had branded her flesh. She came to his place for a drink; she didn't deserve to stumble across a stalker or be caught up in George Trent's psychotic episode.

"If you need a place to stay, I can put you up. This apartment has a spare room."

She pushed her hair over one shoulder. He had obviously embarrassed her.

"There's a lock on the door," he added.

"Oh, I'm not worried about *that*..."

"Is something else bothering you?"

"Nothing."

"Now *you're* the one looking funny."

She shrugged. "This is nice of you."

"It's no big deal. You need a place to crash. You don't have a change of clothes—"

"I...left my stuff downstairs." Her eyes closed. When they opened, they were moist. She had been through more than enough for one day.

"You'd better lie down. You must be exhausted."

He led her down the carpeted hall, to the last door on the right. "It even has its own bathroom."

She followed him in. "Mr. Gates?"

"Lou."

"Thanks...Lou..."

He smiled.

She sat on the mattress. "It's much softer than – than the last one I slept in." She smiled. A strong innocence

295

emanated from her. He wondered if her father had experienced the same thing when his beautiful daughter started going on dates.

He couldn't imagine taking advantage of such an incredible woman.

"You're not leaving, are you?" she asked. "The apartment, I mean."

"I'll probably just turn in." Best stick around. She probably wouldn't want to be alone in a strange place. "It's been a rough day for me, too."

"I'll bet. You look exhausted."

"Are you hungry? There's a kitchen downstairs stocked with tons of food no one's gonna be eating for a while."

"Thanks. I'm all right."

He went back out.

"Lou?"

"Yeah?"

"You really are nice, you know."

"My mother told me to treat women with respect."

She tilted her head. Her hair slid down her shoulder. "*All* the time?"

He felt his pulse hasten. "Most of the time…"

"Well-behaved guys are boring."

"No one's ever accused me of *that*…"

"I figured that out when I saw you wrestling that guy."

"The place needed livening up." He went into his own room, lay down, and tried focusing on more important issues.

The restaurant, for instance. And the lawsuits. Accepting Trent's offer now would probably be the sensible thing to do. And probably the cheapest.

His thoughts automatically shifted to Tiffany. He had never met a woman so good-looking who was so *nice*. That combination didn't seem possible. The few gorgeous women he knew had been pampered, self-absorbed, and shallow. His father once told him that all women were crazy. The better-looking the woman, the crazier she was.

So why didn't Tiffany seem crazy?

Why did she seem so *unreal*?

PART IV - THE SEARCH ENDS

CHAPTER 43

The Committee Regroups

A silver buffet cart filled with steaming food and a large pot of the Club's special brand of Colombian coffee sat in front of the bay window in the Gold Room.

No one spoke. Everyone quietly chose what they wanted, went back to the table, sat, and picked at his food.

Noel Thomas finally broke the tense stillness. "Does anyone know what happened?"

"Doesn't matter, does it?" Miles Ladner smeared cream cheese on his garlic bagel.

"Baffling," Leonard Winslow said. "Trent? Come on…"

Holeridge barely noticed the food on his plate. He was struggling to rationalize Trent's unexpected rampage yesterday in Denner's. Trent was low-keyed and as calm as they came. It simply defied reason. It was even more baffling than the food fight at the church. "I know it's incredible, but we have to face facts. It happened."

"What the hell was that idiot doing with a gun?" Augustus Phelps asked. "A *bank manager* carrying a *gun*? Preposterous."

"He has a carry permit." Holeridge immediately realized how ludicrous that sounded.

"A carry permit allows you to have it on your person. It doesn't entitle you to carry it into a crowded restaurant, take it out, and actually *fire* it."

"That's what concerns me," Holeridge said. "The fact that Trent actually did it."

"He flipped out," Noel said. "It's that simple."

"Trent's one of the most level-headed men I know," Miles said.

"Maybe," agreed Ira. "But he was showing clear signs of stress at our last meeting."

"In what way?"

"Dragging his feet over our restaurant proposal."

"What does that have to do with anything?" Holeridge asked.

"Something was obviously bothering him."

"He felt uncomfortable about asking Gates to sell off his dream." Holeridge shrugged.

"But would he shoot up the place just because of that?"

"This really troubles me," Leonard Winslow said softly. "It's another sign."

"You and your damned signs." Miles tossed it aside with a wave of his hand.

"Bill, you talked to Trent," Augustus said. "Can you tell us anything?"

"Client privilege," Elliot replied. "We scheduled a series of tests with the court psychiatrist after our consultation. That's all I can say."

"Good thing he didn't actually kill anyone."

"Does Stokely know about this?" Ira picked up a sausage link.

"I contacted him," Holeridge said. "He told me he'll do what he can to ensure the bank isn't affected."

"Let's get back to the restaurant." Miles picked up his bagel. "It's the main reason we called this meeting."

Holeridge shuffled over to the buffet for a coffee refill. "I think a different approach is in order. We've been proceeding too cautiously. It's time to get serious."

"Serious how?" Bill Elliot asked. "We never abandon caution. It'll be catastrophic if anyone discovers what the Diocese really is."

Holeridge put down his cup and sat. "No one will find out. Don't forget how old the Legion is. When Old Joe revamped the Order nearly a hundred years ago—"

"I'm not forgetting," Bill Elliot said. "But as an attorney, I know from experience not to underestimate people. Even the stupidest individual shows signs of brilliance at the most inopportune times."

"It's imperative to be cautious," Miles said. "Shit happens the moment you lower your guard."

His appetite returning, Holeridge picked up a sausage link. "Don't worry, I'm thinking clearly on this."

"Tell us what's on your mind," Noel said.

"Bill?" Holeridge asked. "Anything to contribute?"

Elliot unbuttoned his dark blue Baroni jacket and leaned back. "Gates faces lawsuits from every person in that room for what happened yesterday. This'll hang him up for months—perhaps years. His legal expenses will put him in the poorhouse. He won't be able to reopen and will be forced to sell."

Holeridge had a slug of coffee. "Then our worries are over."

"If," Augustus said, "he sells to *us*."

"Two things we're not considering." Alan Crenshaw smeared whipped butter over his English muffin. "What if no one wants to sue?"

"Wouldn't *you* consider a suit if *you* were there during the shooting?" Holeridge asked.

"I was there," Ira said. "I'm not considering it."

"Why not?"

"For one thing, I was able to get out in time. For another, I wasn't hurt. And lastly, it wasn't Gates's fault. This was all on Trent."

"Whose side are you on?" asked Augustus.

Ira shrugged. "I'm a storeowner. I can relate."

"There's the possibility Gates might try something to appease everyone," Elliot said.

"Such as?" Holeridge asked.

"Offering his customers something for their troubles. A free meal, for example."

"You think that would *work*?" Leonard asked.

Ira nodded. "It would work."

Noel laughed. "When I offer a ten percent discount on a few select items in the hardware store, the place is flooded for days. And if I toss some things into a bin, drop the price five percent, and mark it Discarded or Damaged, that bin's empty in two hours."

Ira chuckled. "Folks faced with maybe winning a lawsuit after it's been hung up in court for years, then handing over most of the monies to their greedy attorneys? Or a guaranteed free meal immediately at Denner's? I know what *I'd* do."

"I resent that," Elliot said.

"You disagree that you're all greedy?"

"No, but I resent it anyway."

"What's that second item you mentioned?" Holeridge asked Alan.

"Gates might decide to clean up and reopen."

"He'd have to find a local cleaning service."

"There are dozens in the Wheeling area alone."

Holeridge ate some toast. "What if no cleaning service would venture anywhere near that restaurant?"

"How do you intend to stop a cleaning service from fulfilling a contract with a private restaurant?"

Holeridge didn't reply.

"You're considering outside help," Miles said.

"Maybe."

"Whaddya mean?" Miles deserted his bagel in favor of a cigar. "Hiring outsiders gets rid of all maybes. Idiots have stuck their big noses into the picture every damned time we've gone this route."

"We have several key people on our payroll. Their job is to keep us safe."

"I'm not forgetting that," Miles said. "But I'm nervous. The more bodies involved, the more chances for a screw- up."

"Joe Flynn won't let us down," Holeridge said.

"Not as long as we keep bribing him," Miles said.

Leonard shrugged. "It's like giving a dog a bone. The man's a Neanderthal."

"He knows how to keep his mouth shut," Holeridge said.

"We could use Hawkins on our side," Augustus said. "He's much higher on the food chain. If Flynn hadn't lucked into that cocaine bust, we'd be dealing with Hawkins."

"The man's too honest," Holeridge said. "We've tried tempting him before. He asks too many questions. Only wants to do the right thing. He can't be trusted. It's enough that he's the one actually running the Department. Flynn comes in occasionally to take the credit. Things get done. Everyone's happy."

"Let's get back on track." Bill Elliot checked his Rolex. "You mentioned an outsider. What are you planning?"

"The man I've sent for calls himself a persuader."

"A bone crusher?" Miles scowled.

"This man's subtle and discreet. A true professional."

"Where's he from?" Noel asked.

"We've used him before. About eight years ago. The Hedrick contract."

"Ah. Boy's good. Knows his stuff. He's discreet."

Noel nodded. "We didn't even know he was here until we heard the sad news about Otis."

"If you'll remember, he came to us highly recommended by our Washington contacts and our associates in Hyannis Port."

"I take it everything's all arranged," Leonard said.

Holeridge beamed with pride. "He's on his way here as we speak."

CHAPTER 44

Catty Chick Chat

Fresh and bright in her cream-colored silk blouse and gray skirt, Kathryn scratched something onto her notepad while talking softly on the phone.

Stifling a yawn, Louis poured coffee and went over to the window. Outside, the morning sun turned the roofs of the cars and pickups parked along East Main into dazzling bars of silver.

He was exhausted from a sleepless night, tossing and turning until seven-thirty as his mind relived the shooting. When he finally realized sleep was no longer possible, he decided to start the day with a warm shower. He wasn't ready to go downstairs; there was plenty of time to sift through the rubble. He wanted to enjoy his first cup of coffee.

Kathryn put down the phone. "Feeling all right?"

"Considering I was nearly shot in the face at point-blank range and will probably be sued by fifty people? As fresh as a wilted daisy. How about you?"

"No complaints. And I'm glad you think things are looking up."

"When you've just been knocked flat on your ass, there's nowhere else to look." He sat down across from her and lit a cigarette.

"Such an enlightening morsel for so early in the day." She wrote something else onto her pad. "But honestly, you really should provide less stressful entertainment for your customers. They come here to eat. Crawling on the floor in their good clothes, dodging tossed food and

304

overturned tables, doesn't do much for their digestion. Or their wardrobe."

"Maybe I'll install lava lamps or a pool table."

"That might be more restful than dodging bullets. A mechanical bull for the friskier crowd would work wonders."

Her dry wit amazed him. It made him realize how much he appreciated her.

"Who were you talking to?" he asked.

"I just got a reasonable estimate from a cleaning service."

"How about a tile guy?"

"Still working on it."

"I was told the tile's original, which makes it close to fifty years old. Matching it won't be easy."

"Healthy optimism always makes the day more pleasant."

"Tell me about the cleaning service."

She checked her notepad. "They can be out within the week. I told them what needed to be done and they said they could do it in three days."

"Now all we have to worry about is the tile. We might be able to cover the damaged places with rugs until we come up with something better."

"That sounds good."

"What about Antoine? Anyone hear from him?"

"He called this morning. When I told him what happened, he ranted about Americans being violent. He also said he couldn't possibly work with brutes, bullies, and psychopaths."

"Isn't he the same guy who sleeps with his butcher knife?"

"Different strokes, as they say."

"Too bad we couldn't get Gutier to talk some sense into him in French."

"By the way, what's happened with him?"

"No idea."

"You didn't talk to him?"

"It's hard to talk to someone who isn't there. I've done that a few times before. People assume you're mental."

"Then I take it he didn't formally quit?"

"Don't know. I won't be surprised if we never see him again."

"That's a shame. Now I've got to find someone else. In a way I guess this is a blessing. He seemed strange."

"You mean aside from his disappearing?"

"His tee shirt struck me as odd. I haven't seen an ad for Keds since I was a kid. He's much too young for that."

"Sure you're not an age bigot?"

"I don't think so…"

"A tee shirt bigot?"

"It did bring out the wild woman in me."

"Does your husband know you're a wild woman?"

"Only when he takes most of the blankets."

"We need to find another chef. I don't want to subject Morey to a double workload. That buffet restaurant in St. Clairsville keeps him busy during the week."

"Already working on it."

"You sure are earning your money. Find out anything yet?"

"Two possibles haven't returned my calls. Both work in Pittsburgh."

"Spontaneous violence shouldn't raise a wrinkle on *their* brows."

"Now that's cynical."

306

"How about that? Shoot up a guy's place, stick a gun in his face, and he turns cynical. Can't anyone take a joke these days?"

"Actually, I consider your cynicism one of your most endearing qualities."

"Then I won't subject you to any surprises by changing."

"Please don't do that unless I'm sitting down."

"You're always sitting down."

"You want me to do all this work standing up?"

"No. Please sit, by all means."

"Thank you. And speaking of surprises…what happened to your blond bombshell?"

"Good morning." Tiffany emerged from the hall and went right over to the coffee pot.

Her hair, along with everything else, looked perfect. She wore a gray silk shrug over a turquoise tank top. She also wore form-fitting Capri slacks a shade darker than the pair yesterday, and expensive-looking leather pumps.

"Where'd you get the clothes?" he asked.

"I went downstairs and found my overnight bag."

"That stuff isn't even wrinkled. It's amazing."

She sugared her coffee.

"Tiffany, you remember Kathryn Hayes."

Tiffany smiled. "Ms. Hayes."

"Just Kathryn, Ms.—"

"Please call me Tiffany."

Kathryn shifted her gaze to Louis. He recognized the look very well. Something was on her mind. Best get this out in the open right now.

"Tiffany doesn't have a place to stay. I told her she could bunk here."

"I see…"

"I've got that spare room—"

"Of course you do."

Tiffany cleared her throat. "I think I'll go freshen up."

Kathryn waited until the door closed down the hall before lowering her voice. "Lou...what do you know about her?"

"Well—"

"Where's she from?"

"She mentioned California."

"Is she married?"

"No idea."

"She's trouble."

"How can you say that? You've only seen her once..."

"Twice."

"For maybe two minutes."

"It doesn't matter."

"She's in a bind."

Kathryn blinked above her reading glasses. "A girl like her is always in a bind."

"What's wrong with helping her out?"

"A girl like her always finds someone with a soft heart."

"You keep saying 'a girl like her.' She can't help the way she looks."

"Do you honestly think she was born with those pouty lips? And talk about perky breasts... How many women are that breathtaking in the morning?"

"Maybe she's had work done."

"At her age? She isn't much older than twenty."

"What's her age got to do with—"

"Did you notice her outfit?"

308

"Do you think I'm blind?"

"Tell me what you've noticed."

He grinned. "She looks really great. Perfect. I mean wow. In fact—"

"Do I need to get a bucket of ice water?"

"You asked."

"Those pumps. They're Gucci."

"She has good taste."

"I just saw them in a catalogue. A pair like that runs close to a thousand. But I've never seen them with diamonds on the side. And those rocks look real."

"They can't be."

"Even if they aren't, the pumps look custom—like they were made specifically for her."

He shrugged. "Like I said, she's got—"

"And the pair she had on yesterday. Kitten Heels. Donald J. Pliner Viola, no less."

"What are they?"

"Three hundred, easy, I'd say."

"Like I said, she—"

"Tell me something. Haven't you known women like her before?"

"What do you mean?'"

"The kind that always has some sort of personal crisis going on."

"What if I have?"

"Have *you* ever gone through a personal crisis?"

She couldn't be serious. "Take a trip downstairs. Bring your camera."

"I had to bypass the mess on my way up, thank you."

"Your point?"

She pulled off her glasses and dropped them on the blotter. "Many women skate through life. I'd bet my next paycheck she's one of them."

"You don't know the whole story."

"Lou, you're a nice guy. I don't want to see you hurt."

"How can helping someone possibly hurt me?"

"She's a user."

"She's a sweet girl."

"I agree."

"Then why all this bashing?"

"I'm a woman. I've known one or two users."

"So have I. Not all of them are women."

"A woman has a lot more going for her. Sweetness is merely one of her weapons."

"You're awfully catty this morning."

Kathryn drank some coffee. "Have you ever seen someone like her with a flat tire on the highway?"

"Not recently…"

"You'll have to look fast. And don't blink. All she has to do is stand there looking helpless for ten seconds— less, if she's wearing shorts or a halter top. Then presto— a convoy of men appear out of the blue, fighting over her with one another."

"Like I said, you don't know the whole story."

"I have a few minutes."

"She's carrying around a bruise."

Kathryn's forehead wrinkled. "A…*bruise*?"

"One of those ugly black-and-blue things you get from a sharp blow or slap."

"I happen to know what a bruise is, thank you."

"I wondered."

"*I'm* wondering what this has to do with anything."

"She got it downstairs."

"Don't tell me she was injured while trying to get away from the shooting and now wants you to reimburse her for –"

"Someone attacked her in the bar."

"And this concerns you how?"

He couldn't believe how cold Kathryn was acting. "It happened in my bar, Kathryn. She came in for a drink and someone put the make on her. I'm taking her to the Police Station so she can give them a statement. Then they can find the jerk and get him off the street."

"Then what?"

"I'll give her bus fare."

"To where?"

"Wherever she wants to go."

She sat back and said nothing.

"Nothing wrong with *that*, is there?"

"Not as long as you don't expect to be repaid."

He finished his coffee. "I happen to think people should help one another. We're all stuck here in the same place, aren't we?"

CHAPTER 45

Tracking Down the Blond Angel

Darcy picked up her ten-year-old tan Nissan Maxima at Bob's Bodyworks on South Chestnut and drove the two blocks east on Main.

She parked across the street from Denner's. She had called the school earlier and told them she wasn't coming in because she wasn't feeling well. That wasn't the whole story, but it didn't matter. She didn't want to answer a barrage of questions about Todd and Leon.

There were more important issues to address. The weird guy Todd picked up Friday night, for instance. The guy who could read minds. And disappear. And turn you into Felix Unger. And make you think you could buy booze even though you were only eighteen.

After the food fight in the church and the shooting in Denner's, Darcy realized that weird guy actually could be a demon.

If the events during the last few days were any indication of his powers, Raven faced serious trouble.

Plus the fact that his disappearing and reappearing was bound to cause a heart attack or two if he did it in front of the right person.

The solution seemed both simple and impossible. She had to find a way to send him back where he came from.

The beautiful blond lady knew something about this. Anyone with the power to get into someone else's head had to know about demons and spells.

Denner's looked deserted. Yellow tape stretched across its front. A large square sign, **CLOSED UNTIL**

FURTHER NOTICE, showed clearly in the center of the front door beneath the green canopy.

Was the blond lady inside? Or had she left after Dad showed up yesterday afternoon?

That would just figure.

But what if she hadn't?

Darcy had to find out.

But how? What excuse could she give for going into a closed restaurant?

What if someone asked what she was doing?

Tell them the truth? *A beautiful blond lady came in here yesterday. I have to find her. You see, this guy who wants to be my personal demon bumped into Sheila and me in front of Neely's and—*

That sort of talk would get her into serious trouble.

She had to find some way of nosing around in there without arousing anyone's suspicions. It would help if she knew someone working there but she didn't—not since the place had switched hands. She didn't get to eat there very much because it was so expensive.

What about applying for a job?

They might welcome a new applicant after what happened. It was dishonest, but it would be well worth it if it got her in the door. Once she was inside, she might be able to wander around and see who was in there. And if she bumped into the blond lady—

Then what? Talk about something else that could get her into trouble?

Ma'am, I don't know who you are, but you must be an angel for what you did outside Neely's. You may not think I know what happened, but I could hear your voice inside my head—

313

That sort of talk might work if no one else was around.

But what if someone *was* wandering around? Could she bluff her way through this without looking like an idiot?

And what about the job interview?

No problem. She could call later on and tell them she wouldn't be able to work there because Mr. Crenshaw had increased her hours at the Five'n Dime.

If finding the blond lady would help rid the town of the demon, a little dishonesty might be needed to coax the process along.

CHAPTER 46

Reporting to Hawk

The nameplate on the desk said Nancy Cunningham.

The busty redhead smiled at Louis. Her large green eyes instantly checked out his gray dress shirt and black slacks. She took in Tiffany and her smile nearly dissolved. Louis thought of two jungle cats sizing up one another.

"Hawk isn't in right now," she said. "But he shouldn't be long."

"Would it be all right if we wait? We don't have anywhere else to be right now."

"That'd be fine. I'm really sorry about your place, Mr. Gates. Any idea when you'll be able to open back up?"

"It depends on how much I've got to spend to clean up. And, of course, the lawsuits."

"I'm glad no one was seriously hurt."

"So am I. My bank account's pleased as well."

"If it helps any, we're all rootin' for you."

"Thanks."

Clancy Hawkins' small office was the first room down the hall on the right. They let themselves in and took seats facing the metal desk. Tiffany crossed her legs. She glanced at the clock on the wall behind the desk, then at the half-closed window.

He caught himself staring at those shapely calves as well as her expensive-looking pumps. It made him wonder about the other stuff Kathryn had said about this girl. But it didn't matter. He didn't want anyone causing trouble at his place.

"Your manager," she said softly. "Miss Hayes?"

"What about her?"

"She doesn't like me very much."

"She doesn't even know you."

"You don't know me, either."

"I can tell you're okay."

"But you've only known me a few hours."

"I know that..."

"What *do* you know, Lou?"

"You're soft-spoken, polite, intelligent—"

"I've been told I'm dumb."

"I don't think I've ever met a dumb woman before. The few I *thought* were dumb were able to get what they wanted very easily. Anyway, you don't qualify."

"That's sweet, but you don't have to lie..."

"I'm not lying."

"You sure?" She sounded anxious. "Lots of guys lie so they—"

"I know why they lie. I'm a guy, remember?"

"But you really don't know me. How can you tell—"

"I've got what they call intuition."

Her big blue eyes stayed on him. "Isn't that something women have?"

"If all women have intuition, how come so many of them always fall for the wrong guy?"

"You're right. Before I—before I came here, I always fell for a good line."

"You definitely look the type."

"What type?"

"Easy."

She smiled. "I've been called that a lot. I don't mean to be. Things just happen. Even when I know what a guy's up to, I let him do what he wants anyway."

"Why?"

"I like being fussed over. It makes me feel special. Needed."

He stared at her. How could someone so beautiful and so nice have an inferiority complex?

"I guess that's why I'm so comfortable around you," she said. "You've been fussing over me since—"

"I figure I owe you."

"How?"

"You came to my place for a drink—not to get attacked."

"Is that the *only* reason? Because you think you owe me?"

He didn't reply. He hadn't expected things to turn in this direction so fast. Bad enough he had that brain blip the night before, back in his office.

"Well?"

Clancy Hawkins came in, thank God, and closed the door. "Sorry 'bout the wait." Hawkins ignored the protests of his chair as he settled into it. "Your friend here tells me you found yourself a gentleman a little rough around the edges," he said to Tiffany.

Tiffany glanced at Louis. "Yes, but since I've been staying with Lou, I don't think I'll have any more trouble."

"That's real nice." Hawkins's quick glance made Louis feel guilty. "But just to be safe, we oughta look into this anyway."

Tiffany nodded.

"I hear you're carryin' around a battle scar."

Another nod.

"Care to let me see it? I can have one of the ladies—"

"It's all right." Tiffany stood up slowly. Still nervous, no doubt. She hooked her fingers underneath her shirt and hiked it up just high enough to expose the bruise.

Louis blinked.

The discoloration was not only smaller than he remembered, but darker. It was also two full inches lower and shaped differently.

Hawkins shook his head. "We'll need a picture or two, ya don't mind."

"I don't mind." Tiffany covered herself and sat back down.

"Back in a sec." Hawkins left the room in three quick strides.

"Something wrong?" Tiffany asked.

"Uh…no. Why?"

"You look strange."

"I'm fine."

"You're sure?"

He wasn't sure of anything. He didn't know if it was because of his being elbowed by Trent or because this woman was having a strange effect on him. Being cracked on the forehead could have jarred his vision. But he didn't want to bring anything up right now. "Just thinking."

"About what?"

"The restaurant clean-up. That sort of thing."

"Nothing else?"

"Like what?"

"A woman?"

"What woman?"

"Don't you have someone, Lou? A girlfriend stashed somewhere?"

318

Great. The conversation was headed back there, regardless of what he wanted. He had to stop it somehow. He had enough problems. "I've never been particularly good at stashing women. They always manage to find their way out of the garment bag." He glanced at the door. No sign of Hawkins.

"Come on. A good-looking guy like you?"

"Hard to believe anyone can resist this package, huh?"

"*I* can't understand it. What's their problem?"

He shrugged. "I just always seem to have bad luck with stuff like that."

"What do they do?"

"Who?"

"The women you're having bad luck with."

"The usual stuff. Pluck their eyebrows, shave their legs, hog all the covers—"

"I *mean*, what do they do to make you think you're having bad luck with them?"

"Get married to other guys. Pack up and move. You know, things even a clueless moron can pick up on."

"You're not serious."

Clancy Hawkins finally returned carrying a small silver camera. "Okay... Time to smile and look pretty."

"You've got to be kidding," Louis said.

"I was talking to the lady."

"Good. I'm not exactly in the mood to smile or look pretty."

"Actually, I ain't exactly in the mood to *see* it."

***

Tiffany could tell Lou was upset about something. She hoped it wasn't anything she said. She knew she was

319

flirting with him, but she just couldn't help it. He was the warmest, sexiest man she had ever met.

Her appearance might be the problem. When she caught him glancing at her shirt, she suspected something about her outfit bothered him. She tried picking up his thoughts, but they were muddled. The image of her bruise seemed prevalent. Then she caught a flash of Clancy Hawkins coming back in. Maybe Lou didn't want to say anything until they were alone. Or maybe her flirting had embarrassed him.

What if it was her outfit? The pumps, maybe? Chip warned her about blending in, but she couldn't help it. She loved her new powers. They were *so* much fun...

A trip to the ladies' room might help.

After Deputy Hawkins finished taking his pictures, she excused herself and found the restrooms down the hall.

Her reflection in the smudged mirror told her she looked good. The shrug might be overkill, but it looked so great on her, and—

"What is it with you and bathrooms, muffin?"

A stall door yawned open. Chip came out dressed in a tan janitor's outfit and a white painter's cap mashed over his unruly red mop. His eyes twinkled in the overhead lighting.

"I should ask you the same thing. Nice outfit. Cleaning up?"

"Sniffing around. When you're dressed like this, no one notices you. Besides, once I found the poop on Trent, I needed to keep a low profile."

"Who?"

"The banker with the handy pocket pistol. Don't tell me you've been hauled in." He chuckled. "I knew those puppies would be trouble."

"I'm *not* being hauled in. I came over with Lou—"

"Lou?"

"Yes. Lou."

"Lou who?"

"He owns the restaurant."

"Nice pumps. The diamonds are a tad much, but we all know what they say about females and their best friends. I take it you've decided to stop blending in."

"Yes. And what do they say about females?"

"Where do you want me to start? And what are you doing here? I thought—"

The bathroom door opened.

Nancy Cunningham took two steps in the room and stopped abruptly. Her eyes darted from Tiffany to Chip, then back to Tiffany. "I knew I heard voices." She took her makeup kit over to the sink and opened the plastic case. "Hope I didn't interrupt you two ladies."

Oh boy, Tiffany thought. *He's done it again.*

"She was just leaving," she said.

"You're cold, girl," Chip whispered.

Nancy squinted at her reflection. "Either of you see anything wrong?"

"Please be more specific," Chip said.

"My eyebrows."

"They look fine," Tiffany said, glaring at Chip.

"The funniest thing happened yesterday. This lawyer fella tells me I have one eyebrow. I look in the mirror and sure enough, he's right. I give it a good goin' over with the pencil and wouldn't ya know it? Everyone's staring at me like I'm something from a spooky movie."

"Maybe they were just giving you the business," Chip said. "You know how men are. Real jokesters."

"I thought I'd investigate anyway, so I came in here. Guess what I saw."

"A really thick eyebrow?" Chip asked.

"How'd you know?"

"Just an educated guess."

"It made me look like a stupid clown."

"It looks fine now," Tiffany said.

Nancy turned back to the mirror. "You wouldn't be kiddin' me, would you?"

"Not on purpose."

She shook her head.

"Weird things happen," Chip said.

"Don't I know it," she said. "Would you believe I actually thought I heard a *man's* voice before I came in here?"

"Maybe you've been working too hard," Chip said.

Nancy stared at Chip. "I didn't know our cleaning service used women."

"I'm new. Just jumped off the truck."

"That lawyer fella..." She tilted her head. "He looked a little like—"

"Cousins," Chip said. "But we really don't look alike. He's got that chin thing going on. And that *nose*..." He shook his head and grimaced.

"Yep. Workin' too hard." She snapped her makeup kit shut and left the room, mumbling to herself.

Tiffany crossed her arms. "Did you have anything to do with that poor woman's eyebrow?"

"Baby cakes, I don't do eyebrows. Or nails. Not enough panache."

"The truth, please..."

He sighed. "It was sort of necessary at the time."

She wanted to slap him. "Don't you realize how sensitive women are about their looks?"

"Distraction. I had to get by her to find the shooter."

She could tell he was serious. But she could never understand why men treated women so badly. "Don't do stuff like that, all right?"

"All righty-rooty. If it offends you that much."

"So...what did you find out?"

"Just what we figured. The shooter's clueless."

"Then it was the wolf guy after all."

"Correctamundo."

"But it doesn't tell us where he is now."

"You haven't seen him at the restaurant?"

"No, but I can probably find out from Lou if he's working there."

"Stay with your guy. I kinda think we're running out of time."

CHAPTER 47

Darcy's Interview

The brown-haired lady named Kathryn said, "Do you have a social security number, Miss McGill?"

"Yes, ma'am. Please call me Darcy." She tried peering down the hall. No one. Not even a hint of anyone's perfume besides Kathryn's.

"Darcy?"

"Ma'am?"

"You can give it to me now, if you like. It's not that I'm in a hurry, but since I'm filling out your application—"

"Oh! I'm *so* sorry..." *You're* such *an idiot…* She gave it and fought down the embarrassment.

"How old are you? Eighteen?"

"In two months." As far as she could tell, she and Kathryn were alone. Luckily she hadn't bumped into the demon guy. She hoped he wasn't sneaking around, doing that invisible thing again. Or standing behind her, looking over her shoulder.

Suddenly nervous, she turned in her chair—just to make sure.

"Is everything all right?" Kathryn asked.

"Yes, ma'am."

"You seem restless."

"I'm okay."

"We won't be re-opening for a few days. Since you're the first person applying, I'm sure you'll be called. Mr. Gates is very fair."

"Mr. Gates?"

"He owns the restaurant."

"Is he in now?" She risked another glance down the hall.

"He'll be back shortly. Would you like to talk to him?"

"Does he conduct these interviews?"

"He lets me handle them. If you don't mind waiting, he might want to talk to you when he gets back."

Did the owner even know the blond lady? If he did, how could Darcy ask about her without sounding like a dork? But if there was the chance that he did know her, she had to find out.

"All right," she told Kathryn.

***

Still worried about Lou's odd behavior at the Police Station, Tiffany followed him into the dark, deserted bar. He ducked underneath the counter. A pack of cigarettes appeared in his hand. He picked up a box of matches from the ashtray next to the register.

A bad sign. She had already noticed that he smoked only when something troubled him. And he was avoiding eye contact.

She squirmed onto a bar stool. "Something's bothering you, isn't it?"

"I didn't think it showed."

"Please tell me what it is…"

"Nothing important, really. I'm just wondering why your bruise looks different."

Uh-oh…. Chip had been right; she *didn't* know how to concentrate properly.

"Maybe it's…healing already."

He pushed out a thin plume of smoke. "It's moving around. Bruises don't normally do that, do they?"

"Moving around?"

"You know. Not staying put? Going somewhere? Not stuck in one place? Migratory might even be a good word."

She had no idea how to respond. His beautiful dark-brown eyes made it difficult to think up a good alibi. She wondered how those eyes would look in bed, gazing down at her. How his lips would feel against hers. If she really had substance, would she experience pleasure? Excitement?

Would she be able to enjoy a man's touch again?

"Work with me on this, okay?" he asked.

She had zoned out again. It took her a few moments to remember what they'd been talking about. This wasn't like her at all. And it made no sense. She was dead, yet she felt weak and vulnerable—as if she were still alive.

Was it Lou? His eyes? His smell? His soft voice?

"You must think I'm a ditz." She realized that despite her intentions, she was going to tell him how she felt. "I'm really not. I'm having trouble concentrating right now. It's because of you."

"Me?"

"I feel so…warm around you."

He mashed his half-smoked cigarette in the glass ashtray. "Let's go upstairs. I should check on Kathryn."

"Lou…did you lie to me at the Police Station?"

"When?"

"When you told me you liked me."

"I didn't lie."

"Then why are you doing this?"

"Doing what?"

"Changing the subject every time I try flirting with you."

He ran a hand through his hair. "Are you hungry? Wendy might have brought up some food—"

"See what I mean?"

"I take it you're not hungry."

"You're right. I'm not."

"*I* could use a bite—"

"I am something *else*, though."

He hesitated. "What's that?"

"At a loss. Maybe I am a ditz. I just don't understand any of this."

"Tiffany…"

"If you like me, why won't you at least show some interest? I'm not exactly repulsive, am I?"

He sighed. "I wouldn't use that word to describe you."

"What's the right word?"

"I really don't want to get into this." He glanced at the doorway.

"Why not?"

"I have my reasons."

"Please. Tell me. I promise that no matter what it is, I won't—"

"You're beautiful."

She blinked.

"Hell, that doesn't even cut it. You're gorgeous. Absolutely drop-dead *stunning*." He sounded angry.

Icy slivers broke out on her cheeks and arms. *You're dead—how can this even be happening?*

But the feelings were real. And deep. And *so* wonderful.

"What's wrong, Lou?" she whispered.

"What makes you think something's wrong?" He lit another cigarette.

"You're wearing your mad face. And you're smoking another cigarette."

"I am just a little pissed."

"But why would telling me such a wonderful—"

"I didn't *want* to tell you anything *at all*. It isn't something you tell a woman you've just met."

"Why should it matter when you—"

"You can't say something like that and leave the room and expect life to stay the same."

"Why not?"

"It changes everything. You, me—everything. It's something I didn't want to say…at all."

"If you think I'm beautiful, then—"

"Tiffany, you're too young for me."

"I don't think so. I'm twenty-two and you're probably thirty, maybe thirty-one—"

"Thirty-six in November."

"If I'm attracted to you and you're attracted to me, nothing else should matter. You're attracted to me, aren't you?"

"That's not the point."

"What *is* the point?"

"I'm not interested in anything else going on in my life right now. I've got too many problems. So do you."

Yes. She had forgotten the important issue. It was because of Lou. Because of those eyes. His sexiness…

"Someone's after you," he said. "You can't go anywhere because…"

He stopped talking and rubbed his eyes.

"Because why, Lou?" she asked, and the words
("love me")
drifted brazenly from her mind into his.

The softness in his eyes turned into dazzling swirls of fire.

He pulled her close. She enjoyed the delicious sensations as his moist warm lips pressed tightly against hers.

CHAPTER 48

Mortals are Assholes

Gutril crossed the intersection at Main and Chestnut, looking for prospects. The Darcy girl had his blood up, and he decided to look elsewhere.

Friends. Chums. Pals.

Ridiculous. How could a demon make friends?

More important, why would he want to? Demons were evil. Pulling the good-buddy bit just wasn't standard policy.

Gutril had lived the last three thousand years of his non- existence without forming close attachments. He was a wolf. Wolves stuck to themselves.

Get to know the town.

Its people were nothing but walking slugs. He had stumbled across a dozen people since leaving the Darcy girl. None proved the slightest bit interesting.

This place was definitely the pits. He wondered if he should hitch a ride and look for a livelier place. It would sure beat anything happening here. But right now, he needed a host. The Darcy girl was just too damned *nice* for his taste. He wanted someone interesting. And nasty.

A short, slender old man around seventy-five years old tapped around the corner. His wooden cane supported his stiff, misshapen right leg.

He had never considered an old man for a host. But since he couldn't be choosy right now…

"Hi there," Gutril said.

Bald head lowered, the old man nodded slightly and kept moving.

"Got a minute?"

Using his cane to support him, the old man turned around carefully and peered up at Gutril. "You some kind of wiseacre, sonny?"

"No, I just thought you might be interested in –"

"What?"

Watch it, now. Remember the trouble you had with the Darcy girl. Tell this old coot you're a demon and he'll probably have a stroke. What good was an unconscious host?

Friends. Chums. Pals. That might work...

"How about being my friend?"

The old man squinted. "Don't know ya, sonny."

"If you did, you'd *want* to be my friend."

"Who *are* ya?"

"I'm Gutrillus Canus. I—"

"Who?"

"Gutrillus Canus."

The old man scratched the back of his neck. "Bruce Willis' *what*?"

Bruce who?

"Gu-trill-us—"

"You've got a foul mouth on you, wiseacre..."

These deaf old boys could be a pain in the ass. But if Gutril wanted a host, he was going to have to overlook minor irritations. Even the best mortals were irritating. "You can call me Gutril. I can do a bunch of nifty—"

"You're an idiot."

"What?"

"You heard me. I said you're an idiot."

This was unbelievable. "You wouldn't say that if you knew—"

"Don't bother me." He turned awkwardly.

331

"I can do some nifty tricks. Want to see me disappear?"

"Long as ya do it before I come back out after my coffee, toast, and back pill."

Gutril fought off the redness clouding his vision. "I can make you toss that cane, do a backward flip and grow back the hair on the top of that liver-spotted melon you call your head."

"Leave me be, sonny." The old man hobbled up the street. With effort, he climbed the single concrete step of Jake's Coffeehouse. He turned back to Gutril. "And that tee shirt makes ya look danged stupid."

Gutril trembled with rage as the old man disappeared inside the eatery.

Mortals were assholes. They were even worse than demons.

Time for some venting.

A heavyset middle-aged woman carrying groceries reached the door of the manicure place across the street. Carefully she extended a hand toward the door. Gutril coaxed the doorknob a little to her right, just out of her range. She backed up and tried again. He coaxed it to her left, making her miss a second time. Then he made her ankle move wrong and she fell off the heel. Collapsing to the sidewalk, she shrieked and let go of her bag. It slammed to the walk and ripped open. Its contents rolled on the pavement.

Two teen boys passed the hardware store, chattering away.

Gutril made a slight suggestion

("express yourself with color")

and they both scurried into the store and came out two minutes later, carrying cans of spray paint. They ran over to the first vehicle parked along the curb—a silver sports car. Squealing in delight, the boys uncapped their paints and eagerly sprayed the glittering finish with uneven swirls of navy-blue and yellow.

Gutril grinned easily. He had the urge to go back to the church and have some more fun.

***

After leaving Brittany at the Police Station, Chip headed west on East Main, glancing in each shop window as he passed.

Since rush hour had ended, the streets were fairly empty.

Down the block, a tall, lean figure with rust-colored hair and small glistening eyes argued with an old man gripping a cane.

The dazzling jolt of memory nearly made Chip stumble on the sidewalk.

Neely's Novelties.

The same dude who had been arguing with the two teen chicks...

What Epiphany had told him came back instantly.

Easy.... You don't want him to notice you. Be cool.

Keeping his thoughts focused on the Five'n Dime straight ahead, Chip passed the two figures at a moderate, unhurried clip. Once he reached the corner, he fought the urge to turn around.

Don't even think of looking back. You don't know what he's looking at right now, so don't do anything stupid.

At least he had found Gutril. Now it was time to find some way of staying close without giving himself away.

333

He backed up to the corner of the Savings & Loan and, pressing his back to the cool brick wall, assumed the appearance of its rugged flat surface.

Rushing past, Gutril crossed at the intersection and jogged straight for the Presbyterian Church one block north.

CHAPTER 49

Returning an Earring

Louis struggled to focus on something other than the beautiful woman climbing the steps in front of him. The urge to take her in his arms consumed him. Her sweet scent and her golden curls sliding quietly across her back didn't help. Neither did the easy swing of her hips as she ascended the stairs.

Damn, he thought grimly. *I'm no better than an idiot kid with his first copy of* Penthouse *Magazine. What the hell's happening to me?*

Despite his inner turmoil, he kept his cool. And even though the urge did not subside, he managed to reach past her to open the door without incident.

Kathryn maintained her usual post. A pretty young brunette sat in the chair beside the desk. "Lou," Kathryn said, "this is Darcy McGill. She's applying for a job."

"Darcy." He reached for her hand.

Darcy took it but didn't meet his eyes. Her focus seemed to be on Tiffany.

"You two know one another?" he asked curiously.

"We bumped into each other yesterday," Tiffany said quickly. "Hello again, Darcy. In case you forgot, I'm Tiffany."

"Tiffany," Darcy said, almost in a whisper.

"Is this for a waitress job?" Louis asked.

Kathryn said, "We really haven't gotten that far…"

"I'd…better be heading home." Darcy scrambled to her feet.

"I thought you wanted to talk to Mr. Gates," Kathryn said.

"I'm sorry. I have to get home before Mom sends out the National Guard. Another time, maybe?"

"We'll let you know about your application," Kathryn said.

The girl didn't miss a beat on her way out. She gave Louis and Kathryn a quick smile and a slight nod at Tiffany before pulling the door shut.

"Strange girl," Louis said.

"She was just fine before you came in," Kathryn said. "A little nervous, but they're all restless at that age."

"She left her earring." Tiffany picked up something tiny from the chair.

"Funny." Kathryn shrugged. "I didn't notice anything drop."

"It looks pricey. I better take it to her before she misses it and freaks." Tiffany rushed to the door. "I'll be right back."

"Would you like to know what I've been doing?" Kathryn asked.

Louis watched the closing door. "Interviewing a restless teen with one earring?"

"I talked to one of the Pittsburgh chefs." Kathryn consulted her pad. "He can come over tomorrow or Wednesday. Since you weren't here, I told him tomorrow. I hope that's okay."

"It's fine." Louis gave the door another glance.

"I told him any time in the afternoon. I figured you probably wouldn't want to conduct a morning interview. Is that all right?"

"Great." Had Tiffany caught up to her yet? How long did it take to flag down a girl and toss her an earring?

"Are you all right?"

"I'm okay." *Focus...* He opened the liquor cabinet and took out a bottle of Jack's.

"Lou?"

"Uh-huh?"

"So you're okay with this man's salary."

"Sure. Fine."

"You don't care what he demands?"

What was she talking about? "Of *course* I care."

"You didn't hear me, then."

"I guess not." *Pay attention, dammit.* He put his glass on the desk and picked up a pack of cigarettes.

"How many of those have you had today?"

He lit one. "I'm not counting."

"You should be."

"Kathryn, you're not old enough to be my mother."

"Thank you for that obvious but somewhat irritating compliment."

He could tell he had just hurt her feelings. "I'm sorry, but things have been kind of...strange lately."

"I know. I can't help but notice. I'm here, too, remember?"

"And I'm glad you are."

"You're welcome. Now let's talk about this Pittsburgh guy."

"Fire away."

"He wanted to dictate his salary, but I told him he'd have to talk to you about it."

"Obviously." He glanced at his watch. *Where the hell was she? More importantly, why am I so worried?*

"Lou, what's wrong?"

"Wrong?"

"You're acting like someone cracked open your skull and scooped out important parts of your brain."

337

"Which parts?"

"Those keeping you from being a complete idiot."

"That bad?"

"Tell me." She lowered her voice. "Is it that girl?"

Her question infuriated him. *She's doing it again. What's wrong with her? Sometimes she can be really catty. Is it jealousy? Or—*

The heat subsided. His mind cleared.

What the hell's going on? Why did I just want to strangle Kathryn?

"What about her?"

"Where have you two been? If I'm not being too personal."

"The Police Station. I thought I told you."

"And you came right back?"

"Kathryn, what's this all about?"

"Like I said, you're acting really strange."

She was right. The burning cigarette in one hand and the drink in the other were dead giveaways. He remembered lighting the cigarette; he just didn't remember why. He just smoked two downstairs. And why the drink?

"Where were you before you came back?"

"Downstairs in the bar."

"What were you doing?"

"Talking with Tiffany."

"About what?"

About why her bruise moved, darkened, and grew in size.

The story was ridiculous. Kathryn wouldn't understand. How could she? He couldn't even remember how the conversation ended.

"Her bruise looked different." His voice felt strange.

338

"Lou, are you *sure* you're all right?"

He struggled to remember. *Lou, tell me what's bothering you...your bruise... you're beautiful...*

Then everything went dark.

"You're acting strange again."

"I think I need...some rest."

"Maybe I'll call that chef back and tell him to come over later in the week. Would that be better?"

"Thanks, Kathryn." He stubbed out his smoke. "I'd better take it easy. You're not gonna stay all afternoon, are you?"

"Not unless you want me to."

"It's not necessary. If anyone calls, the machine will grab it."

***

Waiting anxiously in the Maxima, Darcy replayed the scene in the upstairs office over and over.

I'm Tiffany...

Then Mr. Gates said something to Kathryn, but Darcy had no idea what it was. She wasn't paying attention. She couldn't turn away from Tiffany.

The soft voice

("We need to talk outside")

drifted in once again, just as it had yesterday in front of Neely's. It shook her, just as it did the first time. Tiffany's voice

("I'll be out in a few minutes")

drifted in one last time.

She hardly remembered coming outside. Or crossing the street. Or getting in her car.

But that didn't matter. The important thing was that Tiffany somehow understood everything. Darcy had the feeling things might turn out okay. When she gazed into

339

Tiffany's clear blue eyes, Darcy experienced warm relief for the first time since she'd come back from the mine.

Tiffany emerged from the restaurant and crossed the street.

"I'm glad you heard me talking to you," Tiffany said through the open window. Then she circled the car and slid in beside her.

"Who *are* you?" Darcy asked softly.

"You don't want to know."

"I really do. What you did for me in front of Neely's—"

"You needed help. You were slightly overpowered."

"Overpowered?"

"The man you were talking to is a demon."

My God. It was true. Those weren't *just magic tricks.*

"Are you really sure?"

"Positive."

"I thought he was just some weirdo who could do strange tricks."

"I'm afraid not."

"So then…if he's a demon, is he…from Hell?"

"That's where they keep them."

The next question frightened her even more than the others she wanted to ask. "But…how do you know—"

"Let's just say we've crossed paths before."

"Then you're—"

"I'm dead, too."

It couldn't be possible. No way. This beautiful, vibrant lady couldn't possibly be dead…

Timidly she covered Tiffany's hand, flinching at its warmth. "You feel…*normal*."

"But I'm not."

"I don't understand."

340

"You won't—hopefully not for another sixty or seventy years. But let's get back to the wolf guy."

"Who?"

"The demon."

"Why do you call him that?"

"His spirit form is a wolf. His name is Gutril."

"He wants to be my personal demon."

"Of course he does. That way, he can stay here. How do you know him?"

She turned away—partly in shame, but mostly in anger. She didn't want to tell anyone—especially Tiffany—what she'd done at the mine.

"Darcy, I need to know."

"I summoned him." She lowered her head and felt just as small...and as dirty...as the crumpled candy wrapper sitting on the floor near the gas pedal.

"So then, *you* were the one."

She felt like she had murdered someone. Well, she had. Because of her stupid chant, Todd and Leon were dead.

"I didn't realize...what I was doing."

"Don't beat yourself up."

"I can't help it. I've caused all this. Todd and Leon are dead because of me."

"Those two boys?"

"It's a long story. I can't tell anyone what happened without freaking out."

"Forget about that for now. We've got to work on a strategy. Where is he?"

"Wandering around. I had to do something to keep him away from me. He's been weirding me out. Big-time. I told him I'd call him when I wanted him."

"Excellent. This gives us time to work on a plan."

341

Was there truly a way of fixing this? Of making things as they used to be? "A *plan*?"

"We need to send him back where he belongs."

"Is that possible?"

"It is, now."

"What's changed?"

"You."

"Me?"

"Now we've got a trump card."

CHAPTER 50

Bewitched, Bothered, and Befuddled

Louis slouched in the chair, a drink in his hand, the wall clock a grim reminder of how long Tiffany had been gone.

Twenty minutes to return an earring? Then he caught himself.

Why should you care?

He suspected *some*thing had happened between them, yet he had no idea what it was. As Kathryn said, he was acting strange. And he didn't know why.

Nothing happened at the Police Station. Nothing, that is, except for Tiffany's bruise changing. Did he ask her about it? Yes. Downstairs in the bar. Once again, he struggled to recall the images.

As before, everything went dark.

Damn that Trent. That elbow to my forehead scrambled my brains.

He finished his drink and picked up the bottle. Just an inch or two left.

He was drinking too much.

It was no wonder. Watching your restaurant being shot up would make anyone drink too much.

He poured more Jack's and tried to calm himself. And fought hard to remember what happened downstairs.

The door opened.

***

Tiffany peered through the doorway. Lou sat at his desk, drinking whiskey.

The time had come. Since talking with Darcy, Tiffany knew that all she had to do was hook back up

343

with Chip and figure some way of using Darcy to lure the wolf guy back out to the mine. But this had to be taken care of first.

"You were gone quite a while," he said.

She sat down facing him. "Just a few minutes."

"Felt like a lifetime."

She closed her eyes and enjoyed the moment. Then she realized once again that she liked everything about him. He made her feel wanted. Needed. For the very first time, she actually felt *good*...and *comfortable*...and *natural*...in a man's presence.

When she was little, people gawked at her, told her how pretty she was. She suspected even at that early age that her looks might actually be a curse. And when her mother remarried and her new stepfather began making his nightly trips to her bedroom to say goodnight with his hands, she was afraid she could never trust anyone again.

She could trust Lou. She sensed it the very first time she saw him.

She didn't want to be with anyone else. She knew this was wrong but promised herself she would make it up to him, if it was the last thing she ever did.

Just because I was dragged into Hell doesn't make me a demon...

"Did you see Darcy?"

She nodded.

"Was she appreciative?"

"Very. Can I please...have a drink?"

He got up and found a glass on the table near the coffee pot. He poured from the bottle and handed it to her.

He's under my spell but it's not real, just as I'm not real. This wonderful man wants me but would hate me if

344

*he knew I was just a conniving dead girl doing everything
I can to stay out of Hell.*

I'm no better than Chip. No better than the wolf guy.

*No better than Balboa Whip. Or Algernon. Or
Oglethorpe.*

"Something happened downstairs with us, didn't it?"
He was staring at his glass.

"Yes."

"Was it what I think it was?"

"What do you think it was, Lou?"

"Something…wonderful?"

She nodded.

"I told you I don't want anything new in my life right
now, didn't I?"

"You did."

"I also told you you're too young for me, right?"

"Uh-huh…"

"And that you have your own problems."

"I do have my own problems."

"Then why is this happening?"

"Why do you think?"

"I think it's a mistake."

"Why?"

"You're young. I'm old enough to be your…older
brother."

"A girl doesn't care how old a man is. Especially
when she's taken by him. His age just isn't important."

He blinked and looked up from his glass.
"You're…*taken* by me?"

"Can't you tell?

"But I've got these weird, irritating habits. No normal
woman would want to put up with me."

"I'm not normal, Lou."

345

"Believe me. I know."

"Tell me about them. I'll bet they're nothing at all."

"Sometimes I leave the toilet seat up. I also tend to snore—"

She got up, bent over him, and kissed him, long and passionately.

After the kiss, he gazed dumbly at her. She couldn't believe how real it felt. She had completely forgotten she was dead. It made her want to kiss him again.

Most of all, it convinced her that she didn't need her powers. Not for this, anyway.

"I guess the toilet seat thing doesn't matter much," he said.

"I can always put it back down whenever I get the chance."

"How about the snoring thing?"

"I'm a heavy sleeper."

CHAPTER 51

The "Persuader"

Aaron Scheckley never had a regular job.

He never needed one. When he graduated high school fifteen years ago, he realized even at that tender age that the wealthy were indeed different. While most of the population went its entire life facing every conceivable irritation, inconvenience and hardship, the rich paid good money for certain events to sway in favorable directions. The rich liked having things done quietly and quickly. They paid dearly for a particular type of service and didn't care how it was handled as long as the end result met with their approval.

Rich men paid for just about anything, and if you handled their affairs to their liking, they didn't mind paying for your services again.

The work, for the most part, was simple. Since Aaron had always been a loner and never had a personal relationship, eliminating people never presented a problem. The money was good and the hours his own, so there was no problem. And at the rate he was going, he could retire in two years with five million in his account that would enable him to buy that mansion in Bermuda he'd been lusting over.

Aaron had been in Raven several years earlier. It was a nice, quiet little town owned by a group of incredibly wealthy men. His first job involved a local farmer named Hedrick, who didn't want to sell off his land. The process was ridiculously easy. A trip to the local pharmacy, the right combination of the right blood thinners, a midnight visit to the farmer's residence, and a little prowling around in the kitchen. The next morning, Old Man Hedrick got up early as usual, took his medications and went out to milk the cows. He never made it to the barn.

A simple job that took three days of his time and earned him fifty thousand big ones. No fuss, no muss.

Aaron pulled the rented white van over to the curb between Neely's Novelties and the Raven Drugstore & Pharmacy. He always picked white vans for his jobs. White vans were used by phone and power companies, painters and plumbers, as well as pizza delivery and pest control, and were virtually invisible.

Across the street, an unlit sign above a green canopy said, *Denner's Restaurant*. Police tape stretched across the front of the two-story brick building. A men's clothing store bordered its right, the First National Bank its left.

According to the information supplied by Scheckley's employer, a man named Lou Gates owned the restaurant. Due to a shrewd business move, Gates had bought the place out from under its rightful heirs and refused to sell. Gates had become stubborn and obstinate and wouldn't listen to reason.

Because of recent trouble, Gates might consider changing his mind. The expenses of cleaning up and refurnishing the place might prove too much. Word was that his main chef had quit, causing additional problems. Gates would have to make a drastic decision. Aaron's employer desperately wanted the restaurant. Aaron was being paid handsomely to prevent Gates from reopening. If Gates sold in three days, Aaron would earn a bonus of fifty thousand dollars.

Not bad for just a few days of his time. A hundred K for the job, an additional fifty if Gates sold in three days.

The first step, of course, was look around and make sure the damages were extensive enough. If not, step in and coax the process along. The best and easiest way was, of course, to make it look like druggies or bored teen punks had trashed the place. A bunch of broken windows worked wonders in most cases.

No problem at all.

Aaron got out of the van.

CHAPTER 52

The Old Man and the Preacher

From the front pew of the Sanctuary, Gutril had an excellent view of the pulpit, the polished wooden rail, the large stained-glass windows, the carved woodwork, a huge silver cross suspended from chains, and other expensive goodies.

A fire sure would make for some great entertainment.

With fire, everything turned bright and exciting. All darkness vanished. When the Mortanites tossed *paparazzi*, lawyers, insurance salesmen, and other worthless idiots into the fire, it lit up the Valley.

The two little tricks he had done a few minutes earlier reminded him how much he missed using his talents. Host or no, he would do as he desired. He would save the big stuff for later but had no intention of letting a stupid teen twit dictate to him.

For now, he would keep the fireworks down to a low simmer while finding a host. Once he found one, this boring little town would quickly see some interesting fireworks.

The old man's words

(you're an idiot)

jolted him again, turning his vision a murky red.

The rage came back. He gripped the smooth wooden rail until his knuckles turned white.

I have to do something.

But it had to be subtle. A church fire would cause too much commotion. If the Legion had already sent someone up here, it wouldn't take them any time at all to find him.

350

Subtle. Tasteful, perhaps? With his usual boyish flair?

The lanky figure in black passed through an archway.

A preacher. The perfect target.

Far out.

Let the holy man take over the festivities. Anything that happened would be the preacher 's doing. This had suddenly become a win-win situation. If the preacher proved as corrupt as all the other holy men Gutril had known, Raven faced some first-class excitement.

***

Spencer relaxed in a pew facing the stained-glass window. Straight ahead, the last of the day's dying sunlight filtered in.

He needed to be in the basement in a few minutes to help set up Pot Luck. But each time he thought about it, the hair on the back of his neck stood on end and he shivered as if someone had splashed him with ice water. The Purdy incident kept coming back. The heavy throbbing in his gut refused to subside.

He needed to focus, collect himself, and stop acting like a frightened child.

As Pat told him, it was an isolated event.

Maybe so. That did seem highly possible. A food fight in a church cellar. It happened, certainly. But that didn't mean it would happen again.

But what about the restaurant shooting?

It was one of those scary tragedies you read about or saw on the national news. Something that happened to others. A horror you didn't even want to think about because it brought about depression and fear.

351

But it had happened. It didn't happen in another place or another part of the world, it happened here. In Raven. Just down the street.

What was next?

A suicide bomber? A plane smashing into one of Ira Crenshaw's high-rises?

Spencer was a man of God, of peace. Violence repelled him. It represented everything he hated, everything he feared. Bad enough these negative elements existed in the first place. The fact that they had found their way into his church—his town—outraged him.

Pat had been right when she said it wouldn't be fair to punish everyone for the actions of a few. The Military operated this way. When someone did the unforgivable, the entire unit suffered. This not only ensured cooperation, it pitted the wrongdoer against the majority, creating peer pressure and guaranteeing the same crime would not reoccur.

It suited that type of situation. But it had no place in a *church*.

He lowered his head. One last Lord's Prayer, just for good measure.

He felt foolish. It was as if he was ten years old again, running home after watching those horror movies at the local theater in Johnstown, where he grew up.

Fifty years ago. Half a century. Another world ago.

He had been a respected minister for the last thirty years. A pillar of the community standing for truth, honesty, kindness, and the Word of God.

A man who looked evil in the eye.

A grown man suddenly afraid to enter his own church cellar.

Enough. Time to act the part of a mature, capable adult whose actions dictated the behavior of his followers.

Spencer stood straight and tall. Convinced all would be fine once he went downstairs, he left the Chapel.

Movement in the Sanctuary caught his eye. An old man waved from the front pew.

A strange odor drifted over. It was the same foulness he had noticed during the last few days.

He descended the marble steps, where the polished wooden railing separated the podium from the front row of pews.

"Doing Pot Luck tonight, Rev?" the old man asked.

"We open in about half an hour."

"Hope it'll be more enjoyable than Saturday night."

"I'm sure it will be." A shame the old gentleman brought this up. Many were obviously concerned about the violence.

"Sure wouldn't mind having some of that tasty food myself, but I don't wanna wear it home."

"I honestly don't think that'll happen," Spencer said confidently.

"I'm much too old to crawl around on the floor like a youngster."

"I assure you everything will be just fine."

"Rev?"

"Yes?"

"Take care, now. You know how things get outa hand."

"I appreciate that, sir." This sort of talk didn't help. "Things will settle down."

"Hope so. You're an important man. Folks believe in you, do everything you say. They don't wanna let you down."

353

"It's very nice of you to say that."

At least someone cared.

Maybe he *wasn't* losing his grip after all.

CHAPTER 53

No More Donations, Dammit!

Ophelia Grubb and Muriel Dobbins, friends for nearly seventy years, shuffled into the church nave. For the last thirty years, they had spent half an hour each evening in the Sanctuary, saying their prayers. Before plodding back to their modest efficiencies on West Main, they would venture down to the basement afterward to partake in some of the church's tasty vittles. Of course, they invariably met up with many of their friends in the cellar as well—which made for a very pleasant evening.

A tall, elderly gentleman marched briskly out of the Sanctuary, darting out of her path. "Excuse me," Ophelia said, nearly losing her balance.

The man didn't pause in his dash for the doorway.

Goodness gracious... Ophelia couldn't help noticing how much spring the gent had in his step for his advanced years. Impressive indeed, though she considered it rude that he didn't acknowledge Muriel or herself. Some folks were in too much of a hurry these days. Wouldn't stop to say hi even if they were on their way to their own funeral.

"What's this?" Muriel had stopped five feet from the Sanctuary archway.

A faded gold metal box marked *Donations* fixed atop a thick pedestal stood near the stone wall.

Muriel slipped on her reading specs.

"Don't remember this bein' here." Ophelia squinted. Her specs remained in her bag. It was a bother, getting them out. She would gladly let her friend perform the necessary examination.

"Every little bit helps." Muriel opened her change purse and fished for money. She dropped three quarters into the slot, one at a time. A slick gurgling sound resonated when they landed inside the box.

"Sounds damp in there," Ophelia said.

"Downright peculiar." Muriel shook her head.

Ophelia found some change in her purse. Someone probably discovered the box in a loved one's basement and donated it. It smelled like damp soil. No doubt left out in the elements too long. Could be mud and something else lying in there among the change.? "Probably hasn't been cleaned out in a month of Sundays."

Muriel was still shaking her head as she shuffled through the doorway.

Ophelia joined her friend in the Sanctuary.

Choking and gasping exploded from the nave.

Mindful of her arthritic hip, Ophelia hobbled back. Her thirty years as RN in the health care profession had served her well. She hadn't administered First Aid in several years, but that was something a body never forgot.

No one was in the nave.

The Donation box had disappeared.

***

Bent over double behind the bushes, Chip hawked out the coins and a lint-covered sourball.

Just what he needed: a mouthful of foul-tasting change and leavings from an old lady's purse.

After one last hack, he collected himself and rushed down to the corner.

Gutril, back to his original human form, headed east on Main.

Time to find Spiffy and work out their strategy. She told him she'd be at the restaurant, finding out what she could from the owner guy.

Sounded like a good place for a rendezvous as well as a regrouping. But he had to be extra careful not to be spotted while keeping close to Gutril.

Maintaining a brisk pace, Chip crossed the street, keeping at least twenty yards separating him from the lean figure ahead.

Just as Chip passed the entrance of the Raven Meat Market, Gutril abruptly stopped walking.

And spun around.

CHAPTER 54

Tiffany's Plan Develops a Kink

As Lou lay sleeping peacefully, Tiffany snuck out of bed.

It seemed kind of cheap—almost the Hollywood equivalent of auditioning for a big movie part—but it also seemed the best way of acquiring a mortal host.

Since she was new at this, she had no idea if anything else was involved. If she had to recite a certain spell or chant, she was doomed. She couldn't ask Chip for advice—he was her partner, but he was also a demon. She was working by instinct, using her feminine wiles. She knew it was shameful—even selfish at best— but she didn't have much time. And anyway, what was a little deceit if it kept her from having to return to that awful place?

Now it was time to meet up with Darcy and hunt for Chip. They could drive out to the mine and find a way to summon the wolf guy. If they could get him out there, they might be able to trick him into going back down the tunnel.

No problem. You've tricked men before, haven't you? Got them to do whatever you wanted. You were always reluctant to do it, but sometimes it just had to be done.

Look what you have just done... You have seduced and made love to a mortal man, and although you are truly fond of this man—

Forget that, all right? Worry about that when the wolf guy and Chip are both back down and you have all the time in the world to make amends with your mortal host. You can tell him what you did and why you did it, and

358

how you intend to make the rest of his life wonderful to atone for what you did.

But first things first. Finding and tricking the wolf guy...

Before she left the room, she regarded the sleeping figure snoring softly under the sheet. She was so lucky to have found him. They could have a lovely future together. There could never be kids, of course, but did that matter?

You're dead, princess. What about that?

And that other tiny detail? That you've actually been in Hell?

What will you do if Lou doesn't appreciate the fact that you're a demon?

But she *wasn't* a demon. Otherwise, she wouldn't have been sent to Limbo.

Limbo or not, you're still dead. Do you honestly think Lou will want to spend the rest of his life with a dead girl?

***

Aaron Scheckley crept down the dark, bitter-smelling alley.

Cluttered with garbage, the slim passageway barely enabled him to pass freely. As always, he considered himself lucky that he wasn't very large.

Anonymity ruled in this business. When you were of average size and looks, people ignored you. You became invisible. To most, anonymity was an insult. To Aaron, anonymity meant getting things done quietly.

His penlight guiding his way, he stepped over piles of crushed beer cans and smashed cigarette butts, squeezed past overflowing garbage cans, and avoided shattered beer bottles.

In the rear, a five-foot wooden privacy fence spanned the back yard of the restaurant. He had no problem scaling the locked gate.

The lot looked to be around a hundred by a hundred and fifty feet. A dumpster sat amongst some tall grass in the center of the yard. A scrub area butted up to the walkway. A late-model Mustang slept beneath a metal roof on sticks at the opposite end.

The back door would not budge.

From his wallet he removed the special lock-pick acquired several years ago from a former FBI expert. Its non-metallic substance could not be detected by X-ray. It could open ninety percent of all locks made after 1970. It hadn't failed him yet.

He fitted the pick carefully into the slot and twisted it around, listening for the click. A moment later, he slipped through the doorway.

Small tables cluttered the large area. Refrigerators and freezers hummed steadily. A butcher block stood by itself in the adjoining room near the doorway. Beyond it, a hall emptied into another area—probably the dining room. A wide archway on the far left led to a stockroom or loading dock.

The huge stainless double refrigerator grabbed his attention.

A massive freezer stood beside it.

Interesting. If the appliances were unplugged, everything inside would spoil in probably less than twenty-four hours. Gates would go into hock to replace the food.

Curious, he opened the refrigerator door.

Mixed aromas pushed outward, grabbing his senses. Delicious-looking foods crammed the shelves.

Drumsticks. Vegetable plates. Turkey, chicken, and roast beef sandwiches. A large dish layered with cold cuts. Strawberry cheesecake. A bowl stacked with deviled eggs.

He suddenly realized how hungry he was. He never ate on planes. Their freeze-dried stuff made him physically ill.

He picked up a deviled egg and popped it into his mouth. A symphony of tangy flavors assaulted his taste buds. Next, a drumstick. After a couple of those and a few more deviled eggs, he'd indulge himself with a slice of that scrumptious-looking cheesecake before unplugging the works.

Shuffling on the tile behind him made him cringe.

The overhead fluorescents blazed the room with light.

CHAPTER 55

No Respect!

His brief encounter with the town's preacher successful, Gutril went back out into the street and scanned the activity.

Time for some serious fun. Putting that hex on the preacher

(everyone will do as you say)

had whetted his appetite, urging him on.

Three teen boys running across the street, dodging traffic.

A heavyset middle-aged man in a dark suit coming out of the Savings & Loan.

Halfway down the block, the door of Jake's Coffeehouse opened. The crusty old man who called him an idiot carefully climbed down the concrete step, then hobbled down the street.

A hot wave gushed heavily down Gutril's spine.

Idiot, huh?

Maybe this idiot should leave his calling card.

How about giving the old coot a sprinkling of fresh hair?

Gutril focused. A foot-long, unruly tangle of gray appeared just above the shiny crown, sliding down the back of the old man's shirt collar.

There. Call me an idiot, will you? Explain that *to your crotchety friends when you hobble back to the rest home...*

His anger somewhat vented, Gutril resumed his scan of the street. An elderly woman standing at the corner across the street rummaged through her purse.

Gutril coaxed the woman's dentures out of her mouth. They slapped the pavement, skittered over to the curb, toppled over the side, and disappeared down the storm drain.

Two points. Far out!

A fat middle-aged woman pulled along a white toy poodle with a red ribbon attached to the top of its fluffy round head. The pooch stopped and sniffed a brightly painted fire hydrant.

Something odd there. An older hydrant squatted farther down, near the corner. So why was one needed in the middle of the block?

Then he remembered. The Bochner kid ruined the one at the corner, forcing the City to replace it.

The mutt raised its leg and sprayed the side of the new hydrant. The woman yanked on its leash, interrupting the yellow stream. The stray drops darkened the sidewalk. The woman gave the leash another yank, jerking the mutt along.

Gutril gave the hydrant another glance. Strange. For a moment it looked like the damned thing had *moved*.

Your imagination. You already think someone's following you.

He was being paranoid. There was no way someone had already been sent up here. It took them forever to get anything done while everyone was out wandering around in the Valley.

The poodle reached the end of the block and sniffed at something on the pavement. The woman tugged it along while crossing the street.

His mouth watering, Gutril resumed his walk.

The fluffy little thing had just given him the munchies.

***

When no one was watching, Chip straightened out of his fire hydrant position, scurried into an alley, and furiously shook the dog pee from his leg.

It was time to hook up with Travesty. Gutril and his silly shenanigans had turned this trip into an irritating pain in the ass!

CHAPTER 56

How Do You Handle a Hungry Man?

People strolled leisurely down the sidewalk, unaware that a demon had hexed their quiet little town.

Her guilt a heavy weight on her shoulders, Darcy waited nervously in her Nissan. She couldn't stop thinking about a scary story she'd read a while ago about a monastery that had captured the Devil and kept him locked in a room in its basement. Everyone knew about the evil in that room and had been warned what would happen if the door was unlocked. But the inevitable happened. No longer imprisoned, the Devil was free to unleash his unbridled malevolence upon the world.

To Darcy, this situation somehow seemed worse. She not only pulled one out of Hell, but she had also set him upon a town of innocent people. The town where she was born. The place where she had grown up and lived all her life.

How could she fix this?

How could she make things as they were before?

As Tiffany said, the only way was to lure the demon back to the mine.

Darcy kept hoping that this was all a dream. Too many scary books and movies had taken their toll.

But if it's not a dream…if this is actually happening, what can you do to get your life back?

She didn't know. She didn't even know if she'd be able to go back to school. Or what to tell her friends about Todd and Leon.

If she told them the truth, she would become the laughingstock of the school. She'd be known as the girl with her own personal demon. The fruitcake responsible for two deaths.

Three more weeks until summer vacation. Three long, excruciating weeks of stares, glances, whispers, jokes.

If only your car hadn't been at the shop...

If only Todd hadn't picked up that guy...

Out of the corner of her eye she saw something that made her cringe. The demon was walking up the street, heading in her direction.

***

"Who are you?" Tiffany asked.

The man standing in front of the refrigerator was about her height, with small, nervous brown eyes. His hair was shaved down to brown stubble. He was probably in his early thirties. He wore a loose gray sweatshirt, jeans, and black tennis shoes. A half-eaten drumstick protruded from his left hand.

"Didn't mean to scare anyone," he said in a soft, high-pitched voice.

"How did you get in?"

"Door was unlocked."

Lou wouldn't leave the place unlocked. Neither would Kathryn. According to Kathryn, the cleaning guys weren't due to show for another day or two. Best play along. "You're hungry."

"Does it show?"

"The drumstick gave you away."

"You own this place?"

"I'm a friend of the owner. He won't like you sneaking in, but I don't think he'll mind you taking something if you're hungry."

"You're sure?"

366

She didn't feel right about this, but that didn't concern her right now. She had to find Chip. This had to be cut short. "Reasonably."

"You won't call the cops?"

"I'd feel guilty getting a hungry man in trouble. You didn't take any silverware or anything, did you?"

He stiffened. "Whaddya think I am? A common *thief*?"

"Just asking."

"Sorry. I get a little antsy when I'm hungry."

"I understand."

Fifty-thousand-dollar bonus…

The phrase trickled softly into her head.

If Gates sells in three days…

"You're sure he won't mind?"

"Just take what you want."

He was definitely stalling. That wouldn't happen with a hungry man coming across a refrigerator filled with food. But if what she'd just heard had come out of this man's head, Lou faced big trouble.

"If I could just make up my mind—"

"You're not hungry, are you?"

"Famished."

"You should be grabbing anything—"

"There's a lot of great-looking stuff here. I'm confused."

"Have another drumstick. Or a sandwich."

"I'm not really a sandwich sort of guy." He picked up a bowl, glanced at it and put it back. "Red onions. Not my lucky day."

"Please take something. I have to leave."

He picked up another drumstick. "Sure you won't call the cops?"

"I said I wouldn't." She wanted to grab him by the collar and drag him outside.

"You're really sweet," he said.

She wished he hadn't said that. But she could tell he didn't mean it. She was quite accustomed to dishonesty and knew how to recognize it. He probably said it to soften her up.

"I've got an appointment. You're leaving."

***

Her skin cold and tingly, Darcy scrunched down in her seat.

Luckily, she'd parked across the street. The demon hadn't seen the Maxima before, so he shouldn't be suspicious. If he didn't cross the street, she'd be safe.

But where was he going? What was he doing?

He works at the restaurant. Maybe he's going back to pick up his check.

Silly. Would a demon *need* a paycheck?

He worked there for a reason. Maybe to blend in. Or kill time.

But if he goes inside, he might stumble onto Tiffany. That would ruin everything.

Please don't go in there. Please let everything happen the right way...

Something was going to happen. Something bad. She knew it, felt it. But she couldn't let it happen. She had to *do* something. Bad enough all this was because of that stupid chant. She couldn't let Tiffany become yet another victim.

If he passes Denner's, everything might be all right. But if he goes inside, you have to find some way of alerting Tiffany.

Her cell phone. Maybe—

Idiot. Tiffany's dead. Why would she need a cell phone?

Darcy could call the restaurant and tell them—

Tell them what? A demon is on his way inside?

Was there some way she could distract the demon without placing herself or Tiffany in jeopardy?

She could call and tell them she saw smoke coming from somewhere inside the building. That would get everyone stirred up. Maybe she could call the Fire Department instead and have them rush on over. The demon wouldn't like the commotion and he'd have to disappear again. Then maybe everything would be okay.

But first, Darcy had to see exactly where he was going.

Her pulse thumping loudly, she fumbled for the seat adjustment and lowered its back. Her head dropped below the level of the window. The door frame would hide her face from view. She just hoped he wouldn't be looking in her direction when she revealed herself.

Holding her breath, she cautiously raised her head.

No sign of the demon. Or Tiffany.

CHAPTER 57

A Little Mind-Reading to Pass the Time

Once they were outside, the blond babe closed the screen door.

Beautiful chick. Great face and hair. Terrific body. And those boobs...

No way did this chick belong in a small hick town. She looked big city. Someone you'd expect to see dangling from some rich guy's arm. Those fancy pumps looked like they went for close to a grand.

Aaron Scheckley nibbled on his drumstick and tried hard to focus, but all he could think about was how this chick would look naked.

Remember why you're here. Maintain the guise. Just a bum coming in off the street for free food.

He had to make sure he didn't say anything to arouse her suspicions. Best give the illusion he would be on his way, then sneak back inside once she was out of sight.

If only this babe didn't look so damned terrific in those Capri's...

"Do you honestly think that'll work?" She was frowning. "Unplugging the fridge and freezer?"

Shit. Where the hell did she get that?

"Wh-What are you talking about, lady?"

"Once I'm gone, you're going to come back and unplug the appliances. You'll get a bonus of fifty thousand dollars. Lou won't be able to replace all that food. He'll have to sell in three days."

What's going on here?

His employer wouldn't *dare* let any of this slip out. Rich men kept their mouths shut—especially with big money at stake.

Someone had opened his big mouth.

It was obviously a setup. He would be framed if he didn't get out fast.

Wait a minute.

How the hell did she know about unplugging the appliances when I just thought about it five minutes ago?

"Lady, I don't know what you've been smoking, but—"

"You didn't come here because you were hungry. You came to force Lou to sell his restaurant. You should be ashamed of yourself." Her expression had changed from dead serious to harsh. Like Miss Storm, his first-grade teacher. Standing in front of her desk, the permanent scowl frozen on her wrinkled face, her stick-thin arms crossed over her flat chest—

"I'm sure Miss Storm's ashamed of you, too."

He swallowed a cold gooey lump and backed up.

This is weird...really and truly weird...

In seconds, this situation had steered clear of setup and now hovered dangerously close to the unimaginable. Much like those old *Twilight Zone* reruns he had seen on television years ago.

She went down the walk and stopped in front of the dumpster. "The *Twilight Zone* was one of my favorite old shows, too."

Drops of cold sweat tickled the back of his neck. This babe was doing a major number on him. Those big blue eyes held him fast. A tiny spark flared in their centers.

She's reading my mind!

"That's what's wrong with people nowadays," she said. "No one reads anymore."

Jesus... "Lady...how can you do that...mind-reading stuff?"

She shrugged. "Oh, just something I picked up."

She made it sound like it wasn't worth mentioning.

Slivers of ice slid down Aaron Scheckley's limbs, making him tremble.

"What did Lou do to you?"

"Who?"

"The man who owns this place. The man you're trying to ruin."

"L-Lady...this is just...business."

"It's more than that to Lou. It's his livelihood. Did you ever think of that? Or don't you care?"

"Listen, lady—"

"I actually thought you were nice. I felt sorry for you, being hungry and all. But you just want to sneak back here and ruin Lou's business. That's not very nice. I'll bet your own mother's ashamed of you."

A stab of heat slammed him in the pit of his stomach. "That's low, bringing up a guy's mom."

"What do you intend to do with that fifty thousand? Buy a boat or something?"

He had nothing to say. For the first time in his professional career, he actually felt remorseful.

"You *should* feel remorseful," she said.

She did it again...

He had to stop all this before she conned him into doing something stupid, like joining a monastery or donating the fifty grand to some worthy cause. He had to shut her up. A belt in the mouth, maybe?

372

If only this chick wasn't such a *babe*... If she wasn't so damn gorgeous, he would have already hauled off and—

He suddenly froze.

The babe changed into an ugly old hag.

CHAPTER 58

The Lady Vanishes

Crouched in the alley, Gutril probed the cluttered darkness.

Nothing. No rats or mice anywhere amongst the garbage. A cockroach or two and some antsy spiders, but nothing substantial.

A giant bummer, he thought sourly.

All he wanted was a light snack. With the rotten food spilling from the cans, the area should be swarming.

Maybe the little suckers had sniffed him out...

No problem. Denner's Restaurant was just on the other side of the fence. He could check out their dumpster, see what goodies he could find in there. Since it wasn't Garbage Day, it should be packed with three days of trash. Maybe he could find a critter or two wandering around, looking for scraps.

He tilted his head.

Voices were coming from the other side of the fence.

***

"What's going on?"

The shady guy had dropped his drumstick. His eyes bulged.

"Whatever do you mean?" Tiffany asked.

"Your face. It's...*disgusting!*"

Having powers was great. The euphoria resulting from making your breasts a different size and wearing the footwear of your dreams was indescribable.

Tiffany clearly remembered the countless times she wanted to change her appearance as a mortal when creepy guys wouldn't leave her alone.

Creating an illusion was nothing new. Neither was playing a role. Maybe her powers were developing so naturally because of where she came from. Hollywood was the Mecca for creating illusions.

It seemed so funny and ironic that Hollywood and being dead shared so much in common.

"That's a nice thing to tell a girl," she said flatly.

He looked like he was going to be sick. "You're *ugly*!"

"*Such* a charmer…"

"You used to be gorgeous. Now you're roadkill."

Tiffany sighed. "I know I told you just a few minutes ago that you're not very nice but let me put it another way. You're really and truly not very nice. At *all*."

He continued to gape. "Look at you. You're like the hag in that old *Twilight Zone* episode."

"The one in the cabin with those tiny spacemen?"

"Yeah."

"One of my favorites. Agnes Moorehead was in it."

"Who?"

"Agnes Moorehead."

"Well, you're just as ugly as whoever she is."

"She's dead. And thanks."

"She was ugly and gross, and she slobbered. Bitch scared me half to death. And you're welcome."

"Your mother didn't teach you much etiquette."

His cheeks reddened. "Dammit, leave my mom out of this. Where'd your face go?"

"It's right here."

"I don't mean *that* one. I mean the *gorgeous* one."

"The facelift probably stopped working. They said I'd have to have another one in a few years."

"Facelift?"

375

"It's a medical thing. They put you under, slice behind your ears and tighten the skin—"

"I know about facelifts."

"What's the problem?"

"You're *ugly*..."

"You're no Adonis. For one thing, you're too short."

He straightened. "I'm five-eight!"

"You wish. And your voice is too high. How many times have you been called 'ma'am' on the phone?"

"That *hurts*, lady..."

"And being called 'roadkill' should make me warm and fuzzy?"

"This doesn't make sense. Look at you."

"Do you happen to have a mirror?"

His cheeks puffed out. "I think I'm gonna puke."

She coaxed a long white string of imaginary drool out of her mouth. It dropped softly to the grass.

He covered his mouth, turned around and bent double.

She decided to give him some sound advice. She closed her eyes. *Stay away from Lou. Go away and never come back. That evil demon from the* Twilight Zone *episode will come back from the dead and haunt you forever—*

Scratching sounds scraped the privacy fence on the other side of the lot.

Tiffany peered around the corner of the dumpster.

The wolf guy's rust-color hair appeared above the top of the fence.

376

CHAPTER 59

Gutril Finds a Host

Kathryn was going on about Tiffany's Gucci pumps.

She sat behind the desk and fiddled with her reading glasses. She also kept glancing at Tiffany, who sat on Louis's right.

"What's wrong with them?" Louis asked. "I think they're fabulous."

Kathryn shook her head. "They're not real. Sorry, Lou. Your blond bombshell isn't real, either."

"How can you say that? Look at her. She's sitting right there. How can you say she's not real?"

Kathryn shrugged. "Look at that hair – not one out of place. Perfect cheekbones. Perfect lips. Clear blue eyes. She's *breathtaking*." Her gaze shifted to Tiffany. "I'll bet you didn't even have to run a comb through it when you rolled out of bed. I'll also bet you didn't even have to pluck an eyebrow—"

"You sure have been catty lately," he snapped.

"She's too *perfect*, Lou. You told me yourself. She makes the rest of us look…well, pretty bad."

"Is *that* why you don't like her? You're jealous?"

"Among other things."

"You just don't like her being perfect. And nice. And not only that, she thinks I'm terrific. Doesn't even care that I leave the toilet set up."

"What about her famous bruise? Didn't you tell me it moved? How can a bruise move? Lou, figure it out. Tell me how a bruise can move, and I'll admit I'm wrong about her."

"I have no idea how it moved. I only know it did."

"If it did, it proves she's not real. If it didn't, it proves you're losing your mind. Someone snuck up to you, opened up your skull while you weren't looking, and scraped out your brains."

"It's easy to prove. Go ahead, Tiffany. Show Kathryn your bruise." He turned in his seat.

Her chair was empty.

"Tiffany?"

It all came back in a rush. The shooting downstairs. The beautiful golden vision showing up at his doorstep. The trip to the Police Station. The drink. The kiss.

It was a dynamite kiss. But there was more to it than it. Her hair…her beautiful breasts…her sweet smell…

They were making love. But it didn't seem real. It seemed like…a *dream*…

No. It *was* real.

Tiffany was *real*. They just made love.

How could you make love to someone who wasn't real?

He opened his eyes. He was lying naked in his own bed. Alone.

A dream, all right.

Wasn't it?

***

A short, slight male in a baggy gray sweatshirt and jeans circled the dumpster in Denner's back yard.

Something was obviously wrong with the dude. He kept wiping his mouth and mumbling. And looking around as if someone was sneaking up on him. His eyes, glossy and dazed, didn't focus.

Gutril did a quick probe.

Images of monsters. Women with droopy breasts, penetrating eyes and long, sharp teeth. An ugly hag

378

hobbled around in a cabin, long strings of drool swaying from her pointed chin.

This dude had serious issues.

Gutril wondered if it would be worth his time to latch onto a demented mortal. It could be entertaining. Gutril could do interesting things and this boy probably wouldn't even notice.

Cool beans. Might be worth a try.

"Hey, Slick! Want to be my friend?"

No reply.

The mortal circled the dumpster. He picked up a half-eaten drumstick from the grass and studied it. He didn't seem to know what it was. Then he glanced at the building, then the dumpster, and went back to studying the drumstick.

"Want me to turn that into a giant chicken?" Gutril asked.

Again, no reply. The mortal didn't even seem to have heard him.

"How about a T-Rex?"

Slick stared at the dumpster and backed up. The images of droopy-breasted women grew more vivid in his head.

"No need to worry about those ugly women," Gutril said. "If you want to be my friend, I'll do all sorts of things for you. As for those monsters? If you stay away from that cabin—"

Gawking at him, Slick dropped the drumstick. With an ear-splitting whine, he sprinted to the fence, scaling it in a giant leap.

Bummer. Even when you found an interesting mortal to play around with, he screwed everything up.

379

Gutril surveyed the yard. He was certain he heard a woman's voice before scaling the fence. But where was she? And what made that guy go bonkers?

Catching a whiff of something sweet, Gutril approached the dumpster. Something appetizing awaited him inside.

"Gutier?" yelled a voice behind him. "Is that you out there?"

***

Perched in front of the dumpster, Gutier looked like he was about to leap inside.

Louis rubbed his eyes. *I must still be dreaming.*

"Just checking things out," Gutier said.

"You haven't by any chance come across a gorgeous blonde, have you?"

Gutier frowned. "In the dumpster?"

Louis sighed. *Cool it. You sound like a nutcase.*

But he couldn't help it. He hadn't felt the same since Tiffany had come back from returning that earring.

"This blonde," Gutier said. "Is she real?"

Whoa. Louis wanted to pinch himself, find out if this was a continuation of that stupid dream.

"Why do you ask?"

"You look weird."

First, Kathryn. Now, Gutier. I must have a huge sign on my forehead that says, Caution – Shorted-Out Brain Cells.

"Weird how?"

"You've got sleep in your eyes."

He ran a hand through his hair. "That's probably because I just woke up."

"You were asleep? In the middle of the day?"

He was in no mood for this. "Don't ask."

380

"You can't blame me for being slightly curious, can you? You just asked me if a gorgeous blonde's hiding in your dumpster."

Gutier was right. You need to relax, start taking things easy. The shooting had apparently knocked something loose. Focus. Time to start acting the part of a reasonably intelligent human being. "By the way, why did you just walk off the job?"

"It wasn't challenging enough."

"It was stock work. What did you expect? A company car? Expense account? A bevy of half-naked dancing girls following you around?"

"The dancing-girl option sounds pretty good."

"Sorry. The Health Department has a problem with nudity so close to food."

"Put the girls in a separate holding area." Gutier grinned. "That'll work for me."

"I'll keep that in mind."

"Mind if I ask you a personal question?"

"Go ahead."

"Ever given any thought to having your own personal demon?"

Was he hearing things? Did Gutier say *demon*? Louis studied the man's expression. Was he kidding? The grin was still there. And it should be, shouldn't it? This conversation was ridiculous. It was Louis's fault, too. What did he expect? He had just said something about a gorgeous blonde in a dumpster... Then the dancing-girl thing.

The man probably thinks I'm a fruitcake. No wonder he walked off the job.

"Sure," he said, playing along. "Who wouldn't?"

381

Gutier's small eyes lit up. Louis could have sworn they turned red.

"Let's go inside," Gutier said eagerly. "We can talk better."

CHAPTER 60

Leaving Town
Bargaining

The mouth of the alley threatened to devour her.

Darcy stood there, frozen, unaware of what to do next.

It was dark in there. Scary, too. If she squinted just so, it could pass as a grave. It smelled really gross, as well. Garbage cans lined up farther down. Garbage meant bad food. And stale beer. And rats.

What if the wolf guy's waiting for me in there? Can he see me?

She was being silly. *He's a demon. He can make himself invisible. And he wants to be* your *demon. He'll do whatever you say. If he doesn't, he has to go back to Hell. And he hates it down there.*

It made sense but didn't make her feel any better.

A shadow was moving in the darkness of the alley, coming straight for her.

A glint of gold.

It was Tiffany. The welcomed sight brought about a huge jolt of relief.

"What are you doing *here*?" Tiffany asked, out of breath. "You were supposed to wait in your car."

"You were taking too long. I was worried and—"

"Save it." Tiffany grabbed her arm and they both scurried across the street.

"What kept you?" Darcy asked when they slid into the front seat of the Maxima. "And what's that funky smell?"

Tiffany slammed the door. "I was hiding in a dumpster."

"Why?"

"It was the smart thing to do at the time."

"I was sure the demon guy had seen you."

"He almost did. Get us out of here. And step on it."

"Why the rush? And where's your friend?"

"We just ran out of time. We've got to do this ourselves. The wolf guy's inside with Lou. I don't want him doing anything to him."

Darcy smiled. "He's not allowed to hurt anyone. That was one of my conditions."

Tiffany's expression turned grim. "Was another one of your conditions that he couldn't read anyone's mind?"

A chill climbed up her spine. "He's...not allowed to read *mine*..."

"What about anyone else's?"

My God. I've done it again...

"I'm sorry. I guess I wasn't thinking of—"

"Like I said, step on it."

***

Gates closed the screen door. He lingered in the doorway, watching the back yard. The image of a blue-eyed blonde appeared prominently in his head.

Maybe he thought there really was a gorgeous babe in the dumpster.

Bummer. Gates could be just as loony as Slick was. He didn't appear to be, but you never could tell with mortals. Most of them—especially the rich and most successful—were as batty as shithouse rats. The wealthy Chicago pharmacist Gutril had chosen as a host more than a hundred years ago was as loony as they came. But he sure was entertaining. Anyone who had a castle built specifically for torture and murder couldn't be all bad.

Crazy mortals were infinitely more interesting than a half-witted teenage female. With Gates protecting him, Gutril could do whatever he wanted. Everyone came into this restaurant. Gutril would have a ball, and no one would even suspect what was happening.

Gates turned away from the door. "Now…what did you want to talk about?"

"You forgot already?"

"Just making sure I heard you right."

"I mentioned having your own personal demon."

"I heard you right." Gates frowned. "You're *serious* about this?"

"Don't I look serious?" Why were so many mortals skeptical about Hell and its demons? How much proof did they need that malevolent spirits had been manipulating them for the last forty-plus centuries?

"C'mon, Gutier. I know you're a joker and all–"

"What makes you think I'm joking?"

"Demons don't *really* exist, do they?"

Here we go again. Every time he turned around, one of these idiots said or did something to piss him off.

"They exist. Trust me."

"Where are they? *I* haven't seen any. Have *you* seen any?"

This was accomplishing nothing. If the Legion had sent someone up, there wasn't time to stand around and argue. Gutril needed a host. *Now.*

"Like I said. Trust me."

"You've actually *seen* a demon?"

"You might say I know them intimately."

Gates rubbed his eyes.

385

"Something wrong?"

"I keep thinking I'm dreaming all this."

"You're awake. Want me to slap you just to make sure?"

"Thanks, that's all right. Does this have anything to do with Antoine?"

"Who?"

"Our former chef. Remember when I asked you to talk to him?"

"What's he have to do with demons?"

"I'm just wondering if Antoine's a demon. He was sort of a psychopath, you know."

This was going nowhere. He could stand here for the next hour, trying to convince this idiot that there were actually demons wandering around, or he could just leave and start looking somewhere else. "Do you want your own demon or not? I'm serious. And I don't have much time. If you don't—"

(*"Gutril"*)

The tiny voice trickled into his consciousness.

"Gutier?" Gates was watching him curiously.

(*"Gutril"*)

The Darcy girl. The summoning was clearer, but farther away.

"Gutier?" Gates's voice again. One more time and

(*"Gutril!"*)

the summoning, louder and more urgent, was complete.

An image of the woods drifted into Gutril's head. The Darcy girl was calling from the woods.

"Gutier, what's wrong?"

Gutril cleared his head. The restaurant kitchen. Gates was standing near the door, a worried expression on his face.

Gates was an idiot. He didn't even believe in demons and was boring Gutril to death with his stupid questions. The Darcy chick already knew about him and had agreed to accept him. He could work around her goody-goody nonsense and she wouldn't be the wiser. She was calling for him and it sounded urgent.

"Gutier?"

Shut up and take me for a ride…

Gates moved away from the cabinet. Without a word, he crossed the room and hurried toward the dining room doorway.

"Where are you going?"

"My car keys are upstairs."

"Hurry, dammit. We don't have all day."

CHAPTER 61

Darcy's Double Dose of Déjà vu

Trembling with fear as she gripped the wheel, Darcy turned off Raven Road West onto the same path she, Todd and Leon had used only days ago.

Days ago. It felt like years.

And now, the fate of the town she had lived in all her life rested on her shoulders.

"Do you think he heard me?" she asked Tiffany.

"If he bonded with you, he did."

"How will we know?"

"Did you tell him he could stay here with you?"

"If he did what I said..."

Tiffany didn't reply.

"I messed up again, didn't I?"

"I don't know. I'm new at this, too. I just hope he hasn't done anything to Lou."

"Is there a chance he has?"

"I'm not sure. When I was hiding in the dumpster, I heard him say some things that really frightened me."

"Like what?"

"I could have sworn he mentioned demons, but I really couldn't hear much from where I was hiding. But I'm fairly confident that he'll come out here."

"How do you know?"

Tiffany's expression turned grim. "You know about him. You might tell others. He won't like that."

Tiffany's explanation hit her like a splash of ice water. "You don't mean—"

Tiffany nodded.

It keeps getting worse and worse. But I can't let it frighten me.

She struggled to concentrate on the task ahead. They had to get him out here. If he showed up, maybe they'd get lucky. But whatever happened, she was determined to see this through. She couldn't live with herself if someone else was hurt.

They coasted down the familiar overrun path. Just beyond them, the woods cried out in silent desperation. Barbed wire

(Know what barb wire will do to paint and metal?)

blocked their path. She veered to the right, and they eased past a scattered trail of beer bottles. Her thoughts accelerated, becoming disjointed images.

Todd and Leon smoking joints.

She wants to conjure up a demon.

Demons. Heavy-duty.

"Keep going." Tiffany's voice sliced through her guilt, jarring her back to the present.

Darcy coaxed the Maxima through the weeds, past the spot where Todd had parked. "I thought we were going to the mine."

"We have to find the dump."

"That's farther down."

"It's where Chip and I came up."

"Where...did you come up...*from*?" Darcy asked uneasily.

"Hell." Tiffany's voice was barely a whisper.

Darcy stiffened. "You mean –"

"I mean Hell. The Darkworld. Not a nice place, believe me."

"But how…I mean why…a lady like *you*?" She no longer felt the wheel; her fists had gone numb. "How could someone like *you* end up down there?"

"It doesn't matter now." Tiffany's face had become dark and lifeless. Heat radiated from her.

What had Tiffany done to end up in that terrible place? How could a sweet, lovely lady like her—

She was gazing at Tiffany when the Maxima slammed into a deadfall half-hidden in the tall weeds, forcing a gasp from both of them.

Darcy pried her hands from the wheel. "You okay?"

Tiffany pushed open her door and jumped out. "We need to keep moving."

As they trudged up the grassy slope, the approaching gloom of darkness sucked every bit of light and hope from the air.

The dark, swollen mass of the woods quickly enveloped them.

Tiffany stood very still. She seemed to be listening. "We'd better take cover." Then she slipped between some bushes.

Darcy followed.

About twenty yards farther down the wooded path, Tiffany stopped once again. "Someone's coming."

"Is it…him?"

"Possibly."

Tingly shards of fear scraped heavily down Darcy's arms.

Tiffany's eyes glinted. "Darcy, I want you to go on over to those bushes and crawl inside. Don't move or make a sound."

"Then what?"

"You'll know when to come out."

That didn't make sense. How could she possibly know when to come out? And what was Tiffany going to do during this time? She didn't want Tiffany to face the demon guy alone, she wanted to help get rid of him. She'd hate herself if she didn't at least try and help set everything right. "But what will you be doing while—"

"No need to worry. I'll be just fine."

"But I want to help—"

"Darcy, go in there right now and hide. I want you to understand something first. It's not your fault your friends are dead or that the demon's up here. Demons have hundreds of ways of escaping. If they want up here badly enough, they'll find a way."

"But if it wasn't for me, none of this—"

"You got in the middle of this by accident, but soon everything will be just fine."

"Will I…see you again?"

"Just do as I say, all right?"

Darcy wondered what had just happened. Why Tiffany had suddenly changed. Why all the light had vanished from her beautiful face.

"Trust me," Tiffany said softly.

Darcy suddenly realized she would never see Tiffany again. She also realized things might actually turn out all right.

But she still wanted to help. Once the demon guy went back down and things were okay again, she and Tiffany could be best friends.

"But I thought we could maybe—"

Black…

391

CHAPTER 62

Louis Suffers a Memory Lapse
Gutril Gets Suspicious

As his vision cleared, Louis kept the Mustang steady on the winding country road.

He didn't even remember getting in the car. But now he and Gutier were headed north on Raven Road West, toward the Interstate.

What's going on? First, Tiffany disappears. Then I find Gutier sniffing around in the back yard. Now I'm driving out to the Interstate.

Trent probably elbowed me harder than I thought.

"What's going on?" Louis asked curiously.

"Keep driving." Gutier stared straight ahead and chewed his lower lip. He seemed anxious and upset.

"What's up?" Louis asked.

"Just drive."

"Something's up."

"What makes you say that?"

"I took a Psychology course in college. I can tell when someone's anxious and upset. You're chewing your lower lip. That's a definite sign."

"I've got gas."

"You chew your lower lip when you've got gas?"

"Doesn't everyone?"

"*I* don't."

"I give up. What do *you* do when you've got gas?"

Louis shrugged. "Take Tums. Fart a lot. Cuss myself out for having that last helping of baked beans. But I don't chew my lower lip."

"I'm *so* glad you've got your act together. Now turn here."

"But …that leads to the dump."

"Thanks for the tour guide info. Now turn, like I said."

"Why? Nothing there but trash."

"Trash? Is *that* what they're putting in dumps nowadays?"

Gutier sure was being a smartass. But why? And why was he so bent on going to the dump?

"I'm just curious. And a little nervous because I can't even remember getting in the car, and I really can't figure why we've come here in the first—"

Louis's mind suddenly went blank.

***

What seemed like a moment later, he found that he was slumped behind the wheel of the Mustang in a wooded field. Twenty yards straight ahead, Gutier's lean figure descended behind the overgrown slope. To Louis's left, a light-colored Nissan, its front bumper pressed against a fallen buckeye, sat in overgrown weeds. The car looked empty.

Shaky, Louis got out of the Mustang.

A strange flower poked out of the ground near the rear tire. It was very large and seemed out of place. He couldn't remember seeing such a flower before.

Being out here was playing havoc with his senses. He needed to drive back to town and look for Tiffany. Why should he care about Gutier in the first place? That boy was entirely too damned weird.

Louis turned back to the Mustang.

No sign of the flower.

***

Gutril reached the top of the hill.

He was certain the Darcy girl had called him from this area. He hadn't picked up anything when Gates drove past the mine entrance. But he had gotten a clear picture of the woods during her summoning and knew she was out here somewhere.

But why summon him *here*?

And if so, where *was* she? And who was that blonde Gates was worried about?

Something about her tickled his memory.

Her scent…

It suddenly brought it all back.

The Valley of Decay.

It was. Yes. Same hair, same tits, same blank look.

But…how did she get up *here*?

She would only be able to escape if the Legion had ordered her to—

To what? Take him down?

The laughter gushed through him in uncontrollable spasms.

***

The sight of the wolf guy laughing hysterically caused bursts of heat exploding inside her.

Tiffany stepped away from the pine tree.

Seeing her, the wolf guy stopped laughing. "Hey! If it ain't the lost party girl! Cool beans! Ever find your buds?"

"Didn't get the chance."

"What happened?"

"I guess you could say I was shanghaied."

"I figured you were lonely. Needed livening up. I felt sorry for you."

"Lucky for me you cared so much."

"You don't have to thank me now. Maybe later—when I get bored."

His arrogance grated on her. "I'll bet you didn't expect to see me again, did you?"

"I haven't given you much thought. I've been kinda busy."

"I've heard. Food fights and restaurant shootings. How *gauche*."

"We all do interesting things when we're bored."

"A real shame."

He obviously didn't catch her sarcasm. "So…how'd you get up here—what did you say your name was?"

"*Tiffany*. You really should learn about the people you pull into Hell. Or are you just too stupid to care?"

"Ouch. You sound bitter."

"I didn't think it showed."

"Don't take it personal. Anyway, I'm lousy with names."

"You're just plain lousy."

"My, we've got a sizeable chip on our shoulder, haven't we?"

"I was sent here to take you back down."

"Just you? Alone? Without help?"

"Just little ol' me. All alone. Without help."

"This is really far out. Whatever would possess them to use a dumb blonde with silicone boobs and collagen lips to bring me back down?"

"I guess they wanted the job done right, so they decided to send a woman. A woman who isn't dumb at all. And the breasts—as well as the lips—are all mine."

"Let me put it this way. In a word, they screwed up. And there's no way that stuff is real."

"That's three words. And I was born with this stuff, thank you."

"Let's not quibble. Wanna play a game?"

"No, I won't pull your stupid finger." When would this jerk ever learn?

"How about if I change into one of your movie heroes again?"

"Not in the mood."

"How about if I just send you back down where you belong?"

The heat inside her continued to grow. "Not interested."

"You're really being obstinate, baby cakes."

"I'm *trying* to be..."

"You're doing a real bang-up job."

"Thanks *so* much."

"Enough with the chit chat. We need to play our little game. I've got stuff to do, mortals to annoy."

"I wouldn't want to take you away from your true calling."

"I'm *so* glad you understand. Now listen...I'm gonna close my eyes and count to ten."

"Then what?"

"When I open my eyes, once I find you again, it's back down to the Valley for you. Ready?"

"You sure talk a lot."

"Baby, I see why they picked you. You're sassy, ballsy, and probably deliciously sweet wrapped in a bun—"

"Just shut up and count."

He closed his eyes. "One..."

Something swayed in the breeze to her right.

A flower. The same one she saw down below. Its scent was vaguely familiar. In fact, it smelled almost like—

"Two…"

Enough of that. Get away *fast*.

"Three…"

Tiffany slipped quietly into the brush.

CHAPTER 63

The Persuader Retires

Nervous and a little frightened, Phil Holeridge closed the heavy metal door behind him.

"We could all be facing big trouble," Joe Flynn told him five minutes earlier, as he stepped into the Sheriff's office.

"Whatever do you mean?" Holeridge asked.

"The man you paid to get the restaurant back."

"What about him?"

"You better just take a little walk so you can see him for yourself."

"Speak plain, Joe. Tell me what you're—"

"Wish I could. But you'd think I was funny. Or drunk."

Holeridge didn't like the sound of this. "What's stopping you?" he asked softly.

"Go talk to the boy. You'll see what I'm gettin' at."

Holeridge moved hesitantly down the aisle and stopped in front of the last cell.

Wadded up in the corner, his knees drawn up, the pathetic figure hugged his pillow. His face pale and drawn, he stared at the graffiti on the concrete wall. His sweatshirt was damp, the sweat reek strong in the confined space.

"Can you...hear me?" Holeridge asked uneasily.

No reply.

"It's me," he said. "Your employ—"

"Haunted." His raspy voice sounded like a cough.

"W-What?"

The blinking eyes shot to the right, then the left. The pillow lowered. "That place," he whispered. "It's haunted."

"What are you talking about?"

Scheckley nodded slowly, over and over.

"Haunted? By what?"

"Demons."

This was worse than he'd suspected. Even worse than what Flynn had hinted at. Travis had recently arrested someone wandering the streets, rambling about demons and witches. Holeridge hadn't had any idea the man in question was Scheckley. Good thing Flynn had intervened, telling Travis to keep his mouth shut. Talk about a stroke of luck...

"Tell me about them," Holeridge urged softly.

"They live in the dumpster. Behind the restaurant. If anyone messes with them, an evil hag makes bad stuff happen."

"An evil *hag*?"

"She lives in the dumpster, too. She's the queen demon."

Holeridge sighed. "What sort of bad stuff?"

"She can turn into a beautiful woman. She reads minds. And she can make you see things."

"Like what?"

"My mother's been dead for three years but I saw her. I really did. Yep. Sure did." His voice sounded like a child's. "Saw her, plain as day. And my old teacher, Miss Storm. Saw her, too. And *Twilight Zone* episodes."

"*Twilight Zone* episodes?"

Scheckley's blinking eyes darted from one end of the cell to the next. "The hag used to watch them, too, before

399

she became a demon. There was also that one about a robot that came to life…and mannequins…"

Scheckley continued babbling as Holeridge hurried down the hall, where sanity awaited him just beyond the door.

CHAPTER 64

Birth of a Butt-Kicker

"*Ten!*"

Gutril's voice tore sharply through the trees. "Ready or not, here I come!"

He turned around. No sign of her. She certainly knew how to make tracks. But it only stood to reason. A female looking like her would learn early on to move quickly.

Her strong, sweet scent pulled him farther into the woods. Good thing his excellent night vision hadn't failed him. Otherwise, she might slip away.

A strand of golden hair waved at him behind a pine tree just a few yards from the clearing ahead.

Coming, baby...

He could finally have the fun he had planned to have with her before he was summoned up here and—

He stopped moving. Something had been bugging him since he got here.

Where was the Darcy girl? Why summon him here? And why was Blondie here instead of the Darcy girl?

The scene outside Neely's gushed back. The blonde passing, glancing at the Darcy girl.

Who was that skinny redhead?

Sudden movement caught his eye.

Down the grassy slope, a shadow crouched behind the tall buckeye tree.

A fat, delicious-looking Chihuahua crept into view.

***

Tiffany kept her back pressed against the base of the tree and tried not to breathe.

The wolf guy wasn't far behind. She could sense him drawing closer.

But the footsteps had stopped.

Tiffany quietly let out her breath. She knew he could probably smell her, but she was determined to make this difficult for him. Bad enough she had made it so easy before.

She peered around the base of the pine tree. Chip, crawling on all fours, came into view.

Her heart leaped with joy and relief.

How did he get out *here*?

It didn't matter. Now that they were together again, they might be able to do this, once and for all.

The wolf guy's back faced her. He stood motionless, gazing at Chip, who had also stopped moving.

Tiffany kept close to the trees. The wolf guy had obviously forgotten about her.

Chip inched away from the buckeye. The wolf guy crept closer.

Suddenly Chip launched into a doggie mambo of yapping, howling, and snarling.

The wolf guy's features rapidly changed into the furry folds of a wolf. His ears shrunk, their tops forming hairy points. His nose grew into a wrinkled snout. Reddish fur jutted from every pore, covering his flesh. He lowered himself and rested his lean figure on all fours. His back arched, he crept cautiously toward Chip. "Here, doggy-doggy!"

The small hairy red butt provided the perfect target.

A stab of heat wrenched through her.

Violent images stormed by. The Meddaworld. The dark, foul-smelling forest of crippled trees and cold, clammy earth.

In Hell. For eternity. Because of this creep.

She looked down at her feet. The pumps were not made for this. They weren't even suitable for walking in the woods, let alone doing anything more strenuous.

For this job, she needed *tough*. And *powerful*.

Tiffany closed her eyes. Her anger worked for her, instantly creating a clear mental picture of a pair of heavy-duty steel-toed iron worker's boots.

Go, girl...

Let him have it!

She took one more cautious step closer, held her breath...

And thought: *field goal!*

The thump of hard leather-covered steel connected with soft flesh. A high-pitched squeal ricocheted off the trees.

The furry figure sailed ten feet in the air and flipped, executing a perfect backward somersault. When the wolf guy came back down, he landed on the strange-looking flower, now positioned over the crack in the soil where Chip had been only a moment before.

The wolf guy jerked on the ground. His eyes squeezed shut. Drool from his gaping mouth splashed the grass. He appeared to be shrinking as if the air was being sucked out of him.

In just moments, the wolf guy and the flower were pulled into the ground.

Nothing remained but the small, jagged crack puncturing the soil.

Tiffany rushed over and dropped to her knees. "Chip?"

The tiny fissure revealed nothing.

"Chip? Are you down there?"

Silence.

CHAPTER 65

The Trickster Returns
Tiffany Casts a Final Spell

Chip pushed himself out of the hole.

Taffy hadn't budged since he'd dragged Gutril back down. She wore her standard deer-in-the-headlights expression—possibly because she had no idea what happened.

However, he figured his own expression wasn't much different.

That babe had just kicked a sub's ass! He couldn't believe it.

He brushed himself off and fluffed out his hair. Dirt, mashed bugs, and strands of damp roots dropped to the ground beside him.

"Why didn't you tell me you knew how to kick butt?" he asked. "I might have been less of a jerk. Not much, but a little."

She smiled sheepishly. "I guess I just lost my cool."

"Cupcake, you kicked a sub's butt! Any idea what that means?"

"I really wasn't thinking too much about it."

Was this chick for real? She was talking about it as if it were nothing at all. "Well, I'm glad you did. I almost became that asshole's supper."

"So…what happened? Where did you two go?"

He brushed more dirt from his trousers. "I took him back where he belongs."

"You took him down already?"

"Elementary, lamb chop. You did all the dirty work."

"By the way, how did you get out here?"

"Hitched a ride with the restaurant owner guy."

"Lou?"

"Is he the restaurant owner guy?"

"Yes."

"Then yeah. I hitched a ride with Lou."

Her face quickly changed from humble to stupid. "Lou's out here?" she asked softly, looking around.

"Somewhere."

"Where?" Her stupid expression quickly changed to concern.

Ah. A little hanky-panky going on, perhaps?

"How should *I* know? Anyway, I made myself look like a bumper sticker. I believe it said *Eat More Eggs*. Couldn't get in the car; Gutril would've sniffed me out."

"You must have been close for quite a while, then."

"Ever since our little chat at the Police Station."

"What was that flower thing?"

"If I told you, I'd have to kill you."

"I'm already dead."

"Shuckers, I forgot. Well, if you must know, that was my spirit form."

A frown. "You mean you're…a *flower*?"

"Watch how you say that, Miss Infamy—"

"It's *Tiffany*."

"Whatever. One of us is sensitive about his roots—pardon the pun."

"What kind are you?"

"I've already told you my name. Can't you remember anything?"

She crossed her arms. "I wouldn't talk if I were you…"

"Nobody's perfect. But like I said, I already told you—"

406

"Something with a million letters that sounds like Surreptitious Calculator—"

"Cypripedium Calceolus, dammit."

"It's kind of pretty."

"For your information, I'm quite beautiful, stylish and especially dazzling in the morning sunlight. I'm known as the Yellow Lady's Slipper, and I'm extremely rare."

"So that's why you like water so much."

"And eggshells—"

"And dirt."

"Sometimes, my amazingly amorous amigo, your powers of deduction are delightfully delectable."

"Where do you—where does this flower—grow?"

"If you study my heritage, you'll discover I'm also known as the American Valerian, named after Valeriana Wallichii—"

"You're Italian?"

For a butt-kicker, she could be *such* a lightweight...

"Now you're being insulting, Buttercup. The Valeriana Wallichii, which comes from *India*, is used to treat nervous disorders. It's a mild stimulant for depression related to female problems. In this country, the Cherokee Indians used the flower for medicinal—"

"What's this have to do with the wolf guy?"

"Since you already had him lathered up, I distracted him with food. From what I've heard, he's a sucker for a fresh doggy meal."

"*That's* why you made him think you were a dog..."

"I thought I'd lend the moment a nice, subtle touch."

"Kind of scary, though. He looked hungry."

"Good thing you lost your cool. He wanted to turn me into mucilage."

407

"I'm glad it didn't get that far. But why'd you do it?"

"He was after you, wasn't he?"

She blinked. "You did it…for *me*?"

Females could be really disgusting when you were nice to them. "I really wish you wouldn't get so sloppy all the time. It's embarrassing."

"I can't help it. That was really sweet."

"I also wish you'd stop with the insults. I just hoped you'd think of something quick."

"Everything worked out."

"Thanks to your tasteful, tush-terrorizing tootsie. Since you disoriented Gutril with pain, he wasn't in the best position to think clearly. He was probably too busy thinking of a graceful landing. I used my stimulant powers and zapped him senseless when he landed on me. They were waiting for him when we went down."

"Why'd you come back?"

"Guess."

Another dazed look. He wondered if she even remembered they had to go back down. Probably thinking about the ensemble she wanted to wear tomorrow.

"We…have to go back *down*?" she whispered in her little girl's voice.

"I know this will probably tear you up, but—"

"Tiffany!"

The restaurant owner guy emerged from the woods.

***

Guided by the distant voices, Louis reached the clearing. Tiffany and a skinny red-headed young guy in dire need of a haircut were talking in front of a buckeye tree. And Tiffany was wearing what looked like a pair of heavy-duty work boots.

Louis' head pounded.

408

Another blackout coming on?

Didn't matter. There were more important things to address. He needed to know why Tiffany had come out here. Why she was with another man. And why so much sadness shrouded her face as he approached her.

"You're okay?"

She nodded.

"When I woke up and found you gone…"

"I'm fine."

"Where'd you get the work boots?"

She smiled sheepishly. "Had them in my bag."

"Where's your bag?"

The redhead mumbled something.

Without taking her eyes off Louis, she said, "Chip…do you mind?"

"We don't have much time," he said.

"This is important."

"So is this."

"But—"

"Listen. I didn't have time to tell you what happens next."

She turned to the redhead. "Tell me now."

"With him standing there?"

"Just give me a rough idea."

"With him standing there?"

Tiffany smiled at Louis. He thought she was about to say something, but—

Black…

He opened his eyes an instant later.

Tiffany's radiant smile lit up the night. Her companion stood behind the buckeye tree, pulled something from a branch, sniffed it, and popped it into his mouth.

What was going on? Yet another blackout?

Just a moment ago Tiffany seemed so sad. Her face now beamed with happiness while her friend munched on a tree. And she was now wearing her fancy pumps again.

Idiot. You should have had yourself checked out right after the shooting.

"I've got to go," she whispered.

"You're…going away?"

"I'm afraid so." The sadness returned.

This made no sense. "I thought we had…a good thing—"

"It's got nothing to do with you. Or with us."

His head grew hot. Once again a woman decided to end things with him. "I guess I can't shake this streak of bad luck," he said.

"Like I said, this has nothing to do with you. You're the finest man I've ever met. You'll find someone very soon. I promise."

"Why can't you stay?"

She turned to the redhead, who avoided her eyes.

This was obviously another dream. Last he remembered, he and this terrific woman were making love in his bed. It was wonderful. He couldn't even remember it ending.

"Will I ever see you again?" he asked.

Tiffany placed her hands on his shoulders. Her touch made him weak. *You're supposed to be strong*, he reminded himself. But how could he be when a woman like Tiffany was about to walk out of his life?

"One last kiss," she whispered.

Her warm lips pressed against his.

The kiss revitalized him, made him realize things might not be so bleak.

"I'll never forget you," he said.

"Yes you will." She sounded like she meant it.

But how could he possibly forget such a terrific woman?

Why would he *want* to?

"I…don't understand…"

"If I handle this right, you won't have to."

This didn't make a lick of sense.

Maybe true love was never meant to make sense. It was so rare, so pure. Something that takes shape in a single moment and vanishes the instant it grabs your attention. Like a rainbow. Or a snowflake dropping gently onto your cheek.

"Tiffany—"

"Turn around and walk away. Please?"

His heart was breaking. He couldn't do this. He couldn't even though she obviously wanted him to.

He forced himself to turn away. To leave a woman he had known only briefly. A woman who had literally stolen his heart in a single moment. A woman he had grown to love instantly—as if by magic.

The solemn black hulk of the woods leered at him.

This was not right. When you found someone so wonderful, so special, you didn't walk away. And you certainly didn't let the woman of your dreams wander off with another man.

Maybe she wanted to hear him say how he felt. To hear it in his voice, see it in his eyes. Hearing it might change her mind. It might be all she wanted.

Just turn around, give that gorgeous face your best smile—

Black…

CHAPTER 66

The Legacy of a Dysfunctional Demon

Phil Holeridge closed the Gold Room door.

Everyone was understandably restless tonight. Miles Ladner gnawed a fingernail. Bill Elliot performed a steady drum roll on the gleaming surface of the mahogany table. Ira Crenshaw and Noel Thomas swirled brandy and stared at the darkness pressing against the big bay window. Alan Crenshaw squirmed in his seat.

Leonard Winslow and Augustus Phelps hadn't shown yet. Holeridge snuck a peek at his watch. These men were seldom late—especially for an emergency meeting.

"Anyone hear from Augustus or Leonard?" Holeridge took his seat.

Two negative grunts drifted across the table.

Ira said, "I think I saw them on Chestnut about half an hour ago, as I was leaving the store."

Holeridge grabbed a brandy snifter. "I'm sure they'll show."

"Let's discuss this man we hired," Bill Elliot said.

"Agreed," Noel said.

"They caught him running down Church Street, chattering away like an idiot," Bill said.

"Didn't seem to notice the traffic swerving around him, either," Miles Ladner added.

"I intervened in time," Holeridge said. "Very few questions were asked. His cover wasn't blown. We can all breathe easier."

Miles grabbed a toothpick from the silver cup. "What was his fee for this shitstorm?"

Holeridge selected a cigar and lit it. "I don't think the details of the contract are important right now."

"I think they are," Bill Elliot said. "If we can no longer depend on competent help—"

"The man is a highly competent professional." Holeridge hoped he sounded convincing enough.

"Why'd he go nutso, then?"

Holeridge shrugged. "The situation spiraled out of his control."

"Were you aware of a mental problem?" Ira asked.

"I'm not sure he has one." Holeridge wanted to deflect this. Things wouldn't escalate if he didn't let on what happened.

"He was babbling about witches when Travis arrested him."

"Joe Flynn is handling this," Holeridge said. "The man was put on a chartered plane that will land in Washington, D.C., within the hour. He'll be picked up by a team of medical experts. They'll email me their findings."

"Did you talk to him?" Miles asked.

"Briefly."

"Did you get anything out of him?"

They live in the dumpster…behind the restaurant.

"Very little." Holeridge struggled to ignore that strange conversation. He blew a smoke ring.

"Then let's discuss the Presbyterian Church renovation," Noel said. "How's that coming along?"

"It'll have to be postponed," Holeridge said. Spencer's reluctance after Services convinced him they might be pushing too hard. "The Reverend needs more time. We'll all profit if we set this aside temporarily."

413

"Then what about the restaurant?" Bill Elliot asked sourly.

Holeridge reluctantly believed Balbor's absence had left them defenseless. Unforeseen factors stripping away their protective barriers had caused a chain of negative events to unfold.

He chose to address this more positively. "I've analyzed the writing on the wall. Things haven't been favorable since the shooting."

"You can't possibly blame this on Trent," Holeridge said. "There's been a domino effect. You're having lunch and someone at the next table jumps up and starts shooting. It's a near-death experience."

"What are you saying? We're giving up?"

"I think it would be in our best interest."

"Our best *interest*," Bill Elliot said, "is getting another benefactor. None of this would have happened otherwise."

"We've been through this before," Noel said. "It's like beating a dead horse. And it's making us all cranky."

"The last three days have been unduly hectic," Holeridge said. "We all need a break."

Several affirmative grunts echoed around the table.

"Speaking of three days," Ira said. "Why'd you want the restaurant in three days?"

Holeridge sighed and sipped some brandy. Most of these men were fathers. They would understand his dilemma. "My son's birthday is Saturday," he said.

"So?" Bill asked.

"He wanted an arcade."

"So?" from Ira.

Holeridge shrugged. "I figured Denner's was the perfect building."

414

"You wanted the restaurant for *that*?"

"Dammit." Miles shot over a glare. "All this for an *arcade*? For a *kid*?"

Holeridge sank in his seat.

"An *arcade*?" Bill Elliot nearly choked on the last word.

Ira said, "One of those places with loud, annoying games and even louder, more annoying *kids*?"

Noel mashed his cigar in the ashtray. "Tell us you're putting us on."

"I haven't liked this at all, gentlemen. The boy's twelve and—"

"An arcade will turn that block into a den of juvenile delinquents!"

"We offered Gates what?" Miles asked. "Around a mill and a half? Just so you could turn that place into a damned *arcade*?"

"I figured that if the arcade went down, we could turn it back."

"That would be fine," Miles said. "As long as those little idiots didn't make everything a shambles. I know what kids do when they're bored."

"Look what those two idiots did outside my building Friday night," Ira said sourly.

"They weren't bored," Tom Elliot said. "They were drunk."

"Drunk, bored—they still made a goddamn mess…"

"How can kids get bored in an arcade?" Holeridge asked.

"Kids get bored in amusement parks," Miles said. "At football games. Rock concerts. Movie theaters. The last time I took my wife to the theater, some idiot teen sitting behind us spilled a jug of Pepsi on the floor. I nearly broke my neck when I got up to leave."

"How much did we shell out for this fiasco?" Noel asked.

Holeridge had more brandy. "I paid him ten percent of a hundred K up front."

"Then you owe us ten grand."

"No problem," Holeridge said.

"And an apology for such a ridiculous blunder," Ira added.

"You gentlemen have my deepest apologies."

"An arcade for a twelve-year-old." Miles rubbed the back of his neck.

"You have kids, Miles." Holeridge felt the need for some sympathy. "Have you forgotten that classic XK-E you bought your grandson on his sixteenth birthday?"

"That was different. When the moron got bored, I sent it to auction and made a profit of five grand."

A knock at the door.

Holeridge got up, crossed the room, and unlocked it.

Leonard and Augustus came in quietly and took their seats.

"Problem, gentlemen?" Holeridge returned to the table. "It's not like either of you to be late."

Augustus took the brandy Ira handed him. "We were…at the church."

"Discussing the renovation plans?" Holeridge asked.

"That's why we went," Augustus said.

"Initially," muttered Leonard.

"What happened?"

"We talked about…attending Services," Leonard said.

Silence.

"We do attend," Holeridge said cautiously. "It's expected of us as town elders."

"We don't worship," Augustus said. "We sit there and try not to doze off. There's a world of difference between going to church for appearances and going there to worship."

"This is blasphemy." Bill Elliot scowled.

Yes, Holeridge thought uneasily. It *was* blasphemy. Leonard and Augustus had been members of the Committee the last forty years. They never once gave the slightest indication of backsliding. Something unforeseeable must have happened. "What else did you discuss?" he asked.

Augustus loosened his tie. "The Reverend asked us to be ushers."

"And what did you tell him?" Holeridge asked.

Augustus shrugged. "I said we'd...be happy to."

Moaning filled the room.

"What's next?" Miles snapped. "Don't tell us you've decided to lead the swarm in prayer?"

"I think the correct term is flock," Tom Elliot said.

"Swarm, flock, mob—what the hell's the difference?"

Holeridge turned to Leonard, who customarily showed more finesse than Augustus. Perhaps he could clear this up. "Leonard? Something you'd like to add?"

"I...volunteered to help the Boy's Club...with their woodworking projects."

"*What*?"

"This is the end!"

Bill Elliot stood up and nearly knocked over his brandy snifter. "What the hell's going on?"

Holeridge realized how quickly things were going south. Before it turned ugly, they needed to put it to rest. "I think we all should sit back and take a breath," he said. "Leonard? Are you all right?"

"Fine."

"Then why—"

"I'm a carpenter by trade." The trace of a grin touched Leonard's gaunt cheeks.

"We all know that. But…the *Boy's Club*?"

"Spencer asked me. I couldn't say no."

"Couldn't say no to the usher gig, either," Augustus said dryly.

First an usher? Now the Boy's Club? Just days after Trent's rampage in the restaurant? And right after Scheckley went stark-raving nuts?

Better put a handle on this. Somehow.

"This kind of thinking is unhealthy," Holeridge said. "We've all taken an oath."

"Our conjuration attempts haven't been answered," Augustus said, shrugging. "What's left?"

"You were a churchgoer years ago, Augustus. Don't you remember what turned your head around?"

"Our prayers were never answered. My father lost his savings, then his health. My mother died of cancer. Our house was robbed during her funeral."

"When you joined us, your life improved drastically."

Augustus said nothing. The shame in the man's eyes was clear.

"Boy's Club," Miles said sourly. "First this arcade nonsense from Phil. Now *this*?"

"You know something?" Noel said, tapping his chin. "Augustus might have a valid point."

"Don't tell me *you're* gonna succumb to sudden brain loss as well," Bill Elliot barked.

"Without a benefactor," Noel said, "it's almost like we're Christians, anyway—"

"I won't stand here and be insulted!" Elliot backed up. "Especially by a so-called *friend*!"

"These aren't insults," Augustus said. "They're facts."

Holeridge stood. "Gentlemen, *please*…"

Ira said, "I'm leaving if this isn't stopped this instant. It's grossing me out."

"I think we're all just tired," Holeridge said. "Bill, *please* sit."

"This is actually scaring me." Bill Elliot reluctantly took his seat.

Holeridge sat back down and sighed tiredly. "Anything else we need to know?" he asked. "Augustus? Leonard?"

Augustus said, "I told Spencer Ira might consider joining the choir—"

"*What*?" Ira jumped up.

More moaning. Noel covered his mouth to hold back a chuckle.

Augustus shrugged. "Ira used to sing—"

"Fifty years ago!" Ira's face splashed red. "Whatever possessed you to include *me* in your sudden plunge into total idiocy?"

"Spencer asked me."

"So?"

"It was strange," Leonard said softly. "Whatever Spencer asked, we had to say yes."

Augustus nodded. "I got this warm feeling—"

"That's gas," Ira said dryly.

"You've been hexed," Bill Elliot said. "I don't know how that preacher did it, but he hexed both of you."

"I didn't know religious people did that," Alan Crenshaw said.

"They do it," Ira said. "Especially the fanatics. Those people are *scary*..."

"The ones causing the mass hysteria thing you hear about," Bill Elliot said. "They claim to have the touch. They're *touched*, all right!"

"Look at those two." Noel gestured to Leonard and Augustus. "Anyone can tell something's wrong with them."

"They look constipated to me," Miles said sourly.

"We need to clear this up." Holeridge couldn't let Augustus and Leonard join the other side. They were good men. "Leonard? Augustus? You're not saying you want out, are you?"

Their lack of response was disheartening.

"Donating a little of our time won't hurt anything," Augustus said.

"It's been so long since I've done *any* carpentry," Leonard said.

"We need to stay away from Spencer," Noel said. "Bill's right. Our pastor's been touched."

"No problem," Ira said. "Just don't look for me in their damned choir. I've got better things to do."

"Better than serenading the congregation with your rusty old pipes?" Bill said, chuckling.

"Funny," Ira grumbled.

"I think *I* need to have a talk with Spencer," Holeridge said. It was important to set an example. These men desperately needed guidance.

"*I* wouldn't," Bill said.

"No need to worry." Holeridge grinned. "I don't think *any* man can force me to do anything I'm not about to do."

"I don't know," Augustus said softly. "I had no intention of volunteering as an *usher*."

"I don't even *like* kids," Leonard said.

CHAPTER 67

Returning Home

Drifting slowly awake, Darcy rubbed her eyes. The heavy mass of blackness startled her.

Have I gone blind?

Cautiously she crawled out from her nest in the tall bushes.

Nighttime. Orange slivers of moon hiding behind a puffy gray cloud provided a faint swirl of hazy light.

Her arms tingled with stickers. Grass, pine needles, and broken twigs covered her shirt and the back of her neck. She brushed it off. More needles and twigs clung to her hair.

How did I get here?

She phoned the school this morning to tell them she was sick. That was a lie, of course, but she didn't want to face her classmates so soon after Todd and Leon died.

The guilt had taken over. She had been sleepwalking ever since, unaware of anything else.

She struggled to recall the last few hours.

Why did she come here? Closure?

She had no idea. Her existence had taken on the soft, cloudy sensation of a dream. Since Todd and Leon were gone, nothing felt the same.

Conjuring up a *demon*, of all things.

She couldn't believe she'd been so gullible. So silly.

She had to make this right. Coming out here where it all started seemed the most natural thing to do. She couldn't undo what happened, of course.

However, a soft, caressing voice in her head told her she might eventually be able to look in the mirror again without hating herself. And when she finally forgave herself, things wouldn't be so bleak.

Why did she have this strange feeling everything would be all right again?

The harder she tried to remember, the hazier her memory grew. She knew she should be disturbed by this, but she wasn't. The voice in her head suggested some things just weren't worth the bother.

Her subconscious, no doubt. Because of it, her guilt had ebbed into an almost inaudible hum.

It really wasn't her fault Todd and Leon died. If they had stayed at the house with her and listened to the Sabbath until they passed out, they would both still be alive.

As common sense told her, terrible things happened to people all the time. It was no one's fault. It was life.

She descended the grassy slope. At the foot of the hill, dark shapes huddled just beyond the weed-choked rise.

Bags of garbage and tossed furniture.

The dump.

What am I doing here?

Twenty yards from the foot of the rise, a sloped shape *(Cammie?)*

crouched in the bushes like a cat.

Darcy covered her eyes and turned away.

No. Cammie was gone. Todd had turned his beloved ride into a shattered husk of seared metal.

She rushed over to the Maxima and climbed in. Her temples pounding, she flicked on her headlights.

The darkness glowed with a bright sheen of white, jarring the jagged bulk of the woods back to life.

A late-model Mustang.

423

Someone dumping trash?

Two people in the back seat, making out?

Her lights didn't reveal anyone, but they could be slouched down in the seats. She knew better than disturb them.

You had better be getting home.

Home. The mere thought of it brought a smile to her lips. She had never experienced such warmth thinking about it before. Like her friends, she longed for the day when she could venture out on her own to discover what life had to offer.

But right now, she could think of nothing better than driving back to the house.

She knew everything would be just fine once she joined Mom and Dad on the living room couch in front of the flat screen.

***

Consciousness flooded back. Louis surveyed his surroundings.

He was standing about five feet from the driver's door of the Mustang. He remembered a strange flower, but right now he couldn't decide if it was a dream or just another hallucination. The darkness had made everything blurry and indistinct. There was no flower there now.

He also remembered another car being out here.

Now there was nothing.

He obviously needed a checkup.

You don't even know why you're out here.

Tiffany. He'd come out here to make sure she'd gotten on her bus.

Out *here*?

The Interstate cut into the hill on the other side of the slope. No more than a mile down the road. How else could she get on a bus?

So what are you doing out here in the middle of the woods?

Looking for Gutier, no doubt.

He remembered seeing Gutier's slender figure disappearing behind the grassy slope.

Where the hell had that idiot gone?

Another disappearing act, obviously.

Louis slid behind the wheel and turned on the ignition. His headlights splashed a soft curtain of orange fog brushing the grass and into the trees beyond.

What happened to that other vehicle?

Kids wandering around, checking out that haunted mine theory?

When did they leave? And where was he when they did?

Plodding around in the woods, looking for Gutier— where else? He hoped Tiffany had gotten safely on her bus. He wanted to wait until it came but she told him she'd be all right, that she wanted him to head back home. Thanks for everything, she had said.

Everything else was sketchy. He couldn't even remember what he said to her. He recalled someone else waiting with her. Some skinny guy with red hair.

Forget about it. Just drive back to the restaurant, have a strong drink, and sack out. You helped her and now she's going to resume her life. At least she'll be far away from that moron who assaulted her in your bar.

Tomorrow you can check in for an examination. These blackouts are getting scary.

But what about Gutier? Should he just leave him out here?

"Gutier, go to hell. I have better things to do."

He pulled a pack of cigarettes from his shirt pocket, shook one out and stuck it in a corner of his mouth.

Trying to quit, remember?

He tossed them out the window. Then he slipped the car into reverse and backed down the grassy slope.

CHAPTER 68

Tiffany's Legacy

On this cool, clear night, the dark-blue veil of sky brought an easy smile to Edwin Spencer 's face.

He took in some fresh, exhaust-free air and felt the tightness in his limbs loosening. The foulness he noticed filling the air the last three days seemed to have disappeared.

Two sloppy-dressed, bearded men leaned against the streetlight at the corner of Church Street and Chestnut, smoking cigarettes.

"Have you gentlemen had supper?" Spencer asked.

Both glanced in his direction but said nothing.

"You'd better go on in before the food runs out. I hear the pot roast is excellent."

Without a word they tossed their smokes and bolted inside.

Amazing...

Since Spencer left the Chapel, everyone had obeyed his every word. A short while ago, Mary Ann Riff, who hadn't been to Services in years, agreed to participate Sunday. Before that, an emaciated gray-haired man bringing a burning cigarette into the cellar had, at Spencer's request, gone back outside without a word of protest and tossed it.

And to top off this strange but pleasant phenomenon, Augustus Phelps and Leonard Winslow, two of Raven's most arrogant elders, generously agreed to donate their time to church activities.

Such obedience humbled him, to say the least.

427

Across the street, a dark-haired man got out of a late-model Mustang and trotted over.

"I'm Reverend Edwin Spencer," he said, smiling broadly. "I hope you're hungry."

They shook hands.

"Lou Gates. I own Denner's. I was on my way back to the restaurant when I caught a whiff of something wonderful coming from your church. It stopped me cold."

"Oh, dear. Denner's." Spencer's cheeks flushed. "I'm sorry about what happened, Mr. Gates."

"So am I. Call me Lou."

"I hope you'll be reopening soon. My wife and I love your place."

"I take it you'll come back when we're open?"

"Definitely." Spencer attempted a gamble. "Are you a churchgoer?"

"Haven't been in years."

"Could I possibly persuade you to attend Services this Sunday? Around eleven?"

Lou tugged at his earlobe. "I'm usually busy with Sunday brunch, but since we won't be open for a few days, I think I can make it."

My goodness, Spencer thought, grinning. "Excellent."

"What *is* that heavenly smell?"

"Please come in and join us," Spencer urged. "We're having pot roast."

"I thought this would be a soup kitchen type of gig. You know, canned chicken noodle, maybe chowder once in a while with an actual chunk of clam in it—"

"We've always been fortunate to have our friends helping us out. Our Ladies Club donated their time and effort for tonight's feast."

Inside, the food line had dwindled.

"Help yourself," Spencer told Lou. "I'll look for a table. We can talk, if you like."

"Talk?"

"If you don't mind my saying so, you look very tired. Maybe I can help."

Lou sighed. "The shooting took a lot out of me."

"I honestly don't know how you've managed to keep your wits about you. I still can't believe what's happened in this town the last few days."

"Yeah. Weird things you only read about going on in other places."

"I'm wondering why the weirdness has stopped."

"You think it has?"

Spencer hadn't smelled the sourness since leaving the Sanctuary. By his calculations, that happened two hours ago.

"I honestly think so," he said, feeling better than he had in days.

***

Rae Larson picked up her ladle, glanced up at the man sliding his tray in her direction…and froze.

Denner's. Yes. She had seen him there a couple of times, but only at a distance. But now that she saw him close-up, she couldn't believe how handsome he was. His beautiful dark-brown eyes locked onto hers, sending a shimmer of warmth through her limbs.

"Hi."

"Hello." As soon as it escaped her lips, it became a whisper. She wondered if he even heard it above the clatter of dishes.

"Everything looks great." He wasn't staring at the food.

"I've seen you at Denner's, haven't I?"

429

"No doubt. I own it, so I have to spend a lot of my time there."

"Really?"

"You weren't there during the shooting, were you?"

"I heard about it. I'm so glad you're okay."

His forehead wrinkled. "My head's been kind of muddled lately, but I'll live."

"How badly…were you hurt?"

"Just roughed up a little. Nothing to worry about. Anyway, I'm glad you weren't there."

Suddenly she hated her stupid paper hat. But somehow it didn't matter. He seemed to be focused on her eyes. "Will you be able to reopen soon?" she asked.

"Next week."

"I'm *so* glad. I love your place. The food's fantastic. So is your music."

"You like jazz?" He seemed surprised.

"I've always been a sucker for big band stuff."

"I'll make sure my Basie, Ellington and Ferguson recordings are in the lineup."

"And Doc Severinsen?"

"It wouldn't be the same without Doc."

"I think I'd like to come over before you reopen," she said. "Maybe I can help with the clean-up."

"You don't have to do that."

"I'd enjoy it. Just tell me when a good time would be."

The smile stayed on his face. "Any time you come over will definitely be good."

She ladled him out an extra portion. His eyes lingered on hers. He thanked her, then took his tray over to where Reverend Ed sat near the door, stirring his coffee.

"Something wrong, honey?" Pat Spencer asked over her shoulder.

"Everything's fine." She couldn't remember being so excited. For the first time since her divorce, she actually wanted to start living again. "I feel wonderful."

"You sure?"

"Yes. Why?"

"Ever since you gave that man his dinner, you've been polishing your ladle with your apron."

EPILOGUE

Leaving Raven

Tiffany followed Chip down the grassy slope.

It seemed like years had passed since they had gone down this same path. Years since she'd discovered she was dead and would no longer have to worry about finding the right agent. Or that her breasts might be too small. Or that she might not have next month's rent ready.

It was all behind her. Everything. Illness. Aging. Heartbreak.

When she thought of it that way, death didn't seem so bad. And since she now possessed powers, the road ahead looked less bleak.

Except for a few things.

She not only sent away the only man she'd ever loved, she'd placed a spell on him that would put him in the arms of the first good woman he encountered. You couldn't do much worse than that.

"Why so quiet, sweet cakes?"

"Sending Lou away was difficult," she said, a lump in her throat.

"It wasn't exactly a picnic to watch, either."

It was time to start thinking ahead. "Now tell me what we're doing."

"They've got another job for us."

"That's what you said just before I sent Lou away. Really? Another job? Up here?"

"Now why, pray tell, would they want us to do something down there?"

It didn't seem possible. In fact, it seemed much too good to be true. "You mean we really can stay up here? Really and truly?"

"Don't burst a blood vessel."

"Does it show that much?"

"It would help if you weren't showing so many of those lovely pearly-whites. Someone might mistake you for a jack-o-lantern and shove a candle in your mouth. But don't get too comfortable. We'll probably have to go back down after this."

Another reprieve. Her second in three days.

"Why would they allow us to stay up here?"

"We're saving them the agony of getting everyone together to send up two more inferiors. Lately they've been having a helluva time rounding up everyone. With so many mortals down there lately, the subs and supers love wandering around, looking for something interesting to scrape up."

"Then it has nothing to do with our sending Gutril back down?"

"Demons aren't noted for their generosity, muffin."

"I don't care. I'm so grateful, I could—"

"*Please* don't get sloppy again. You'll wilt the petals."

"Sorry. Sometimes I can't help it."

He sighed. "You wouldn't be half bad if you'd stop being so damned *nice*. And disgustingly *sweet*."

"I don't like hurting people."

"It can be *so* much fun…"

"It's not fun when it's happening to *you*…"

"But you're dead now. Mortals can't hurt you anymore. Why should you even *care* about them?"

433

She shrugged. "I just think things could be better for everyone if someone gave them a helping hand. Life can be tough. If people had a little help, everyone would benefit. The world would be a happier place—don't you think?"

"Sorry for the yawn." He lowered his hand from his mouth. "I think I just dozed off."

Sometimes he was so *impossible*...

"Tell me something," he said. "Your powers. Have they grown much?"

She hesitated. "I'm not sure what you mean."

"Aside from tweaking your cup size and those cute little tricks with your wardrobe, not to mention that shoe thing. Can you do any mind-reading or manipulation?"

"Of course not." She didn't know how he'd react if she told him the truth.

"A couple of things just aren't clicking."

"Like what?"

"The restaurant owner dude, for example. When you looked at him, he turned into one of those comatose figures you see running a funeral parlor or hosting a TV news program. You weren't by any chance trying to make him your host, were you?"

She swallowed. "Why would I do *that*?"

"It only works for demons, lamb chop. You're not a demon."

Darn... She hadn't thought of that.

"You should've asked me if that's what you had in mind. We *are* a team, aren't we?"

"But I wasn't meant to be a demon. I wasn't sent to Hell, so why should I be a demon?"

"You ended up there."

"That doesn't make me a demon, does it?"

"Yes...no... Jeez Louise, you ask some screwy questions."

"You mean I ask questions you can't answer."

"Just tell me the truth."

"About what?"

"The restaurant owner dude. You did a number on him, didn't you?"

"A *number*?"

"When he looked at you, he turned into a slab of meat. With eyes. Big, bulging eyes."

"How can I do a number on anyone without knowing how?"

"You've got powers. You may not think you do, but I can tell. I already told you, they grow while we're up here. Something about the open air."

"That's right. That Bible thing you told me about. But wouldn't I feel differently if I had more powers?"

"Precious, I'm not exactly the right gentleman to ask."

She hoped she satisfied him for the moment. But she couldn't help wondering how her powers as a non-demon were growing while Chip's powers as a demon remained the same.

"He got to you, didn't he? It wasn't just one-sided."

"How could you tell?"

"That kiss. And that frothy conversation you two had. For a moment I thought someone stuck me in the middle of a sappy soap opera. You really need to stop the mushy stuff. You'll give everyone a bad name."

"If everyone down there has a *good* name, it wouldn't be Hell, would it?"

He thought that over. "You know what, lamb chop? I think that dumb blond act is just an act."

435

"I'm surprised you figured it out."

They edged down another wooded slope.

"So where are we going?" she asked.

"You don't care, do you?"

"Not as long as it keeps us up here."

"Ironic, isn't it?"

"What's that?"

"Down there, the demons chased *you*. Up here, you're chasing *them*."

"You're right. What's that make me?"

He shrugged. "A dead girl chasing demon guys?"

"How about demon chaser? It sounds more dignified."

"I prefer the term demon butt-kicker."

"That makes me sound really *bad*..."

"You *are*, muffin cake. What makes you *really* bad is that you don't *look* bad."

"Most guys I knew in Hollywood would agree with you."

"Just make me a promise."

"Depends on what it is."

"Promise me you'll *try* to do interesting stuff this next time around."

She knew she could easily keep that promise. "Whatever I do from now on will be *very* interesting."

He stopped walking. "I don't think I like the sound of that, but it'll have to do for now. Ready to wave bye-bye to good ol' Ohio?"

The thought of never seeing Lou again racked through her, but she had to let it go. She couldn't pursue a lasting relationship with a mortal man. If she had used her powers correctly, he'd already forgotten her. And Darcy would revert back to the sweet girl she was before all this happened. That in

itself was well worth the sacrifice. If she could do some good and keep some of the bad from happening, she'd feel just fine. It would be her revenge for being sent to Hell. "I think so," she said.

"You sure?"

"Why do you ask?"

"We might have to do a lot of walking."

"So?"

He pointed to her feet.

She had changed the steel-toed work boots back to the Gucci pumps. Now it was time for another change. She closed her eyes and covered her feet with a nice pair of tan slip-ons by Merrill. "How's that?"

"Very stylish."

"Now…where do we go?"

"You need to stop asking stupid questions. Put a little faith in your spirit guide."

"You're my spirit guide?"

"And they say females are dense. But to answer your last irritating question…they told me to leave this tacky little cow town and get on the Interstate."

"In which direction?"

"South, my merry maiden of mirth."

"And we hitch again…"

"Can't slip anything past you, can I?"

"But where to?"

"Have I *ever* led you astray?"

"You mean since we've been together?"

Steam puffed out of his ears. "No, I mean since you were born. Of *course* I mean since we've been together.

When else could I have led you astray? That is, if I have—which I haven't."

She didn't want to make this too easy. It might give him an ego complex. He was already too much of a smartass. "Let me see…"

"Ah. A whiff of doubt has drifted into my proboscis cavity."

"You *are* a man, aren't you?"

"When the occasion calls for it."

"And you do have issues you need to fix, right?"

"But even with my tiny flaws, have I led you astray?"

"Not yet."

"It would be both stupid and unhealthy to break up such a talented act. Me with my tricks, wit, boyish charm, excellent style, tasteful humor, limitless mental acuity…and you with your looks, hair, bodacious boobs, and especially those butt-blitzing bunions."

"Are you gonna turn yourself into a homely stick-girl again?"

"I could make myself appear as a *priest*…"

"That would look good. Ralph and Sandra Sedarski's only daughter thumbing along the Interstate with a priest."

"I thought your name was LeBouf."

"My real name is Sedarski."

"I can understand why you changed it."

"It's not as bad as Centipede Calorie-bluster—"

"*Cypripedium Calceolus*. Don't make me hit you now. You can really be a pill at times, Tiffany."

She stopped walking. Had she heard him correctly? "*What* did you just call me?"

"Isn't Tiffany your name?"

"I didn't think you'd *ever* get it right."

"I'm not very good with names."

"You're *horrible* with them! With mine, anyway. But with those big nasties down there, like Oglethorpe and Beer Swill and Belching Waiter? You've got *them* down perfectly."

He rubbed his eyes. "Honeykins, I honestly hope you start getting those right before we go back down. Demons tend to get nasty when they're insulted."

"When aren't they nasty?"

"That's beside the point." He yanked a plug of grass from the ground and sucked on its roots as they walked.

"You actually *like* that stuff?"

"One can never get enough roughage."

"Good point."

"I tend to act silly and slightly unmanageable when my chemistry's off."

"Good grief. I can't imagine…"

They descended the slope that led to the Interstate.

ALSO BY DAVID BERARDELLI

THE APPRENTICE
DEMON CHASER II
STEPPING OUT OF MY GRAVE
COLORS
DEMON CHASER III
IN ANOTHER REALM
BEYOND RECOGNITION
THE NIGHTMARE COLLECTOR
DEMON CHASER IV
DEMON CHASER V
BEYOND GUILT
REDEMPTION
A RIPPLE IN TIME
YESTERDAY'S JOURNEY
ENLIGHTENMENT